Emma allowed Charles to lead her to one of the French doors that opened onto a veranda.

Flambeaux cast dancing flames that reached for the stars and sent golden light into the garden. Twenty steps down and they were surrounded by the heady, musky scent of blooming roses and twining honeysuckle.

Charles turned to face her and his eyes danced with amusement and tenderness. "I had wanted to pursue you slowly. I see it is not to be."

Flummoxed by his words, she stood mute, taking shallow breaths that did nothing to ease the sense that she was racing toward something that would change her life forever.

The scents of growing flowers mingled with the intoxicating smell of the man standing too close to her. But she didn't move away. Her legs were incapable of saving her.

His head bent so his warm breath fanned her face, caressed her lips just seconds before his mouth touched hers. She stood transfixed.

Never had she thought to experience anything this powerful.

* * *

The Rake's Redemption
Harlequin® Historical #206—February 2007

GEORGINA DEVON

has a bachelor of arts degree in social sciences with a concentration in history. Her interest in England began when she lived in East Anglia as a child and later as an adult. She met her husband in England, and her wedding ring set is from Bath. Today she lives in Tucson, Arizona, with her husband, two dogs, an inherited cat and a cockatiel. Her daughter has left the nest and does Web site design, including Georgina's. Contact her at www.georginadevon.com.

The Rake's Redemption

GEORGINA DEVON

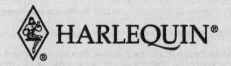

HARLEQUIN®

TORONTO • NEW YORK • LONDON
AMSTERDAM • PARIS • SYDNEY • HAMBURG
STOCKHOLM • ATHENS • TOKYO • MILAN • MADRID
PRAGUE • WARSAW • BUDAPEST • AUCKLAND

ISBN-13: 978-0-373-30515-5
ISBN-10:   0-373-30515-X

THE RAKE'S REDEMPTION

Copyright © 2007 by Alison J. Hentges

First North American Publication 2007

Chapter One

Miss Emma Stockton looked around Lady Jersey's filled-to-overflowing ballroom. Everyone who was anyone in the *ton* milled about, some dancing, many talking. It was a fashionable crush.

She felt Amy shift beside her. 'Em, might I go to speak with Miss Julia? She's with her mother.'

Emma glanced in the direction her younger sister indicated. 'Yes, but remember, if anyone asks you to dance, you may only do so twice and then not consecutively. And no waltzing.'

Amy pouted but nodded before moving away.

Emma watched her headstrong sister as worry gnawed at her stomach. It seemed they went nowhere that Amy did not flaunt Society's rules. Had she thought more about it, she would have never told her not to do something. It only provoked Amy's stubborn streak into action. But it was done. She would keep a close eye on her spoilt sister.

She sighed and cooled herself with a delicate ivory-and-lavender silk fan that had belonged to her mother. The torpid air moved slowly.

She stepped farther into the room, thinking she would get a glass of punch, when she spotted *him*—the Honourable Charles Hawthorne. Although in her jaundiced opinion there was nothing honourable about the man.

He moved with an animal grace few men possessed. His hair, as dark as Whitby jet and just as glossy, was cut short in a Corinthian style that suited his masculinity to perfection. His broad shoulders seemed even wider than normal in the perfectly fitted black evening jacket, and his narrow hips and strong thighs could not have looked better if he padded them with sawdust. He was everything a maiden might want in a man.

Too bad he was a rake of the first water. Even worse that he pursued her younger sister in a manner guaranteed to ruin Amy before she even had a chance to meet an acceptable young man. And more than anything, Amy needed to meet an eligible party.

Their brother and father continued to gamble what little was left of the family wealth and to sell off land and homes as fast as others sold horseflesh in an effort to keep ahead of their debtors. Had her engagement to Lord George Hawthorne, Charles Hawthorne's older brother, ended in marriage things might be different. But that had not happened.

As she looked at him, Charles Hawthorne turned to look at her as though her attention drew his. His dark eyes met hers and a frisson skittered down Emma's spine. She told herself it was apprehension. Nothing more.

She stood and watched him move in her direction. Part of her wanted to turn away and run, fearing the fascination he held for her. But a stronger part wanted to confront him and tell him to leave her sister alone. Either way, by the time her feet seemed capable of moving, he was upon her.

'Miss Stockton,' he drawled, making a leg that showed his physical attributes and natural grace at their best. 'What a pleasure to see you here.'

She grimaced at him and managed to incline her head in what she hoped was a superior nod. No matter how her stomach twisted in what might be attraction as easily as dislike, she could not bring herself to return his compliment. She settled for, 'Mr Hawthorne.'

He smiled as though he understood perfectly her dislike

for him, his fine lips quirking at one corner. 'I hope Miss Amy is with you?'

She scowled even as she felt a flush of anger mount from her neck to her freckled cheeks. Being a redhead was not easy when one tried to appear collected.

'Amy is here under my protection. I do not wish you to approach her.'

His smile turned into something calculated. 'Of course you don't.'

'I don't suppose you would consider leaving?' Even as the words left her mouth she regretted them. They made her look weak, as though she could not control her sister.

'I could. But I have no plans to do so—yet. Perhaps later. There are other haunts where my presence is more appreciated.'

She nearly choked on her indignation. 'A gentleman would not allude to such establishments in front of a lady.'

He shrugged. 'I am sure you don't consider me a gentleman.'

'No, I don't.'

'Then we understand one another.'

Her eyes narrowed. Before she could say the scathing words welling in her mind, Lady Jersey joined them and put black kid-leather-covered fingers on Charles Hawthorne's forearm.

'There you are, Charles.' She smiled graciously at Emma. 'And Miss Stockton. I am so glad you were able to come. I saw your sister with Julia Thornton.'

'My lady, thank you for inviting us.' Emma made a short curtsey to the older woman, who was also one of the patro-nesses of Almack's, the *ton*'s most sought after arena for in-troducing young ladies to marriageable gentlemen. Lady Sally Jersey was a woman no one wanted to alienate.

Lady Jersey waved the thank-you away. 'If you will excuse us, Miss Stockton, I have something to discuss in private with Mr Hawthorne.'

Emma forced a gracious smile to her lips and backed away. She hoped the woman was going to take away Charles Hawthorne's entrée to Almack's and have him booted out of this ball. It would be safer all around for Amy, who was too young and flighty to go against her own desires where the wretched man was concerned.

One glance at their laughing faces, the glow of pleasure on Lady Jersey's features and the way her fingers remained on Charles Hawthorne's arm, told Emma she was going to be disappointed. The older woman seemed to be reveling in the charm only Charles Hawthorne could exert.

Emma snorted in disgust.

Charles allowed Sally Jersey to steer him away from Emma Stockton, but he watched the younger woman long enough to see her snort. He nearly laughed.

'Now, Charles Hawthorne,' Lady Jersey said, drawing his attention back to her. 'I hear your business establishment is making you a very wealthy man. How long has it been? A year now? Two?'

He looked down at the slightly plump and very socially powerful woman and gave her his best smile, the one that promised secret things. 'Two, but Lady Jersey, surely you should not be talking to me about something like that. Trade is so dirty.'

Her mouth pursed but her eyes danced. 'I suppose if I were a strait-laced chit like Emma Stockton I would not mention it to you. Or her headstrong sister, Amy, whom you pursue so brazenly and who, I must admit, encourages you shamefully. But I am a matron of the world. I know that sometimes we do things considered unacceptable by society in order to survive.'

'Ah, so experience has its privileges and its delights.' He allowed the look he gave her to speak volumes.

She flushed, a feat not easily accomplished by someone of her character and experience. 'You are a rogue, Charles Hawthorne. And a rake. But charming in all cases.' She tapped him lightly with the closed fan she held. 'I find I cannot bring myself to bar you from Almack's—in spite of your unusual method of feathering your nest. Just yet. But be careful. There are others who feel more strongly than I, who would prefer to see our doors closed to you. They say your family name and personal attributes aren't sufficient to overlook your involvement in trade. Were you a woman your fate would already be sealed.'

'How fortunate for all involved that I am not a female,' he murmured.

She chuckled and again swatted him with her fan.

He bowed deeply to her. 'But you are not small-minded, and I thank you for defending me. Life would be vastly boring without Almack's to entertain me every Wednesday.'

She laughed up at him. 'Take a care, my fine young buck, that you don't allow your sarcasm to overcome the honey of your words.'

'I shall,' he promised, returning her amusement with his own. 'Would you care to dance? It is a waltz.'

Her eyes narrowed appraisingly. 'Perhaps. It certainly would do much for my standing as a woman.'

He guessed at the cynicism underlying her words. 'You need no increase in your standing, Lady Jersey. But I need to boost mine.'

'Nicely said.' She inclined her head regally. 'I believe I will endeavour to help you.'

He held his arm for her to place her fingertips lightly as he guided her to the floor. Several heads turned. Some people smiled. He noted Emma Stockton was not among those who approved. No matter. He did not live his life to please her. Actually quite the opposite. Her pique at him over her sister was one of the few things he looked forward to. It seemed every other woman toadied to him to some degree. She was a breath of fresh air with her disapproval.

He smiled at the woman in his arms, but his thoughts were on a particular ginger-haired woman.

Emma watched the byplay and wondered at his skill. With no visible effort he was charming one of the most important women in London society. How could she expect someone of Amy's inexperience to resist a man who could bring a woman of Sally Jersey's age and experience to heel?

When he led Lady Jersey out for the waltz, it was all she could do to keep her mouth from dropping. He was the most audacious creature. If rumour were true, and she found there was normally a kernel of truth in everything, he was as wild with his money as he was with women.

She watched the couple, unable to turn her attention elsewhere. Whatever else she thought of the man, he was a delight to behold. A sigh escaped her. He was not for the likes of her or her sister. Just as his older brother had not been for her.

Emma forced her gaze elsewhere as she smoothed the lavender folds of her evening gown. She had purchased it many years before, the fine damask silk and simple lines perfect for half-mourning. She was fortunate the subdued colour complemented her complexion and hair even though it was not the first crack in fashion. But that was as far as her vanity would go. Having only received one offer of marriage and then having had to decline because her future groom carried on openly with another woman, she accepted her lot as a spinster. Many married men kept mistresses, but most were more discreet than her former fiancé.

When she had Amy respectably settled in marriage she would look for a job as a governess. Her education had been thorough, and by then she fully expected the males in her family to have gambled away everything.

In the meantime, she must find Amy.

A quick look around showed Amy in the midst of a group of young men and women close to her age. They all seemed to be enjoying themselves immensely. Emma decided to find the punch she had originally been interested in before Charles Hawthorne had sidetracked her.

She found the refreshments in a side room and filled a cup with punch before returning to the ballroom. The waltz was just ending. Automatically, before she even realised what she was doing, her gaze found Charles Hawthorne.

He made his bow to Lady Jersey and added a kiss to the

back of her hand as she laughed up at him. When he took his leave, he sauntered toward Amy, who turned to him with a brilliant smile on her face. Amy's full red lips and sparkling blue eyes, framed by golden curls, seemed to make her shine in the warm glow of hundreds of candles. He took her proffered hand and raised it to his lips.

For an instant only, Emma nearly felt the pressure of his flesh on the back of her hand before she shook off the unsettling sensation. She moved toward the couple without conscious thought. She was Amy's chaperone and she had a duty to protect her.

Helplessness settled over her like a heavy mantle as she watched the couple move to the dance floor. Knowing she could not reach them through the throng of people, she bit her lip in consternation as Amy curtseyed and her partner bowed in the opening moves of the dance. All she could do now was wait—and be thankful it wasn't a waltz. The dance was only done in private homes and considered too fast for a young woman in her first season.

She tapped her foot and waited for Charles Hawthorne to return Amy to her side. Instead, when the dance ended, the couple headed to a pair of open French doors. She wasn't surprised, yet still, fury clawed up Emma's spine. That man and her sister flaunted her dictates at every turn.

Even if she ignored every person between herself and the doors, they would still be outside much longer than she liked and by the time she got there, they might have moved on. If she remembered correctly, Lady Jersey had a beautiful garden. She had to follow them.

Charles escorted the young minx into the cool night air. A dimple showed in her cheek and her brilliant blue eyes peeked up at him through thick blond lashes. He knew he should have refused to bring her out here without a chaperone, but Amy Stockton intrigued him. As experienced as he was, and he was very experienced, she always managed to amuse him with her hoydenish ways. Very often she crossed that fine boundary between acceptable and not, and she seemed to care nothing for the consequences.

Then there was Emma Stockton. He found it very entertaining to watch Amy's older sister sputter and futilely try to clip the wings of this chick.

He settled Amy near a wrought iron bench close enough that the light from the ballroom fell onto the girl's skirts. A damask-red rosebush climbed the stone balustrade behind her, scenting the warm air.

'What can I do for you, Miss Amy, that is so secret we must come out here?'

She gave him a smile nearly as roguish as the one he was famous for. 'Well…you are a rake and you do flout conventions all the time.'

He nodded, wondering where this was leading and beginning to think he was going to have to bow out of her proposed escapade—and he didn't even know where her wiles were heading. Not even he would compromise a girl barely out of the schoolroom.

'I am all those things, but that does not mean I am your pet monkey to do as you bid me.' He kept his tone light to counterbalance the baldness of his words.

She sat down and beckoned him to join her. He shook his head and propped one elegantly clad foot on the base of the balustrade. 'I think not,' he murmured.

She pouted. 'But you won't be able to hear me if you insist on staying so far away.'

'You amaze me with your audacity, Miss Amy. Don't you know well-bred young ladies keep their distance from men of my reputation?'

'Oh, pooh! As though I care about that. I am in London to enjoy myself.'

'And to find a suitable husband.'

'You would do very nicely.'

He shook his head and wondered what he had got himself

into. 'I have no intentions of marrying anyone, let alone someone as young as you are.'

'You are not being very gallant.'

Her brows drew together into a ferocious frown that he was sure normally got her whatever she wanted. He had used that ploy himself when he was younger and it had always worked. It was time to burst her bubble before the two of them got into something he could not extricate himself from.

'I am being blunt and honest.'

'Then why do you always come to my beck and call?'

He pondered that. 'For the pleasure of doing as I please. You see, like you, I have been spoilt and am used to having my own way.'

'Exactly.' She gave him a triumphant smile. 'That is why I know you are just the one to do this.'

He raised one brow.

'Oh, yes.' She was so excited her breath came as though she were running. 'There is a masquerade tonight. I want to go.'

He stepped back from her. 'Then go.'

'Don't be stupid. I need someone to take me.'

'Ask your sister.'

'Ask me what,' Emma Stockton said.

Her voice was so cold that Charles immediately decided to see how far he could provoke her. It was a pastime he found entertaining.

He turned and watched her stride across the balcony until she stood barely a foot from them. Her auburn brows formed a tight *V* and her usually full, peach-tinted lips formed a thin line of anger and disapproval. He found himself delighted.

It always amazed him that he reacted to her this way. She was not voluptuous or even particularly beautiful, but she was striking and for some reason he couldn't understand— didn't want to spend the time trying to understand—she always made him want to bait her.

'Your delightful sister has plans for later this night. I told her that she should ask you.' He kept his voice to a soft drawl, which he knew would irritate her. It always had in the past. Ennui was so difficult to assuage.

Emma turned her attention on her sister. 'Amy?'

The younger Stockton scowled at her sister for all she was worth, while casting appealing looks at Charles. 'Really, Em. It is nothing. Mr Hawthorne is making something big out of something that doesn't exist.'

Charles nearly shook his head in amazement. Instead he laughed. He couldn't help himself. The girl was a minx and the person assigned to control her couldn't. He nearly pitied Emma Stockton.

'What is so amusing, Mr Hawthorne?' Emma Stockton's voice dripped acid. 'I find this entire situation skirting the boundary of acceptability. But then, I suppose, you already know that and choose to do as you wish. It seems to be a trait in your family.'

Her sarcastic words, perfectly aimed, sobered him. 'If you had a sword, Miss Stockton, you would have scored a very solid hit.'

'I know that.'

'Oh, stop bickering you two,' Amy's light voice intruded. 'You are ruining the evening. It is supposed to be about fun and excitement and the two of you make it seem awful.'

Charles found he could not look away from Emma Stockton, no matter what the girl said. The woman seemed fit to explode. Colour mounted her high cheekbones and her grey eyes seemed lit from within. Suddenly, he had had enough of taunting her.

He made a brief leg. 'I will be about my business, ladies. I wish you a good evening—what is left of it.'

He departed without a backward glance, glad to be away before Emma Stockton went up in flames. Even he, as selfish and hedonistic as he was and bent on entertaining himself during a dull Season in any way possible, didn't want to be around for the fireworks he knew were to come.

* * *

Emma felt Charles Hawthorne's departure in spite of herself. It was as though the warmth had fled, leaving only her cold anger at him and her sister.

'Amy, you know you should not be out here with a man of Charles Hawthorne's ilk. Think of your reputation.'

Amy defiantly met Emma's gaze. 'There is nothing wrong. The doors are open and—' she half turned and swept her arm in an indication of the gardens below '—there are people walking on the paths. Nothing would have happened.'

Emma wondered if she had ever been this headstrong and bent on achieving her own purpose no matter what the cost. She didn't think so. From the first, she had realised someone needed to be responsible and help Mama. Her anger softened at the memory.

'Amy,' she said gently, 'it is not a matter of anything happening. Exactly. It is a matter of propriety, and young girls don't go outside alone with a man like Charles Hawthorne.'

Amy stood so they were eye to eye. 'Well, we might have been brother- and sister-in-law. Surely that counts for something.'

'Amy,' Emma said reproachfully, 'you know better than that. If I had married Lord Hawthorne, things would have been different. But I didn't, so you can't use that as an excuse. Society will forgive much in a man that it won't forgive in a woman. Always remember that.'

'Humph!'

Amy made to flounce around her sister but Emma grabbed her sister's arm and held tight. 'You still haven't told me what the two of you came out here to discuss.'

Amy simultaneously tossed her head and tried to wriggle from Emma's grasp. Emma let her go.

'Nothing.'

'Amy.' Emma felt her patience shredding.

'Oh, all right. There is a masquerade. I wanted him to escort me because I knew you wouldn't.'

Emma gasped in spite of herself. 'You are the most brazen

girl. You would have ruined yourself for a couple of hours of pleasure.'

'No, I wouldn't. I would have worn a mask. No one would even know who I was.'

'So, is he taking you?'

Amy half turned away, giving her sister a look from the corner of her eyes. 'And if he is?'

'Don't goad me, Amy. I am not in the mood for it.'

And she wasn't. Already she found herself wanting to lock her sister in her room with only bread and water, but Amy wasn't a child anymore even though she acted like one. Next, she wanted to land Charles Hawthorne what her brother Bertram would call a facer. But she would do neither.

'You are never in the mood for fun, Emma. That is the problem with you.'

Emma glared at Amy.

'Oh, all right. No, he isn't taking me.' Her voice fell. 'I was surprised. He is always game for anything.'

Emma silently groaned at her sister's naiveté. 'And what if you had been recognised? He might be reckless, but he's not stupid. Your reputation would be in shreds and someone might start thinking he should marry you—something I very much believe he has no intention of doing.'

A flush spread across Amy's fair face. 'He certainly made that plain.' She smoothed the fine white muslin of her gown, her eyes not meeting Emma's. 'But men change…if they want something badly enough.'

'No, they don't.' Emma snapped the words, hearing the fatal misunderstanding so many of her sex seemed to have regarding men. 'They don't change.'

'You don't know that,' Amy persisted. 'Besides, Em, I am tired of this conversation. And he is not taking me to the masquerade. So, as far as *you* are concerned, things couldn't be better.'

Emma would have begged to differ, but knew it did no good to argue with Amy when she had her mind made up. All she could do was try her best to be an obstacle in the young girl's reckless path. To lecture Amy would only make her sister try harder to achieve what she ought not.

Chapter Two

Emma alighted first from the hired carriage they rented when need dictated. They lived in a genteel yet shabby part of London. The walk to Lady Jersey's ball would have been too far, even for women raised in the country. Delicate ballroom slippers were not made for long distances and wearing one's half boots and carrying one's slippers to a fancy ball was not done.

Amy followed Emma. 'Em, what engagements do we have tomorrow?'

Emma turned to pay the coachman, who tipped his hat before driving away. She moved to the front door, pulling a key from her reticule. 'I believe we are at home tomorrow afternoon, Amy. At night, we should have been at a rout at the Princess Lieven's but it has been postponed until the next evening.'

'Nothing tomorrow afternoon,' Amy murmured.

Amy's voice held impatience and something else that Emma always dreaded. Excitement. She didn't need Amy to say any more to know her sister had arranged or was planning something that would not be to anyone's liking but Amy's.

'Why do you wish to know?' Emma worked to keep the growing apprehension from her tone. Provoking Amy to further indiscretions was the last thing she needed to do.

'Oh, nothing.' Amy waved her gloved hand in an airy sweep. But there was a sparkle in her blue eyes that spoke of mischief.

Rather than press the issue, Emma said, 'Then you had best get some sleep.'

A glance at Amy showed the young girl had missed Emma's irony. Yes, Amy was definitely concocting something.

Emma inserted the key in the lock and pushed open the door. No servants waited up for them. It wasn't fair to ask their old butler, who did many other things now because they were short of staff, to wait up. Nor would she ask the housekeeper who now filled in as lady's maid. They rose at dawn, so she would not ask them to stay up until dawn.

Emma watched Amy trip blithely up the stairs, a bounce in the girl's step that spoke of suppressed energy and excitement. Amy was enjoying her first Season immensely.

Emma remembered her own and wished she had been as young and unconcerned. But she had been twenty during her first Season. Her debut had been delayed three years while she nursed Mama and then for the year of mourning. When she'd finally come to London, she had known above all else that she needed to marry well.

The only man with the position and wealth to help her family and who had proposed to her had been Charles Hawthorne's older brother, Lord George Hawthorne. It was to have been a marriage of convenience and both of them had known that. Then Hawthorne had met another woman and his actions with her had been so blatant that Emma had felt herself constrained to call off their engagement. While she had not expected a love match and had not been heartbroken, she had been humiliated. Nor had she wished to keep another person from finding happiness. For the most part, the only thing she regretted was that now Amy needed to marry well. Amy deserved better than that.

Her shadow wavered against the wall, catching her attention from the corner of her eye. A single candle burned in a brass holder set on a table. Nothing else adorned the entryway of the rented house. Her father and brother had sold off the silver long ago to pay gambling debts. Debts of honour.

She stared at the flame for only a few seconds. Crying over spilt milk or badly needed money frittered away for pleasure that did no one any good was not going to change anything. The best hope Amy had was to marry well. If the man could also pay to get their father and brother out of debt, then so much the better.

Charles Hawthorne could not fill either of those requirements. No matter that he was a devastatingly attractive man with a devilish charm even she found hard to resist.

Thank goodness he had not agreed to take Amy to the masquerade. Emma knew too well she would be hard-pressed to keep so close a watch on her sister that Amy could not escape or make it uncomfortable for Emma to prevent her. She nearly chuckled aloud at the picture of herself stretched on the floor across Amy's bedroom door, for that is what she would have to do to keep Amy in check. Or tie her sister to the bed.

However, she had no doubt something else equally unacceptable would arise, for Charles Hawthorne had made it clear he had no intention of changing his atrocious behaviour where Amy was concerned. He would ruin her sister without a second thought, and Amy would let him.

Too much was at stake. She dared not let Charles Hawthorne and Amy continue down the path they were on. She had to do something to stop the man. The well-being of her sister and their entire family depended on Amy marrying well.

Yet, if she thought Amy loved the man she would think seriously about trying to convince their father to allow the match. But she knew her young sister well enough to know Amy enjoyed the notoriety of his attention because he was considered unattainable by every woman in society. Amy did not love Charles Hawthorne. Nor did he love her. That knowledge allowed Emma to entertain plans to sever the connection with a clear conscience.

But what to do about Charles Hawthorne?

A door opening down the hallway caught her attention. Who would be up at this hour? She had told all the servants to go to bed, and Amy had mounted the stairs. Footsteps echoed on the bare wood.

'Who is there?'

'Just your brother,' Bertram Stockton drawled, his tall, skinny frame silhouetted by the light coming into the hall from the open door to the room he had just left. 'Where have you been? It's rather late to be out unescorted.'

His criticism raised her hackles.

'We have been to Lady Jersey's ball. We took a hired carriage since we do not have one of our own—for reasons you know very well. And I am old enough to not need an escort and to be a proper chaperone for our sister.' Her irritation was instantly replaced by concern, for London and Bertram were not a good combination. 'What are you doing in Town?'

His hazel-eyed gaze slid away from her. She knew he was going to lie to her. Perhaps it was better. She knew all too well why he was here, and she could do nothing to stop him.

His gaze returned to her. 'I am up to check on you and Amy. Disturbing rumours have reached Father and me about Amy and Charles Hawthorne. After what his brother did to you, Father decided it would be best for all of us if I came and stayed. Provide a brotherly presence and all that. Besides which, the man is not someone we wish in the family. A rakehell of the first order. No, not at all what we wish for Amy.'

'But a rich rakehell,' Emma said, unable to stop the sarcastic retort. 'We could use that commodity.'

Most days she felt no bitterness toward her brother and father for their recklessness at the tables, knowing there was nothing she could do to stop them. She tried to clean up the mess they left behind. Mother would want her to.

One day after Emma had got into a fight with Bertram over his gambling debts and the hardship they created, Mother had explained that some things were better left unsaid. Harsh words changed nothing and only created trouble between the people involved. Emma had followed that advice since, although at times like tonight, it was hard not to let her anger burst out.

She closed her eyes and willed herself to release the destructive emotions. They did no one any good, least of all herself. She could not change anything.

'Your tongue is sharp tonight, sister.'

Emma took a deep breath and opened her eyes. 'I am tired and surprised to see you. You sent no note so there is no room ready for you.'

'The housekeeper saw to all of that.'

'When did you arrive?'

'An hour ago. You were out.'

'You woke Mrs Murphy?'

'Naturally.' He shrugged. 'That is why one has servants.'

He was right, of course. 'There is not much available. We have had to move once already and our spare rooms are at a premium.'

'And they are of less than top quality.'

She bristled. 'And why do you think that is, brother?'

He had the grace to flush. 'Mama always managed to make do.'

A pang of guilt because of her ire assailed Emma. Their mother had been wonderful. She had kept the houses that eventually became one house as though they still had an income of consequence. Whenever something had happened, Mama would smile and say, 'Your Papa is an impetuous man, but he is always generous and loving.' She had said the same about Bertram, and it was true more often than not. Then Mama would shoulder the new burden with a smile on her face.

It was because of Mama's memory and her love for her husband and son in spite of anything they did that Emma kept going, kept trying to stay one step ahead of the trade people and money lenders. Mama would want her to.

But things had become worse after Mama's death. Both Papa and Bertram gambled unchecked, and there was no Mama to look on the bright side.

'Mama had more to make do with.' Emma's exhaustion laced the words.

Right now, with Bertram standing in front of her, and knowing he would gamble away still more money and heirlooms while he told himself he was providing brotherly support and protection, it would be very easy to feel defeated. Emma squared her shoulders. She would not feel sorry for herself. She would look on the bright side and carry on. Mama would want her to.

'We would not be in this position if George Hawthorne had not acted dishonourably or if you had held him to the engagement.' Bertram's voice was both accusing and whiny.

Emma looked at the brother she loved in spite of his faults and wondered when the boy who had shown her how to trout fish and joined her in madcap escapades had changed to the man standing before her. This man was weak, and he blamed others for his situation instead of himself. Regret filled her heart for what Bertram had become.

'We had this discussion at the time, Bertram. I did what I thought best.' She did not want to continue in this vein. It led nowhere. 'Now, I am going to bed.'

Even as he opened his mouth to continue, she turned her back to him. When she heard his voice, she ignored it and went up to the next floor and her room. Tomorrow would be a long day with Amy to curtail and Bertram's gambling to worry about.

Emma looked up from her third cup of hot chocolate, one of her few indulgences, as Gordon, the butler, entered the breakfast room. She smiled at the old man who had begun service with her family as a footman and was now at the pinnacle of achievement.

'Yes, Gordon?'

'Miss Stockton, you remember requesting us to keep an eye on Miss Amy?'

Emma set the half-empty china cup down and carefully

folded her hands in her lap. Something had happened which she would not like.

'Yes, I do.' She was glad her voice sounded calm when she really wanted to scream in frustration.

'Well, Miss Amy has just sent one of the hired kitchen girls on an errand.'

'Do you know what kind?'

The butler shook his grizzled head. 'No, Miss. The girl was gone when Cook told me. Seems Miss Amy got to the girl just as Cook entered the kitchen to prepare your breakfast.'

Neither he nor Cook could question Amy. Emma sighed. 'Where is Amy now?'

'I believe she went back to her room.'

'No doubt back to bed. It's very early considering the time we returned last night.'

She rose and dusted toast crumbs from her plain black bombazine dress. She had bought it the first year after Mama's passing. It was still in too good a condition for her to be rid of it, although the harsh lines and dark colour were not the most flattering for her.

'Thank you, Gordon.' She went past him into the small hallway and made her way to the stairs before stopping. 'Is my brother at home?'

'Yes, Miss. I believe Master Bertram is sleeping.' He cleared his throat, an unconscious habit he had when he thought he should say something but didn't want to.

She would help him. 'Did my brother come in several hours ago?'

'Yes,' Gordon murmured.

She wasn't surprised. She had expected Bertram to go out after their talk last night. In fact, she would have been shocked had he not.

'Thank you again, Gordon.' Somehow she found a smile for him, knowing it was weak but the best she could do.

Emma turned back to the stairs and mounted them slowly, keeping her back straight even though it felt as though the weight of the world rested on her. She was not surprised by anything the butler had told her. Both her siblings had acted just as she expected them to. But the consequences of their actions would make life more complicated for her.

When she had promised Mama that she would care for them and Papa, come what may, she had never expected it to be this difficult. Now all she could do was her best.

Emma rapped on Amy's door. When there was no answer, she entered. She was in no mood to cater to her sister.

Amy sat up in bed, her blond curls spread around her shoulders in glorious disarray, her cheeks rosy with excitement and her blue eyes dancing. Emma had no doubt Amy's note had precipitated something Emma would not like and that Amy would like very well.

'Good morning, Em.' The younger girl was all innocence.

Emma moved into the room. 'Good morning, Amy. I hear you have been to the kitchen.'

Amy blushed and Emma marvelled at how beautiful her sister was. When Amy refused to look at her, Emma sighed.

Amy tossed a curl over her shoulder. 'I went for a bite. I was hungry.'

Emma made a moue of irritation. 'Amy, when will you stop these high jinks? I know you gave a note to the hired girl. I am sure you sent it to Charles Hawthorne. I don't know what you said, but it is not done. Not done at all.'

Amy's face paled into obstinacy. 'You carry on as though Charles Hawthorne can single-handedly ruin all my chances. Really, Em, you worry too much.'

Emma spluttered in her sudden anger. 'You do not worry enough!'

'Pooh!' Amy threw back the covers and slid out of bed. 'If you know exactly who I sent the message to, then why are you berating me? I'm surprised you haven't sent another message telling him to ignore mine.'

'Then you did send it to him.'

Amy's attention snapped back to her sister. 'You didn't know.'

Emma shrugged. 'A calculated guess based on what I know of you. You just confirmed my suspicion. Thank you. Now I shall send a note.'

'Don't forget,' Amy said, mimicking her sister's tone, 'it isn't done to send a message to a single man one isn't related to.'

'You should have remembered that before you put me in this position.' Emma didn't try to keep the tartness from her voice. 'I have had enough of this, Amy. If you don't behave, I shall tell Father you must return to the country.'

Amy pulled on her finely woven wool robe, for it was still cool in the mornings, particularly since Emma ordered no fires to be lit in order to save on costs. 'You know he will not agree. I am the fatted calf.'

There was only a touch of bitterness in the younger girl's words, but it was enough to stop Emma. Neither one of them was happy with the position they found themselves in. Neither one of them had created this situation, but both of them were paying for it.

Emma's anger melted. Amy was only doing her best to enjoy her first and only London Season. She would be wed all too soon, sacrificed on the altar of gambling.

Unable to swallow her sorrow for her sister, Emma said, 'You are too young for this and I wish I could spare you, but I cannot. Just as you are correct in saying Father will not allow me to send you home.' She went to the door, turning back to say, 'I will tell Mrs Murphy you are up.'

Emma left, feeling worse than when she'd arrived. Added to that was the requirement to send a note to Charles Hawthorne telling him not to do or respond to whatever was in Amy's note. One complication after another.

In her room, Emma sat down at the scratched and stained writing desk and pulled a piece of thick paper from the drawer. The note to Charles Hawthorne was not easy. Several copies later, she was satisfied enough to sand the sheet before folding it into a twist. She would give it to a footman who had been born on their family estate. She could trust him not to speak of this. Once that was done, she could settle into her daily supervision of the housekeeping and accounts.

That afternoon Emma sat near the window in the parlour that looked out on the back garden, using the afternoon light to see. She looked up from her darning on a pair of silk stockings when Gordon entered and cleared his throat.

'Yes?' She smiled at the elderly butler.

His brow furrowed. 'Mr Hawthorne is at the door, Miss Stockton. He says he is come to take Miss Amy driving.'

Emma's stomach seemed to plummet in a pleasurable sensation and her fingers tingled. Her weakness tightened her mouth. The man was nothing but trouble.

'He ignored my note,' she muttered.

'It would seem so, Miss.'

'Please send him away.'

She ignored a traitorous pang of disappointment. He was not to be trusted and he was only amusing himself with her innocent sister. He was nothing to her.

'Yes, Miss.' Gordon said the words without inflection but the gleam in his eye told Emma he would enjoy doing her behest.

The door closed behind him just as Amy's raised voice came from the foyer. Emma didn't have to think. She knew if she didn't get to Amy, the chit would take off with Charles Hawthorne and the devil take the hindmost. She dropped her darning without a qualm, even though there was the chance it might come undone. Seconds later, she was in the hallway.

'Amy!' She marched to the couple. 'And you!' She turned to glare at Charles Hawthorne.

He was dressed casually but impeccably. His navy jacket fit his broad shoulders as if it had been moulded to him. His buff breeches were equally tight, showing muscular thighs that, try as she might, Emma couldn't quite ignore. And his top boots were shined to a mirror glow. He held his beaver hat in gloved hands.

He quirked one black brow and said with a sardonic drawl, 'Miss Stockton, how nice of you to come and see us off.'

Emma halted several feet away from them and forced her attention from the man to her sister. 'Amy, you are not going driving.'

Amy tossed her head, her blond curls bouncing beneath the brim of her stylish straw hat. Her mouth was a mulish line. 'Of course I am, Em. There is nothing wrong with accompanying a gentleman in an open carriage through Rotten Row. It is nearly five and everyone will be there.' She slanted a sly look at Charles. 'And it will do wonders for my reputation when the other gentlemen see me squired by Mr Hawthorne.' Her gaze slid back to her sister. 'Even you must admit that Mr Hawthorne sets the tone.'

Emma closed her eyes briefly and wondered why she even bothered when Amy was so determined to throw her reputation to the wind. When she opened her eyes, it was to Charles Hawthorne's ironic grin.

'Much as it pains me to seem so arrogant,' he said, his tone saying nothing of the sort, 'your sister is correct. I am generally considered a paragon of fashion.'

Emma snorted before she realised it. Scarlet suffused her face but she would not let herself look away from his now laughing eyes.

'It is true, Mr Hawthorne, that no one has ever accused you of modesty.'

He made her a mocking half bow.

'No matter how attractive such an attribute would be for you,' she finished before turning back to Amy. 'You are right, it is perfectly acceptable. And the weather is delightful. I believe I shall accompany you.'

Amy's mouth dropped before she gathered her wits. 'But, Em, where will you sit? Mr Hawthorne drives a high-perch phaeton that will only hold two and his tiger.'

Emma considered her dignity for a second before throwing it to the wind. 'I shall sit between the two of you.'

'We will be tight as clams,' Amy groused, using a term she had coined when young. She had tried to open a clam bought at the fish market and been unable to. Ever since, when something was hard to open or tight, she used the phrase. 'Really, Em, it is too bad of you to be this way.'

Ignoring Amy's words, Emma said, 'I will only be a moment to get my hat and a pelisse.'

Not waiting for an answer, she hurried up the stairs to her room. She rummaged through her closet for the pelisse and hat, yanking the short jacket on without bothering to button it and cramming the hat onto her head with no regard for her styled hair. She trusted the old butler to do his best to delay them, but she was not giving that pair the opportunity to leave before she got back down.

She arrived downstairs breathing quicker than when she had left, but they were still there.

Amy continued where she had left off. 'It will be horribly crowded with three. I wouldn't wonder if Mr Hawthorne will be so cramped that his driving will be affected. That would not be good, for I know he is considered a fine whip.'

Still smiling, Charles said, 'Thank you for the compliment, Miss Amy. I shall do my best not to lose your trust in my abilities.'

Emma cut him a look, wondering if he had meant the double entendre his words had implied. His countenance showed nothing but good humour. Perhaps her thoughts dwelt so much on his possible seduction of her sister that she read meanings into his words that weren't there. Somehow she doubted it.

She moved to stand between them. 'Shall we be on our way?'

She heard Amy's huff of irritation and ignored it. She just wished she could as easily ignore the sense of Charles Hawthorne's nearness. She wanted nothing to do with him yet her body betrayed her. She straightened her shoulders, determined to control herself, and marched through the door Gordon held open.

Outside was a magnificent ebony barouche that would hold four people comfortably. The top was down for the fine weather and the crest of Lord George Hawthorne, Charles's older brother, adorned the door. The urge to turn on the odious man who had let them carry on thinking he was in his racing carriage was nearly too much to resist. He had made fools of them.

Instead, she allowed the footman, dressed in the Hawthorne livery, to open the carriage door and assist her. She sat facing the magnificent team of four matched bays and patted the velvet-covered seat beside herself to indicate Amy was to sit there.

Charles Hawthorne placed himself with his back to the horses. They were no sooner settled than he signaled the driver to start. The carriage moved forward with a smoothness that spoke volumes about the quality of the vehicle. Emma remembered riding in this carriage once with Lord George Hawthorne. She had enjoyed the movement then as well.

Her eyes met her host's and she suddenly regretted her determination to join the pair. He had such an unsettling effect on her.

'A tuppence for your thoughts?'

His deep voice penetrated her senses, seeming to sink into the depths of her being. There was something about this man that spoke to her of things done in dark, private places even though she deplored his morals and the way he led his life.

'Oh, la, Mr Hawthorne,' Amy said. 'I am thinking of what an enjoyable drive we shall have.'

His voice tinged with irony, he replied, 'I hope we will.'

Emma was grateful to Amy. She must have made a mistake when she had thought he was asking her. A silly mistake.

Against her will, Emma listened to the man exchange quips and banter with her sister until they turned smartly through the gate and into Hyde Park, taking their position in the throng of carriages and horses promenading on Rotten Row. Anyone who was anybody, and many who weren't, crowded the park at this time of day during the Season. It was the height of fashion to be seen here, and Emma, always honest with herself, had to admit being here did Amy no harm.

Amy beamed, her Cupid's bow mouth open to show perfect white teeth. She raised her gloved hand every few minutes to wave at an acquaintance. Emma decided that much as she had not wanted them to come here with Mr Hawthorne, it pleased her to see her sister so happy. Surely Amy would soon receive an offer.

Charles Hawthorne sat directly across from Emma and when she wasn't careful, her knee brushed his. It was an unsettling sensation, she decided, as his knee grazed hers for the sixth time. Much as she hated to admit it, the experience was so startling she kept count.

Darting a glance at him and seeing the amused curve of his fine lips, she wondered if he meant to touch her in so intimate a manner. Immediately, she decided not. He was interested in Amy, not her. She had too many freckles and a spare figure that not even the high-waisted gowns in fashion flattered.

He could have his pick of the ladies of the *ton* or those not so high in the instep. He would never give her a second glance if he weren't pursuing Amy for reasons Emma knew had to be far from honourable.

'A tuppence for your thoughts, Miss Stockton.'

Warmth spread through Emma's body at his use of her name and made her wonder if he had really meant her the first time. She chased that thought away. Everything about this situation was disconcerting.

'I am wondering why everyone wants to be in London when the countryside is at its best at this time of year.' She couldn't help a wistful glance at the green trees and emerald grass. 'There are days when I miss home very much.'

His eyes intent, he murmured, 'How very interesting. I thought you enjoyed London.'

She met his gaze without thought. 'I don't know why you should think anything about me, Mr Hawthorne. You don't know me.'

'I know some things.'

'Such as?'

He glanced at Amy and shrugged. 'That you have been in London for the Season these past three years. That your family's country estate is in Yorkshire. That until three years ago, you were in mourning. You did not come to Town until after that.'

She listened to him, thinking he must have heard everything from his older brother when she and George Hawthorne had been engaged for all of three months just two years before. It seemed a lifetime.

'You are well-informed. I would have thought me too boring a subject to hold any interest for a man of your persuasions.'

As soon as the words left her mouth, she regretted them. They sounded as though she were begging for a compliment, not as the insult they should have been. Why did this man— with nothing to recommend him that she valued—manage to make her feel disturbingly alive?

'You don't have a high opinion of me.'

'No, I don't.'

'Em, how can you be so rude?' Amy's voice cut into what had seemed a small cocoon where only Emma and Charles Hawthorne existed. 'If I said such a thing, you would threaten to put me to bed with only bread and milk.'

Emma shook herself, thankful to Amy for interrupting a discussion that was becoming too revealing. She angled to smile at her sister. 'I might have done so several years ago, but you are too old for such measures now.'

'Hah! And thank goodness for that.' Amy laughed. 'I have seen that glint in your eyes many times these last weeks. You always have it when you wish to discipline me.'

Bantering with her sister eased some of Emma's uncanny awareness of the man sitting across from her. Even when his knee once more touched her own, she managed not to feel as though her stomach spiralled. She was more aware of him than she wished.

Charles Hawthorne raised his hand to wave and the carriage slowed. They paralleled a dark-haired, dark-eyed, vivacious woman who sat on a prime piece of horseflesh as though she had been born to the saddle.

Harriette Wilson, the famed courtesan, smiled at Charles Hawthorne.

Emma's face paled and her fists clenched. This was not done and showed a tremendous lack of respect on the man's part toward her and her sister. She glared at him.

'Harriette,' he said, his fine voice making the name sound like a caress, 'how are you today? You look in fine mettle.'

The woman smiled back, her entire body seeming to light up. 'Charles, you devil, I am in great spirits.' Her teasing gaze turned challenging. 'Do you intend to introduce me?'

His grin widened. 'I would not have hailed you if I did not.' He turned so his intensity held Emma like a vise, his countenance as serious as Emma had never seen it. 'Miss Stockton, Miss Amy, I would like you to meet Miss Wilson. A friend of mine.'

Emma nodded her head. Good manners and an innate tendency not to hurt others kept her tone pleasant and kept her from looking away without acknowledging the introduction. 'Pleased to meet you, Miss Wilson.'

Amy's voice rose. 'Miss Harriette Wilson? *The* Harriette—'

Emma cut ruthlessly across her sister's excitement. 'That is enough, Amy. I am sure Miss Wilson has no desire for her name to be shouted for all to hear.'

The mounted woman laughed and her attractive face turned beautiful. No wonder men thought her irresistible. Emma found her appealing.

'I am not shouting,' Amy said indignantly.

Emma scowled at her, hoping to quiet her.

'I am delighted to make your acquaintance,' Harriette said solemnly.

Tension Emma had not seen before eased from the courtesan's stiffly held back. Harriette Wilson had expected to be snubbed. Emma felt sorry for the other woman who had much more freedom than any respectable female, but also suffered more slights and less security. Upon the realisation, Emma gave the other woman a slight smile, her only regret being that Amy was in the carriage and being introduced to Britain's most well-known, sought after and successful courtesan. This would do Amy's reputation as much damage as being pursued by Charles Hawthorne.

For her sister's sake, Emma regretted her show of friendliness but she could not have done differently. It was not Harriette Wilson at fault here, but Charles Hawthorne for stopping, and she would tell him so at the first opportunity.

Chapter Three

Nearly an hour later, they swept through the gate and out of
Hyde Park. Emma still fumed.

'Did you enjoy your outing?' Charles Hawthorne asked
Amy, a knowing gleam in his eyes.

The young girl sparkled in the afternoon sun. 'Very much
so.' She laughed with enjoyment. 'And you are such a rogue
to introduce us to Harriette Wilson. Although, I must admit
to being fascinated by a woman who earns her living like that.'

Emma did nothing to disguise her groan. 'Amy, if you
please, that is more than enough. Ladies do not discuss wom-
en like Miss Wilson.'

'Oh, pooh! Ladies don't do anything that is interesting.'

Even as she silently agreed with Amy, Emma knew she had
to stop Amy's fascination with the other woman right now. 'You
seem to be doing quite a few things that are interesting to you.'

'Sarcasm?' Charles Hawthorne murmured. 'It will accomplish nothing.'

Emma gave him a bland look. Right now was not the time
to let him know what she thought of his actions. She was
spared any further temptation to do so with Amy present by
the carriage pulling up to their house.

Charles Hawthorne hopped out and turned immediately to

help Amy down. She giggled. 'Thank you, kind sir.' Her eyes
flirted as she allowed him to guide her to the front steps.

'My pleasure.' He put his gloved hand over hers where it
rested on his forearm.

His head bent to Amy's and he said something Emma
couldn't hear as she followed behind, having been helped
down by the groom. No doubt he was flirting as outrageous-
ly with Amy as she was with him. A tiny ball of frustration
and another emotion Emma didn't want to examine formed
in her chest.

She reached them just as the front door opened. 'Amy,
please give me a few moments alone with Mr Hawthorne.'

Amy looked from one to the other. 'So you can scold him?'

Emma ignored the challenge in her sister's voice. 'Please
honour my request.'

'Don't let her box your ears, Mr Hawthorne. She has a
predilection for that.' Amy tossed her head.

'I am more than capable of taking care of myself, Miss
Amy.' He took Amy's gloved fingers and raised them to his lips

A flush of pleasure made the already pretty girl beautiful
'You always know exactly what to do.'

Emma thought she would lose control and step between the
two like a knife cutting through cloying syrup. She managed
not to do so by a strong effort of will.

The door closed behind Amy before Emma turned to Mr
Hawthorne, who looked at her with one black brow lifted as
though daring her to do her worst. It was more provocation
than she could resist.

'How dare you flirt with her in such a way, kissing her
hand! It is much too sophisticated for a girl like her. Save it
for a more experienced woman. Isn't it bad enough that Amy
allows you to pursue her in a most unseemly manner when all
and sundry know you have no intention of offering marriage?'

His blue eyes were nearly black and impossible to read
'Would my pursuit be acceptable if I intended marriage?'

She blinked. His answer was totally unexpected. 'Do you?'

He grinned. 'No, but you seem to put such emphasis on that being the reason my interest isn't acceptable.'

'You are twisting my words and you know it.' She took a breath to try and ease the beating of her heart. 'You are the most odious man.'

'I try.'

His sardonic words sped her pulse in spite of herself. 'You try very hard and always succeed. How dare you introduce us to Harriette Wilson.'

'Not *that woman?* You surprise me.'

Now it was her turn to flush. 'She is a person even though men consider her something to be bandied about. I do not fault her for doing what she must to survive.'

'Neither do I.' He met her gaze, his serious look brooking no argument. 'I respect her as a woman who moves in a man's world, and does so successfully. I will not be a hypocrite and ignore her when I meet her out—no matter who is with me.'

Unwilling respect blossomed in Emma. No other man of her acquaintance would have been so bold and flouted convention to introduce the infamous courtesan. None would even acknowledge her if they were with a woman of their own class.

'Then you did not introduce us to irritate me or disgrace Amy?'

'Contrary to what you think, I stopped for the reason I told you.'

Emma searched his face for the truth. She could not tell what he thought, but his mouth was not curled into the sardonic smile he seemed to have perfected. An unwelcome awareness of him penetrated her anger, which was already crumbling because of his reason for introducing the courtesan.

She realised he stood too close. She could see the fine lines around his eyes and the dark stubble that would soon need to be shaved. A hint of pine mingled with that of starch. His breath smelt of mint. Under it all was the richness of a man's scent, musky and exciting. The day had turned unaccountably warm.

She stepped backwards and her half boot left the step. She tottered. His hand shot out and grabbed her arm. His fingers held her through the layers of material, seeming to sear into her flesh. A shiver coursed her spine, first like ice then like fire. The last thing she wanted was to react to him like this.

Anger at her own weakness made her voice harsh. 'You can release me.'

His gaze hardened. 'And let you fall off the step?'

She notched her chin up and set her back foot down onto the next level. 'I won't fall now.'

His hand fell away. 'You are welcome.'

She felt a blush of embarrassment mount her cheeks. There had been no call to be rude no matter what his touch did to her. Her mama would be appalled if she had seen this. 'Thank you.'

He stared at her, his gaze going from her eyes to her cheeks to her lips. Against her will, she felt the heat consuming her intensify. Heaven help her if he ever did anything more. She was a fool. An utter fool.

'Good day, Miss Stockton.'

He turned on the heel of his mirror-polished Hessian and strode to the carriage, where he opened the door himself and leapt inside with the grace of a natural athlete. He did not glance back at her when the vehicle started forward. It was she who continued to stare.

The man was insufferable. He had to be for she could not allow him to be anything else. Becoming enamored of him would do her no more good than it did Amy. Less.

Charles stared straight ahead as he was conveyed to his brother's town house to where he would return George's carriage. His fingers still tingled from touching Emma, and the scent of sweet peas lingered in his mind. His stomach tightened. Obviously he had been too long without a woman if he was reacting to a spinster like Emma Stockton.

The drive had been as entertaining as he had expected when he chose to ignore Emma Stockton's note ordering him to refrain from doing whatever her sister had requested. There was very little that gave him as much pleasure as provoking her. But the unsettling problem was that he responded to her physically as well as mentally.

He was jaded. Nothing more. Upon longer exposure to the woman's tiresome meddling, she would lose her allure.

The carriage pulled up in front of George's house and Charles shook his head to clear his thoughts. The last thing he wanted was to forget himself and mention the Misses Stockton. He and his sister, Juliet, had been down that path many a time and not to his good. Juliet was a strong woman who spoke her mind, and she didn't like his dallying with Amy Stockton.

He exited the vehicle and went inside, nodding at the family butler. 'Good afternoon.'

'Good afternoon, Master Charles.'

'Is anyone at home?'

'Lord and Lady Hawthorne are in the salon with Master Robert. Lady and Sir Glenfinning are with them.'

Charles considered visiting his siblings, but decided against it. He would send a note of thanks to his brother instead of doing it in person. He was in no mood to watch Juliet with her new husband, a liaison he had been against. Adam Glenfinning reminded him too much of himself to make a good husband.

'Please have my horse sent 'round.'

The butler nodded. 'Will you be in the saloon?'

'No, I will wait out front.'

'Yes, sir.'

Charles watched the old retainer motion to a nearby footman, who was sent to the mews. Not many people could afford to house their horseflesh in the city. George could.

Charles quickly stepped outside. Clouds bunched up overhead and a breeze moved the tree branches. He sniffed, smelling moisture in the air. It would likely start raining before he got home.

A groom leading Charles's horse came around the corner. Charles tossed him a coin and mounted the large bay gelding. If they hurried, they would beat the worst of the weather.

The rain started just as he turned the corner of the street where his house was situated. He settled the bay before running to the back door and into the kitchen.

The aroma of roast beef and potatoes hit him like a warm blanket. Alphonse, the French chef he employed, stood by the spit, supervising the basting of a large piece of meat. He was a tall man with a rotund middle that spoke of good eating. Grey hair stuck out from under the white hat he wore, giving him a wild look he did not deserve, and his bushy grey mustache was the envy of every young boy who worked for him.

The chef turned. 'Monsieur.'

Charles grinned. 'That smells like heaven, Alphonse.'

The Frenchman nodded his head regally, knowing the compliment was only his due.

A small black-and-white whirlwind sped across the slate floor, coming to a sliding halt at Charles's feet. Bright brown eyes and a black button nose peered out from a mop of hair while a long pink tongue lolled nearly to the ground. Soft barking sounds told Charles he was loved.

Squatting down, Charles ruffled the dog's long ears. 'How have you been, Adam?' The mutt of disreputable breeding looked up at him. 'Very well, I take it.' Charles glanced at Alphonse. 'Has Adam been impertinent?' Charles knew the answer.

'But of course. He demands the best slices.'

'Just like his namesake,' Charles muttered, thinking of his sister Juliet's new husband.

He loved this dog that had been a stray, even though he had named him after his unwelcome brother-in-law, who was also of dubious lineage. It had been one of his more subtle rebukes to his sister during her affair with Adam Glenfinning. As usual, it had done no good. Juliet had gone her own way.

For a moment the picture of Emma Stockton as she had looked on her porch not more than an hour ago flooded his

mind. Her hair had spiralled from beneath the brim of her un-
fashionable straw hat. Her grey eyes had been challenging yet
vulnerable, a trait he was beginning to find caught him off
guard more than he cared. Even the freckles marching across
her short nose in no pattern or order drew his admiration.

He shook his head to get rid of the portrait. He was not the
sort of man to dwell overly long on a woman, particularly one
who fit none of his criteria for beauty. She was too thin and
too tall, along with everything else about her that irritated him.

'Woof!' Adam's wet tongue on Charles's hand came immediately after the demand for attention.

Charles stood. 'You are a demanding scoundrel.' The dog
seemed to smile as though he knew there was no rebuke. 'I am
going to my office. Alphonse, please bring me something to eat.'

'Yes, monsieur.' There was a pause. 'And what about that
canine monster you spoil so shamelessly?'

'He will need sustenance as well.'

'Humph!'

Charles smiled as he left the kitchen. Alphonse might fuss
and complain, but more than once Charles had caught the
Frenchman *accidentally* dropping a piece of meat on the floor.

Adam trotted close at Charles's heels, his sniffing getting
louder as they neared the office. The room was near the kitchen
so the tantalising smells made Charles realise he was as hungry
as Adam. They would eat while he balanced his books, a duty
that had started as tedious and which he now found satisfying.

It was nearly midnight that evening when Charles looked
around and realised he had made a mistake. He had allowed his
cronies to talk him into coming to Crockford's gambling hell.

It was his first time in such an establishment in nearly
three years.

Candles were everywhere, lighting a scene of licentious
pleasure. Men lounged in chairs, bottles of liqueur beside them.
A few demireps clung to the arms of their protectors. Several
green-baize-covered tables were crowded by gamblers.

A man sat at a faro table with a visor over his eyes and his coat turned inside out, hoping for luck—or, perhaps, having luck. Charles knew all too well what the man was feeling: the thrill of waiting for that winning hand; the need to play again and again no matter what happened. It was like taking another sip of alcohol. The need intensified rather than diminished.

The urge to join a table was nearly overwhelming. All his hard-earned abstinence seemed like nothing. He should never have come.

His hands broke out in a sweat. Moisture beaded his brow. He needed to leave.

He managed to smile at the man nearest him. 'I have decided this place is a bore,' Charles drawled, glad the need didn't show in his voice. He sounded as bored as he claimed to be.

The other man raised one brown eyebrow. 'As you wish, Charles. I will stay awhile. Crockford's is known for its high stakes and I feel lucky.'

Charles smiled again. 'Luck is a fickle lady.'

The man shrugged. 'As is any woman.'

'So be it.'

Charles took one last look around the crowded room, knowing as he did so that he tempted himself. But he also knew he was strong enough to resist. He had learned the hard way what ruin this vice could bring.

He turned away and sauntered toward the door. Several men watched him, a knowing look in their gazes. His downfall was not *ton* gossip, but nor was it secret. He nodded to acquaintances, determined that no one would know how hard this was for him.

A flurry of activity caught his eye just as he neared the exit. Some of the richest men in England circled a table more crowded than the others.

Charles knew someone was betting heavily and either winning or losing. He could not resist even though he knew that going over exposed him more than he should to the urge to gamble. Better not to even go near.

But go he did.

Faro. Sinclair Manchester was the bank and Richard Green was the lamb.

Memories flooded back. Five years ago he could have been Green.

Charles kept his face void of the anger and pain building in him. How dare Manchester fleece such a young boy?

Manchester was a tall, thin, effete man who dressed impeccably and seemed to mince when he walked. His silver-tipped ebony cane, which leaned against the wall behind him, was an affectation as effective as the quizzing glass hanging from his waistcoat. His sandy brown hair was cut in a perfect Brutus, the wisps dressed to frame his narrow and angular face. He was a dandy.

Charles considered himself a Corinthian. The two of them could not be a greater contrast. Particularly in the present situation. He turned to Green.

The boy's blue eyes were wide, his pupils dilated. His blond hair was cut short like Charles's, and his lapels were reasonable. He could turn his head. Perspiration dotted his brow. His smile was forced.

'Charles,' Manchester's light tenor voice said, 'come to pay us a visit? Join in. I am very lucky at the moment.'

Charles flicked him a glance. 'Perhaps, later, Manchester.' He turned to the young man. 'Good evening, Green. I see you play deep.' Charles watched the young man, wondering how he was going to get him out of this and deciding the sooner the better.

'Y-yes.' His stiff smile widened into a rictus.

'Perhaps you shouldn't.' Charles turned back to Manchester. 'If you will excuse us, Green and I have things to discuss.'

'Really, Hawthorne, don't be a wet blanket.' Manchester raked in the chips piled before him.

'Ah, but I must,' Charles drawled, placing his hand on Green's shoulder and squeezing as he shifted the boy away from the table.

'Ah, ex-excuse me.' Richard Green went where Charles steered him, but said over his shoulder, 'I will make my vouchers good tomorrow, Manchester.'

A twinge of pain caught Charles unawares. Seeing this youth, not yet a man and no longer a boy, in such a pass brought back unpleasant memories of where his reckless disregard for money had eventually landed him. Gambling deeply was only for those who had been left a fortune, not a younger son. The discomfort was enough to make him thrust Green roughly toward the door so the boy stumbled before gaining his footing.

'Keep moving,' Charles said through clenched teeth. 'You are not staying here.'

Green's eyes widened until they seemed to be two blue china saucers. 'But, the night has just started.'

'Be quiet.' Charles scowled at the young man. 'You are foolish beyond bearing.'

'I-I s-say, you c-can't order me about.'

Charles's brows rose. 'Can't I? I am doing so and you will thank me for it.'

The boy's red face blanched. 'You are Charles Hawthorne?'

'Yes, and you are on your way out.'

He realised Green had been so deep in the fever some people experienced while gambling that the boy hadn't heard Manchester's greeting. The realisation increased Charles's anger. He propelled the youth toward the front door and through to the street.

'I hope your carriage or horse is nearby because you are leaving.'

'I—'

'Yes?' Charles held him. 'You what?'

'You go too far. You have no right to do this.'

The young man's words finally penetrated the red haze that seemed to surround Charles. He unclenched his fingers that gripped the boy's arm like a vise and let his hand fall away. Seeing this child in straits he had been in and paid dearly for had made him forget the circumstances. All he could do was throw the fool out.

'You are going home, Green. You play deeper than your pockets. This is a gambling den, not a shearing house.'

The youth drew himself up straight, coming just short of Charles's six-foot height. 'I will do as I please.'

'Not if I have any say.' His flat voice brooked no argument. 'And a word of warning. You may think you are immune to the repercussions of your behaviour, but you are not. No one is.'

Seeing a hackney coach coming around the corner, Charles motioned for it to stop. The driver pulled up and Charles yanked open the door and pushed Green inside.

'Go home.'

He slammed the door shut and turned away, ignoring the boy's sputtering anger. If only someone had done as much for him.

Chapter Four

Amy tweaked Emma's paisley shawl. 'When are you going to get new gowns? These are so old-fashioned.'

Emma pulled the shawl over her shoulders and kept moving toward an open settee in Princess Lieven's ballroom. She was not about to give Amy the satisfaction of seeing that her comment had hurt. Amy knew why Emma had no new gowns.

Amy was peeved because Emma had refused Charles Hawthorne's offer to escort them here. The man was too brazen. He wasn't family, and his bringing them would have set tongues wagging. Especially after the ride in Hyde Park yesterday.

She reached the seat and sank down with a thump. Graceless, but she didn't care.

Amy sat beside her, careful to spread the skirt of her pink muslin gown so it wouldn't wrinkle. 'You ignored me.' Her tone and posture were a challenging pout.

Emma swallowed a sharp retort. Her voice was still more acerbic than she intended. 'You know why, Amy. So don't vent your displeasure over something we both know can't be helped.'

'Humph!'

Amy angled away, her back an unyielding wall between them. For an instant, Emma raised her hand to touch her sister's shoulder. All they had was each other. Then she let her arm fall. For once she wasn't willing to be conciliatory. She was tired and worried and wanted to be done with all this. She didn't want to apologise for something that wasn't her fault.

Amy stood abruptly. 'I am going to find Julia Thornton.'

For a second Emma considered telling Amy to remain. Then she shrugged. Denying Amy would only make her more rebellious. At least Julia would have her mother with her or be surrounded by a bevy of young men and women closer to Amy's age.

As Amy flounced away, Emma turned her attention to the other guests just as Charles Hawthorne made his bow to their hostess. Sensation chased down Emma's spine. She told herself there was a draft. The man had offered to escort them here. It shouldn't be a surprise to see him, and there was no other reason for the funny feeling that engulfed her.

Nor should it be a surprise to see him make his way toward her. He likely thought Amy would be back immediately.

Emma watched him in spite of all her good sense. He was the most sensual man she had ever seen. Everything about him indicated that he was a rake. His black hair with the lock that insisted on falling over his forehead made him look like a pirate—or what she imagined a pirate would look like. His broad shoulders swung loosely in a well-fitted evening jacket. His muscular legs with their long length and strong shape showed to perfection in tight-fitting breeches. He was perfect.

'Enjoying something?' He stood before her with a sly smile on his sharply handsome face.

She jolted and blinked and wondered where her common sense had gone as she gave him a curt nod. 'Mr Hawthorne.'

He made a perfect leg. 'Miss Stockton.'

Her eyes narrowed at his mocking tone. 'What brings you here, Mr Hawthorne? My sister is elsewhere.'

'So she is, Miss Stockton.'

Emma felt her temper sizzle, intensifying the warmth spreading across her cheeks. 'Then you had best be on your way.'

'I thought I might linger here.' He indicated the empty spot by her.

The breath caught in her throat, and she forced herself to speak coldly. 'I think you would be very bored, Mr Hawthorne.'

'I think not.'

Without further leave, he sat beside her. His thigh barely brushed hers, bringing back the uncomfortable awareness of him that made her chest tight. This wasn't supposed to happen. Emma tensed to rise but his hand clamped on her forearm. She paused.

'Do you want to give the gossips more ammunition?' he murmured.

She glanced around to see many eyes on them. She sank back down and muttered, 'How dare you put me in this position. It is bad enough that you do this with Amy. It is a shame you insist on including me in this mockery.'

He quirked one eyebrow. 'Why do you think this is a mockery?'

'Isn't it?'

He didn't speak for long moments, his gaze meeting hers. 'I don't believe so.'

She told herself her heart wasn't lodged in her throat. A warm glow started in her stomach and spread out. 'Well, I do. I told you no earlier, and you are not a man who likes to be told no. I believe you are amusing yourself at my expense and I want this to stop.'

'Then dance with me and I will leave afterwards.'

'Absolutely not.' Particularly as she recognised the music the orchestra was starting to play. A waltz.

He shrugged. 'Then I will go and ask Miss Amy.'

Emma blanched, knowing her sister would accept to spite her and to accomplish a coup that would make her the envy of all the other silly young chits. A waltz with Charles Hawthorne.

Emma felt like she had been outmaneuvered, and she knew she was outgunned. 'Surely you jest. It is my sister you are interested in.'

For a fleeting moment she thought he looked disgusted, but it was over so quickly she decided she had imagined it. He looked his usual arrogant, confident and mocking self.

'Are you sure?'

'I am no fool.' But she began to fear she was. She wanted this dance he had maneuvered her into. Wanted it badly. 'But you have forced me to accept.'

He stood and extended his gloved hand. She dropped her gaze, unwilling to see him study her as she put her fingers into his.

Gloves separated their flesh, yet Emma felt like his warm skin touched hers. This was crazy, she thought, sucking in a deep breath and looking up at him, determined to act as though this dance was the last thing she wanted.

His dark eyes held hers. Was there a question in his? Did he wonder what she thought?

She notched her chin higher and turned to the floor. He led her out. She turned to face him, his strong jaw at eye level for her. He had a dark shadow on his cheeks that gave him a reckless air he didn't need. He was already overpoweringly attractive.

The scents of musk and male wafted over her, mingling with the smell of burning wax from the hundreds of candles. Dimly she sensed other people moving around. The sound of the orchestra was muted. It was as though she stood in a room with only this man. Everything else might be in her imagination.

His right arm circled her waist and held her firmly in place a foot from him. The regulation distance. Anything closer would be considered scandalous.

Her mind told her they were adequately separated. Her senses told her he pressed her to his chest. It seemed she felt his heart beating against hers and his warmth enveloping her.

He moved and his hand guided her to move with him. She felt melded to him, as though they had danced like this before. Blood pounded through her body.

'Are you feeling well?'

His deep voice flowed over her and twined around her. All her aversion to him seemed to have gone up in smoke the instant he touched her. No wonder Amy made a scandal of herself for this man. And how could she blame her when she, an older woman who had once been engaged to this man's brother, was now following him in a dance that mimicked things done between a man and a woman in dark places?

Emma shook her head. 'Well? I am as well as can be expected when coerced into a dance I did not want.'

'Are you so sure of that?' He gave her a knowing look that seemed to see through to her racing heart.

'You gave me no choice.'

He swung her in a circle, forcing the breath from her lungs. If not for the firm hold he had of her waist, she would have stumbled.

'Liar.'

She dragged in air. 'I am not. You threatened to ask Amy if I did not agree.'

'I gave you a choice.'

'A very poor one.'

They moved rapidly around the room, circling and circling, skirting other couples. His arms never faltered, supporting her strongly and her body felt safe to follow his lead—wherever that might go.

'But a choice.' He finished the discussion, his tone brooking no more argument.

Her hackles rose. 'A poor choice is no choice at all. I know that too well.'

His mouth thinned and she thought he would say something, but the music stopped. They stopped with it. She stepped from his embrace and tried to pull her hand free from his. He held tight.

'Let me go.'

His mouth curved into a smile that held no humour as he brought her fingers to his lips. Even through the gloves she felt the firm softness of his kiss. An arc of fire coursed its way up her arm. Her determination floundered.

He released her and bowed. 'Thank you, Miss Stockton, for a very informative dance.'

She stared at him, the heat still coursing through her. 'Informative?'

He turned away as though he didn't hear her. She stepped toward him, wanting to twirl him around and demand what he thought he was doing, toying with her as though she was a plaything. Instead she pivoted on her heel and moved in the opposite direction from him.

Somewhere in this room was the settee she had taken refuge on earlier. She reached it seconds before Amy descended on her.

'What do you think you were doing?' Amy said, her voice a whispered screech. 'I thought he was a disreputable rake that no respectable woman should associate with. Yet, you *waltzed* with him.'

Emma's fingers still tingled from his touch. Now they shook with irritation. 'He is everything I always say he is, but he gave me no option.' She steeled her voice. 'And I am old enough to do as I please.'

'So, you like him.' Amy's blue eyes were grey with anger. 'That is why you tell me to stay away from him. Because you want him.'

Emma's raw nerves snapped. 'Don't be a ninnyhammer, Amy. It is bad enough that you are flighty.'

Amy's rosebud red mouth formed a perfect *O*. Her eyes filled with tears. 'How could you, Em? First you dance with the man I am attracted to, and then you insult me so.'

Emma's head began to pound. This was getting out of hand. She rose. 'I think it is time we left.'

Amy stepped back. 'No. I have promised Mr Kennilworth a dance. I shan't shirk my duty.'

Sharp words about Amy's frequent failure to honour her word hung on Emma's tongue but she bit them back. Things were so bad she did not want to make them worse. 'When you are done, we are leaving.'

Amy sniffed and turned away, her shoulders stiff. Emma watched her young sister and wondered what mischief Amy would get up to now. Likely she would manage to dance a waltz with Charles Hawthorne even after Emma's sacrifice to prevent it.

She longed for a hot drink and a warm bed. What should have been a pleasurable outing in the home of one of the *ton*'s most powerful women had turned into a nightmare thanks to Charles Hawthorne. The man should be ousted from Society.

Emma rubbed her temples, hoping to ease some of the tension pounding through her head. Perhaps a breath of fresh air would help. She made her way to the open windows, watching for Amy as she went.

Amy was where she said she would be. Emma knew her sister didn't care much for Mr Kennilworth, but she had used him as an excuse to remain.

Emma stepped into the cool night air with a sense of relief. Nothing would happen during the country dance.

The music filtered to a murmur that failed to muffle the sound of female voices. Several feet away, their backs to her, two women laughed. Emma retreated, not wanting to interrupt them. She heard her name and froze.

'Did you see Emma Stockton in Charles Hawthorne's arms? She looked absolutely besotted. No wonder she chides her sister for chasing the man. She wants him herself.'

The second woman giggled. 'As though he would be interested. He is playing with both of them.'

'So true.'

Emma felt the blood leave her face before raging back as mortification claimed her. The cool night was suddenly unbearably warm.

She twisted on her heel and sped back into the hot, crowded ballroom. The dance was only half done. What would she do? She felt like the fool she had chided herself for being. Surely she hadn't looked besotted. She couldn't stand the man, no matter what her body did. Her mind found him despicable and…and…

How could she have reacted to him so much that others noticed? She had thought she had more self-control.

She paused inside the doors, out of view of the two women, and scanned the room. Amy curtseyed to Mr Kennilworth as the dance ended.

Emma's nemesis laughed at something Princess Lieven said before she swatted his arm with her closed fan. Very much as Lady Jersey had done. Were all of them susceptible to him?

She looked away.

What was happening to her? She had never felt this way about George Hawthorne. Truth be told, she had felt nothing for him. That was why it had been easy for her to break their engagement. Her only regret was that her action had necessitated Amy marrying for money regardless of anything the girl might feel.

'Are you feeling all right, Miss Stockton?'

Emma jerked as *his* rich voice came from just behind her. Her fingers trembled as she twisted around. 'I am fine. Please go away.'

'Touchy.' He stood his ground, his eyes darkening.

Her headache returned with a vengeance. 'Mr Hawthorne, I am merely watching my wayward sister flirt with the latest object of her attention.' She tried to keep her unease out of her voice and realised she sounded tired and petulant.

'She is a handful.'

'Quite.'

He chuckled. 'George would sympathise with you.'

She stiffened at the name of her former fiancé. 'Are you referring to your peccadilloes?'

He wore a rueful expression. 'What else? I'm sure my past isn't a secret.'

In spite of her distrust, growing attraction and overall sense of being out of her depth, she replied, 'I only know what I have seen this Season. You dabble in trade to great profit and do as you please without regard to others. The last is very like Amy.'

'Yes, Miss Amy and I share a dislike for being dictated to

and for wanting our own way. Perhaps the youngest child is like that.'

'Spoilt.'

He smiled. 'Exactly. But sometimes we go too far.'

She sensed he spoke about something besides their shared willful disregard for propriety. 'Such as?'

'Here you are, Emma,' Amy's hard-edged voice intruded, 'entertaining Mr Hawthorne. Again.'

For the first time in many years, Emma felt as though she was in deeper water than she could navigate. Charles Hawthorne seemed ready to confide something intensely private, a trust she was not sure she wanted. And now Amy's biting words showed again how hurt she was by the situation between Emma and Mr Hawthorne. There was only one thing to do.

Emma took a deep breath. 'Amy, dear, it is time we left.' She took Amy's arm and started moving even as she said, 'Good evening, Mr Hawthorne.'

He did nothing to stop them, and Emma found herself ridiculously grateful for his restraint. She knew that if he had tried to delay them, Amy would have allowed it. She propelled her sister to the entry, hoping no one else would intercept them and that Amy would not dig in her heels.

Neither happened.

They reached the front door where a footman retrieved their wraps. Emma released Amy. Already she felt as though she had overreacted.

Things were falling apart. Amy's headstrong rush into adventure, Charles Hawthorne's pursuit, Bertram in London and, worse than all of the others combined, her own reaction to Charles Hawthorne.

Amy stepped outside and Emma belatedly followed. Their hired carriage was nowhere. It wasn't scheduled to pick them up for another two hours.

Amy, blond brows furrowed, turned on Emma. 'Now what will we do?'

Two women alone, the last thing they could do was walk.

Hoping to see a hackney coach, Emma moved to the kerb so the flickering light from the gas lamps lit beside the imposing door cast her shadow onto the cobbles. The crush of coaches filled with guests still arriving filled the street. Carriages would arrive until the morning sun lit the eastern sky as members of the *ton* moved from one party to another.

'Let me help,' Charles Hawthorne's voice intruded on Emma's simmering nerves.

'Did you follow us?'

'And if I did?'

She glared at him. He was the last thing she needed. He was the source of all her problems, or so it seemed. 'I have had quite enough of your help to last me a lifetime, thank you.'

His face inscrutable, he looked from one to the other. 'Is Bertram coming for you?'

Amy's laugh was brittle. 'I should think not. He is in some gambling hell losing what little we have left.'

Emma gasped. 'Amy!'

Amy's mouth turned mulish. 'It's the truth.'

Everything was unravelling. 'It is none of Mr Hawthorne's concern.' She rounded on him. 'Just as our situation is none of your concern.'

'Then how will we get home?' Amy's pale blond hair was coming undone from the spray of white roses that was her only adornment.

Emma wanted to shout at her, but there was nothing to say. They had no way home unless a hackney carriage appeared out of thin air or their hired coach miraculously materialised.

She darted a glance at the man responsible for this awful situation. He stood watching her, his face unreadable. If he had only left them alone.

She was sure the freckles stood in stark relief on her nose and her cheeks shone like ripe apples. Not an attractive picture—and just the thought of that made her angrier. She ground her teeth, even as she realised this fury was not like her.

Emma took deep calming breaths, refusing to meet his gaze. People milled around them, some looking, others careful not to.

'We are presenting the polite world with fuel for its wagging tongues,' he said dryly.

He was right.

'Emma, we should accept Mr Hawthorne's offer of help.'

Emma scowled at him. 'Are you in your brother's barouche or must we all squeeze into your phaeton?'

He had the grace to look mildly embarrassed, nothing more. 'I hadn't anticipated this situation, Miss Stockton.'

'I imagine you didn't.' The tart words were out in a trice. He brought out the absolute worst in her.

'I am in my phaeton.'

'Well, that solves it.' She wondered where her vaunted self-control had gone as she noted the acid in her tone. She should be speaking calmly and rationally, not like a fishwife. 'We cannot all cram into that vehicle. It would not be at all respectable.'

'Nor is this bickering in public.' Amy's voice cut across them.

'The pot calling the kettle black,' Charles murmured.

Emma cast him a sharp look but said nothing. Amy was right. But she could not allow her young sister and herself to pile into his phaeton. They would be much too close.

'I shall get a sedan chair.' Charles moved to the street and hailed two down. Turning back to them, he said, 'I will walk along side until you are safely home.'

'Sedan chairs are for old dowagers,' Amy's disgusted voice rang out.

Emma nearly laughed. It certainly cut across the retort Emma had planned to make. Her fury of minutes before seemed to evaporate and for the first time since her waltz with Charles Hawthorne, she felt as though her mind worked properly.

'We have no need of those, Mr Hawthorne. We are country girls and quite capable of walking home.' She looked at the still crowded street. 'It is just that I don't believe it would be safe.'

'Then I shall escort you.' When she opened her mouth to decline his offer, he added, 'Or hoist you into my phaeton.'

'Neither, thank you.'

She was proud her voice was calm and not burdened with fury. Her lapse had been momentary and would not repeat itself.

'Then how do you propose to get home?'

'Here is our hired carriage,' Amy said, moving toward the vehicle. 'It is early.'

'Thank goodness.' The heartfelt words followed on the relief Emma felt.

Charles moved into the street and motioned the coach to stop. Without waiting for the groom perched on the back to dismount, Charles opened the door and handed Amy in. She gave him a radiant smile that put the lie to her former peevishness.

Emma noticed he did not kiss her sister's hand even though Amy let it linger overlong in his. An unwelcome, piercing relief lanced Emma. She refused to study the sensation—or try to name the cause of it.

Instead, she walked to the carriage door, ignoring Charles Hawthorne's outstretched hand. She lifted her skirt and put her foot on the carriage step. He took her arm to steady her. Instantly awareness of him flooded her: his smell, the warmth of his hand on her arm. He was a man it was impossible for her to ignore, try as she might.

Better that he did not touch her, but she knew from her previous experiences with him this evening that he was too strong for her to make him release her. He would have this his way just as he had had everything else his way this evening.

'I am sorry for all the trouble I have caused you tonight,' he murmured.

Surprise held her immobile as his barely audible words wafted against her neck. He was apologising? She could not believe her ears.

Turning her head, she gazed at him, realising too late that only inches separated their lips. A dip of her head and his mouth would touch hers. Just this once, she wanted to close the distance and let her senses rule her head. Her eyes widened in shock at the realisation.

As though he knew what she wanted, his fingers tightened on her arm and his mouth parted. His eyes were as dark as the sky behind his head. Emma knew it was her imagination only that whispered he would kiss her. Her wanton desire for something she knew was wrong and the illusion caused by unclear lighting. Nothing more. She wouldn't let it be anything more.

'You have done more damage than an apology can rectify,' she finally managed to say, her voice breathy. 'Let me go.'

He held her a moment longer. She thought he would say something. Her stomach tumbled.

He released her and stepped back. 'You are right, of course.'

His tone was flat, as though he felt nothing, and she was infinitely glad she had not reacted on her unbidden response to him. It was her need that had prompted her to think he meant to kiss her. He did not care for her.

She hurried into the carriage and sank into the seat opposite Amy. The vehicle lurched forward. Emma fell backwards before righting herself and squaring her shoulders.

'I saw you.' Amy's words were an accusation. 'You want him.'

'Don't be ridiculous.' She closed her eyes, unable to look at Amy when she said the words.

Emma admitted to herself that she lied. It was not that she wanted him in the sense of love and permanence, but for just this small period of time she wanted to feel his arms around her and his lips on hers. So, yes, she did want him.

When she opened her eyes, Amy was a dark silhouette in the unlit interior. Emma hoped she looked the same to her sister because she knew the blush on her face would tell Amy the truth.

She was always honest with Amy no matter how hard it might be at times. She had prided herself on that openness. Now Charles Hawthorne was the cause of her first untruth to her sister. Just another thing to hold against the man. She nearly sobbed in regret.

They did not speak the rest of the drive.

When the coach stopped, Amy bolted from her seat and out of the door. Emma alighted and saw Amy had used the key in her reticule to let herself into the dark house. Now there was a wedge between them when they needed each other the most.

She turned to the coach driver and offered him the money. 'Thank you.'

'No need, ma'am. 'Is Lordship paid me.' The driver gave her a gap-toothed grin, indicating the amount had been more than adequate.

Emma forced a smile and turned away. She wanted to push her money into the man's hand if only to prove to herself that she did not need or appreciate Charles Hawthorne's act of generosity. But that would solve nothing. She had to control herself.

The glow from the single candle Gordon kept burning when she and Amy were out cast a puddle of pale light at her feet. The rest of the street was dark. No one fashionable lived here to be entertaining in the small hours of the morning.

She shivered in the cool air and followed Amy into the house.

Charles stood watching the hackney coach long after it disappeared around the corner. The tip he'd given the driver should ensure Emma Stockton and her sister got home safely and with promptness. It was the least he could do after causing the rift between the sisters.

He turned to look at Princess Lieven's glittering mansion. It had been an impulsive decision to come here, based solely on boredom. He had wanted to irritate Emma Stockton by offering to escort them, and when that failed, he'd wanted to amuse himself by pursuing her at the ball. He had not realised how it would escalate.

Even he, spoiled and filled with ennui, had been uncomfortable with the argument between the sisters. He had underestimated Amy Stockton's infatuation with him, something he rarely did. That's what came of meddling with schoolroom chits.

It was bad enough that he had found himself reacting to Emma Stockton's nearness. She was a prude and high in the instep, traits he did not care for. Yet, he had nearly kissed her.

It must be the scent of sweet peas she wore. He had always liked them. It could not be her.

Irritated with himself and his behaviour, he pivoted on his heel and strode down the street. A few minutes later, he remembered his tiger and phaeton were at Princess Lieven's. He stalked back and signaled a footman to call for his carriage.

Chapter Five

Having slept suitably late to compensate for not getting to bed until six in the morning, Charles sauntered into White's Club in the early afternoon. He moved towards the bow window where Beau Brummell, Alvanley and others had once sat to watch any female brave enough to walk along St. James.

He nodded to several acquaintances and angled to where his brother sat near the window reading *The Times*. Charles sank into the overstuffed leather chair closest to George. His brother was tall and slim with golden brown hair and matching eyes. Their sister took after George.

Charles stretched out his long legs with a sigh of pleasure. 'What are you doing away from your beautiful bride and bouncing baby Robert?'

Lord George Hawthorne looked up and smiled at his brother. 'I was reading the paper, quietly minding my own business.' His gaze shifted to his brother's coat, and he rolled his eyes. 'And what are you doing with a sweet pea in your lapel?'

Charles grinned. 'Answer my question and I'll answer yours.'

'Just like old times, huh?' George set down the paper he wasn't going to read for awhile. 'I left Rose and Robert in the company of Juliet. Adam is at Tattersall's looking at horseflesh. They plan on touring the Continent, and he wants to take his own conveniences.'

'Oh, Adam.' Charles scowled as he thought of his disreputable brother-in-law.

'Still on that note?' George shook his head. 'He's reformed, and he makes her happy.'

Charles's scowl lightened marginally. 'True on both counts, but that doesn't mean I have to like the situation.'

'What about you and the Stockton chit? Is your behaviour any better?'

Charles bristled. 'You are no one to be talking about the Stocktons and how we treat the women in that family.'

George paled but he held Charles's gaze. 'You are right. I did poorly by Miss Stockton. The only redeeming feature of that incident—which I tell myself—is that I did not love her and she didn't love me. Ours was to be a marriage of convenience. I am now married for love and happier than I have ever been, and Miss Stockton has the chance to find a man who will value her like I could not have.' He stared into space for a minute. 'Love is a powerful emotion. I found just how much it could change me.' He looked back at Charles. 'I hope some day you have the experience.'

'Yes, yes.'

Charles found himself unwilling to talk about Emma Stockton and her finding a suitable marriage partner. Something about the topic made his stomach twist. Nor did he want to talk about finding love. So far, he was not impressed with what love had made his siblings do.

'As for the sweet pea in my lapel.' He grinned again. 'I am performing a test.'

One of George's golden brows rose.

'Yes, a test. To see how many sheep there are in the *ton*.'

'Sheep in the *ton*? In other words, how many men will have a sweet pea in their lapel by this evening or tomorrow.' George shook his head. 'You are incorrigible.'

Charles made a mocking bow from his sitting position. 'I try.'

Even as he bantered with George, raised voices caught Charles's attention. Glancing in the direction of the commotion, he saw a group sitting by a window. One of the men was Bertram Stockton. All Charles's former ire at his brother-in-law, the injustices done to Miss Emma Stockton and young Green several nights before, and other emotions he could no more describe than he could banish, surfaced.

'What is that good-for-nothing doing here?'

George looked over his shoulder. 'You mean Stockton?'

'Who else?'

'I imagine the same thing we are. Looking for company and entertainment on an otherwise boring afternoon.'

'He shouldn't even be in London.'

George's eyebrow rose again. 'And why is that?'

Charles gave him a scathing look. 'Because the man is in debt—he's deep in the River Tick and likely going deeper. He will make it impossible for Amy Stockton or Miss Stockton to make suitable marriages because of the family debt they will expect their prospective husbands to pay off.'

'Ah, that explains your interest and irritation.' George drawled the words as he put one hand up to cover the smile he couldn't stop. 'And what about your past? Aren't you the pot calling the kettle black?'

Charles sat up straight. 'My peccadilloes are in the past. And what I did only impacted on me. My losses made no difference to your future or Juliet's. I hurt no one.' A muscle in his jaw twitched. 'I learned the hard way and don't want to see anyone else in the position I was in several years ago.'

'I am sorry for that.'

Charles knew George blamed himself for the plight Charles had got himself into. 'Don't be. I did it to myself and I am doing my best not to do it again. My business interests pay me well even though trade is not considered respectable by the *ton*. I do not gamble anymore and I stay within my means. It was a hard lesson to learn.'

'I know. I didn't know any other way to help you.'

'There wasn't.'

Still, if he let the memories take him, they were painful. He did his best to keep them at bay. Just as he stayed away from gambling dens, knowing how hard it was to resist temptation. The other night had been the first time in three years that he had entered a gaming establishment. But his club was different. More than gaming went on here.

'I am merely out to make enough money to do the things that are important to me.'

'And those things are…'

Charles waved a hand to indicate White's. 'Belonging here. Good horseflesh. My estate…'

'And women.' George's voice held a hint of exasperation.

Charles's eyes flashed. 'You are certainly on your high horse today. I shouldn't think what I do is any concern of yours.'

George smiled gently. 'Everything someone in my family does is of concern to me. I care for you.'

'I am not duelling and I am not breaking any laws.' Charles felt as though he were in the witness box defending himself to a judge. 'Nor am I going to mend my current ways.' He sighed. 'I have made the only major change I intend to.'

George nodded. 'And I know it was hard for you. I admire your strength. But think how hard it was for you and maybe you will find a little compassion in your heart for Bertram Stockton.'

'I didn't lose my family's fortune and force my sister to put herself on the Marriage Mart to save us from ruin.'

'True. Even when you lost everything, I was able to cover your debts. Today you are more careful with money than I am even if you are still reckless with women.' He paused to consider. 'But then, women encourage you shamelessly.'

Tired of the subject and more than a little defensive, Charles stood. 'I am going to go and see what is going on.'

'It really isn't any of your business,' George said reasonably.

Charles looked down at him, his black brows a *V* of ire. 'Someone must stop the man from gambling away what he doesn't have.'

'That someone isn't you,' George said pointedly. 'And you don't know if they are gaming.'

Charles stared at his brother, knowing George was right. His impulsiveness and tendency to fight for the underdog— or in this case, underlady—had nearly put him into a position that was untenable for him and for the Stockton ladies. It was not as though he was engaged to either one of them or owed them more than common courtesy and manners required. No matter that baiting Miss Emma Stockton seemed to occupy more of his thoughts than it should.

He sat back down with a thud, his usual gracefulness gone. 'You are right.' Charles beckoned for one of the waiters. 'A bottle of port.'

'A little early isn't it?'

'No.'

As though the waiter's movement had started a chain reaction, Bertram Stockton broke off whatever he was saying to the man beside him and looked at Charles. Their eyes met. Charles looked away without acknowledging the other man, giving Stockton the cut direct. He was being unreasonable, but couldn't help his anger over the burden Emma Stockton bore. She was an underdog.

The port arrived at that instant and Charles sniffed the cork, approved the wine and then accepted the glass poured by the waiter. He took a long swallow, wishing he could wash away the bad taste left in his mouth from Stockton's presence, and knowing he couldn't. So he watched the man who was to blame for Emma Stockton's situation.

Charles finished his wine and poured another glass. He didn't even like Emma Stockton. He merely enjoyed irritating her and even that was to stop. He had no wish to further compromise either her or her younger sister. Nor did he want to be responsible for another rift between the sisters.

Perhaps it was time to stop provoking Miss Stockton.

Bertram Stockton said something to the man he was with and turned and headed toward Charles. Charles's eyes narrowed to slits as he watched Stockton approach. The man had nerve after receiving a direct cut.

'Charles Hawthorne.'

Charles gazed up at the man who had a paler version of Emma Stockton's red hair and hazel eyes instead of Miss Stockton's striking grey ones. He was in no mood to be polite.

'I don't believe we have anything to discuss.' Charles's tone would have chilled every bottle of wine White's had.

Stockton turned an unbecoming shade of red. 'I am not here to discuss anything with you.'

'Good,' Charles drawled. 'Go away.'

'Gentlemen,' George interjected, 'it is time my brother and I left.' He stood. 'Good to see you, Stockton.'

Stockton turned his attention to the man who had all but jilted his oldest sister. 'I can't say the same, Hawthorne.' He turned back to Charles. 'As for you. Leave my sister alone.'

Charles stood. His height and lean physique gave him the advantage over the other man. 'And what if I don't?' He insolently took another sip of port.

'Then we will meet on the field of honour.'

Charles nearly spewed the wine at Stockton's absurdity. 'You jest. From what I hear, you can't fence and you can't fire a pistol from ten feet and hit the target, let alone fight with your fists. What field of honour do you propose we meet on?'

Every word had been meant to insult, and the mottled red on Stockton's face gave Charles a modicum of satisfaction. When George put his hand on Charles's shoulder and squeezed hard, Charles didn't need the reminder that his behaviour was irrational, not to mention rude to the point of being inexcusable. He already knew that. But he couldn't seem to stop himself.

On one level, Charles sensed the attention of every man within sight. Still, he focused on the man in front of him as time seemed to stand still while he waited for Stockton's response.

Stockton was tall and thin, with a dusting of freckles across his nose and cheeks. He looked like a youth even though

Charles knew him to be at least George's age. His clothes were of the latest style. His Hessians gleamed in the watery sunlight coming through the nearby window. A quizzing glass hung from his waistcoat pocket and his gloves were pristine. His shirt points were high enough to make it impossible for him to turn his head. A dandy.

Stockton took one of those immaculate gloves from his hand, the gesture not as smooth as Charles knew the man would have liked. The fine kid-leather stuck as though Stockton's palm sweated.

A tiny cruel smile formed on Charles's perfect mouth. Anticipation tightened his gut. He refused to think about the emotion or wonder why he felt it. He just waited.

A quick swipe and Stockton's white glove slapped Charles's jaw. The impact made a sound like that of a shot, and though it wasn't loud, Charles was sure every man in the room heard it.

'That is for introducing my sisters to Harriette Wilson. The entire town is talking about them.'

Fury leached the colour from Charles's face. Stockton was right, he shouldn't have introduced the women to the courtesan and particularly not in Rotten Row. Still, a challenge was a challenge.

'Pistols,' Charles stated without hesitation.

As the one challenged, it was his right to choose the weapon. He would have preferred fists for the sheer pleasure of the physical exertion, but that was more ungentlemanly than even he was prepared to go. Nor was it considered a duel, and this was a duel.

'Send your second 'round.' Stockton's voice was flat, his face so pale the freckles stood out like splotches. 'Do not see my sister from this point on.'

Charles's smile widened, showing white, predatory teeth in a slash. 'I shall do as I please, when I please, Stockton. Best you learn that now.'

Stockton pivoted on the heel of his boot and strode off, not

sparing a glance for anyone else. Charles wondered that the
man left what appeared to be a game of chance, a pastime
Stockton preferred before all others.

'The fox is in with the hens now,' George said dryly. 'I've
seen you do some harebrained things before, but this takes the
wager. Whatever got into you?'

Charles shrugged and swallowed down the remainder of
the port in one long gulp that made his Adam's apple move
above the perfect crease of his cravat. 'The man irritates me.
Always has.'

George frowned. 'You don't even know the man above a
passing acquaintance.'

Charles looked sideways at his brother as he carefully set the
empty glass on the table. 'I know *about* the man. That is enough.'

George shook his head. 'Don't you mean, you know his
sister?'

Charles glanced around, saw all the attention still on them and
motioned with his hand. 'White's isn't the place to discuss this.'

George moved to the door. 'This wasn't the place for any
of this.'

They collected their beaver hats, canes and top coats from
the servant and exited onto St. James Street. Charles set his
hat at an angle and swung his ebony cane with its silver tip.
Now that it was done, he felt a fierce gladness. There was no
going back from a duel of honour.

'It isn't your place.' George's sober voice intruded on
Charles's thoughts. 'Stockton had the right of it. You have
been paying a too marked attention toward Amy Stockton.
She's barely out of the schoolroom. It isn't like you to pursue
someone of her innocence. Nor is it proper. And that is just
for starters. I won't mention the *introduction* which is indeed
the latest crim con.'

Heat rose in Charles's cheeks. 'Was it right for you to
pursue Rose when you were engaged to Miss Stockton?'

'No.'

'Then leave off, George. Stockton is a cad who has wagered his family fortune until there is nothing left. Emma Stockton became engaged to you in hopes you'd bail her family out of debt. When you put her in the untenable position of having to call off the engagement because of your far from respectable behaviour, you put paid to that plan. Now she is considered the spinster on the shelf and Miss Amy is the fatted calf set on the Marriage Mart as the sacrifice for her father and brother's vices.'

George's voice cut sarcastically through Charles's tirade. 'And you have appointed yourself seducer and knight in shining armour all in one package? You're overdoing it.'

Some of the jauntiness left Charles's walk. He knew George was right. What George had done had been wrong, but that didn't make what Charles had just done right.

George continued. 'Not to mention what this duel will do to Miss Amy and Miss Stockton's reputations when it gets about. As you say, Miss Stockton is on the shelf, but Miss Amy *had* the opportunity to make an advantageous marriage.'

'*Had* being the key word?'

Disgust at George's honesty and his own stupidity made Charles as sarcastic as his brother. He had botched things up, but there was no going back. If he retracted his acceptance of the duel, he'd be branded a coward and his standing in the *ton* ruined. All the social pleasures he enjoyed would be denied him. His way of life would be over. He was not ready to give that up merely to keep from meeting Bertram Stockton at dawn.

They were halfway to George's town house when the rain started. 'Bloody nasty ending to a bloody nasty day,' Charles groused.

George looked at his younger brother, who had never been known for his patience and often known for his impassioned impetuosity. 'You can still back down.'

'No. I can't.' Charles stared at the rain-slicked cobbles, feeling the water drip from the brim of his beaver hat. He slapped his thigh with the ebony cane and cursed his own stupidity. 'It would ruin me.'

'I see.'

Charles stopped and rounded on his brother. 'No, you don't. You have everything. I have to make my own way in the world. I am doing that through trade. Already I am on the fringes of acceptable society. If I were branded a coward, not even my male friends would acknowledge me. Bertram Stockton isn't worth the sacrifice.'

George's eyes widened and he stepped back. 'I didn't realise you felt that way. I can arrange a larger settlement for you.'

Charles sighed and ran a hand down his face, wiping away the water that dripped from the brim of his hat. 'No. No. I don't envy you the inheritance. Never have. But I never want to repeat my stay in the Fleet. And my business investments will ensure that.' He paused. 'If I back down, I will be a laughing stock. It is bad enough already being a criminal.'

His mouth twisted. He turned away and stepped forward, trying to ignore the fact that things were getting too complicated.

A carriage pulled up alongside them and one of the windows opened. Adam Glenfinning leaned out.

'Care for a ride?'

George grinned. 'You are in the nick of time. I can feel the wet sinking through my coat, and I know it has ruined my boots.'

Charles scowled at the man who had recently married his sister. 'I'll walk, thank you.'

Adam looked at him as though he wanted to say something very scathing. 'Suit yourself, old man.'

George glanced at Charles. 'I'll walk with you then.'

'No,' Charles said. 'Go with Adam. Just because I am deranged enough to stay in this downpour doesn't mean you should.'

George studied his brother for a long moment. 'I'll see you at the house then.'

Charles nodded and waved them on, continuing to trudge through the wet. The last thing he should have done was to provoke Bertram Stockton into challenging him. He had honestly not thought the man had the stomach to do so. He had misjudged him and now he had to face the man and delope for he could not in good conscience shoot the man when he was right. And he had to consider what to do about the reputations of the two Stockton sisters. He was the worst thing that could have happened to them.

He groaned. This was complicated.

Inside the carriage, George sat opposite Adam and took off his wet beaver. 'Ruined.'

'I wasn't in the nick of time?' Adam said with a sardonic twist of very fine lips.

His brown eyes held a glint of amusement that went very well with the deep creases bracketing them. He was a large man with not an ounce of fat on him. Unlike his wife's brothers, he was not a style setter, but his clothes were well-made and well-fitted.

George scowled. 'Might as well tell you. It will soon be all over Town, just so Juliet doesn't find out until it's over.'

'Juliet?' An ominous note crept into Adam's usually mellow baritone.

'Yes, Juliet. She will go to great lengths to stop it.' He scraped back a lock of hair that had fallen over his high forehead. 'Bertram Stockton challenged Charles to a duel and Charles has chosen pistols.'

Adam's brows rose. 'I should have thought you would be the object of Stockton's wrath, not Charles.'

A hint of colour darkened George's cheeks. 'Yes, one would. But no, it is Charles because of his marked pursuit of Miss Amy Stockton. It seems he has been treading a fine line of respectability and Stockton is here to put a stop before it goes too far. Not to mention the latest gossip about Charles introducing both Stockton chits to Harriette Wilson.'

Adam whistled softly. 'I hadn't heard that one, having just come up from the country. Wait until Juliet finds out. She will box Charles's ears.'

'If he lets her get close enough,' George said ruefully.

'And now a duel.'

'Unfortunately for Stockton,' George said, 'Charles is a crack shot.'

Adam leaned back into the well-cushioned seat. 'Then there is no problem. Stockton will miss and Charles will aim for a target other than his opponent.'

'That would be the best course of action.' George shook his head. 'But for some reason, Charles has it in his head that Stockton deserves to be taught a lesson. He provoked the confrontation, as I'm sure you'll hear when the story spreads.'

'Then we had best set this duel up quickly.' Adam's eyes crinkled as he smiled. 'Your sister has a very efficient network of gossip gatherers.'

'Are you volunteering to be one of Charles's seconds?'

'Who else? Whether he wants to acknowledge me or not, we are related and nothing will change the fact.'

'He does have plenty of cronies who would stand by him.'

'I know, but the least said the best. And not just because of Juliet. It seems your family has twisted ties with the Stocktons, and instead of getting better, they become more complicated.'

'So true,' George said as the carriage pulled up in front of his town house. 'Thanks for the ride, Adam. I shall be in touch shortly.' He stepped out and turned back. 'And give my love to Juliet.'

Adam smiled, his entire face warming. 'Gladly.'

Emma smiled at Gordon, who held a tray with a single heavy, embossed envelope. She took what was obviously an invitation. 'Thank you.'

The butler left the room, and she broke the seal and read the contents. Mr Stephen Kennilworth and his widowed mother were inviting Amy and her to the opera. Tonight.

Exhaustion ate at Emma. After getting home from Princess Lieven's last night, she had been unable to sleep. Her mind had refused to stop replaying what had happened between her and Charles Hawthorne. Around dawn she had fallen into a restless sleep only to be awakened at nine by Amy demanding to go to the lending library.

She had hoped they would stay home this evening, but this was something she could not refuse. Mr Kennilworth was very well off. And he was young. Amy could do much worse.

They must go.

Chapter Six

Emma, with a barely civil Amy behind her, entered the door of the opera box Mr Kennilworth had reserved. Amy had been dismissive of the invitation, but Emma had accepted for them both. Mr Stephen Kennilworth was a wealthy man in search of a wife.

The Dowager Mrs Kennilworth already occupied one of the front seats, her impressive bosom swathed in mauve silk, her neck circled by chains of pearls. Three ostrich feathers, attached to grey curls by a diamond and pearl clasp, fanned forward from the back of her head. The scent of money seemed to waft from her.

Emma smiled as she dipped a curtsey. 'Mrs Kennilworth, thank you for inviting us.'

The Dowager inclined her head. 'My pleasure, Miss Stockton.' She turned her piercing blue eyes on Amy. 'And Miss Amy.'

Amy made a shallow curtsey, her lips turning up stiffly. 'Ma'am.'

'Sit beside me, child,' Mrs Kennilworth said to Amy. 'I wish to know you better.'

The smile on Amy's mouth froze as she took the seat. Mr Kennilworth sat behind his mother and Emma behind Amy.

Emma hoped Amy would mind her tongue. The girl might not be interested in the man, but it wouldn't do to alienate his mother who was a powerful hostess in the *ton*. Gossip about them was already rampant.

Emma wished her sister did return Mr Kennilworth's regard. Things would be so much easier. Bertram's gambling debts would be paid, and Mrs Kennilworth could do much to stop the wagging tongues. Emma would hope for the best.

Unwilling to eavesdrop on the conversation between the women for fear of hearing Amy say things she shouldn't and knowing she could do nothing to stop her sister, Emma looked around.

Nearly all the boxes were filled. Everyone seemed to be here. Most of Society came to the opera to see and be seen, not to watch the stage. The gentlemen also came to see the actresses and singers. While it wasn't spoken of, Emma was very aware of what went on. Just as she had known about Harriette Wilson.

A full, unchecked laugh filled a moment of silence. Emma turned her head to see Miss Wilson holding court in an overflowing box. The courtesan sat like a jewel in the midst of a bevy of the most powerful and influential men in the *ton*. Charles Hawthorne sat beside her.

A knot formed in Emma's throat.

He turned his head and saw her looking at him. Heat mounted her face, starting at the low cut of her lavender gown and rising to her hair. She jerked around.

'Mr Kennilworth,' she said, 'I am remiss in not complimenting you on the fine pair of horses you have. They made the ride here everything one could hope.'

She knew her voice was brittle and feared her eyes glittered, but there was nothing she could do. The hard knot remained in her throat and made speaking difficult.

He beamed at her. 'Thank you, Miss Stockton. I am very pleased with them.'

'And well you might be,' she murmured, determined to not let *his* presence interfere with the evening.

She stretched her mouth wider in a forced smile, and refused to give into the urge to glance back at Harriette Wilson's box. She should not be surprised that Charles Hawthorne was amongst the men buzzing around the courtesan.

Thankfully, the gas lamps dimmed and the first act began. Emma focused her attention on the stage, ignoring the part of her that wanted to take surreptitious glances at the courtesan's box. What should have been enjoyable because she loved music, was torture.

Drat that man.

After an eternity, the intermission came.

Amy twisted in her seat to say something to Emma only to stop, her eyes widening. 'Isn't that— '

Emma cut across Amy. 'Wasn't that wonderful, Amy. We are so fortunate Mrs Kennilworth invited us.' When Amy continued to stare, she said pointedly, 'Aren't we?' She nudged Amy's chair with her foot.

The younger girl looked down, then up at Emma. The anger Amy had felt all day flared in her blue.eyes but her voice was honey sweet. 'Yes, aren't we? I vow we might have had to stay home tonight.' She batted her lashes at Mr Kennilworth.

Emma swallowed a reprimand at her sister's provocative exaggeration. Amy was not a child, even if at times she acted like one. Still, the urge to box her ears was strong. She was grateful when Mr Kennilworth smiled as though he took every word at face value.

'Might I escort you to get refreshment, Miss Amy?' The look on Mr Kennilworth's face was that of a man smitten.

Amy's gaze bored into Emma. Emma knew Amy wanted her to tell the man no, but it was perfectly acceptable to do so in a public place so she said nothing. While Amy wasn't infatuated with the man, he would make a good husband. He obviously adored Amy, and in many ways, her sister could make a much worse match.

Reluctantly, Amy rose. 'Yes, that would be nice.'

Emma knew Amy's smile was false and heard the displeasure in her sister's voice. She hoped Mr Kennilworth did not. She said a silent prayer that things went well as she watched the pair leave.

'Miss Stockton, please join me.' There was an underlying tone of command in Mrs Kennilworth's voice as she patted the seat Amy had just vacated.

Emma moved, wondering what had brought about this order before deciding it was a way to ensure Amy and Mr Kennilworth sat together when they returned. The Dowager was definitely a matchmaker. Emma smoothed her skirt over her knees and turned an enquiring look on the older woman.

'I wish to be perfectly open with you, Miss Stockton.' Her tone was prim and bordered on censuring.

Emma hoped her countenance showed none of the unease she began to feel. In her experience when someone wanted to be perfectly open, things were not going well. She shouldn't be surprised. No mother wanted her son to marry into the ramshackle family the Stocktons were becoming.

'Please be so, ma'am.'

'Good. I have watched you closely and know you are a sensible young woman, and had hoped Stephen would fix his interest on you. But he has not.'

Emma blushed even as relief filled her. While she would have accepted Mr Kennilworth's courting had he been interested, she found herself unsettlingly glad that he was not. She did not want to look deep enough to find out why that was.

'I am flattered,' she managed to say in a stilted voice.

'Yes, I thought you would be.' The Dowager's tone was smug. 'But it is not to be. He is interested in your sister, who has shown herself to be flighty and…perhaps, too high-spirited at times. Particularly in her dealings with Mr Charles Hawthorne. I do understand this is her first Season and she is young, and he is a handsome rogue.' She smiled, but it was tight. 'I consider myself to be very free-minded in that regard. Once she and Stephen are married, Miss Amy will settle down.'

Relief mingled with unease as Emma listened. Much as

they needed Amy to marry well, she would not wish this dragon on anyone, least of all high-spirited Amy. But unless Amy said she absolutely, under no circumstances could tolerate marriage to Mr Kennilworth, it seemed their problems were about to end.

Mrs Kennilworth cleared her throat and stared pointedly at Emma. 'It is your brother who concerns me.'

Emma's shoulders tightened but she managed to remain smiling even though she had a good idea of where this conversation was headed. 'Bertram is here to lend us countenance.'

'Harrumph! Then he had best curb his proclivities.' A hint of acerbity entered the Dowager's tone. 'Particularly if the rumours I hear have any truth in them.'

Emma's smile slipped. This was not the time or place she would have picked to discuss Bertram's gambling. 'I am afraid I don't know what rumours you are referring to, ma'am.'

Mrs Kennilworth's blue eyes narrowed as she took a long minute to study Emma's face. 'Perhaps you don't. But I must tell you, as they pertain directly to Stephen's reason for inviting you and your lovely sister to join us tonight.'

Emma wanted to look away from the other woman's pointed gaze, but refused to do so. She was not a coward. She might be discomfited, but that would be nothing new.

'Please do tell me.' She was proud her voice didn't waver. She made a conscious effort to unclench her fingers where they held her reticule in a death grip.

'It seems your brother has lost a great sum of money.'

Emma blanched. Still more losses. This was her worst nightmare and Bertram hadn't been brave enough or concerned enough to tell her. She had to learn it from this odious woman. The large opera house suddenly seemed cold in spite of all the lit candles and hot bodies that crowded every box and every corner.

'Bertram only arrived last week. Surely the rumours are exaggerated. He is here to lend us countenance.' She laughed lightly, trying to make a jest of it, to include the other woman in her amusement. 'It seems Father thought I was not old enough to be a proper chaperone.'

'You are a very mature young woman, and I have no complaint about your ability as a chaperone. But I do wonder at your father's judgement in sending a young man known for his gambling weakness to Town.' She paused, her gaze boring into Emma. 'Because, I assure you, the rumours are true. Stephen was there.'

Emma's stomach clenched and she wished more than anything she could stop Mrs Kennilworth from saying more. She couldn't call Mrs Kennilworth a liar. That would be beyond the pale, and the woman was likely correct. Emma's worst fears about Bertram's visit had happened.

'Bertram has many fine qualities,' she finally managed to say, determined to defend her wayward brother.

'I am sure he does. But his penchant for losing money, while similar to many in the *ton*, is a handicap for a family such as yours.'

Emma's hands clenched automatically at the criticism. She might berate Bertram, but it was not this woman's place to disparage him—even if Mrs Kennilworth was right.

She pasted a cold smile on her face. 'I can see you think so, ma'am, but Bertram only does what many others do. Nor can I believe it is of import to you.'

The Dowager sniffed. 'Then you aren't the intelligent young woman I had thought since I told you from the first that my son is honourably interested in Miss Amy.' Under her breath, she added, 'Perhaps it is better that Stephen is interested in your flighty sister.'

Emma's nails bit into her palms. 'Perhaps.'

'Since Stephen is considering asking for your sister's hand, I feel it is my duty as his mother to look out for his best interest.' She sniffed and her expression took on a look of love and pride. 'While we are very well off financially, Stephen—and very few men for that matter—should not be burdened with the amount of debt your brother has incurred during his

stay in London. I wanted to make you aware of this. I am sure
you understand.'

Emma stared at the woman, wondering at her audacity in
discussing this situation at all, let alone in a public place. She
wanted to tell the Dowager not to bother but knew she had to
keep her expression and voice cordial even though anger
simmered through her.

'I am not ready to discuss this here or at all, Mrs Kennilworth. It seems to me, Mr Kennilworth should talk with my
father.'

The words were close to a verbal slap and shock narrowed
the older woman's eyes. Emma knew she had cut too close to
the bone for this woman who wanted to meddle freely while
trying to make her interference appear as helping.

A knock on the door to the box came as a relief. Emma did
not want to know what Mrs Kennilworth would say or do next.
She only hoped their visitor had not heard any part of the discussion.

Mrs Kennilworth angled in her chair to see who was
there and turned a bright shade of puce. 'Mr Hawthorne.
Do come in.'

Emma's stomach seemed to drop to the floor. Resisting the
urge to turn and look at him, she kept her face pointed toward
the stage and wondered why she felt so glad to have him
here. It was because she did not want to hear another word
about Bertram. Nothing.

'Mrs Kennilworth, how pleasant to see you here tonight.'

His rich voice flowed over Emma and his presence felt like
a hot coal at her back. Perhaps she would look at him. What
could it hurt? Not to do so would be rude. She turned to him
and immediately felt heat rise in her face.

He was impeccably dressed. His Corinthian style suited the
lean, muscular lines of his body. His black hair shone from
the many candles, and his blue eyes looked almost as dark as
jet and just as sharp. She licked dry lips.

'And you, Miss Stockton.'

He bowed to both of them. Emma managed to keep the smile on her face. To her right, she noticed the Dowager flick open her fan and start rapidly cooling herself. The other woman's reaction was exactly what Emma needed to realise how silly they both were. Charles Hawthorne was a very attractive man, but he was just a man.

'Mr Hawthorne, how nice of you to visit,' she paraphrased Mrs Kennilworth.

He gave them a wicked grin. 'It seemed the two of you were having a cosy chat, and I thought I might join.'

Emma kept the smile on her face and wondered exactly what he meant. The man was a cipher.

Mrs Kennilworth coughed. 'We were discussing matters that need to be resolved, but nothing that can't be settled later. Please have a seat.'

Instead of sitting, he gave her a brilliant smile—the one he had used to good effect on Lady Jersey and the Princess Lieven. Mrs Kennilworth was no more immune than the previous two. She simpered at him.

'Thank you, ma'am, but I find myself hoping Miss Stockton will stroll with me during the intermission.' He turned to her, his expression devilish. 'Miss Stockton?'

Emma's heart skipped a beat before speeding up. 'Yes, thank you.'

She rose, telling herself she accepted only to escape the Dowager and the mortifying conversation the woman insisted they have. After the trouble Mr Hawthorne had caused between her and Amy, she was *not* interested in the man.

He extended his arm. 'They are roasting chestnuts just outside the entrance.'

She hesitated a second before setting her fingers on him, afraid of what her reaction would be. Her touch was light and his evening coat was thick, yet she felt as though his skin scorched her. The breath caught in her throat as though a searing wind swept over her.

It took great difficulty to speak. 'I like chestnuts.'

He smiled down at her and the world ceased to exist. 'I thought you might.'

Vaguely, Emma heard Mrs Kennilworth clear her throat. 'I trust you will return shortly, Miss Stockton.'

Somehow Emma managed to take her gaze from Mr Hawthorne's face. 'Of course, Mrs Kennilworth.'

The older woman moved her fan rapidly, her bright blue eyes moving from Emma to Charles and back again as though she weren't quite sure what she saw and had to study the situation carefully. A shiver of unease rolled over Emma's shoulders. The last thing she needed after her siblings' antics was to have rumours start about her. It was bad enough the two women at Princess Lieven's had talked about her and Charles Hawthorne.

Yet, she wanted to go with him, if only to escape the Dowager and their private conversation. She began to realise how perverse she was.

He swept her from the box and into the crowd of people milling about in the aisle and in the foyer. Heads turned and eyebrows rose. She kept her attention straight ahead.

'Another Hawthorne after being jilted by the older one?' she heard a man mutter in an aside to the woman beside him. Mortification flooded Emma's cheeks at the reference to her broken engagement to Charles's brother. She lifted her chin and continued walking without looking to see who had spoken.

Charles stopped. 'Ah, Mandeville. I see you are socialising after your long sequester in the country.'

The man turned brick-red. 'Escortin' m' sister.'

'Yes, I believe I understand.'

Emma listened to Charles's condescending voice and wondered if the other man realised he was being mocked. The dark glitter in Mandeville's eyes told her he did.

'May I introduce Miss Stockton?' Charles asked. 'This is Mr Mandeville.'

Emma made a small curtsey as the man made a slight bow. 'How do you do.'

He studied her. 'Pleased to meet you, Miss Stockton.'

She forced a smile to brittle lips. This night seemed to go from bad to worse.

'We are looking for her sister, Miss Amy Stockton,' Charles added, his tone bored and piqued at once, as though they were truly looking for her sister.

'She is with Mr Kennilworth,' Emma supplied.

'Saw him with her just minutes ago,' the woman beside Mandeville said, humour lacing her words.

The voice was familiar and Emma looked at the woman for the first time. Harriette Wilson, with a glitter in her dark eyes that said she was enjoying the situation immensely. Definitely not Mandeville's sister.

'Miss Wilson.' Emma acknowledged their prior introduction, knowing she should have ignored the woman, but unwilling to do so.

'Miss Stockton,' the courtesan responded.

'You know one another?' Mandeville's tone was intrigued and slightly scandalised.

'We have met.' Emma felt nothing but contempt for the man and it showed in her voice.

'Interesting,' Mandeville said.

'No more so than your being in her company, Mr Mandeville.' Emma narrowed her eyes. 'At least I have the courage to acknowledge my acquaintance.'

For the second time in the encounter Mandeville turned an ugly shade of red, but said nothing. Satisfaction surged through Emma even as she wondered at her own audacity to speak so to a man she didn't know. She was never this bold in defending herself. Her brother and sister, yes, but not herself.

Mandeville had tried to shame her and to her regret she had been ready to let him. Now, seeing how he treated the woman at his side, she wondered that she could have walked by without confronting him for his insult. She owed Charles Hawthorne for doing the brave thing and forcing her to follow his lead.

Emma wanted to turn her back on him and finish her response with the cut direct, but knew better than to add fuel to the gossip she was sure he would start. Harriette Wilson's face mirrored Emma's thoughts.

'Mandeville,' the courtesan said tartly, 'Miss Stockton is too much of a lady for you to say anything snide about her.'

He snickered. 'I don't have to say a thing. Everyone who is watching us will say more than enough.'

Emma glanced around to confirm what he said. Not many people looked at them, but the speculative or scandalised expressions on the ones who did told her more than enough. When the curtain went up on the next act, the topic of conversation wouldn't be the opera.

Still more to lay at Charles Hawthorne's door. She was appreciative that the man had insulted Mandeville for his slight to her, but that was outweighed by the continuing difficulties he caused.

She smiled at Harriette Wilson and ignored her companion. 'I believe I must continue looking for my sister. Excuse us.'

Charles shifted to allow her to move toward the entrance. She moved forward briskly.

'You said nothing,' she accused him.

'I didn't need to, Miss Stockton. You and Harriette were doing a much better job than I could have ever done.'

'Ha!' She smiled at his compliment in spite of herself. 'Being linked with the most famous courtesan in England will not do wonders for my reputation.'

'Then you should have ignored her presence.' His face was solemn as he maneuvered her through a small group of people near the entry doors. 'Wait here. I will be just a moment getting the chestnuts.'

She watched him go while his words rang in her mind. Why hadn't she pretended the other woman wasn't there? Everyone she knew would have.

He returned with a paper cone filled with the hot nuts and held it out to her. 'Have one.'

Still pondering her reaction, she took a chestnut, peeled and nibbled. 'Thank you.'

'Here you are!' Amy's voice was an accusation. She stopped beside Charles but looked at Emma. 'I thought you and Mrs Kennilworth were staying in the box.'

Mr Kennilworth stood beside her, looking bewildered and disapproving at the same time. Emma pitied him, having often felt that way around her sister.

'Mrs Kennilworth and I were talking when Mr Hawthorne joined us, Amy.'

Charles smiled devilishly at Amy. 'Miss Amy, it is my fault. I wanted to get hot roasted chestnuts and wanted company.' He held out the cone, his eyes telling her to help herself to what he offered.

Emma wanted to yank the chestnuts from him, her pleasure in the treat gone. How dare he continue to provoke reactions from Amy that were unacceptable in a girl her age.

'Why, thank you, Mr Hawthorne.' Amy batted her blond eyelashes and took a nut.

Charles offered the nuts to Mr Kennilworth. His expression was bland now. Against her will, Emma admired his social proficiency.

'No thank you, Mr Hawthorne.' Stephen Kennilworth looked as though the last thing he wanted was something from the infamous rake. 'I believe it is time Miss Amy and I returned to my mother.' He turned to Emma. 'Will you join us, Miss Stockton?'

Emma knew the polite question was more of an order to join them. In Mr Kennilworth's world, single ladies did not stay with men of Charles Hawthorne's stamp. Just as respectable ladies didn't know or acknowledge courtesans. She thought she would stay with Mr Hawthorne out of pique if nothing else.

One black brow lifted as Charles watched her. 'I must be leaving.' His amused voice held the hint of an emotion Emma couldn't identify. 'My party awaits me.'

Disappointment lay heavily in Emma's stomach even as she admitted to herself that he had saved her from making still another bad decision. By all rights she should return with Mr Kennilworth.

They said their goodbyes, Amy doing nothing to hide her disappointment. 'Do call tomorrow, Mr Hawthorne,' she said sweetly, ignoring Emma's frown.

Charles Hawthorne darted an amused glance at Emma. 'I fear I am busy tomorrow, Miss Amy. Perhaps the day after?'

'Oh, yes, please do.'

Amy beamed and Emma wanted to scream.

Hours later, Emma watched Amy take her leave of Mr Kennilworth and his mama.

'Thank you, sir and ma'am.' Amy smiled, her rosebud mouth barely curved. 'I enjoyed the opera immensely.'

Mr Kennilworth beamed. 'I am so glad, Miss Amy. Perhaps tomorrow—'

'I believe we are busy tomorrow, Stephen,' Mrs Kennilworth cut across her son. 'Good evening, Miss Stockton. Miss Amy.' She nodded regally.

Emma smiled and followed Amy from the carriage, thankful the horrible evening was over. Things could not have been worse. Mr Kennilworth had been the only one talking after they returned to the box. Mrs Kennilworth had looked as though she wished nothing more than to boot the Stockton women from her presence. And on the way home, Amy had been marginally polite and shooting arrows at Emma.

Emma went through the entryway of their rented house just as Amy flounced around her. The butler stood holding the door as the young girl turned to Emma.

'I won't marry that milksop!'

'Thank you, Gordon.' Emma undid the frogs on her opera cape and allowed the butler to take it from her shoulders before turning to Amy. 'I wouldn't want you to have to marry him.'

'What?' The look on Amy's face said she had expected a fight.

Emma would have smiled if she hadn't been so tired and so discouraged. 'He is too much in his mama's pocket to make a good husband.'

'You wouldn't?'

Emma nodded to the butler. 'You may go now.'

She didn't want the entire household to know about the conversation she and Amy were about to have. Not even the old and loyal retainer.

'No, Amy, I wouldn't. The man is wealthy and could pay all of Papa and Bertram's debts, but the price on you would be too great.'

Amy's rosebud mouth nearly dropped. 'Why, Em, I...I...'

'Let us go into the drawing room, Amy. I need to talk to you.'

She put a hand on Amy's back and urged her into the room before Amy could dig her heels in. The girl was amazed at what she'd just told her, and glad from the dazed look on her face, but when she heard the rest Amy would be far from happy.

Amy moved near the unlit fireplace and shivered. 'It is freezing in here, Em. Can't we have a fire?'

Emma looked at the coals, piled and ready to light, and gave in. The cost would be minuscule all things considered. She found the flint and lint, and struck a spark as Amy pulled an old, patched chair closer. The fire caught and Emma blew to fan the flames.

Amy stripped off her white gloves and held her hands out. 'That feels so good. It may be summer, but it is cold early in the morning—or late in the night,' she ended with a giggle.

Emma smiled. If only she didn't have to wipe the pleasure from her sister's face. But she did.

Emma pulled another rickety chair close and followed Amy's example. She doubted the cold bothered her as it did Amy, but still the warmth felt nice. 'I am glad you like it.'

Amy closed her eyes and leaned into the heat. 'I wish I could go to Italy. I hear it is lovely and warm in the summer. Much warmer than here.'

'I wish you could, too, dear. And perhaps one day you will.'

'When I marry a rich man?' Amy opened her eyes and looked directly at her sister.

'Yes.'

'That is why you told Gordon to leave and brought me in here, isn't it?' She frowned. 'Although it's not likely to be Mr Kennilworth, the mama's boy.'

Emma met Amy's eyes. 'Yes.' She pulled her hands from the warmth and folded them in her lap. The position was one Mama would take when she had unpleasant news to impart.

'Then get on with the reasons for why I must marry.' Amy's blue eyes bored into Emma.

'While I think Mr Kennilworth would probably not be a suitable partner, it is time you found someone. Quickly.'

A look of weary knowledge moved over Amy's delicate features. 'It is Bertram and Papa, isn't it?'

Emma sighed. The situation was one she shouldn't discuss with a girl Amy's age, but Amy was the one being sacrificed. She felt it only fair to tell her the truth. 'Yes. Bertram has been gambling heavily while he has been here. It seems more so than normal.'

Amy's mouth curled. 'While he has been protecting our reputations?'

It hurt to hear the sarcasm in her young sister's voice. Disillusionment was a tough pill to swallow and she wished Amy did not have to be put through this. But there was no other alternative. Guilt moved through her. She should have married George Hawthorne in spite of his carrying on with another woman. Amy would not be in this position if she had. But that was the past, and she could do nothing about it.

'I'm afraid he has gone so deeply that Mrs Kennilworth felt compelled to discuss the problem with me. That means everyone is aware.' She took a deep breath, not wanting to say the rest, but knowing she had to. 'You must find someone to marry quickly before every eligible bachelor decides we are too big of a financial burden.'

Amy's fair complexion turned purple, a sign of anger. 'So, not only am I the fatted calf, but now I'm to be led to the slaughter before I even have a Season. How unfair.'

'I am so sorry.'

The urge to go to Amy and gather her close was strong, but she knew Amy would not want that. The young girl was too angry at the moment and needed time to fume.

If only she had held George Hawthorne to their engagement. If only Bertram didn't gamble as though he had a fortune to lose. If only…if only…

Amy jumped to her feet, her hands clenched, her mouth a tight line. 'So who should I chase to ground?'

The instinct to correct Amy's use of hunting cant gave way to compassion and Emma said nothing. The girl had a right to her fury.

'Well?'

'Is there anyone you think you could stand to marry, dear?'

Amy glared at her. 'Don't try to be Mama and come all gentle and calm, Em. Even Mama could not make this look or feel good, so you certainly cannot.'

Emma flushed, torn between being hurt at Amy's harsh words or disappointed that she had tried to be like Mama and failed. She had struggled against the odds to make things work out and now were falling apart. Mama would have found a way to keep everything from crumbling. Mama would have made it all right.

She had failed. Again.

'I didn't mean to sound like Mama, Amy. I'm only trying to make this as easy as possible.'

'Nothing about this is easy or fun.' Amy stomped to the far wall, turned and stomped back. 'This is all Bertram's fault. Instead of talking to me about finding someone to marry, why don't you shout at him? Send a note to Papa telling him what Bertram is doing and demand that he be ordered back to the country. Goodness knows that might not be enough to make him leave.'

Amy was right and they both knew it. Even if Papa would order Bertram home and that was doubtful.

'I will write Papa a note.'

'For all the good that will do.' Amy kicked the fire grate. 'Ouch!' She hopped back, her satin-covered foot in the air.

'That had to hurt,' Emma said in sympathy.

'Blast!'

'Amy!'

All the starch went out of the girl and she sank to the chair. Tears ran down her cheeks.

'Oh, Em, I hate this. This is my first and only Season. It was supposed to be fun. Not horrible—' she hiccupped '—like this.'

Emma left her chair, fell to her knees in front of Amy and wrapped her arms around her sister. 'I know, sweetheart. I know.'

Amy sobbed onto Emma's shoulder, her tears soaking through the wool of Emma's gown. Emma said nothing. Sometimes all she could do was hold Amy and love her. If only things could be different.

Chapter Seven

Hours later, Emma tossed from side to side, the bed covers tangling in her legs and nightdress. The night's events kept running through her mind. First Amy's open disdain for Mr Kennilworth, then Mrs Kennilworth's disclosure about Bertram, followed almost immediately by Charles Hawthorne and another meeting with Harriette Wilson. Last, but always woven in with Emma's sense of guilt, came Amy's tears.

Emma felt like a prisoner stretched on a rack made up of failure to prevent awful things happening to the people she loved. And why didn't she just ignore Harriette Wilson? The woman was a courtesan, after all.

Sleep eluded her as the answer to her question appeared. She didn't ignore Miss Wilson because the woman was honest and open and…and she liked what she saw of her. So, if she was going to be part of her sister's problem, she might as well shoulder all the responsibility that was hers.

Emma groaned and sat up, her mind whirling around the situation. She finally settled on her brother as the issue to resolved first.

Bertram had to be stopped before every eligible party in London crossed Amy off his list of possible brides. Not that she considered Mr Stephen Kennilworth eligible. It had been made clear the man was tied to his mother's ample and controlling apron strings. He would not do for Amy. But someone must be found.

Flinging the covers aside with a burst of frustration that sent them tumbling to the opposite side of the bed and spilling onto the floor, Emma swung her legs to the side. The chill early morning air hit her like a splash of ice water. Gooseflesh chased along her arms as she grabbed her woollen robe and yanked it on. Standing, she tied the belt and slipped her feet into cold slippers.

She needed a cup of hot chocolate. Cook was still abed, but the coals in the kitchen would be banked and ready to be lit. There would be some bit of milk left and the cocoa was in a jar in the pantry. The drink always soothed her and cleared her mind. She needed that badly.

Minutes later, Emma passed through the foyer and heard the door knocker. She jumped, the light from her lone candle jiggling and casting dancing shadows on the walls. Who could be knocking at this hour?

She went to the door and peered through the peephole. The full moon cast the man outside in silver. Bertram. Why was he knocking when he had a key? Unless he had forgotten it or lost it, both of which were possible.

The inclination to let him stay outside was strong. The last thing she wanted right now was to see or speak to her brother. She was raw inside and he was the main reason. If she had to deal with him now, there was no telling what she would say.

He pounded on the door again, this time louder.

Emma sighed. He would only continue to beat on the door until he woke someone up. She let him in.

He stumbled inside, his beaver hat falling to the floor. His straw-coloured hair lay in limp wisps around his forehead, and the flickering light from her candle made the freckles on his nose look like moving dark spots. His eyes were swollen.

'Why didn't you use your key?' she asked, knowing the answer, but wanting him to confirm it.

He drew himself up stiffly. 'Don't have it.'

The sweet smell of port rolled over her with his hot breath. She stepped back and suppressed a sharp reply. Confronting him in this condition never did any good. Her mood would make it worse.

'I see.' She turned away, needing a cup of hot chocolate more than ever.

He moved to block her. 'I have a fairly large debt of honour to pay tomorrow.' His words were only slightly slurred.

The import of what he said was like a blast breaking down the wall of her control. Those words were everything she had dreaded to hear from him. Everything Mrs Kennilworth had led her to expect to hear.

She should angle around him and leave. Now. Instead, she glared at him. 'Fairly large?'

Anger seethed from her. Anger at him. Anger at Amy, mingled sharply with the guilt she felt over Amy's situation. She should have held Charles Hawthorne's brother to their engagement. Then none of this would matter. Anger at herself joined her mounting fury.

He swayed. 'Yes. We will have to find something to sell.'

'We?' The urge to slap him was so strong she set her candlestick on the nearby table and clasped her hands behind her back. 'Why don't you send a note to Papa. The two of you are the ones who should deal with the situation you are in.'

He twirled his ebony cane. 'That won't be necessary.'

The words were slurred just a bit, but she understood him. She refused to be pulled into a solution for his weakness.

She shook her head. 'There is nothing here to sell.' She spread her arm to indicate the worn table and brass candlestick. The mirror on the wall was old and its frame nicked and faded. 'Nothing.'

He frowned. 'You or Amy will have to sell one of your baubles if you can't find something else.'

She ground her teeth together. 'Amy and I have nothing of value. Tonight she wore flowers in her hair and a satin ribbon around her neck—'

'And you wore Mama's pearls.'

'Yes, I did. They are all I have of her.' And they gave her comfort when little else did.

He leaned closer while putting one hand against the still open door for support. 'They should fetch enough for my needs.'

She blanched. 'They are mine, and I won't give them to you to throw down that black hole you call gambling.'

'They are Papa's. He lets you keep them, but they belong to him, and we both know he would agree that they should be sold to pay my debt of honour.'

He was right. Papa would tell her to give him the necklace. A debt of honour was always paid.

Devastation swept over her like a storm wave crashing to shore. Tears threatened to spill from her eyes. She would not cry in front of Bertram. Not anymore.

A memory flickered. She had been six and fallen and skinned her elbow. Bertram had been the first to reach her. As a much older ten—or so it had seemed at the time—he had kissed her scrape. She had cried then.

The memory disappeared amid her current anguish. 'Debt of honour, Bertram?' Her voice was hoarse from the effort not to cry, but anger strengthened her. 'You have no honour or you would have stopped before reaching this point.'

His face darkened and she knew she had pushed him too much, but she hurt. The pearls were all she had left of Mama, and she knew Papa would order they be sold. It wouldn't matter to Papa that she had asked for them after Mama's death as a tangible reminder of the mother she had loved so dearly. He would take them back and sell them without a second's thought.

Bertram slammed the door shut and stood with only a slight waver. 'You know nothing about honour, sister.'

She looked at him and wondered that he could be so drunk yet continue saying things that hurt so much. She struck back.

'I know nothing of an honour that continues to put hardship on those dependent on you. Is honour losing your inheritance at the gambling tables and forcing your sister into a marriage of convenience to pay your debts with no regard for her wishes?'

He drew himself up straight. 'You are a shrewish harpy and know nothing of the matter. My gambling debts must be repaid.' Only the slight glassiness of his eyes revealed how inebriated he was. 'And I do take care of you and Amy.'

She snorted. 'By making Amy a fatted calf to your weakness and selling the only thing I have left of Mama? That is a strange form of caring.'

He slumped from tiredness and too much wine but caught himself. He looked down his nose at her. 'People in our class marry for money all the time. It is Amy's duty and she will be happier for it. As you would have been.' He struck a pose that was ruined when he wobbled. 'Because you didn't marry Lord Hawthorne, I must take care of the situation you have created by your selfishness.'

She stared at him speechless. He must be more drunk than she had thought. He had always been a voluble drinker, but tonight he was besting himself.

'A situation I created?' She wondered what tangent Bertram was heading down now.

'Yes. Because you refused George Hawthorne, Amy had to come to London much too young. Then you have been unable to keep her from compromising herself with Charles Hawthorne.'

Emma's mind reeled. Bertram spun one situation after another. Yet everything he said was true, except...

'She has not compromised herself with Charles Hawthorne.'

He laughed, a short, harsh sound. 'As good as. She flirts shamelessly with him, and you allowed him to introduce both of you to Harriette Wilson.' He paused for breath, his figure stiff with indignation. 'Harriette Wilson is a whore. But I am going to take care of that. When I am through, no one will say another word, and Amy will be able to marry even the highest stickler.'

Emma began to think Bertram was lost in a world of delusions. This often happened when he had too much alcohol. But this time he was more dramatic than his norm.

A sense of unease nagged her. 'What have you done?'

He drew himself up and squared his shoulders. 'I have challenged Charles Hawthorne to a duel. That will take care of everything.'

His pompous tone and posture did nothing to prevent the sudden clenching of Emma's stomach. Her immediate fear for him made her sharp. 'You challenged him to a duel? You can't shoot and you can't fence. What kind of duel are you planning? One where you commit suicide?'

His lips thinned, and for a second there was the hint of uncertainty in his hazel eyes. It was gone as quickly as it had come. 'I intend to fight him for Amy's honour. When I win—as I will since I am in the right—Amy's name will be unblemished.'

She gaped at him and wondered if he'd been inebriated at the time of his challenge. That was the only thing she could think of to explain his craziness. 'Did you just do this? This evening?' she added at his blank look.

'No. I did it several days ago. At White's.' He smirked. 'George Hawthorne was there as well.'

Emma reached behind, feeling for the wall and its support. What more could happen? 'Before or after you lost a great sum of money?' Perhaps this was why he had played so deeply. Fear.

'After.' He looked down his nose at her. 'I didn't gamble from fear, Emma.'

The tears she had managed to hold at bay when confronted with the loss of Mama's pearls threatened once more. This was horrible. She had to do something.

'Call off, Bertram. You must.'

His eyes widened in surprise. 'Can't do that. Even if I wanted, which I don't.'

'Yes, you can,' she persisted. He would be killed. Furious as she was with him, she didn't want to lose him. He was her big brother. She loved him. 'No one even knows about the duel. Do they?' she added, when he shook his head as though she were deranged.

'Everyone who was in White's knows. And, by now, likely everyone who wasn't.' He moved toward the stairs, the rigidity of his body beginning to slip. 'Can't call it off. I'm right.'

He didn't wait for her response but turned and went up the steps. It was as though he'd told her what he wanted and now he was through and going to bed. He'd dropped his cannonball and left her to deal with the knowledge as best she could.

Emma stared after him, her mouth open. What could she do? She had to do something.

How could she prevent Bertram from meeting Mr Hawthorne? If she announced it to the *ton*, she would be considered vulgar and that would hurt Amy still more. Ladies did not know about such things. If she told a Member of Parliament, he would likely ignore her. Duelling was illegal, but everyone did it, even the highest in the land. The only penalty was if a man killed his opponent. Then the winner had to flee to the Continent.

In a daze she moved to the kitchen, the thought of hot chocolate sliding down her throat to a grateful stomach drawing her. Vaguely aware of what she did, she prepared the hot drink and poured it into a large, cracked mug. She twisted the mug so the crack was away from her mouth and took a sip of the burning drink.

Warmth spread from the center of her body to her extremities. She realised her fingers and toes were nearly numb. Chills took her.

She set the mug on the large wooden trestle table so the drink wouldn't slop onto her and buried her face in her hands. She had to do something.

Inspiration hit. She jerked her head up and stared at the fireplace. She would ask Charles Hawthorne to call off. He had nothing to lose by doing so, and he was in the wrong. That would solve everything.

But how to do it?

She grasped the mug and wrapped her fingers around its heat before picking it up and drinking more. She was glad to note that with a solution her fingers had stopped shaking.

She drank everything before a plan came.

Only later did she realise she hadn't once considered that Charles Hawthorne could be harmed by Bertram. Mr Hawthorne was an experienced rake who had duelled several times. His reputation on the field of honour told her that he was not the one in danger.

She closed her eyes in exhaustion.

Emma watched Amy leave with Julia Thornton and Julia's mama. She had pleaded exhaustion to avoid going with them to Almack's.

This was the only chance she would get. She hurried upstairs to her room where she still kept the black hat with a veil she had worn at Mama's funeral. She would wear her black cape as well.

It took only a moment to fetch the hat from the top shelf of her armoire. It took longer to pin it in place so the veil completely covered her face.

Looking in the mirror, she decided no one would recognise her when she visited Mr Hawthorne. Definitely not him until she told him who she was.

The only thing that might give her away was Mama's pearls. So far she had been unable to make herself give them to Bertram. She knew she would have to at some point, but the longer she had them the more she hoped to keep them. But that was a futile hope. Bertram's debts wouldn't disappear.

She reached up to finger the lustrous necklace, rubbing each pearl as she made her way to the clasp. Her fingers trembled and it was several long minutes before the heavy strand fell from her neck into her hands.

She closed her eyes to keep from crying. It was as though another part of Mama had disappeared from her life.

She took a deep shuddering breath. She had not been successful at trying to take Mama's place. Perhaps it was time for her to be herself and to live her own life.

For a moment longer, she allowed herself to hold the pearls. Then she dropped them into the silk bag she had dug out of her drawer this morning.

On her way out of the house, she stopped in Bertram's room. She left the pearls on his shaving stand.

Charles Hawthorne looked up from the open ledger where he diligently, and with a great deal of satisfaction, entered the figures of his latest trading enterprise. Sometimes his skill at business surprised him. It always brought him satisfaction.

Every time he walked into his town house or visited his country estate he appreciated his business skill. He had made enough profit in the last three years to buy a very nice property in London and to get his once depleted country home back to a place where it supported itself. In a couple of years it would once more provide income. He got great satisfaction from creating after he had allowed his gambling habit to be so destructive for so many years.

A discreet cough drew his attention from his pleasurable thoughts. His manservant, Stoner, stood in the open doorway, his bulky chest filling the space.

'What?' Charles put down his quill.

'Guv'nor, there is a woman 'ere to see you. Quality by the looks of 'er.'

Always one for a challenge or a mystery, Charles unfolded his lean, well-muscled frame and stood. 'A lady? Here?'

Stoner shrugged. 'Best I can tell. She's wearin' an 'at with an 'eavy veil and a thick black cape. But the material is good and 'er mannerisms are those of a lady.'

A spark of interest had Charles sitting forward in his chair. He squelched it. The only lady he knew who had the recklessness to visit him in his home was Amy Stockton. Not a situation he wanted.

However, if it were her sister—which would never happen... 'A lady of quality doesn't visit a man she isn't related to.'

Stoner shrugged again, being a man of few words. With his scarred face and broad, beefy shoulders and arms, all he had to do was look at someone to make them step back and leave him alone.

Charles suppressed an irritated frown. Stoner was good at what he did, and if he didn't speak much, then that was the way it was. Although, since patience wasn't one of Charles's virtues—and there were many who said he had none, usually women—it was hard not to take the hulking man in front of him to task for being so taciturn. However, Stoner was an excellent judge of character. If he said the lady was quality, then Charles would bet a monkey the lady was—if he still bet.

'What does she want?'

'To see you, Guv'. What do they all want?'

Charles's guard was up, but his interest was piqued. If she was Amy Stockton, he would send her packing. If she was someone else...

'Send her in.'

Stoner turned and left without word or movement to show acknowledgement, but Charles knew the man would do exactly as told. He had found Stoner near starvation when the two of them had been cell neighbors in debtor's prison. When he got out, Charles took Stoner with him. The man was fanatically loyal.

Wondering what a woman of his own station was doing seeking him out, Charles turned one of several ladder-back chairs in his office so he could straddle it. An outrageous pose for a man to take in front of a woman of sensibilities, but he had learned long ago that often the unexpected got the best results.

He knew how gambling could get into a man's blood and destroy his life. That was why Bertram Stockton disgusted him. The man was too weak to mend his ways, so he let his obsession ruin his family.

After the debacle several nights before with Amy Stockton, he had not gone out of his way to run into the Misses Stockton. He regretted the part he had played in the dustup between the two sisters. Baiting Miss Emma Stockton chased away his ennui, but not even for the entertainment it provided in an otherwise dull Season, did he want to cause more problems for her than she already had.

This mysterious woman would be his diversion tonight.

A small smile of anticipation played around the corners of his mouth. This meeting would surely enliven an evening that so far had been spent in the satisfying, but far from entertaining, occupation of updating his accounts. He could hire a man of business, but he found pleasure in personally entering the fruits of his outré enterprise in the ledger.

The door opened again and Stoner ushered in a woman covered from head to toe in black. Even her hat, with its near-opaque veil, was black, as were the half boots peeking out from the hem of her skirt, which showed beneath the bottom of her black cloak. She was definitely dressed for secrecy.

He smiled. The dark colour and enveloping folds of the cape did nothing to keep him from remembering the tall, slim, elegant figure underneath with a narrow waist, small breasts and—he would swear—long legs. Nor did the hat and veil disguise the tilt of the woman's head. And nothing could conceal the liquid grace of her walk or the illusive hint of sweet peas wafting from her. He knew only one woman who wore that fragrance.

He smiled. He had decided not to further inconvenience her, and instead she came to him. It was the last thing he expected from the prim and proper Miss Emma Stockton. His interest in her grew.

He stifled a laugh and instead smiled and stood, motioning to another straight-backed chair. He would play her game for awhile and see where it led.

'Please have a seat.' After a quick turn of her head to take in the entire contents of his office, she sat with her spine ramrod stiff and not touching anything. His smile widened. 'I would offer you refreshments, but all I have is Scotch whisky. No sherry since the last lady visitor drank it all.'

Her shoulders stiffened. 'I imagine you have quite a few *visitors*.'

He resumed his outrageous position straddling the chair, hugely enjoying himself. Her voice confirmed what he already knew. This was indeed a very brave and determined lady.

'Enough visitors to keep things interesting. But what can I do for you? It isn't often I entertain a lady of quality here.'

'That is abundantly obvious from your manners.'

He would swear he heard her sniff from behind what she thought was the disguising curtain of her veil. He wondered how long it would take her to reveal herself and her reason for coming here, although, truth be told, he had a good idea. This had to be about Amy Stockton.

He rested his forearms on the back of his chair. 'But you are not my usual visitor.'

Her hands, covered in black kid gloves, clutched the top of a matching reticule. He was glad they weren't on his neck because she would be strangling him. A tiny spark of sympathy for the position she found herself in blunted some of his humour. He always felt sorry for the unfortunate, and his visitor was definitely that. He admired her courage and determination.

'You realise,' he said softly, 'that if you are discovered, your reputation will be ruined.'

This time she snorted. 'As though you would care. You are a debauched rake and seducer of innocents. What would one more reputation be to you?'

He winced, but only briefly. There was some truth in what she said. 'I don't seduce innocents. I may flirt and sometimes be a little outrageous, but I do not seduce.' He paused. 'Unless the lady invites me.'

'Hah! One would never know it from your behaviour—'

'Towards your sister, Miss Stockton?' he asked.

She jerked. 'How do you know?'

He was not about to tell her how he really knew. 'An educated guess. I can't think of another lady who would visit me here—unless it was your sister, but her voice is higher and more breathless. Or, my sister. She *might* be harebrained enough to come here, but at least she is married—if not respectably so—and she is my sister.'

He frowned at the memory of his sister and her recent marriage to Adam Glenfinning, a rake of the first order. Charles had fought their liaison and lost. Juliet was strong willed. Juliet was as strong willed as the woman sitting across from him.

'The man she married is no worse than you, Mr Hawthorne. At least he has never been involved with a chit fresh out of the schoolroom.'

'Like your sister.'

'Exactly.'

'What if my intentions are honourable?'

She snorted again. 'What if they are? You are not exactly an eligible party.' She waved one graceful arm to encompass their surroundings. 'Even though you are successful, trade is not considered acceptable behaviour for a member of the *ton*. Although, you don't seem to have suffered for doing it.'

His enjoyment rapidly evaporating, Charles asked, 'What exactly do you want? Visiting my home is more disreputable for a woman than making a living in trade is for me. I am the member of a respected family. I would have to do far worse than importing and selling goods for Society to close its doors to me.'

He heard the sharp intake of her breath and knew he had hit his mark. It was small satisfaction. He didn't want to hurt her. He didn't want to hurt anyone. But she had struck a sensitive spot, and he found himself unable to let her comments go. 'You might even be recognised. After all,' he drawled, 'I knew who you were.'

'You heard me speak.'

'True.' He let her think that was how he had recognised her. 'Since I know who you are and since no one will enter here without my permission, why don't you lift your veil so I can see your face when you insult me.'

She said nothing for long seconds before lifting the veil from her face. She had a very fine pair of grey eyes and they glared at him. A wisp of silky, flame-coloured hair teased the outer corner of one dark brown winged eyebrow.

As though the room were suddenly too hot, she also undid the clasp of her cape and allowed the heavy black garment to open at her neck. Underneath was a black dress with a modestly scooped neckline.

'Pleased?' Her rich contralto voice was edged with sarcasm and dislike.

'Very much.'

Charles allowed himself to enjoy the rich cream of her exposed skin. He imagined it would be as soft and silken as it looked. A sensual delight.

But something was missing. He frowned. 'Where are your pearls? I have never seen you without them.'

She moved like lightning. Grabbing the edges of her cape, she gripped them together and redid the clasp at her neck. 'What I wear is none of your concern.'

He studied her. She was right, but from her actions he would bet a monkey that they were gone to pay one of her brother's gambling debts. But she would never tell him that. He let the subject die.

'I presume you are here to warn me away from your sister.'

'One would think.' Acid dripped from each word.

He began to think he had the wrong reason. But surely she didn't know about the duel. No man of honour would tell a woman about a duel. It wasn't done.

'Yes, one would think that.' He was not about to be the one to let slip the confrontation in White's.

Her fine mouth sneered. 'But that is only one of your transgressions against my family.'

She did know. He sighed, the fun of the encounter nearly gone. 'And what is the real reason you are here?'

She twisted her reticule until one of the strings holding it closed snapped. 'Please don't duel with Bertram.'

He realised how hard it was for her to swallow her pride and ask him for something as well as risk her reputation in order to do so. But he could not give her what she wanted. His pride would not allow him. 'It is Bertram's place to call off, not mine. He did the challenging.'

She swallowed hard, the creamy skin of her neck moving. He wished he could ease her discomfort. But the price would be too high.

'You can back out.'

He shook his head. 'I could, but I won't. I will not be branded a coward.'

'No one would think you a coward.' Her laugh was shaky. 'You are known as a crack shot. Bertram can barely hit a barn from twenty feet. You will put a bullet through him while he is still aiming.'

Unreasonably, he wanted to comfort her. 'I will delope.'

She snorted. 'I don't believe you. To do that would be to admit the reason Bertram challenged you is valid. You have said it is not—no matter how much you flirt with Amy.'

'Do you doubt my word?' He kept a tight rein on the anger her insult prompted. 'I am not used to someone calling me a liar.'

She stared at him, as though trying to figure out how serious he was. 'I can't believe you would admit to the world that Bertram is right by shooting to miss.' She looked away, looked back. 'People would then expect you to offer for Amy if your attentions have gone too far.' When he didn't immediately refute her, surprise rounded her eyes. 'Do you intend to do so?'

The urge to let her think so was strong. He wished to make her pay for doubting his word. 'Perhaps. Didn't I ask you earlier what you would do if my intent was matrimony?'

Chagrin pulled her brows together. 'I told you your suit would not be welcomed.'

'Then I could ask for Miss Amy's hand in the knowledge I would be safe.'

She looked momentarily nonplussed. 'You could, but I believe you are trying to make me worry because I doubted your word.'

It was his turn to look surprised. 'You are an astute woman.'

'I have studied you carefully.'

'Really?'

'In an effort to stop you from carrying on with my young sister. Nothing more.'

'Of course,' he murmured, hugely enjoying himself again.

He watched the barest hint of colour mount her cheeks as the meaning of her words and his reply dawned on her. He wondered if she would blush if he kissed her, something he found he wanted to do. It was an unsettling realisation. She was nothing like his usual flirts.

She stood abruptly, nearly knocking over her chair. 'If you refuse to call off the duel, then I have no reason to stay longer.'

Charles stood and paced behind his desk. Action in all things was better as far as he was concerned. 'I am sorry your visit was wasted.'

Her full, peach-tinted lips thinned. She took a deep breath, and he could not help but follow the rise and fall of her bosom or what was visible of it through several layers of clothing. His imagination provided more than enough to make his own breathing quicken before he rebuked himself. He didn't even like the woman. But he had learned early that desire and like don't always go together.

Her gloved fingers tangled in the cords of her reticule. 'Please consider again and bow out of the duel—and leave my sister alone.'

'You don't want much, but I am sorry I shall have to disappoint you.' He kept his voice soft, but his anger at her brother and father's failure to take the responsibility of protecting their women simmered in his gut. It joined the stew already brewing from her insult.

Her retort was full of barely controlled anger. 'No, you aren't or you would do what I asked. But I will do something, be assured of that. I cannot allow you to meet Bertram. You will hurt him. Nor can I let you continue making Amy the focus of your attentions, for you will ruin her chances of making a good marriage.'

'I will harm your brother by shooting in the air and ruin Miss Amy's chances on the Marriage Mart by flirting with her?' Sarcasm dripped from his words. 'I beg to differ with you.'

She smiled but it wasn't friendly. 'You always do.'

'I hardly think so.' He moved to the front of his large mahogany desk and rested one hip on the top. 'In fact, my attentions will likely draw the interest of others to her.'

Her mouth turned down. 'Not the type of interest we want.'

'You want a rich man, preferably with a title, who is besotted enough to bail your father and brother out of the River Tick.'

'And why shouldn't we? That is what the Marriage Mart is all about.'

Her high cheeks flushed, and he found himself intrigued by how the colour played against the light sprinkling of freckles across her small tipped nose. In spite of her not being anything like the women he was normally attracted to, he had always been intrigued by her. She was very like his sister Juliet in personality, which boded no good for him if it came to a confrontation, for Juliet always won. He had a feeling this woman would, too.

'No reason. But you are right. I hardly fit your parameters.' He caught her eyes with his. 'My brother did—or so we thought.'

Her mouth thinned to a blade. 'A gentleman would not mention that.'

He shrugged. 'You have already made it abundantly clear you do not consider me a gentleman.' He paused to choose his words carefully before speaking softly. 'George should not have done what he did to you, and I apologise for that. But I won't brand myself a coward by calling off the duel because of what my brother did.'

'What your brother did in the past has nothing to do with the present.'

Her voice was cold enough to freeze a fire. He didn't blame her. He had been out of place, but then so had George when he had made it impossible for the woman sitting here to stay engaged to him. Not that Charles didn't love his brother and his new sister-in-law and think they were a much better match than George and Miss Stockton would have been. But that didn't make things right. Still, it really was none of his business.

'A word of warning,' he said. 'The type of man you are looking for will either be too young to be a good husband or too old to fulfill his duties.'

Her blush deepened. 'You are blunt.'

He shrugged. 'It serves no one to beat around the bush, no matter how easy that might be. I have always found honesty serves me best. Perhaps you would do well to consider it yourself.'

She bolted to her feet, and he knew he had gone too far. So be it. He was tired of this situation and would do as he pleased no matter what she might ask.

'My male relatives and my past are none of your business, Mr Hawthorne.'

'True, but they are all bound up in the reason you are here.'

Her eyes narrowed, and he knew she would gladly see him in Hades at this instant as she said through clenched teeth, 'I see I have wasted my time—'

'And possibly damaged your reputation.'

'If someone recognises me, which I doubt. You have no company and I made sure no one saw me arriving. And I am disguised.'

'Just because you saw no one doesn't mean no one saw you.'

She lifted her chin. 'I believe I have not been seen and that you made a lucky guess. Nothing more.'

'Perhaps.'

A sigh escaped her. 'I have wasted my time. I had hoped to appeal to the side of you everyone says you have. The side that helps the underdog.' Her voice turned flat. 'I was wrong.'

His eyes narrowed. Whether she knew it or not, she had just

scored a hit. 'I am not going to tell you again that I won't shoot your brother.'

She pulled the veil back over her face, muffling her voice. 'I wish I could believe you.'

His patience gone, Charles turned his back on her and went to the table where the decanter of Scotch and glasses were set. He poured a stiff drink as the door to his office shut with a bang. He drank the liquor in one long swallow.

Shortly after, the door opened again and Stoner stuck his head in. 'You certainly know 'ow to charm 'em, Guv'nor.'

Charles looked at the other man with a jaundiced eye. 'When I want to charm a woman, I do. Come in and close the door, I need to know something and I don't want anyone else privy.'

Bushy brows raised, Stoner did as instructed.

'Did any of the servants see my visitor?'

A knowing smile curved Stoner's fleshy lips. 'One of the maids and a footman, but they're used to women visiting here.'

Charles frowned. 'Did any seem interested in more than a superficial way—as though they recognised her?'

Stoner scratched his bald head. 'Don't think they would. She moves in different circles from them.'

'Well, keep your ears open. I don't want the lady's reputation ruined no matter how stupid her visit was.'

If possible, Stoner's brows went higher. 'Right, Guv'.'

Charles's frown intensified. 'Don't read anything into my words that isn't there. I may have a reputation as a rakehell, but I don't ruin ladies of quality—no matter what the one who just left might think.'

'Right, Guv'.' A smile that was just on the border of a knowing grin split Stoner's craggy face.

'Don't smirk, Stoner. It isn't manly.'

The other man's face went flat but there was still a gleam in his brown eyes. 'Interested in this one, ain't you?'

Charles didn't like the implications of Stoner's words.

'I am most definitely not interested in the woman. She is

dull and too strait-laced for my tastes. I am merely concerned for her safety as I would be for anyone who needs protection.'

'Right, Guv'.' The smile still played around Stoner's thin lips.

Charles put his empty glass down a little too hard. 'Go away and do what I told you. I still have a lot of work to finish here.' He looked down at his accounts and back. 'And see that she gets home safely. She likely turned right when she exited the front door.'

'Right, Guv'.' Stoner's tone was a smirk.

Charles scowled at the numbers which just minutes before had marched down his ledger with gratifying success. Now they were just figures.

Miss Emma Stockton's assumption that he would just quit what he was doing because she asked intrigued him. Why would she think he might?

Particularly the duel. To back out would ruin his reputation. There was nothing she could do to convince him to pull out. But her sister...

Until now, he had pursued Amy Stockton because it amused him, or so he had thought. This evening's visit made him realise what he had truly enjoyed was watching Emma Stockton's reactions to his attentions to her younger sister. And he hadn't really cared about much else.

Was he that self-centred?

Disgusted at himself and the unwelcome introspection his visitor had brought, he flung down the quill, leaving a splat of ink on the paper, and rose. He would take a walk through his domain. Get his mind off the encounter.

Chapter Eight

Emma stepped outside and into rain. She realised her fingers shook. The encounter with Charles Hawthorne had been difficult, having learned long ago from her father and brother that confronting a man who has made up his mind was like standing against a dashing carriage. But she had to try.

If only that were all of it. If only the man didn't make her body feel things she knew were improper for an unmarried woman to have towards a man. If only he would not duel Bertram and would leave Amy alone. She took a deep breath to get better control of her reaction.

The young, burly footman she had brought for protection materialised from the shadows where he had been waiting. The hackney cab she had hired to bring them was long since gone.

She swiped at a blur of water that obscured her vision. The street was empty. Likely they would have to walk home. Her shoulders slumped for a moment before she berated herself into standing straight.

Failure lay on her like a rain-doused cape, but she was not defeated. She would think of something to keep Charles Hawthorne from meeting Bertram. And when that was done, she would figure out how to make the man stop paying such marked attention to Amy. Nothing was impossible, only very difficult. Particularly anything having to do with that dratted man.

'Miss,' the footman said, opening a large umbrella which was already too late to protect her from the downpour, 'I hope your visit was successful.'

She glanced up at him, his face blurred in the dark and the rain as she moved under the meager protection of the umbrella. He was stepping over the boundary of propriety, but he had grown up with her at her family's country seat, so she answered him.

'I doubt it, David.'

She had counted on a facet of Charles Hawthorne's personality that didn't seem to be there—compassion. It must be that he only offered it when doing so did not hurt or inconvenience him.

But she was not going to dwell on her disappointment. She was going to develop a plan to stop Mr Hawthorne.

With a determined stride, she struck out in the direction of the rented house. It was quite a walk from this part of London to the respectable, if shabby, area where she lived.

The rain increased, and Emma found herself trudging through puddles that were impossible to avoid. Her boots soaked through to her stockings, and her skirts clung like seaweed to her legs. Her hat was sodden in spite of the cape's hood, and she sucked the soaked veil into her mouth with every breath. She flipped the black material off her face and thought about taking the hat completely off and throwing it in the ditch, but money was tight and she might be able to salvage something of it. And, heaven forbid, if someone who knew her drove by…she would need the veil.

Mr Hawthorne had been correct when he had said she risked her reputation with this visit. And not just hers. Amy would be equally tarred if word spread that Emma had visited the man. Combine that indiscretion with the introductions to Harriette Wilson, Amy's unabashed pursuit of the rake and now the upcoming duel…

They would all be ruined. Except Charles Hawthorne.

She reached the corner, thankful for the fitful light coming from one of the windows. This part of London didn't have gas lighting. A shiver coursed her spine as she turned right.

'Miss.' David's voice was barely audible in the downpour and because he spoke softly. 'I think we need to take shelter until this lets up. Let me find an urchin and have him find a hackney coach.'

Without missing a step, she said, 'If you can find one in this downpour I will be surprised, but willing to fork over a penny.'

Before he could reply, a coach pulled up beside them and the door opened. David stepped in front of Emma, holding the umbrella like a weapon. She edged back.

Charles Hawthorne's servant stepped out. 'Come to give you a ride home, miss.'

She gaped at him, while rain streamed down her chin. 'Give me a ride home?' She echoed him, totally nonplussed by this turn of events. 'Who sent you?'

He shook his head, water droplets flying from his hat. 'Who do you think, miss? I've no intention of doing you harm.' He eyed David, who still held the umbrella like a bludgeon. 'Nor your man here.'

Should she accept his offer? This was a gesture she had not expected. She looked the closed carriage over and saw it had no crest or other means of identification. It was now dark enough and miserable enough that the likelihood of someone seeing it and recognising them in it was slim to nil.

She motioned for David to move away. 'We are grateful for your help.' She stepped forward.

The mountain moved to one side and held the door open for her as he gave her his hand to help her up. She entered and sank onto the wine-coloured velvet seat. Realising at the last minute that her drenched state would ruin the upholstery, she jumped up.

'Not to worry, miss,' the servant said with a twisted smile. 'Mr Charles plans on replacing the upholstery soon.'

Before settling back down again, she leaned out the door to find her footman. 'David?'

David folded the umbrella and said, 'I shall ride up front, miss.'

He didn't mention her name, for which she was thankful, although with her veil up, Charles Hawthorne's servant would recognise her the next time he saw her. But there was nothing she could do about that. She also knew David rode outside to make sure the carriage went where it was supposed to.

The mountain got back into the carriage, making it rock on its leather straps. She studied the man for a long moment, the flickering light from the inside lantern casting shadows across his blunt face and crooked nose. He returned her gaze without hesitation.

'Thank you for fetching us. We likely would not have found a hackney coach.'

He nodded. 'That's what Mr Charles thought.'

There was a formality in his words that made her think he usually referred to his employer in more casual terms. Interesting. Curiosity pricked her. 'Have you been with him long?'

His face impassive, he said, 'Long enough.'

She looked away from his closed face and wondered what sort of man Charles Hawthorne really was. He had been pursuing her young sister with a disregard for propriety that was disturbing, yet he engendered loyalty in a servant who looked as though he belonged in a boxing ring, not a private home.

She shook her head, totally confused by the man.

Minutes later, Emma gave Charles Hawthorne's servant one last look as her own servant handed her down from Hawthorne's coach. Stoner returned her gaze without flinching.

'I won't tell anyone, miss.'

'Thank you.'

She turned away and hurried through the rain to her front door and into the foyer. A single candle burned in a brass holder.

'You may go to bed, David.' Weariness crept into her voice. 'I won't need you again tonight.'

'Yes, miss.' He bowed before leaving.

Emma watched his retreating back and wondered what she was going to do now. It was obvious that Charles Hawthorne had no intention of changing his behaviour.

Emma took off her soggy hat, looked at it and sighed. In the flickering light from the lone candle, it was abundantly obvious there was nothing to be saved. Still another thing sacrificed on the altar of gambling and debts and getting her sister married to a rich man who would solve all their problems. A man who wouldn't leave Amy for another woman before they even wed. And now the duel.

Too much was at stake. She had to do something. The well-being of her entire family depended on her.

But what to do about Charles Hawthorne?

Mad as he had made her tonight, he had also shown more insight than she was comfortable with. He had remembered her pearls and noticed them gone. She caught a sob. She wasn't a watering pot, and Charles Hawthorne was not the totally self-centred man she had thought him to be—although close.

A door opened down the hall and Bertram appeared. 'Where have you been? It's rather late to be out unescorted.'

A frisson of unease slithered down Emma's spine to be immediately replaced by irritation. 'Where I have been is my own concern, Bertram.' He came closer and she smelled port. 'Are you inebriated again?'

His hazel-eyed gaze slid away from her. She knew he was going to lie to her. His gaze returned to her. 'I have had some port, but I am far from incapacitated.'

He could be so pompous even when he sounded vulnerable. He had been drinking more than was normal the last couple of days. She wondered if he feared the duel. 'Is there something wrong, Bertram?'

Sullenness rolled from him in waves. 'Nothing that couldn't be alleviated if you kept better control of Amy or if you had married George Hawthorne instead of releasing him.

He would have married you from honour and kept the other woman as his mistress.'

Emma's mouth dropped in shocked horror at what he said. 'Bertram!'

He pouted. 'It's true.'

'It is time I went to bed, Bertram,' she managed to say when she got her fury under control. 'I suggest you do the same.'

The urge to berate him and point out exactly why they were in this position was nearly impossible to resist. She managed not to, mainly because everything Bertram said was true. He just left out his and Papa's part in the debacle.

Bertram's voice seemed to follow her up the stairs. 'I am going out.'

She didn't look back even as fresh despair engulfed her. He was going to lose more money. 'Take care of yourself.'

'As though you care.'

She turned back to him. 'I do care.'

Not waiting for his reply because she knew she would not like it, Emma continued up the stairs to the next floor leaving a trail of water and mud behind her. The poor maid would be busy tomorrow, she thought, as she entered her room and closed the door.

Charles returned to his office after looking out the front window to see that Emma Stockton was nowhere in sight. Stoner must be taking her home.

Charles flung himself into a comfortable leather chair pulled near the fire and propped his feet near the grate. Warmth penetrated the soles of his shoes.

The dog, Adam, flopped down on his pillow, kept near Charles's chair, with a resigned sigh. Charles dropped his arm so his fingers could scratch the fluff of hair behind the dog's ears. 'Yes, I know, Adam. Damned difficult, this waiting.'

Adam looked up with soulful and understanding brown eyes.

'I wish everything in life were as simple as a full belly and warm fire.'

Adam flicked one ear as though he understood perfectly.

'Yes, I know,' Charles continued. 'I'm going dotty. Next it will be bedlam.' He stared at the dog's brown, nearly black, eyes and would have sworn he saw commiseration in them.

Emma woke up the next day to the maid she shared with Amy, who was also the housekeeper, and a steaming cup of hot chocolate. The sweet, rich smell made her stomach growl. She hadn't eaten much dinner last night, knowing the visit she was going to make. Then there had been the encounter with Bertram.

The headache that had made it difficult to fall asleep threatened to return. She closed her eyes and counted slowly to twenty, trying to keep all other thoughts from her mind.

'Here, miss, you'll be needing this, I've no doubt.'

Emma opened her eyes to smile at the woman who had been in service with the family before Emma was born. Funds were so tight that they couldn't afford to employ a separate maid and housekeeper. In most houses Betty would be called Mrs Murphy, but they had long ago dispensed with that. Betty had been Betty when she was the nursery maid. She would always be Betty.

'Thank you, Betty.'

Emma pushed up to a sitting position and took the drink, downing the hot beverage in several greedy gulps. She closed her eyes, relishing the peace and pleasure of the moment, knowing it would disappear all too soon.

'Tsk.' Betty bustled around the room. 'Here is more.' She fetched the pot of hot chocolate and poured another cupful.

'Thank you.' Emma smiled at her. 'You always know what I need before I do.'

'Harrumph!' The older, plump woman blushed to the roots of her silver hair. 'A sad thing it would be if I didn't.'

Emma's smile widened but she made no reply. Betty was as modest as she was caring and efficient.

She noticed Betty was hustling about as though something

bothered her. 'Whatever is the matter, Betty, that you cannot settle down?'

The older woman paused with Emma's morning dress clutched in her hands. 'Master Bertram is up and about. He wants to talk with you immediately.'

Emma snorted. So, Bertram was still upset over last night. Since she had refused to tell him where she had gone, he was going to pester her until she did. Well, she was made of sterner stuff than that as he would soon find out.

She threw the heavy covers to one side and slid to the floor, her feet landing on a threadbare throw rug. She quickly put on her nearby slippers. Her thick woollen gown kept some of the chill in the unheated room from reaching her skin.

'I'd best hurry then, since I intend to eat breakfast before speaking to him.'

Betty shooed her to the dressing table and pressed her onto the chair. Emma saw herself in the mirror. She looked a fright.

'I should have braided my hair before going to sleep last night.'

But she had been thinking too much on what to do about Charles Hawthorne. She would pay for her negligence of the night before when Betty dressed her hair. The older woman would be gentle, but the tangles would take a long time to straighten out and would be painful in the process.

Bertram was going to wait longer than he liked.

What a mess everything was.

Over an hour later, Emma entered the breakfast room to find it empty and the fire blazing merrily. Gordon, the butler, entered behind her.

'I will bank the fire, miss. Mr Bertram is in the parlour.'

Emma jumped. She had not realised the butler had followed her in. She had been too preoccupied with Bertram.

'Thank you, Gordon.' She smiled at the butler. 'I will have a piece of toast and an egg before joining my brother.'

The butler bowed and left to tell Cook.

Emma sank into the chair where a fresh pot of hot chocolate had been placed and poured herself another cup. This was the one luxury she allowed herself, for chocolate was not inexpensive. She savoured the drink until her piece of toast and soft-boiled egg arrived, hoping all the time that Bertram would leave her in peace until she finished eating.

She even left the fire burning. Today she felt she needed all the comfort she could get.

The last bite of toast was a memory when Bertram slammed into the room. 'Emma, I told Gordon to tell you I was in the parlour. Why have you taken so long?'

Emma took the final sip of chocolate before looking at her brother. Even now, she could see vestiges of the young, mischievous boy he had once been. She could even remember playing hide-and-seek with him down by the stream where Father would fish for trout. The memories softened her reply.

'I am eating breakfast first. Then I had planned on meeting with you.' She carefully folded the many-times mended linen napkin and laid it beside her empty plate before standing.

Bertram pivoted on his heel and strode from the room. Emma followed, refusing to look at the butler who she knew was studiously not looking at her. Gordon had been with the family as long as Betty, and like the housekeeper he had nearly a fatherly interest in what was happening to the family. Not to mention how the finances would impact on her ability to provide for him in his old age.

She entered the parlour behind her brother and noted still another coal fire. The room was nearly warm enough for her to take off her shawl.

Bertram stomped to the fireplace and placed one immaculately shined Hessian boot on the grate. She sat in the chair nearest the fire and waited. Taking the offensive only made Bertram defensive and accomplished nothing. That much she had learned from watching Mama deal with both husband and son.

'I will get right to the heart of the matter, Emma. You must refuse to let Amy continue seeing Charles Hawthorne. The man is a rake with no title and he is totally unacceptable.' He took a deep breath and added, 'Why have you not been able to keep Amy away from him?'

Emma looked at her folded hands until she could get her emotions under control. 'Charles Hawthorne is accepted everywhere, Bertram. There is no way to avoid him if I intend to take Amy about.'

Bertram's light blue eyes chilled. 'Then I must start to accompany you. What is today's schedule?'

The light at the end of this tunnel was that as long as Bertram was with them he would not be gambling. 'We have a visit to pay Lady James this afternoon. We have no plans for this evening.'

While she spoke Bertram's eyes glazed over with boredom. Too bad.

He took a deep breath, squared his shoulders and looked as if he were facing a firing squad. 'Very well, then. I shall go with you.'

Emma rose, realising that taking Bertram uninvited was not the thing to do. And she could escape before he started asking where she had been last night. She was surprised he hadn't asked that first. He must truly be worried about the rumours linking Amy to Charles Hawthorne. Or had he been too inebriated last night to remember?

'I must send round a note to Lady James to see if she has room for you. If you will excuse me, I will see to that immediately. When I find out, I will let you know.' She moved to the door, paused and looked over her shoulder. 'Will you be here?'

He removed his foot from the fire grate and nearly did a shuffle. His actions told her what his answer would be. She swallowed a sigh of frustration.

'I will be at my club. Send the message there.'

Emma left the room, praying he would not lose more money, but knowing he would. She could not force him to leave London, particularly since Papa had sent him.

But she could and would do something about putting a stop to Bertram's impending duel with Charles Hawthorne. Right after she took care of the new work Bertram's latest decision had caused.

Chapter Nine

$Emma$ dabbed rose water on her temples because that is what her Mama always used when she had a headache. Then she pulled her old robe around her shoulders and sent Betty, who had watched everything with a critical eye, to fetch Amy and Bertram.

Leaning back in the mound of pillows on the bed, Emma closed her eyes and told herself she had to do this. It was the only thing she could think of to stop the duel between her brother and Charles Hawthorne. Bertram was a young man who fished well and gambled. He was not a crack shot, and rumour said Charles Hawthorne was the best shot in the *ton*. The two could not—would not—meet.

She heard Bertram's irritated voice before she saw him. 'What is the matter now? I am on my way out. Can't this wait?'

Betty said something but Emma couldn't hear the housekeeper's lowered tone.

'Oh, if she insists.' Bertram came through the bedroom door without knocking.

Emma hadn't expected anything else since she had known this would irritate him. Anything that interfered with his plans irritated him these days. He could do with a rest in the country, but she knew better than to say that.

'Thank you for coming, Bertram.'

She put all her effort into sounding tired and in pain, which, if she were honest with herself, didn't take much. She was exhausted and worried her plan would fail—and it must not.

'I am on my way out, Emma, so this must be quick.'

She saw the colour in his cheeks and wondered if his quick words had made her flush, too. This wasn't the time to let her anger over everything get the better of her—as it had the last time she had spoken to him.

'Then I am glad I caught you before you left. I have the headache, and Amy has just been invited to a ball where all the most eligible bachelors will be.' She stared hard at Bertram, putting into her look all the things she could not openly say. 'It is imperative she attend. You must take her.'

He returned her stare, his chin setting belligerently. She recognised the expression but she was not going to give in to him. Not tonight.

'I have an engagement.'

'You have a duty.'

His face darkened so that his straw-coloured hair seemed to stand out in bright relief against his narrow features. '*You* have a duty. You are the one who is Amy's chaperone.'

She nearly shook her head in frustration. 'I am not feeling well, Bertram. And Papa sent you here to lend us respectability. You must take Amy tonight in my stead.'

'Then Amy can stay at home.'

Something snapped in Emma, and she wondered fleetingly if this was how she would be from here on. Always losing her temper? 'How selfish do you intend to be, Bertram? First you gamble so that Amy must marry for money, then you drag her name through the mud by challenging Charles Hawthorne and now you refuse to help Amy find the rich husband you have made it imperative she marry.'

He drew himself up, the red that had filled his face draining away. 'You speak harshly.'

'You made me.'

She was not going to back down and allow him to do as he wished tonight. Both he and Amy had to be gone from the house. The only way to ensure they were both gone and she remained was for him to take Amy to the ball.

'What is going on?'

Amy's light voice came from the doorway where she stood, dressed for the ball. Her fair hair was in artful disarray with a spray of pansies tucked into a nest of curls. Tall and slim, her youthful figure was shown to perfection by a pale pink muslin gown, drawn up under her bosom and accented with deep violet ribbons the colour of the flowers in her hair. Her blue eyes were luminous and, at the moment, filled with curiosity.

'We are having a discussion, dear,' Emma answered before Bertram could say something cutting or petulant. 'I have the headache, and Bertram must take you to the ball.'

Amy looked from one to the other. Her previous pleasure seeping away until her rosebud mouth formed a downward turn. She moved to stand by the bed.

'Then I know exactly what is happening.' She looked her brother up and down. 'Bertram has plans already, and he refuses to change them to escort me.' She tossed her head and turned to Emma. 'Well, I can go to the ball by myself. That will solve everything.'

Emma closed her eyes for a moment, wondering why everything seemed to get worse. 'No,' she said, keeping her mounting anger from her words, 'that won't solve anything, Amy. You know you cannot go by yourself.'

'Well, then why doesn't Bertram seem to know that?' She rounded on him. 'For I know you have refused to take Em's place, you selfish thing. All you think about is your own pleasure.'

Bertram backed up a step. 'No, I don't.'

'Don't dare say that.' Amy closed the distance between them. 'What happened to the big brother who used to spend time showing us how to fish or how to walk in the forest so we didn't make noise? I know. He got lost in the man who has decided that he shall do whatever he pleases regardless of the cost to others.'

Bertram's fists clenched as though he wanted to push her away but he didn't move. Emma realised Amy's bitterness over her situation ran deeper than she had realised. If only the girl could find a man she could care for, things might work out.

'All right. I will escort you.' Bertram pivoted on one polished Hessian. 'Give me time to change. I am dressed for an informal gathering, not a ball at Lady Cowper's.'

Emma sighed in relief. It had not been pretty watching Amy and Bertram, but Amy had succeeded where she had failed. Now her plan could be put into effect.

Amy sank onto the bed. 'I am sorry you don't feel well, Em, for I wish above all things not to have Bertram take me. He is such a boor that he will be sure to pout or behave poorly the entire time.'

'Yes, I am sure he will make things uncomfortable. But be happy you get to go.'

Emma couldn't keep a bite of dryness from her tone. If she were truly unwell with the headache, Amy's self-interest would be hurtful. As it was, she accepted it with irony.

Amy caught her meaning and had the grace to blush. 'I did not mean to say that I don't care that you are sick. I know how uncomfortable it is to lie abed. I just…'

'Yes, I know. You just do not want Bertram as your escort. But you must.'

'Yes, that is it exactly.' Amy jumped up. 'I will go and get my shawl and everything and be ready when he is. He is upset enough without being kept waiting.' She paused in the doorway. 'I hope you feel better.'

Emma knew the words were Amy's way of apologising. She smiled. 'I am sure a night at home will do wonders. Go and have fun.'

Amy beamed. 'I shall do my best if only to spite Bertram.'

Emma laughed, sharing Amy's sentiment. 'Then you shall have a great time.'

'Yes, I shall.' Amy pirouetted one time to show off her ensemble, then flipped a wave to Emma and was gone.

Emma sank gratefully into the pillows. Now she had to wait for Betty to return with the news that the two were off. Then the next part of her plan could be put into action.

What seemed an eternity later there was a knock on the door. 'Enter.'

The housekeeper came through. 'They are gone, miss.'

Emma threw back the covers and slipped from bed. She took off her robe to show a practical gown of kerseymere in a muted heather colour. She glanced at the older woman who frowned back.

'I know you don't approve, Betty, but I am at my wit's end and can think of nothing else to do.'

'Humph! You could kidnap Master Bertram. That would put paid to the duel.' She bustled to fold Emma's robe. 'And you should know nothing about that, either. That is men's business.'

'True, but Bertram let the news spill so now I must stop it—or at least try. As for kidnapping Bertram, what would I do with him? Send him to father? He would only come back and challenge Mr Hawthorne again.' She went to her desk, sat and pulled a piece of paper. 'No, the only way to ensure the duel doesn't happen is to have Mr Hawthorne fail to show. Then Bertram will have no need to challenge him again.' She picked up a quill and dipped it in ink, muttering, 'Not that he had any reason to do so in the first place.'

She made the note brief. The less said the better.

Please call upon me. My servant will accompany you.
Sincerely, Miss Stockton.

She waited several minutes for the ink to dry before standing and turning to Betty.

'Please get David here.'

'You don't have to do this.'

Emma turned away from the servant. 'I do not intend to discuss this. Fetch David.'

She heard Betty leaving and turned to look out the window. It was just starting to darken outside. Summer with its long days and short nights was perfect for the *ton* to socialise through the warm months. By the time her note reached Charles Hawthorne it would be dark and many of the people they knew would be indoors at some social gathering.

Would he come?

He had no reason to do so. She was no one to him. He might come if she said Amy wanted him, but he would know she would never send for him to appease Amy. Likely he would come from curiosity—and the chance for amusement at her expense. He seemed to like needling her.

She twisted the paper into a screw for delivery and started pacing. So much hinged on him coming. If he did not, she would have to do something else. What could she do to ensure he came? Nothing.

She heard David's boots on the hall flooring and went to the door before he could knock. Stepping outside, she looked him over to make sure he was inconspicuous. He wore dark clothing and a woollen cap.

He made her a bow. 'Miss.'

Emma gave him the note. 'Please deliver this to Mr Charles Hawthorne. We were there two days ago. Wait for his reply. Escort him back here.'

David nodded as he took the paper. 'And if he doesn't want to come, miss?'

Emma's stomach did a dive when the footman voiced her own fears. She stood taller. 'He will. If not with you, then on his own. Tell him I am waiting for him.'

'Yes, miss.' The young footman bowed, but there was a troubled look on his face.

She turned away, not wanting to see her doubts on his countenance. This had to work. Otherwise, she would have to kidnap Charles Hawthorne from the streets, which would be next to impossible. She would never know where he would be, so she would never be able to have her servants at that location. And Charles Hawthorne was never about alone. No, this had to work.

After David left, she went down to the drawing room to wait. She ordered tea to ease some of her tension and sat by the window to drink it and have a biscuit. She must find patience.

Charles looked up from his ledgers as Stoner entered the small office. Adam rose from his rug at Charles's feet and bounced to the heavyset older man.

'Adam thinks you have come to see him.' Charles set his quill aside and templed his fingers in front of him.

Stoner closed the door quietly behind him. 'I wish I was 'ere to do just that, Guv', but there's a man at the door who gave me this note for you. Same one as was 'ere several nights ago.' He handed a twist of paper to Charles. ''E won't leave, either. Says 'e's to wait for your answer and to escort you.'

One black brow rose as Charles took the note. He untwisted it and read the brief lines, wondering what was going on. The only reason she had to ask him to call on her was the duel. He knew she had no intention of trying to seduce him or even trying to get to know him better. She made no attempt to hide her disgust of him.

Damn Bertram Stockton for getting drunk and telling his sister of their meeting.

Charles knew she intended to ask him again not to go through with the duel. And again he intended to tell her he would. His reputation was very important to him. Not even for Emma Stockton—to make up for what George did to her—would he jeopardise it. When a man lost everything else, he still had his reputation.

But he would go and see her.

He rose and tossed the note into the fire. No one needed to know what was on that paper or where he was going, except for the servant who waited. But Stoner would know since he recognised Miss Stockton's man.

'Stoner, tell the man I will be along.'

Stoner watched him through narrowed eyes. 'It's that Emma Stockton, ain't it?'

Charles kept his face bland. 'Whatever gives you that idea? I get billets-doux from women all the time.'

Stoner's scowl intensified. 'You ignore them. She's the only one I ain't seen you ignore.'

Charles turned away from his valet's regard, feeling uncomfortable for no reason he could explain. 'Just tell the man I will be along.'

'I don't like it, Guv'.'

It was on the tip of Charles's tongue to tell Stoner that he didn't like it, either. But there was a tightness in his muscles that occurred when he was excited, usually when he was doing something even he recognised as risky. And he felt anticipation even though he knew what she wanted.

Charles jerked at the sound of the door slamming behind Stoner. The man made his displeasure felt.

But what did he himself feel about Emma Stockton, that he was willing to visit her? Desire?

He scowled. She wasn't in his usual style. Not at all, yet he found her challenging—arousing. Images flitted through his mind: His loins tightened pleasurably.

She stood up to him, something most women failed to do. Usually, women fawned on him, not berated him. Perhaps it was her total lack of interest in him that he found intriguing. She was different, and thus presented a challenge to him.

That was it.

He wasn't attracted to her for any reason other than he wanted to conquer her. And he would.

Having decided why he was going to do her bidding this once, he made quick work of it. Within fifteen minutes he was out of the door.

He would walk. She didn't have a stable, and he might be

staying longer than it would be comfortable to tie his horse up in front of her residence. He was many things, but he had no desire to ruin her reputation. Although people would think it was Amy he visited.

He headed out, the exercise easing some of the unexpected tension he felt. Her footman trailed behind.

It seemed an age to Emma. Night had fallen. No more coaches rumbled past the front of the house. Had Charles Hawthorne refused?

She rose and went to the door of the room. She paused with her hand on the knob. What could she do if he didn't come?

A discreet knock made her jump back. 'Yes?'

Gordon opened the door, his gaze going beyond her. 'Mr Hawthorne.'

Emma scurried back into the center of the room. Relief made her knees felt weak. She certainly wasn't reacting to the anticipation of seeing and sparring with Charles Hawthorne.

'Show him in, please.'

The butler nodded, still not looking at her. She knew he disapproved, but she had no other choices.

Charles strode into the room, his hat in one hand and a silver embossed ebony cane in the other. He handed both to the butler and turned to her.

Her breath caught at the sight of him.

The familiar lock of hair slanted across his broad brow and his blue, nearly black, eyes sparkled. His navy coat fit smoothly across his broad shoulders, yet looked casual, as though he could take it off without his valet's assistance. His leg muscles rippled under the snug black material of his pantaloons.

He made a perfect leg, with only a hint of mockery in his eyes. 'Miss Stockton.'

She gulped air and managed, 'Please be seated.'

She indicated a large chair pulled close to the roaring fire she had told Betty to make. They might be strapped for money, and Charles Hawthorne might know that, but she intended to treat him as though money were no object. Her pride would allow nothing else with this man.

Never taking his attention off her, he moved with liquid grace and sat.

'Would you like tea or something stronger?' She was determined to be the perfect hostess.

'Something stronger.'

His smile was sensual and knowing, as though he imagined she had asked him here for something personal and intimate. She shook her head to clear it of such nonsensical thoughts.

'Port?'

'That will do.'

His tone indicated that he did not care for the wine, but he had to. Everything was prepared. 'Do you like it?'

He shrugged. 'It is not my favourite, but I have been known to drink it.'

She made a moue of relief. 'It is Bertram's favourite so it is what we have.'

'Ah, your brother.'

His words held a wealth of distaste. She could understand how a man like Charles Hawthorne might not like her brother. He was everything Bertram was not.

'Yes, my brother.' She forced a false brightness into her voice. 'He is the reason I asked you here.'

His mouth curled. 'I thought as much.'

She held up her hand. 'Let me call for your refreshment first.'

His dark eyes seemed to bore into her, as though he heard the falseness in her words. A frisson chased down her spine.

'As you wish.'

Heat rose in her stomach as though she had just taken a sip of a very hot drink. It was the kind of feeling that mixed delight with discomfort. This was not going to be easy.

Only after the port and biscuits were served and Gordon gone, did Emma let herself look at her guest again. His scent of musk and bergamot perfumed the air. It was a heady combination. The man had too much influence over her body as it was.

'You know why I asked you here.'

He nodded. 'Of course, and I wonder that you think you can change my mind. I have already refused.'

'I have to try again.' She spread her hands. 'Bertram is not as skilled as you.'

He shrugged. 'Then he should not have challenged me, as I told you before.'

She sighed. 'I know, but he did. You can call it off.'

His fingers tightened on the stem of the wineglass but he took a deep drink. 'I told you two nights ago why I won't, Miss Stockton—Emma.'

Her stomach knotted at his familiarity even as the milky richness of his voice stroked her nerves. He was a man who knew how to tantalise a woman even as he violated Society's conventions. 'I did not give you permission to use my first name.'

He gave her the smile she saw him use on other women, the one that promised things proper ladies didn't talk about. She licked dry lips and wondered why she felt as though she had lost control of this discussion.

'No, you didn't, but you want something very badly—something that only I can give you. I think that entitles me to a few liberties.'

Heaven help her. This moment she wanted to give him a few liberties. She shook her head to clear it of the disturbing picture of him taking her hand and then... 'If I give you permission to address me so casually, will you call off the duel?'

He cocked one black brow. 'I would certainly be more inclined to do so.'

She knew he had no intention of honouring any promise no matter what he said. Disappointment mingled with frustration, the mix replacing the knot of ardour in her stomach. 'But in the end you won't.'

He shook his head. 'No, I won't. I told you last night that to do so would impact unfavourably on my reputation. There have been times when my good reputation was all I had left in the world. I won't do anything to jeopardise that.'

She could understand his reasoning, but she didn't like it. 'Then why did you come here when you knew what I wanted and that you would refuse?'

He drained the glass of port, poured himself another from the full decanter, and drank it in one long swallow. 'Maybe I wondered what incentive you would offer to change my mind.'

She watched him swallow the rich red wine, her fingers curling in tension. Soon.

She transferred her attention to his face, only to have his eyes meet hers. Was that desire she saw in his? She was going crazy. A man like him would never want a woman like her. Even his brother had not wanted her, and he was not nearly as sensual as this man.

Somehow, she managed to ask, 'And what do I have that would be enough?'

His lips pulled back to show strong white teeth as he took a deep breath. His gaze held her. She began to tremble in spite of the warmth from the fire.

'Become my mistress.'

She gulped in surprise. She had not expected this. Deep inside she felt a liquid warmth that seemed to spread to her limbs, making her feel languid and excited. Her body was a confused mix of pleasure and anticipation even as her mind told her he had just insulted her. She turned her face so she couldn't see his eyes darkening.

'How dare you.' She knew the words were inadequate. They didn't say anything of her turmoil or of the anger she should be feeling but for some reason wasn't feeling enough of. She had not been cold enough.

He laughed, the dark rich tone twining its way down her body to centre in her lower abdomen. She felt hot and full and disturbed in ways she had never experienced before.

He leaned forward in his chair so that he was close enough

for her to see the black line that circled the navy blue of his irises. He needed a shave. The dark shadow of hair on his jaw gave him a dangerous air that tantalised her.

She edged as far back in her chair as she could go.

'Afraid?' he taunted her.

She pulled air into lungs that suddenly felt empty. She wished the fire was dead. She burned. Bravado was her only defense against what he did to her. 'No.'

'Prove it.'

She stared at him, her entire body tingling in fear… dread…or worse, anticipation. 'What do you want?'

'A kiss. Nothing more.'

She studied him and knew that even one kiss would be one too many. For some reason she couldn't understand, he drew her like no other man ever had.

'If I give you that kiss will you withdraw from the duel?'

'So, we are back to that.'

'I never left it.'

His smile called her a liar. He poured himself another glass of the port. 'No, I won't, so this conversation is over.'

Her heart skipped a beat at his nonchalant tone. He had gone from seducer to philosopher. Confusion and embarrassment engulfed her. He had thrown out the offer to see if he could discommode her, and she had shown him that he could. The wine had to work before things got worse.

He drank down his third glass and stood. He swayed slightly.

She froze. Was it working?

'I am beginning to feel funny.' His voice was fuzzy.

'For not liking port, you are doing a credible job of consuming it.' She managed to make her voice acerbic instead of showing the anticipation she felt. 'Perhaps you have had enough.'

He stumbled and suspicion twisted his features. 'Have you done something to this wine?'

She hid her sigh of relief behind a cough. 'You have drunk so much.'

His eyes narrowed. 'I have finished five bottles of wine before and walked home.'

'You mean, stumbled home.'

'It doesn't matter. I got home. Now with just three glasses of port I am getting dizzy.' He took a step towards her. 'What did you put in it?'

He towered over her, his powerful body limned by the fire behind him. The breadth of his shoulders quickened her pulse. His black hair tumbled over his forehead. His eyelids slanted across dark eyes.

She licked dry lips. 'A sleeping draught.'

'I had not thought you the devious sort.'

His words were barely slurred, but it was there. Soon he would sit back down. She found herself truly sorry to have done this to him. But he had left her no choice.

'I have done what I had to. I have to protect Bertram.'

His laugh was harsh. 'If he felt the same way about you and your sister, you would not have had to do anything.'

The words were like a sharp barb that stuck in the space below her heart. 'That is neither here nor there.'

He sank back into the chair he had just left, looking disheveled, even vulnerable. For an instant the urge to brush the hair from his forehead nearly overwhelmed her. This was the man who had insulted her by asking her to become his mistress. This was not a man who needed her comforting.

'What are you going to do with me?'

She watched him. 'I am going to secure you somewhere until the time for the duel is past. I believe it will only be three days.'

He shook his head only to stop abruptly and close his eyes for a moment. Opening them, he said, 'I told you I don't intend to hurt him.'

'I can't take the chance.'

'You could try trusting me.'

Even in his drugged state, he managed to affect her. She really wanted to trust him, but she dared not. So far, she had not been able to trust any man in her life. Not her father or brother or Charles's brother. No, she dared not believe he would delope. She couldn't take the chance he would seriously hurt her brother.

His eyes closed and his mouth relaxed. The tension drained from the muscles in his face.

She moved to the fireplace and pulled the tattered bell cord to summon the men who waited in the kitchen. Soon he would be asleep, if he wasn't already.

Mama had slept quickly after receiving the draught. Emma had remembered that and sent Betty that afternoon to the chemist to get the medicine. Mama would not approve of what she had just done, but that could not be helped.

Gordon and David didn't knock. They entered quickly, knowing she expected them.

'Quickly,' she said, 'tie his hands. We don't know how long he will be affected.'

David whistled low. 'How much did he drink?'

She twisted her hands together, beginning to think he had taken too much. 'Three glasses.'

Gordon stared at Charles. 'He must have the constitution of an ox. I put the entire bottle in that decanter. I would have expected him to pass out sooner.'

Emma gasped. 'He said he could consume a great deal of wine.'

The footman shook his head. 'And anything else, miss.'

For the first time, fear that she might hurt him made her uneasy. She had never meant to harm him. Only make him easier to subdue.

She narrowed her eyes to better see if Charles's chest rose and fell. His white cravat fluttered and relief made her giddy. He was fine.

'Is the upstairs room ready?' Her voice was harsher than she intended. She told herself it was not relief for Charles Hawthorne but edginess over what she was doing.

Betty slipped into the room. 'Yes, miss.' She glanced at their prisoner. 'I started a fire, seeing as he won't be feeling well.'

'Of course.' Emma could not begrudge him the warmth since it was her doing that put Charles Hawthorne into this position. 'Perhaps we should bind his wrists to be safe. I have heard he practices at Gentleman Jackson's on a regular basis.'

The footman's eyebrows rose. 'He's a regular bruiser, ain't he?'

Gordon lifted one of Charles's eyes. 'He is completely under, miss. I don't think we need to worry about anything but getting him up to the attic room.'

'You are probably right.'

Still, apprehension ate at her. He would be a formidable adversary if he awakened before they were ready. As it was, they would have to secure him to the bed.

She watched as the footman took his shoulders and the aging butler took his feet. Charles Hawthorne was a well-muscled man and he had to be heavy. For Gordon's sake, she wished they had a second footman to help, but they did not.

What seemed ages later, she followed them into the attic room in time to see them lay her prisoner on his back on the bed. Charles didn't blink or in any way indicate he was aware. She pulled two silk stockings from her pocket and handed them to David.

'Use these to secure his wrists to the headboard. The last thing we need is for him to try to escape or to attack the first person who comes here after he is awake.'

'Yes, miss.'

The footman wrapped the silk around one wrist at a time and tied Charles to the bed. Only then did some of the tension that had driven Emma all night begin to ease. All she had to do now was somehow keep him here until after the duel was scheduled to take place. Only three days.

'David,' she said, 'I know you have been up since before sunrise, but someone needs to stay with him. Please make up a pallet and stay here, and come for me when he wakens.'

The young footman nodded.

Emma took one last look at her prisoner. He looked like a

fallen angel—a dark angel. His coat had been unbuttoned but left on. It pulled across his well-muscled chest. When he woke up, he would be nauseous and he would ache from being trussed up, but she could not help either of those things.

He should have agreed not to meet Bertram.

Chapter Ten

Charles's mouth felt like it had been dragged through the gutter. And his head....

He kept his eyes closed and his body still as he took inventory. He was on his back. His arms felt like they were being pulled from their sockets. His chest was bound. He decided his jacket was still on. As were his boots, breeches and stockings. He was fully clothed and couldn't remember when he'd last been this uncomfortable.

He opened one eye. It was dark except for a sliver of sunlight slashing across the white ceiling. There wasn't enough light to see much. He tried to sit up and couldn't. His hands were pulled up over his head and seemed to be bound to something hard. He twisted his head to the side and up to see his left wrist tied to a headboard using a woman's stocking. He also saw a young man sprawled on a makeshift pallet across the doorway.

The footman who had brought him Emma Stockton's note.

The last thing he remembered was drinking her port and realising it was drugged. She had kidnapped him.

Charles smiled. She was a very resourceful woman who would do anything for her family. His admiration for her increased, as did another part of his body as he thought of her.

He realised, with wry humour at his own expense, that his offer to make her his mistress in exchange for him not to duel with her brother wasn't far from what he wanted.

She entertained him. She aroused him.

The man on the pallet stirred and Charles came back to his situation. He was her prisoner, a position he didn't want to be in for long. Or at least he didn't want to be bound to her bed under these circumstances.

He flexed the muscles in his arms and swallowed a groan of pain. She had him trussed up tight, as though he were dangerous. A compliment to him, but this would make it more difficult for him to escape—and escape he would.

He inched himself closer to the headboard until he could reach the stocking with his teeth. The delicate material smelled of sweet peas and woman. With a jolt to his groin, he realised these were her stockings.

When he closed his lips over the silk, he tasted and smelled her. The ache that had started earlier intensified as he filled his mouth with the smooth stocking.

It was an effort of will to tear the material with his teeth. He felt as though he bit her when he wanted to lick and kiss the delicate skin these stockings had covered. He groaned and shook his head to rid himself of the image of her pale skin close to his mouth. He made himself shred the silk until there were runs in several places and holes in others.

His breathing deepened.

'I say, sir,' a sleepy voice said, 'you should not be doing that.'

Charles jerked. He lay still for long seconds, willing the urgency in his loins to subside. The last thing he needed was for the guard to realise he was aroused by chewing on Emma Stockton's stockings.

Reluctantly he took his mouth from her stocking. He finally spoke when he was sure his voice would not give away his body's state. 'What else would you expect me to do?' Exasperation crept into his tone. 'I don't have the time to lie here trussed up like a Christmas goose.'

The young man looked uncomfortable. Not surprising. Footmen didn't help kidnap members of the aristocracy.

Instead of replying to Charles's irritation, the young man scrambled to his feet. 'Miss Stockton needs to know you're awake.'

Charles's rebellious body reacted to her name. He called himself ten times a fool. Even if she was interested in him, he didn't have the wealth her family needed. And he was in trade. Not that he was interested in her. His body wanted her, but that wasn't unusual for him. Women fascinated him.

'Ah, yes,' he finally managed, 'the daring Miss Stockton. I would like to speak with her.' He was glad his voice didn't give away the heat coursing through him.

The servant turned red. 'You've no call to use that tone of voice when talking about Miss Stockton. She's a lady who deserves respect.' He added belatedly, 'Sir.'

So the prickly woman was loved by her retainers. Charles hadn't thought about it before, but he wasn't surprised. If her determination to protect those she loved extended to her servants, then they had every reason to be loyal to her.

He said nothing.

'And you must stop tearing at the ties, sir.'

Curious and feeling provocative, Charles asked, 'Do you know what these are?'

The young man turned beet red, his blond hair sticking out. 'Yes, sir.'

Charles would feel sorry for the footman if he didn't feel so unsure himself about what he felt for the dratted woman. He realised he wanted the young man to feel as uncomfortable about his bindings as he did. 'Why didn't you use rope?'

The footman shuffled his feet. 'Miss Stockton gave me those. Thought they would be easier on your skin than rope—sir.'

Charles snorted. 'Well, they aren't.'

She would think that. A more experienced woman would have known how provocative these scented silk stockings were. They were worse than any rope. Rope might cut and burn his wrists, but these intimate clothes had touched forbidden areas of her body and caused more damage to his mind. He had thought his attraction to her was merely because she openly disliked him. He was beginning to realise it was more.

He wanted her as a man wants a woman. He wanted her beneath him, her legs around him, her lips begging him. He closed his eyes and bit the inside of his cheek to erase the picture of her flush with pleasure—pleasure he gave her.

'Sir?' The footman's voice was worried. 'Are you sick? I will get a pan.'

Charles stifled an uncomfortable laugh. Was he sick? Certainly, but not the way the young man thought. 'I don't need a pan. Get your mistress.'

'Promise not to chew the bindings while I'm gone.' He looked stubborn.

'I'll be damned if I promise anything. If you can't fetch Miss Stockton before I work my way through these, then you are too poor a guard to be here.'

The young man's eyes flashed, but he kept his mouth shut. He quickly gathered the bedding from the floor in front of the door and piled it on a chair by the window. He looked at Charles before leaving.

Charles counted to ten after the door closed, then moved back up in bed and continued to gnaw at the silk stockings. He would be free when she arrived as long as he kept himself from the tempting fantasy of how the stockings would look on her.

She had nice ankles, she likely had nice legs. He wanted to taste her skin, run his tongue along the satin of her inner thigh just above where the garter would hold her stockings. Desire washed over him like heat lightning, tightening his loins. He groaned.

The door opened and the scent of sweet peas joined his vision.

'What are you doing?'

Her voice sent a rush of blood to the part of his body that troubled him. He spoke harshly. 'What does it look like? I am eating your stocking. Would you prefer for me to eat something else?' He met her eyes with his, doing nothing to hide the need that rode his body like an unsatisfied woman.

She flushed as her gaze went from him to the damp stocking and back to him. 'Are you hungry?'

He looked at her and wondered if she knew what they were talking about. Didn't she know he wanted her when it was evident in his voice and the aroused state of his body, which he doubted his pantaloons hid?

'Yes, very hungry.' Desire held him in a vise as his gaze moved over her. She was demurely dressed in grey but her ankles peeked below the hem. He could see the outline of her left thigh, a thigh the stocking he had just released might have covered yesterday.

His need increased. He closed his eyes to the sight of her, dazed that she had this power over him. He would have never thought it. She wasn't his type of woman.

'Are you ill?'

Was that worry in her voice? He thought it might be. Another part of him wondered why the idea made his stomach knot pleasurably, much like it did when he made love to a woman. She wasn't for him. No matter what his body thought.

'Are you feeling guilty?' He countered her with sarcasm, hoping to put paid to his response to her and to hide the thickness in his throat.

Her shoulders hunched then straightened. 'Certainly not. I am merely concerned that you will be sick on the clean sheets.'

'Not very clean since your henchman put me in bed with my boots on.'

Her light brown brows furrowed. 'I am sorry. I left them thinking they would make you comfortable.'

He laughed a short bark that did nothing to ease his discomfort. 'They also left my coat on. It was damned painful when I woke up.'

Dismay moved over her features. 'Then I owe you several apologies.'

'I think so.' For the raging fire that coursed through his body if nothing else.

She stiffened and eyed him as though he had gone too far. Did she finally realise the state he was in? Any inexperienced Miss would be affronted at his blatant arousal.

'But if you had agreed with my request,' she said, 'none of this would have been necessary. So, it could also be said that you brought this on yourself.'

Her voice was cold, but did nothing to dampen the heat in him. She didn't know he wanted her or she refused to acknowledge that she knew. He didn't know which and wasn't sure it mattered. He had to control himself better than this.

His eyebrows rose. 'I did not issue the challenge. Your brother did.'

'I am sure you did something to provoke him.'

'I merely treated him as he deserved.'

'So, you did provoke him. I thought as much.' She moved toward him, her fine grey eyes narrowed.

He studied her, wishing his body would let him think clearly. Still, he saw no reason not to tell her the truth. 'I don't like the way he gambles so that you must shoulder the burden of trying to marry off Miss Amy. A burden your brother continues to make harder to accomplish by continuing to gamble and lose.'

'You are concerned about me?' She stopped inches from the bed, disbelief in her widened grey eyes. 'I don't believe you. I think you provoked him out of perversity. Although, I don't understand why our concerns should take even a moment of your time.'

He tried to shrug and winced as the bonds kept him from moving. He ignored her last comment. 'I don't like to see anyone taken advantage of.'

Her face showed her puzzlement but her voice was cold. 'So because you don't like his gambling, you insulted him so that he challenged you.'

This time he stopped himself before shrugging. 'Your

brother isn't known as a dueller. In fact, I didn't think he would challenge me.'

'You think him a coward.'

Yes was on the tip of his tongue, but he didn't say it. 'Bertram said he was protecting his sister's name.' A stupid reason, but he didn't need to say it out loud. He had a feeling she agreed.

She sighed and stopped her momentum. Head cocked to one side, she curled her lips. 'We both know he has only made things worse. I am sure that as soon as word of your duel gets out—as we both know it will—tongues will wag about Amy more than before. Everyone will believe there is something for Bertram to avenge.'

Sympathy for her situation nagged at him. 'And I did not help matters by playing along with your headstrong sister.'

'Are you apologising?' she asked in wonder.

Was he? 'Perhaps. I will definitely apologise if you release me.'

She shook her head, and he thought she actually regretted what she was about to say. 'I can't. I know you keep saying you won't hurt Bertram, not on purpose, but you might by accident. He is silly and irresponsible, but he is my brother.'

'You believe that I don't intend to hurt him?' Did she trust him now? A cool wash of pleasure moved over him.

She looked embarrassed and her gaze slid away from his. 'I…I think you plan on not hurting him. But you might, so…'

'You won't let me go.'

She shrugged. 'I will let you go if you write a note to him begging off.'

He forgot and tried to shrug, even though his tightly fitted jacket and trussed-up arms made it painful. 'No. It would be the worst possible thing I could do for my reputation.' He stared at nothing for a moment, wondering how much of himself to reveal to her. 'There was a time when my reputation was all I had. If I call off, I will be branded a coward. Cowards are looked down upon. I won't do that.'

'I thought you would go back to that.' She moved to the door. 'Can I have you brought something to eat and drink?'

His admiration for her evaporated along with the desire that had held him in its grip, when he realised she intended to leave him like this. The beginning of anger took their places. 'How do you think I will feed myself?'

It was obvious from the look on her face that she hadn't thought that far ahead. Another time, he might have laughed at her consternation, but he was in no mood.

'I shall think of something.'

'You do that,' he said, putting all his frustration and discomfort into his voice. 'You do exactly that.'

She gave him one last look and closed the door. He listened to her footsteps until they faded. For long moments he lay gazing at the ceiling, which was now well lit by the morning sun filtering through the thin white muslin curtains.

Somehow he had to escape. He wasn't about to let a woman hold him captive, and he wasn't about to let his reputation be ruined because of a whining, worthless thing like Bertram Stockton. He might be a rake and willing to live with that appellation, but he wasn't a coward.

And to hell with what his body wanted.

He knew there was more to Stockton's challenge than his sister's reputation. It was the contempt he felt for the man and that Stockton recognised. He wouldn't be surprised if Bertram Stockton didn't despise himself and his behaviour but was too weak to change.

Goodness knew he understood. He had descended into Hell before finding the strength to stand up to his gambling addiction. Only he hadn't dragged his family into Hell with him. That is what really stuck in his throat about Emma Stockton's brother.

Emma stood at the door to the servant's room in her attic where Charles Hawthorne lay—her prisoner. A shiver of excitement coursed through her. She had dreaded having to kidnap him and now there was a part of her that was thrilled to have him at her mercy. This was a very dangerous thing she did.

The weight of the tray holding a pint of ale, a hunk of bread with butter and a slice of cheese brought her mind back to the problem. He had to be fed. She couldn't hold him for three days without giving him sustenance. But she couldn't release him to eat, either. He could easily overpower her.

She would have to feed him. Or a servant. Or not. She wasn't sure which.

She toed open the door and entered. He lay on the bed, a piece of her stocking in his mouth. He had tried to free himself again.

She turned abruptly away to set the tray down. She needed a moment to compose herself. When she had decided to have him tied with her old stockings, she had thought the silk would be easier on his skin. She had never considered that seeing him bound with a piece of her intimate clothing would make her stomach feel funny. And with a silk strand dangling from his well-shaped lips he was so tempting she had to do something to stop her thoughts.

She was not a loose woman. She was no Harriette Wilson to be aroused by a man who was not her husband. Nor did she want him for a husband. She just wanted him to leave her family alone.

Taking a deep breath, she turned around and faced him. 'I have brought you some food.'

He spit out the piece of her stocking. 'How am I to eat it?'

She took another deep breath and made an instant decision. 'I am going to feed you.'

An arrested look stilled his features. 'You are?'

Her palms started tingling, and she told herself not to be silly. He was harmless no matter how dangerous he looked this moment. And she didn't care for him. She didn't even like the man.

But the tingling spread up her arms.

'Yes, I am going to feed you.' She lifted her chin. 'As you

no doubt know, I have few servants so those I have are very busy. They don't have the time to care for you.'

He smiled in a way that told her he was more than willing to be cared for. 'But you do.'

Heat moved over her cheeks. Drat being a redhead. She cleared her throat. 'I am making time because I am the one responsible for you. Nothing more.'

His eyes darkened. 'Nothing more.'

She had known this wasn't a good idea, but she truly had no one else to do it. Turning her back to him, she pulled a small table to the bed along with a wooden chair. The tray just fit on the table. She sat down and took the napkin and unfolded it.

Angling to face him, she placed the linen square on his chest without looking at his face. Musk and bergamot mingled with the smell of fresh bread and ale. Her head seemed to swirl, and she had to put a hand on his shoulder to steady herself.

Heat flared where she touched him. She yanked her hand away.

'Are you feeling unwell?' His voice was raspy.

She glanced at him. His eyes were nearly as black as the lock of hair grazing his eyebrows. She nearly pushed the errant strand back but caught herself. She was behaving very strangely.

'I am fine. I didn't get much sleep last night.'

The excuse was weak and she knew it. But she didn't want to admit to him or herself what was really happening. Because it couldn't be happening. She wouldn't allow it.

'Neither did I.' He grimaced. 'Although I don't remember tossing and turning.'

She noticed there was the start of a twinkle in his eyes as though he teased her. She responded with a smile before catching herself. 'We are both not at our best.' She settled for that. 'I am sure you are hungry.'

'Release me.'

'Would you promise not to escape?'

He shook his head. 'No. I need to be at that duel.'

'As you say.' She picked up the pint of ale. 'Can you lift your head enough to drink this?'

'I can try. Otherwise, you will have to help me.' A wicked grin showed white teeth.

'I don't have to do anything, Mr Hawthorne. But I might be persuaded to help you.'

'Since my predicament is your fault, Miss Stockton.'

Instead of going back to the same argument, she held out the pint. He raised his head, and she put the edge of the mug to his mouth. When he closed his mouth to signal he had had enough, she took the mug away. He had foam on his upper lip.

She set the half-empty mug on the table, picked up the napkin and wiped his mouth. The cloth caught just a little on the roughness of his beard. This was the closest she had ever been to him, and her body was behaving worse than it had during their waltz. She resisted the urge to run her finger along his jaw and feel the black stubble that gave a ruthless cast to his features.

'You must want a shave,' she managed to say around the tightness in her throat.

'You can do it for me.'

His answer was so provocative she gasped. 'I would likely slit your throat.' Thankfully her voice hadn't been husky. It was bad enough she wanted to do more than feed him. It would be beyond bearable if he found out.

He chuckled deep in his throat. 'Would that make you feel bad?'

She realised he was teasing her. The knowledge brought warmth to her body. 'I should feel bad if I hurt anyone.'

'Of course.'

His voice was a soft drawl that slid over her senses like satin on bare skin. She shivered. 'Cheese?'

Not waiting for him to answer, she broke off a piece of the strong yellow cheese and brought it to his mouth. He opened his lips slowly, his gaze never leaving her face.

'Feed me.'

Her heart missed a beat. Did he mean what she thought? Was he talking about something besides food—as he had been earlier when talking about her stockings? Even now, an hour later, the heat she'd felt when she first saw him with her stocking in his mouth returned. The intensity made her want to fan herself. Instead, she stuffed the cheese between his teeth.

'I don't have long.'

She kept her tone businesslike even as her fingers shook from the touch of his lips. This was more intimate than any kiss on the palm. No gloves separated their flesh. She picked up a second piece of cheese.

'No, you don't.' His eyes held her prisoner. 'Kiss me.'

Her gaze locked with him for long minutes. It would be so easy to lean down and place her lips on his. So easy…

She moved until her mouth was inches from his. His breath was warm on her face.

She put her lips on his.

He didn't move. She pressed down, marveling at how he let her control the kiss. But she didn't know what to do.

'I…' she breathed against him.

'Open your mouth,' he said, his lips moving like butterfly wings against her flesh.

She did and his tongue flicked her skin. Fire burst where he touched her. Her stomach clenched in pleasant waves.

He wanted to deepen their contact, but she knew that if she allowed him to do so, she would be lost. She pulled back.

'I am not a loose woman,' she managed to say around the desire that tightened her throat.

'You are a desirable woman,' he said, his face flushed and his eyes hot. 'Let me show you the passion between a man and a woman. Kiss me again.'

Chapter Eleven

S he dropped the piece of cheese that she had unconsciously squeezed.

Inanely, she noted that while Gordon or David hadn't taken off his coat or boots, they had undone his cravat. They must have thought that would make him comfortable. Who would have thought the sight would make her feel so uncomfortable when coupled with his order to kiss him.

She dragged in a shuddering breath and opened her eyes. 'No.'

'Afraid?'

'Yes.' The whisper left her before she realised it.

'You should be.'

His words moved over her like molten lava, leaving a sense of scorched nerves and tingling heat. She was unable to look away. 'I should?'

'Oh, yes, Emma Stockton.' His mouth curved into a sensual line that tempted her.

'Why?' Another whisper that took her by surprise, but it was impossible for her to do anything else. His sensuality held her as surely as chains.

'Because I was serious last night when I asked you to be my mistress.' He took a deep breath that brought her attention back to the tantalising dark hairs on his chest. 'I want you.'

Her attention jerked up to his face. She couldn't believe what he'd just said. She didn't. His words broke the spell. He didn't want her. He could have any woman he wanted. And to taunt her with an offer of mistress not wife—it was beyond acceptable.

'You jest.' Frost dripped from each word, her pride shielding her from his sensuality.

'No. I don't ask a woman to be my mistress unless I mean it.'

'Just as you don't ask any woman to marry you.' Anger, caused by pain she hadn't expected, fuelled her rejection.

'You wouldn't marry me even if I did ask.' His eyes held hers. 'I don't have the money to bail your family out of debt. And I'm a rake. Remember?' Irony tinged his words.

She sat back away from him. 'True.' Every word he said was true, so why did his illicit offer, instead of an honourable one, hurt?

'So,' he said, his lips curving, 'will you accept my offer or at least kiss me again? Deeper. Let me show you what passion between a man and woman can be?'

His mouth beckoned to hers. Another kiss wouldn't mean she accepted his insulting offer. And she had decided to enjoy herself more. And the pleasure he had already ignited in her was just the beginning. Yet…

She resisted, sure that if she gave in, she would open herself to even more humiliation than she already felt. Somehow, she kept from leaning into him and resting her fingers on his exposed chest.

'I don't believe you.' With a conscious effort, she stood and stepped away. She folded her hands into the skirts of her dress so he wouldn't see them shake. 'I must go now.'

'Emma—'

She turned and left, unsure if what tortured her was his teasing her with the possibility of desire she knew he could ignite in her. Or was it the realisation that she had just managed to walk away from something she wanted more than she'd ever wanted anything else in her life?

So what if he only offered her a place as his mistress? It was more than any other man had ever offered her. And she wanted him.

She was a ninnyhammer.

Charles twisted his neck to watch her leave. What had he just done?

Asking her a second time to be his mistress had been the last thing on his mind, or so he told himself. But he wanted her—badly. Marriage was out of the question, even if he had the kind of money her family needed. He wasn't ready to marry and have to put another's needs before his own.

But the idea of having her for his lover felt better the more he thought about it.

Later that day, Emma looked at the tray with Charles Hawthorne's lunch and wondered if she dared send Betty with it. After this morning, she knew being alone with the man was the last thing she should do.

Even now, hours later, her lips tingled after their kiss.

She turned toward Betty, intending to tell her to feed their guest. But Gordon came in, his normally calm countenance flushed.

'Miss Emma, there is a *man* here.' He drew himself up straight and pulled down his vest. 'He says you know him. His name is Stoner.'

Emma blanched. 'Stoner?'

'Yes, miss. A big burly fellow. Looks like he was in the ring.'

Emma's knees felt like noodles, and she slid down to sit on one of the kitchen ladder-back chairs. 'Stoner.'

The old butler stood watching her, waiting for instructions. 'Yes, miss.'

'Where is he?'

'In the parlour.'

Emma pushed an errant strand of hair from her face. She should have anticipated this. Charles's servant would have recognised David and known immediately who sent the note. Now what?

'Tell him I will see him shortly.'

Gordon made a curt bow before wheeling around. Emma had to think of something. She couldn't let Charles go yet. She had two more days.

She didn't think they could drug Stoner, even if they had any of the sleeping draught left, which they didn't. Would he believe her if she told him Charles left last night after talking to her? He would have to.

Thank goodness Amy was at the lending library with one of her female friends and Bertram still slept. He had brought Amy home last night and immediately gone back out, not returning until the morning sun was well up. She never thought she would be grateful to Bertram for his ramshackle ways, but today she was.

The smell of mutton and potatoes came from the food Charles Hawthorne wasn't going to get just yet. She glanced at the tray and wished the only problem she had was whether she or Betty was going to feed the man.

She stood and smoothed down the front of her skirt before marching out of the kitchen. Gordon stood in the hallway. She nodded to him as he opened the parlour door for her.

Not waiting to be announced, she entered and said, 'Mr Stoner, what brings you here?'

Stoner stood by the window looking out at the crowded street. He held his hat in both hands in front of his waist. His coat was heavy and had seen better days. He looked like a man who was uncomfortable but doing what he knew was right. She almost pitied him, but his being here was the worst thing that could happen to her plan.

'I have come to get Mr Hawthorne, miss.'

She smiled and hoped he couldn't see the falseness of it. 'Mr Charles Hawthorne?'

'Yes, miss.'

He moved into the centre of the room. She didn't ask him to take a seat. She wanted him out of here as soon as possible. 'Why would he be here?'

She wanted to tell Stoner that Charles wasn't here, but her tongue seemed unable to say the lie. It was bad enough she had the man trussed up in one of the servant's beds. She didn't want to add untruthfulness to her list of sins.

Stoner turned the brim of his hat around and around while he studied her. 'Because you sent him a note to come and see you last night, miss, and he hasn't returned.' His voice was slow and steady, sure in what he said.

She had known he would recognise David, but still she blushed. Already she had crossed several lines a proper lady didn't. Visited a man in his home and then sent him a private note. The kidnapping was just her crowning achievement.

'Perhaps he has gone to visit a…friend.' She hoped to imply a woman. 'Surely that is not unusual.'

Stoner just looked at her, saying nothing.

She couldn't continue to meet his gaze. She was glad he didn't agree with what she'd said. Even though she thought it likely Charles had a mistress, regardless of what he had said to her just hours before, she didn't want it confirmed. But she also didn't want Stoner to press her further. She was not a good liar.

'Do you remember what time he left, miss?'

His noncommittal tone told her he didn't believe her. Her tension mounted. She waved a hand in airy dismissal that she didn't feel. 'No, I don't. We discussed…' Likely the man knew about the duel and it would be easier on her to be truthful when possible. 'We discussed my brother.'

'And then he left?' The big man's voice was gentle, but his eyes were sharp.

Emma took a deep breath. He was forcing her to lie or tell the truth that Charles was upstairs. She cudgeled her mind for a way to get around his point-blank question. 'He left this room.'

Very gently Stoner asked, 'Did he leave this house, miss?'

It was too much. Somehow he knew, but he had no proof. Was it really so unusual for Charles to spend the night away from his place of business? The idea gave her a funny sort of pleasure that she quickly pushed away. Right now, she had to get rid of this man.

She stiffened her shoulders. 'I am very busy, Mr Stoner. If there is nothing else, I must end this discussion.'

He stopped twirling his hat. 'When you tell me where you have Mr Hawthorne, miss. Otherwise, I will be forced to search the premises.'

His impertinence made her mouth drop. 'You shall do no such thing.'

He stepped toward her, and she found herself backing up before she realised what she did. She stopped. 'Do not think you can intimidate me, Mr Stoner. You are in my house. I can have you thrown out.'

'I don't think so, miss. I am very determined and Mr Hawthorne is my responsibility.'

'He's a grown man. He can take care of himself.'

Stoner's face became mulish. 'He can, but something is wrong.'

'Just because he didn't come home last night? He is likely at his mistress's house, and you are worried over nothing.'

There. She'd put the thought into words, and now Stoner would agree that Charles was likely at his lover's house. She would know beyond doubt that he had a woman. It was not her concern, no matter how tight her chest had suddenly become.

Stoner shook his head. 'Might 'ave been once, miss. Not for a long time now.'

'Really?' Even as the word left her mouth, she clamped her teeth together so hard they clicked. The tiny dart of relief that seemed lodged in her chest meant nothing. Just as Stoner's words meant nothing.

She took a deep breath, and a different tension replaced the one Stoner's words had just relieved. Hope. She knew how fragile hope was. It was with you one second and buried under disillusionment or loss the next. It was an emotion she had no reason to feel in relation to the man held prisoner in her house.

Besides, she had no reason to think Charles's lack of mistress was because of her. Perhaps he really was interested in her sister and had broken with his lover in order to be free to court Amy. And if that was the case, his offer earlier to make her his mistress was even more reprehensible. The man was incorrigible.

But this was not her business. Nor did it get Stoner out of her house. 'Then you will have to find some other place to start your search if he is not with a woman.'

'I will start it here, miss.'

She marvelled at his persistence. It would be much easier for him to leave and wait for Charles to come home. This servant acted as though his employer was the most important thing in the world to him.

'Why are you so persistent? Surely his being gone over night is not unusual. Besides, he is your employer, not part of your family.'

'I owe 'im me life, miss.'

Shock held her speechless. She didn't know anyone who owed his life to another person, other than a child to a parent. But this was different.

She choose her words carefully, not wanting to worry him more than he was but, at the same time, unable to allow him to find Charles. 'I am sorry you are worried about Mr Hawthorne, but it is time you left. I can't imagine he will come to harm.'

Stoner's mouth thinned. 'I will search your house, Miss Stockton. I know he is here.'

'What if he got mugged?' Desperation made her voice rise. She didn't want to make the man suffer by thinking Charles had been harmed, but she couldn't let him search the house. She had two days to go.

'I think 'e is 'ere. He didn't come 'ome. If 'e isn't 'ere, then I will consider that some 'arm 'appened to 'im.'

Emma moved to block the door. Her fingers twisted in the

folds of her skirt as she warily watched the big man. She didn't think he would hurt her, but he was very loyal to Charles.

'Please move, miss. I don't want to 'ave to lift you.'

For the first time, she saw uncertainty in his eyes. He didn't want to use force with her. It made her like him. 'I am not moving, Stoner.'

His hands balled into fists, and she feared she had pushed him too far. Then his fingers uncurled and he stepped toward her. She took a deep, shaky breath and stood her ground.

The door opened behind her and struck her back. She stumbled and barely managed to maintain her balance. Before she could turn around to see who was here, she heard Bertram's voice.

'What is going on here, Emma? Gordon tried to deny me entrance to my own parlour. I—'

'Bertram!' She groaned.

He stopped just inside the room, and his eyes widened into hazel saucers. 'Who is this man?'

Before she could reply, Stoner spoke. 'I'm Mister Charles 'awthorne's man.'

Bertram's shoulders stiffened. 'What are you doing here?'

Emma's shoulders slumped in defeat. Bertram would demand more answers than that one. He would do what Stoner had been unable to do and force the truth from her. Why had Bertram picked today of all days to wake early?

She wanted to scream, so said nothing.

Stoner looked from her to Bertram, and she would swear distaste darkened the man's eyes. But why? He didn't know Bertram.

'I'm 'ere to fetch Mr 'awthorne.'

'Well, this is the last place he would be.' Bertram was at his haughty and chilly best. 'Be on your way before I call my servants to throw you out.'

Stoner planted his feet wider, like a bull getting ready to charge. 'You can do as you think right, Mr Stockton, but I ain't leavin' until I've searched this 'ouse.'

Bertram yelled over his shoulder. 'Gordon, get David. I want this servant thrown out. Now.'

In seconds the aged butler and young, strapping footman were in the room. Apprehension ate at Emma as she watched her two servants size up Charles's one. She knew David wasn't strong enough and Gordon was too old. She stepped forward to prevent the violence she saw brewing.

'Stay put, Emma,' Bertram ordered. 'Charles Hawthorne's servant is leaving, and David will see to it.'

She looked at her brother and wondered at his obtuseness. Anyone could see David was outmatched.

'Yes, sir.' David stepped forward, his face white but determined.

'No.' Emma started to move between the men.

She was too late. In one quick, efficient movement, Stoner drew back his left arm and then punched it forward. His fist connected with David's jaw. A loud 'crack' filled the tiny room. David rocked back on his heels and tumbled to the ground. He sat, looking dazed.

'Oh, no.' Emma rushed forward determined this time to put herself between the two men. She faced Stoner. 'Enough.'

Bertram pushed her out of the way so her knee hit the wooden arm of a chair. She sank onto the cushion with a thump.

'Get up, man, and hit him back,' Bertram ordered, hands on hips, his face furious.

David lunged to his feet only to stagger. A cut bisected his chin. Several bloody spots marred his plain blue jacket. His hand went to his face and came away red. Anger turned his blue eyes black. He moved forward.

'Stop it! Stop it now!' Emma jumped up, ignoring the flash of pain in her knee. 'This isn't worth anyone getting hurt. Stop!'

David took a swing. Stoner ducked and came up with another facer. The footman slumped to the floor.

Emma rushed to him, but stopped when he glared at her out of the eye Stoner hadn't hit. 'Gordon, fetch Betty.' She rounded on Stoner. 'I said stop this.'

Stoner stepped back, cradling his right hand. 'He attacked me.' He looked at Bertram. 'On orders.'

Emma wrung her hands. The only way to stop this was to do what she didn't want to do. But there was no other choice.

'And I will order him again,' Bertram said, disgust twisting his face.

Emma stared at her brother. Why was he so vehement about this? She knew he didn't like Charles, but to continue to thrust David against a man of Stoner's size and capabilities was unpardonable.

She rounded on her brother. 'And I will order David to stay where he is. This has got to stop, Bertram.' She turned back to Stoner. 'He is upstairs. In the servant's quarters.'

'What!' Bertram's voice was loud enough to carry through the house. 'What are you saying?'

She blanched but stood her ground. 'Charles Hawthorne is here.'

Bertram's mouth fell open. He snapped it shut. His body quivered with anger. 'Charles Hawthorne is here? Why? What have you done?'

She could not remember ever seeing Bertram this incensed. She notched her chin up. 'I kidnapped him.'

'Kidnapped him!' Bertram advanced on her.

Stoner moved as though to intercept Bertram. Emma glanced at the man and saw determination and apprehension on his face. She shook her head.

Bertram turned on him. 'How dare you.'

Stoner stood still.

Emma wondered if things could get worse, but doubted it. 'Mr Hawthorne is tied to the bed, Stoner. I'm sure he will be glad to see you.'

Thankfully her voice was calm. She certainly didn't feel that way. Her heart pounded so hard, she wondered it didn't thump out of her chest.

Stoner looked from brother to sister.

'It will be all right,' she said softly, realising he was worried about her. 'Go to the second floor and turn right. He's in the first room.'

'That won't be necessary.' Charles Hawthorne's cold voice came from the doorway.

Emma whipped around and stared. 'What? How did you—'

'How did I get loose?' His smile was like a sharp sword. He extended his wrists. Blood dripped from the abrasions that circled his skin like manacles. 'I twisted until the stock—bindings loosened enough to pull my hands through.' He met her gaze. 'I have a duel to make.'

She marvelled that even now he had managed not to say her stockings. He was protecting her from Bertram's further censure, for she knew that if Bertram found out she had bound Charles with her intimate garments he would be incensed even beyond what he was now.

Stoner moved to his employer's side, watching David.

Bertram looked at them. 'I will be there early. This was not my idea, whatever you might think.'

Charles sneered. 'I never thought it was. It smacks of too much sense.'

Bertram tensed so he looked drawn up tight by a rope. 'Get out.'

'Gladly.' Charles turned his back on them as though they were nothing and went to the door, where he paused and turned back to them. 'If you need me, Miss Stockton, send your footman.'

Emma closed her eyes, not sure what she saw in his and not able to deal with anything else. In his offer to protect her, he had added insult to Bertram's injury.

She turned away as the door closed.

Bertram moved until he was only inches from her, his face puce, his fists clenched. 'What are you doing? Isn't it bad enough Amy's reputation is being jeopardised by that man? Now you have to go and keep him in our house.' His eyes narrowed. 'That is why you insisted I accompany Amy last night. You weren't sick. You planned this.'

'I had to do something.' Even to her ears, she sounded weak and defensive. 'I couldn't let you meet him in a duel.'

The colour left Bertram's narrow face. 'You couldn't! You couldn't! You are not the one to make that choice, do you hear me? I challenged him and I will meet him. And if you try to stop me, I will tie you to the same bed you bound him to. Do you understand, sister?'

She nodded. Nothing she could say would improve matters. Not only had her kidnapping failed to accomplish her goal, but it had created an even greater rift between her and her only brother.

And the argument had been in front of David, Gordon and the just-arrived Betty. They might be old family retainers, but what had just happened between her and Bertram was ugly. She had insulted Bertram's manhood, and he had told the entire household that her position was under him. Their dirty laundry was well and truly aired.

Bertram had also been unable to mask his pain at her lack of confidence in him. Hurting him was worse than anything else. When she'd concocted this scheme, she had not thought to get caught and hadn't even considered how Bertram would feel if it came to light.

What a mess.

It was on the tip of her tongue to beg his forgiveness, but she turned away instead. She had done what she thought best. She was not going to keep apologising.

She closed the parlour door behind Bertram as he stormed from the house and hoped no one would follow. She felt drained and beyond despair. Everything had gone wrong.

Moving to the window so the sun warmed her, she looked outside. She noted with surprise that it was still early afternoon. So much had happened, it felt as thought the entire day had passed.

As she turned away, movement caught her attention.

Charles and Stoner passed by her window on their way home. Charles looked disturbed, his gaze on her house. He said something to the older man. Stoner shook his head. The two of them continued on.

For a moment, Emma wondered what they talked about. Then exhaustion hit her. Too much had happened and it had all happened badly.

She pulled a chair to the patch of sunlight and sank down, her knee protesting. She would have a bruise where it had hit the chair arm when Bertram shoved her. It didn't matter.

Automatically, she tucked a loose strand of hair behind her ear. Something hot to drink would be nice, but she didn't have the energy to go to the bell pull. Nor did she want to be disturbed. The hot drink could wait.

She stared outside and wondered what else she could have done. Let the duel go on even knowing Bertram would likely be hurt? Perhaps she should have.

Perhaps she should have trusted Charles. But it was hard for her to trust a man. She had lost count of how many times her father and brother had told her and told Mama they would not gamble, or would not gamble deeply, and then had.

Perhaps it was time she stopped worrying about what they did. Nothing she tried made any difference.

It would be nice not to fret over other people when she could do nothing to stop them or to help them. For once, she would like to do exactly as she pleased.

Her mouth firmed. For once, she would like to enjoy herself.

Chapter Twelve

Charles shivered in the cold predawn air as he glared at Adam Glenfinning. 'What are you doing here?'

Glenfinning pulled the lapels of his great coat closer to his neck. 'Good morning to you, too.'

Charles clenched his hands at his sides to keep from landing the fellow a facer. The last person he wanted here was his sister's new husband. 'Good morning, Glenfinning. Now you can go.'

Glenfinning cocked his head to one side and studied Charles in the faint grey light of the rising sun. 'Why do you dislike me so much? To the best of my memory—and I will admit there are things I don't remember—I have never done anything to you.'

Charles started pacing, all the while keeping his gaze on his brother-in-law. 'You married my sister.'

Puzzlement rearranged Glenfinning's fine features. 'I would think you would like me then, for I believe I have made her as happy as she has made me. I know you love her.'

Charles stopped in midstride and pointed a finger at the other man. 'You are a rake, Glenfinning. Always were and always will be.'

'Ah.' Enlightenment moved over his face even as the

rising sun illuminated the stubble and lines of irritation on Charles's. 'You think I will be unfaithful to Juliet.' His jaw hardened. 'I won't.'

'Hah! Once a rake, always a rake.'

'Speak for yourself, Charles.' Glenfinning frowned. 'I am happier with Juliet than I have ever been in my life. I have no intention of doing anything to hurt her or jeopardise the love we have between us.'

Charles twisted away, not satisfied with the reassurance Glenfinning had just given him. In his experience, a man who dallied all his life would continue to do so. That is how he thought he would be. No woman had caught his attention and regard enough for him to forsake all others for her. He had assumed the same would be true for a man of Glenfinning's reputation. He and his brother-in-law were very similar.

He spun back around. 'Do you swear that?'

Glenfinning shook his head. 'You are obstinate. Juliet is as well, so I know the trait runs in your family, or I would feel obliged to challenge you myself—to protect my own honour.'

George Hawthorne strode up to them, looking from one to the other. 'Charles...'

Charles drew himself up. 'I had to be sure he treats Juliet well or he will be the next person I meet here.'

Exasperation sharpened George's voice. 'You have to stop measuring Adam by his past and your current behaviour.' George turned to Adam. 'Has the surgeon arrived yet?'

'No,' Adam answered, 'but I expect him shortly.'

Charles stomped his feet in their practical Wellingtons, looking at Glenfinning. 'So you are involved in this.' He gave George an accusing look. 'And here I thought you were the one who took care of all the details.'

George stared down his younger brother. 'Adam is part of the family now and wished to be involved. We both figured that if we shared the responsibilities things would go quicker and smoother. The last thing we wanted was for Juliet to learn of this.'

Charles took off his hat and tossed it to the ground in frustration. Everything they said made perfect sense. 'No telling what she would do.'

'Exactly.' Glenfinning and George answered simultaneously. Then both laughed.

Charles watched them with a jaundiced air. The two seemed in good accord, which only irritated Charles more. He didn't think he could change his behaviour just because he married, he still wasn't sure Glenfinning would. Even though the man seemed to love Juliet. Hell, he wasn't sure he could be faithful to one woman even if he loved her.

The image of Emma Stockton formed in his thoughts. She had the look of resigned determination she wore so often. The picture shifted to the defeat that had slumped her shoulders when Bertram had confronted her about the kidnapping. He had nearly told Stoner to wait while he took care of her brother.

That was two days ago and now he was waiting for the idiot, who was late. He should have known this would happen. 'Has my opponent arrived yet? I don't see him.'

'Neither do I.' George put a hand on Charles's shoulder. 'Maybe he won't.'

'He'd better,' Charles said. After all he went through because of this duel, Stockton had better show or he would call the man out.

'I see carriage lights,' Adam said.

Charles squinted down the road and saw a closed carriage in the early sunlight. 'That's probably the surgeon.'

Minutes later the coach stopped and an older gentleman stepped down. He carried a black bag. 'I am sorry I'm late.'

'That's fine,' Charles said. 'You are here ahead of my opponent.' He did nothing to mask his sarcasm.

The surgeon looked around. 'I will stay. The rains last night made the road difficult in places. He will likely be late.'

Charles grunted and started pacing. Patience was his weak point. He heard Adam near their carriage and the click as the box that held the matched duelling pistols opened. His brother-in-law was going to make sure they were in operating order. Charles knew they were. He had cleaned and oiled them last night.

He stopped at a tree and wondered how long he should wait. If Stockton didn't show, it would be no disgrace to Charles. Perhaps it would be better if the man failed to appear. But right this moment, all he wanted was for something to happen.

When he deloped the way he planned, he would be tacitly agreeing that Stockton's reason for challenging him was correct. While he agreed it was right to a certain extent, his dallying with Amy Stockton had never been to the point that it would truly damage her reputation. No matter what Bertram and Emma Stockton insisted.

The rumble of wheels caught his attention. He twisted around to see another coach. Stockton. Charles wasn't sure if he was disappointed or glad. Now they would meet, and he would delope. He had promised Emma Stockton he wouldn't shoot to hit even knowing what his action would imply.

He stepped away from the tree so his opponent would see him. He had a question to ask.

The carriage drew to a halt, and he watched Stockton exit. The man was dressed all in black, even to his shirt and cravat. Stockton was making sure he did not present a target.

Charles sneered as he neared the other man. 'Before we start this farce, Stockton, I want to know what you did with your sister's pearls.'

Bertram Stockton's cheeks glowed but his eyes shot darts. 'That is none of your business.' He turned to leave.

Charles shot out his hand and gripped the back of Stockton's coat and yanked. Stockton stumbled and managed to stay on his feet. 'You haven't answered my question.' Charles poised himself.

Stockton sniffed. 'I needed them, such as they were.'

Charles simmered. 'Where did you pawn them?'

Stockton looked him up and down. 'So that is the way the wind blows now. It won't do you any good. And if you importune Emma, I will challenge you again.'

Charles gritted his teeth. If they weren't about to duel, he'd land the idiot a facer. 'Where?'

Stockton's hazel eyes narrowed. He mentioned a shop. 'But they will be gone by now.'

'You are a weasel as well as a coward.' Charles could barely restrain himself. If only he hadn't promised this bounder's sister that he wouldn't shoot to hit. But he had, so he stood impotently and watched the man walk away. 'Coward,' he muttered.

'A cautious man often lives to see the next day,' Adam murmured.

Charles scowled at him. 'Or a coward.'

'Either one,' George said, moving between Charles and Stockton. 'How do you do, Bertram.'

Stockton looked George up and down. 'Quite well until I saw you.'

Charles marvelled at the man's idiocy. George was a crack shot.

'I would think it is Charles who worries you.' George's voice was soft, but there was iron beneath it. 'He always hits what he aims at.'

'Right is on my side.' Stockton turned his back to them.

'Then I wonder why you are dressed all in black,' Charles said, deciding the man could use a slap.

Stockton ignored him or didn't hear him.

George moved to Charles's side. 'Let it be. He has a right to dislike me—as we both know.'

'True, but that doesn't mean I like to see him treat you rudely.'

Adam joined them, looking from one to the other. 'We have a duel. I have met with Stockton's second and everything is ready.'

Charles took off his coat to allow better movement. He made a blazing target in his immaculate white linen shirt. He doubted it would matter. Stockton was known as a man who couldn't hit a wall ten feet away.

Confident he would be home and back in bed shortly,

having been up late with his clients, Charles took the pistol from the case Adam held.

'Good luck,' Adam said quietly. 'Not that you need it.'

There was a sincerity in the other man's voice that made Charles really look at him. It surprised him to see sincerity and concern in Adam's eyes. Adam cared what happened to him.

A pang of remorse hit Charles. He had never been nice to Juliet's new husband. He suddenly realised their altercation this morning had been more about what he felt about marriage and fidelity than what was happening between his sister and Glenfinning.

He had judged Glenfinning by his own measure and found him wanting. What did that say about him? He didn't want to think about it right now.

Charles stuck his right hand out to shake Adam's. 'Thank you for the support and for putting up with me.' For the first time since he'd known the man there was no sarcasm or dislike in Charles's tone.

Adam gave him a surprised look before taking his hand and shaking it. 'I'm glad we're finally over that hurdle.'

George moved to them. 'I see you've finally mended your fences. Good.' He spoke to Charles. 'Adam is going to count. Stockton thinks, and he's likely right, you would have an advantage if I do it.'

Charles laughed. 'Like the time you counted the number of trout you'd caught and were one off and I knew by the tone of your voice that you had exaggerated your catch.'

'Something like that,' George said ruefully.

'You never did that,' Adam said.

George smiled. 'I don't remember, but Charles can't be wrong.'

'But right now,' Charles said calmly, 'we must get on with this show. Stockton is champing at the bit.'

His opponent was pacing and slapping his hands against his thighs as though he was cold. Stockton's second held the pistol box.

Adam moved to a position in the center of the field. Charles followed and put his back to Stockton, who had also taken his position.

'On my count of twenty, turn and fire.' Adam's voice was low and solemn.

Charles didn't bother to nod.

'One…'

Charles started pacing. He would aim for the ground at Stockton's feet. That would ensure the bullet didn't go astray and possibly hit someone else.

'Twenty!'

Charles turned, raised his arm and pulled the trigger. Two bangs drowned out the usual sounds of morning. A puff of dirt showed where the ball from Charles's pistol lodged in the ground.

Nearly simultaneously, a searing pain shot through Charles's right shoulder. He staggered back, dropping his right arm and just barely managing to hold onto the pistol. His eyes widened in disbelief.

'I've been hit.'

George was at his side. 'Let go of the pistol.'

Charles looked at his brother and started laughing. 'He hit me. The man considered to be the worst shot in London hit me. I wouldn't believe it if I didn't have this damnable pain in my shoulder.'

The surgeon arrived. 'Let's get your shirt off.'

Stockton stomped up, shoulders back, a smirk on his face. 'That will teach you to dally with a young girl.'

'You were lucky or I was unlucky,' Charles said. 'Nothing else.'

'I was right.' Stockton pivoted on the heel of his Hessian and strode to his carriage.

Charles marvelled that the man could be such a pompous ass. It was even more amazing that he could be the brother of Emma and Amy Stockton. Amy might be a flighty chit, but she wasn't pompous.

And Emma…he wasn't sure what Emma was really like. She was an enigma he suddenly realised he wanted to unravel.

'Ouch!' he said when the surgeon probed his shoulder.

'Help us here, Charles.' George tugged at his shirt. 'You might think this is nothing, but you are bleeding a lot.'

Charles gritted his teeth as his brother pulled the sleeve down his arm, making the material tear away from the wound. The hole was high enough up that it was difficult for him to see but he knew it wasn't fatal.

'It could have been worse,' Charles said, shock finally entering his voice. 'The shot was entirely luck, not something Stockton planned. He could have hit me in the head.'

'That's a novel way to look at it.' Adam joined them. 'Remind me to have you as my second the next time I fight a duel, Charles.'

It was on the tip of Charles's tongue to ask the man why he thought he would be his second then remembered his earlier realisation that he judged Adam harshly because he judged himself that way. Instead he said, 'I'll be glad to help out any time.'

Adam smiled. 'Thank you, old man. Now we must get you home and in bed.'

'I think not. I am not about to be coddled because of this scratch.' Stubbornness thinned his lips.

The doctor snorted as he probed the wound deeper and Charles winced. 'The ball is pretty deep. Do you want me to dig it out here or wait till we get you home?'

Charles swallowed a groan. 'This is damned inconvenient. At home.'

'Duels often are.' The doctor put a pad of linen on the wound. 'Lift your arm so I can secure this.'

Charles did as ordered and winced. 'That hurts.'

'Never said it wouldn't.'

'Are all surgeons like you? Taciturn?'

The older man smiled for the first time. 'Don't know. I suspect the ones who attend duels are. It's a stupid way to lose your life.'

The man was right. He had been in one other duel and had winged his opponent. Now he knew how it felt.

'I think it's time we left,' George said in the silence.

Charles followed his brother and Adam to the carriage. He shook off George's helping hand and climbed in, swallowing a groan of pain. The ride home was not going to be comfortable.

Emma paced the parlour, her robe flaring as she made each pivot, waiting for Bertram to get home. She had lain awake all last night and had heard him leave several hours ago. It was still unfashionably early.

She prayed her brother wasn't hurt. All she had thought about was Bertram being injured. Belatedly, she thought about the possibility that Bertram might hurt Charles. Then she laughed, a tight, high sound that did nothing to lessen her tension. Bertram was a deplorable shot. There was no possibility of him hitting Charles Hawthorne.

She heard the rumble of carriage wheels and rushed to the front door in time to see her brother jump down from a high-perch phaeton driven by one of his gambling cronies. Bertram laughed at something the other man said before coming toward the house.

Relief flooded her. Bertram wasn't hurt. She had fully expected him to be hurt in spite of what Charles Hawthorne had promised.

Even as relief eased the tightness in her chest, she felt bad for doubting Charles. Just because his brother had treated her poorly and just because Charles himself was a rakehell, didn't mean he didn't honour his word. He had just proven it by not shooting Bertram. Shame at misjudging him brought the blood to her cheeks.

'I shall see you this evening,' Bertram said over his shoulder to the man driving.

His voice yanked Emma from her uncomfortable thoughts and she stepped back into the shadows of the foyer, not wanting to be seen. The last thing she needed was for

Bertram's friend to notice her and say something to someone else. It was not done for a lady to know about what had just happened.

Bertram whistled as he entered, stopping when he saw her. Belligerence flowed from him. 'What are you doing?'

'Waiting for you.' She was glad he wasn't wounded, and since he wasn't, she allowed his attitude toward her to make her waspish. 'I was worried. It seems my fears were groundless.'

'Because you thought Charles Hawthorne was a better shot than me.' His tone attacked her.

Emma's hackles rose. 'Isn't he?'

'Not this morning.' Smug satisfaction filled his voice. He smirked.

Emma turned away, not wanting to fight. Exhaustion from no sleep and the constant worry that had accompanied her knowing about the duel had eaten her energy. She had not waited for Bertram with the intent to argue with him.

'I am glad you are unhurt,' she said softly, wanting to leave it at that.

'And that I am the better man.'

She looked back at him. At one time she would have agreed with him, but she wasn't sure now. Too many things had happened since Bertram had come to London and none of them had been expected.

Her brother had an expectant look on his face, like someone with a secret he could barely keep. A secret that threatened to burst from him. She began to wonder what had happened.

'What do you mean you are the better man?' Apprehension tightened her throat.

'I hit Charles Hawthorne in the shoulder.'

'What?'

'Didn't expect that, did you?'

Fear for Charles followed closely on her surprise. 'Is it a bad wound?' she finally asked when she felt she had her voice under control and it would show none of her apprehension for the other man.

He shrugged. 'Don't know. The surgeon was there and Charles Hawthorne was standing when I left.'

'You left without knowing?'

'It didn't matter to me.'

She looked at him, wondering when he had become so callous. 'I see.'

He stiffened as though he heard the disapproval in her voice. She was sorely disappointed in him.

'Would you rather he had hit me?' He pouted, his bottom lip as far out as a small boy might do, yet he was a man.

She wondered when he had become so belligerent. 'No. I am glad you are unharmed.'

Better to leave it at that. But what about Charles? How badly hurt was he?

'You don't act like it.' His mouth curled petulantly, much like Amy's when she was feeling put upon.

In a moment of spontaneous affection, she went to him and kissed him on the cheek. 'I am very, very glad you are unhurt, Bertram. I was so worried for you that I didn't sleep last night and got up right after you left. I paced the parlour until you got home.'

Mollified, he smiled. 'That is more like what a sister should feel.'

'I do love you, Bertram.' Silently she added *I just don't always like you and what you do*. The same could be said of her feelings for Amy and Papa and Charles Hawthor— She caught herself. 'I need to get some sleep.'

He muttered something, but she moved quickly to the stairs. She needed a lot of rest. Exhaustion was the only reason she could think of for what she had just thought about Charles Hawthorne.

But first she had to know. 'Gordon,' she called the butler as she made her way to the kitchen. He appeared in seconds. 'Please send David to me.'

The old servant eyed her with misgiving, but said nothing. He nodded and left.

Emma entered the kitchen, knowing Bertram would never come here. She smiled at the cook. 'A pot of hot chocolate, please.'

The rotund woman who ran the kitchen like her personal fief smiled. 'Yes, miss.'

Emma sank onto a chair pulled up to the plank table. Hot chocolate and a message.

David arrived minutes later.

'David.' She looked at him, noting his eye was still bruised from Stoner's punch and the cut on his chin still red. 'I want you to go to Charles Hawthorne's home.' Heat moved up her neck and settled in her cheeks. Like so many other things recently, this was completely unlike her. 'Find out if he is… Find out how badly he is hurt.' The words were out past the constriction in her throat.

She needed to sleep. Exhaustion was the only explanation she could come up with for her concern.

'Yes, miss.'

'Now, please.'

His eyebrows rose though he managed to keep the rest of his countenance impassive. He would make a good butler some day, she thought absently.

'Yes, miss.'

She drank down her hot chocolate and waited for his return. Then she would go to bed.

Simultaneously, in another part of London, George Hawthorne said to his brother, 'Drink this.' He handed Charles a bottle of Scotch.

Charles moved uncomfortably on the coverlet of his bed. Stoner stood at the foot watching impassively, but Charles saw the twitch in his servant's jaw. Adam Glenfinning was gone, so that hopefully Juliet would be none the wiser.

The surgeon stood patiently by, waiting for George to get the spirits down Charles. 'When you're ready, I'll dig out that ball.'

Charles scowled from one to the other. 'George, why don't

you go home. I'm sure Rose is missing you.' He hated for people to see him this weak.

The surgeon dug in his bag and pulled out a pair of forceps. 'Bring that brace of candles closer,' he said to Stoner, who did as ordered.

The alcohol started to take effect on Charles. 'That makes me feel better.' Sarcasm dripped from each word.

'Angle the light to the right.' The surgeon positioned himself so he was on the side of the bed closest to Charles's wound.

'Right, Guv'.' Stoner shifted, keeping the candles so the wax wouldn't drip on Charles's bare skin.

Banging started downstairs. Charles thought the noise came from the back door, but that was the least of his concerns. Adam started barking from his spot at the foot of the bed. The dog looked at the door to the chamber and back up at Charles, torn between whether to defend the home or stay and protect and support his master. His barks became whines of unease.

'Pardon,' Alphonse, the French chef, said as he eased quietly into the room.

Charles groaned. 'What is this? The King's privy? Can't I have some privacy while I'm being tortured?'

George put a soothing hand on Charles's unhurt shoulder. 'Charles.'

'Yes, I know.' Charles sighed heavily. 'What is it, Alphonse? I don't care what you prepare for dinner tonight.'

The surgeon tsked. 'I can see you aren't going to be one of my better patients. Be still.' He doused the wound with the leftover Scotch.

'Damnation!' Charles gritted his teeth and kept from jumping out of the bed through sheer willpower.

'Monsieur,' Alphonse edged to the bed, careful not to get in anyone's way. 'There is a young man here. He says his name is David and he wants to know how you are.' He rolled his eyes. 'He is most persistent and will not leave until he learns.'

'What?' The effort to keep from shouting in pain made Charles's voice flat. 'I don't think I heard right.'

George glanced from Charles's white face to the chef and back. Realisation dawned in George's eyes. 'It seems your opponent is more concerned about your condition than he let on.'

Charles grunted as the surgeon dug in his skin for the ball. 'Likely wants to know if he needs to flee to the Continent.' He gasped and drew in a long breath which he let out in an equally long exhalation. 'Tell him Stockton's trip can be postponed. I am going to live.'

'Yes, Monsieur.' Alphonse slipped from the room as quietly as he had come.

Adam settled back to faithfully watch everything being done to his idol. His tongue lolled and he finally lay down, careful to keep Charles in sight.

The surgeon exclaimed in triumph, 'Have it.'

'Thank goodness,' Charles said, exhaustion hitting him like a runaway carriage. He settled into rest when the man poured more Scotch on the wound. Charles jerked and looked at the surgeon. 'Was that necessary?'

'I don't want to take chances, Mr Hawthorne. You just told the servant of the man who shot you that you weren't going to die. You won't from the actual shot, but you could if gangrene sets in. A precaution.'

George smiled. 'It seems that with care, Charles, you will live to duel again.'

'Don't intend to do that for a while,' Charles grumbled. 'Now can I rest?'

A ripple of relieved laughter moved through the room. Adam jumped onto the bed.

Charles eyed his canine admirer. 'You have your own bed.'

Adam's brown eyes stared into Charles's blue ones. The dog's tongue lolled out into a canine grin. He circled twice and plopped down at the foot of the mattress, his head facing Charles.

'I believe he intends to keep you company,' George said, humour in his voice.

Charles grunted and let his eyes close. He needed rest. Exhaustion was the reason he had hoped the Stockton servant had been sent by Emma. For a moment, he had thought she was concerned about him. Stupid. All she cared about was her precious brother.

He dropped into slumber.

Chapter Thirteen

The news reached Emma the next day. That afternoon she sat in her parlour with a smile frozen on her face as her unwelcome guest, Mrs Kennilworth, regaled her with Bertram's exploits the night after the duel.

'I must tell you, Miss Stockton, that I seriously considered letting Stephen approach your father for Miss Amy's hand.' She shook her head and tsked. 'I can no longer, in my capacity as a mother, allow that.'

Emma nodded and wondered if Mr Kennilworth, over on a corner sofa with Amy, was any more entertaining than his mother. From the look on her sister's face, she doubted it.

She smiled politely. 'I am sure Mr Kennilworth understands your reservations.'

'He most assuredly does.' The Dowager Kennilworth made a moue of distaste. 'He is the one who told me. But I am sure you already know.'

The look on the Dowager's face told Emma she didn't want to know whatever Mrs Kennilworth hinted at. Undoubtedly, it was about Bertram. Or the duel. Both were subjects she dreaded. And Mrs Kennilworth had already been the bearer of more bad news than Emma wanted in a lifetime.

Thank goodness David had brought word immediately that

Charles Hawthorne was doing well, or she would be worried that Mrs Kennilworth's news would include Charles. Much as the man irritated her, she found herself thinking and worrying about him. But there was nothing she could do. What a conundrum.

She had not seen Mr Hawthorne since the duel. It was as though he had disappeared from London. But that had nothing to do with her current discussion. She hoped.

Emma's smile slipped only a little. 'I am sure there is no need for you to tell me anything.'

Mrs Kennilworth's eyes narrowed. 'Then you will understand when an offer is not forthcoming. After all—' she flicked open her fan and waved it vigorously in front of her face, as though just the discussion heated her '—when a man already in debt to the point of ruin loses a small fortune, one cannot expect a prospective husband to bail the family out.'

Emma's smile disappeared completely. Her nightmare was happening. She managed to say, 'I agree totally, Mrs Kennilworth. One can only hope to get out of the potential embarrassment as quickly as possible.' She looked away from the disagreeable woman. 'Luckily, you did not approach my father.'

That would remind the Dowager that this conversation should not be taking place. She might be chaperoning Amy, but their father was the one who would determine who Amy wed.

The Dowager ignored Emma's last comment. 'I knew you had uncommon good sense, Miss Stockton. It is truly a shame your brother doesn't share that with you.'

Emma abruptly stood. She had endured more than enough. 'I am getting the headache, Mrs Kennilworth.' She rubbed her temples for emphasis. 'I am sure you understand.'

The other woman nodded sympathetically. 'Yes, yes. I am so sorry to be the one to tell you.' The look of smug satisfaction on her face belied her words.

Emma led the way to the door. 'Amy, Mr Kennilworth and his mother must be leaving.'

Mr Kennilworth looked mutinous, but he was used to following his mother's lead. He rose and followed the Dowager out the door. Amy stayed seated, a look of utmost relief on her delicate features.

Emma closed the door with precise care. What she wanted to do was slam the heavy oak so that it jumped on its hinges with a satisfying bang.

She returned to her seat and stared at nothing. She needed privacy to deal with the anger simmering inside her. Bertram went from one disaster to another with no regard for anyone else.

Mama's pearls flashed through her mind. They would not be enough for this. They had gone into the ravenous maw of Bertram's gambling just as everything else had, and none of it was enough.

'Em.' Amy rose and sat beside her sister. 'What is the matter? You look as though you just lost—as though Mama had just died.'

Emma gave up trying to smile and allowed her mouth to turn down. There was no sense in keeping the truth from Amy. The news would be all over the *ton* by this evening when they went to Almack's. If they went.

She took Amy's hand and squeezed. 'Bertram has once again lost a great sum of money. Mrs Kennilworth took much delight in telling me.'

'Well, that should stop Mr Kennilworth's courting.' Amy tossed her blond curls. 'Don't look so shocked, Em. One must find the bright side of everything.'

Emma closed her mouth. 'You do have a point, dear.' What bright side could she find? Then she knew. 'I believe it is time we went to the country for a while. Preferably before we are evicted for failure to pay rent.'

Amy's insouciance went up in smoke as she jumped to her feet. 'The country! I am not even halfway through my first Season.'

Emma craned her neck to look at her sister. 'I know, but with this extra financial burden, we will not be able to sustain even a semblance of Town life.'

'You say that because you prefer the country. I don't!' Amy flounced to the door and turned back. 'Well, I won't go. You can't make me.' She stormed from the room, slamming the door behind her.

Emma remained seated, her small burst of gratification at going to the country buried under Amy's justified fury. They had come here for Amy. She deserved to enjoy her one and only Season before entering matrimony with a man she likely would not love and would be fortunate to like.

And there was Charles Hawthorne. Against her will, a memory of him trussed up in her attic bed filled her senses. He made her feel as though life was electrifying. Now she would never see him again.

They would go to the country, and if Amy was lucky, she would marry some small land-owning squire. She herself would go into service with an equally unpretentious family since no one of consequence would hire her after this latest debacle of Bertram's. She would spend the rest of her life raising other women's children.

She told herself it could be worse. Already it seemed there was emptiness where her heart should be, as though she had lost something she couldn't even name. She buried her face in her hands.

In another part of London, Charles lounged with his feet propped on his desk. A half-empty decanter of Scotch sat on a table beside him and a full glass in his hand. Every time he moved, he winced.

'Damn Bertram Stockton. The man is a lousy shot, yet he winged me.' He drained the glass, grimacing as the strong spirit burned its way down his throat and hit his stomach with a small explosion.

Adam looked up and cocked one ear. He made a muffled whine of enquiry.

'Yes,' Charles looked at his canine companion, 'the man is a menace.'

A knock at the office door preceded Adam's namesake; Sir Adam Glenfinning entered without waiting to be asked. 'Drowning your pain, I see.'

Glenfinning sat in the vacant leather chair that just a week ago had held Emma Stockton. Charles frowned at him. Glenfinning smiled back as though he visited his disapproving brother-in-law every day.

'What brings you here uninvited?' Charles felt as surly as he sounded. He had come a long way to accepting Glenfinning as his brother-in-law but not completely, and the throbbing in his shoulder made his temper short.

'You.'

'Then go away. I don't need you. Didn't need you at the duel, but you insisted on being there. Don't need you now. The surgeon got the ball out, and it's just a matter of time before I heal.'

Adam's fine mouth curled in a sardonic grin very similar to the one Charles was known for. 'That is why you have drunk nearly an entire decanter of aged Scotch.'

'What I do is my business.'

From his rug by the fire, Adam, the mutt, stood and growled low in his throat. Adam, the man, glanced at him and laughed.

'Call your guard dog off. He doesn't scare me.'

A sly grin spread over Charles's face. 'Adam, behave yourself.'

The dog sat down on his haunches, but kept his attention trained on his namesake.

A look of surprise, quickly followed by appreciation moved over Sir Adam's countenance. 'Nicely done, Charles. Did you christen him before or after your sister and I married?'

'After,' Charles said, some of his surliness leaving as he found humour in the situation.

'Since you have such a finely tuned sense of ironic humour,' Glenfinning drawled, referring to the fact that he was a bastard and the dog a mutt, 'you should be laughing hysterically at what has become of Bertram Stockton since he hit you in the duel. It seems only fitting since the man gained entry to some of the most notorious gaming hells in London because of his successful encounter with you.'

Disgust warred with anger in Charles. Anger won, but he did not intend to show Glenfinning how deeply the new knowledge affected him. He flicked his fingers as though tossing away something of no importance. 'Should I? The man has no honour and his family suffers for it.'

Sir Adam turned serious. 'As yours did not so many years ago?'

Charles flushed and carefully set his empty glass down. How many lessons was this man going to teach him? 'That was different.'

Adam raised one black brow.

'Yes, it was,' Charles answered his unwelcomed guest's implied contradiction. 'My family didn't like my gambling to excess, but it didn't pauper anyone. My sister didn't have to marry for money to bail us out of the River Tick.'

'True.' Glenfinning steepled his fingers and watched Charles over them. 'You have been holed up like a wounded animal for the past four days. Stoner says you haven't even been to the Bank of England to check on your business account.'

Charles set his empty glass down with a clunk. 'No, I haven't. Do you think I want people to see me like this, to know Bertram Stockton did this? Not bloody much.'

Glenfinning continued to study him. 'Have you heard the latest *on dit* about the man?'

Unease started in Charles's stomach, making the warm tingle of the Scotch feel like acid. 'Don't tell me he traded on his new notoriety to gain access to more gambling.'

Glenfinning laid his palms flat on his knees. 'Then I won't tell you.'

Charles screwed his eyes shut and clamped his lips together. There was no reason to spew his anger at Glenfinning. But it was hard not to let go with the condemnation and fury he felt about Stockton's selfishness.

And why did the man's selfishness matter? Charles wasn't

impacted by Stockton's actions. No one could force him to wed Amy Stockton, and he didn't have the blunt for them to want him anyway.

Emma Stockton's worried face as she asked him not to meet her brother rose in his mind, followed quickly by the arrested look in her hazel eyes after she had pressed her lips to his. She had been attracted to him. He knew she had come close to kissing him again, deeper. His body responded to the idea and he looked away from Glenfinning not wanting the man to see anything in his eyes.

More calmly than he felt, Charles finally said, 'The man has no regard for anyone but himself. It's a wonder the women in his family aren't more self-serving.'

A strange smile crooked Glenfinning's mouth. 'You admire Amy Stockton?'

Seeing another face with red hair and freckles that refused to be ignored, Charles missed the irony in his brother-in-law's voice. 'I feel sorry for her. It is Emma Stockton I admire. She continues to do everything in her power—and she has too little power—to ameliorate the results of her sibling's actions.'

'Ah…' Glenfinning sat back in his chair. 'So that is the way the wind blows.'

Charles snapped back to awareness of his guest. 'What are you implying?' he asked ominously.

Glenfinning looked as innocent as a man of his experience could. 'Only that you seem mighty interested in your brother's former fiancée.'

Charles pushed to his feet and towered over the other man, thinking the position would give more emphasis to his words. 'Nonsense. But I do feel sorry for her plight. *I* wouldn't want to chaperone Amy Stockton or to feel responsible for a loose screw like Bertram Stockton. Nothing more.'

Glenfinning stood so their eyes were on an equal level. 'Of course. I mistook your concern for a more serious emotion.'

'You did mistake it.' Charles met Glenfinning's gaze and changed the subject. 'How badly is Stockton duped?'

'Oh.' Glenfinning's voice turned nonchalant. 'I don't know for certain.'

Charles's foot started to tap. 'I am sure you know very closely or you wouldn't have come here to tell me.'

Glenfinning laughed. 'Nearly three sheets to the wind and you keep your wits about you. I heard you have a head hard enough to withstand a hammer hit.'

'Compliments will get you nowhere,' Charles said sourly, although he was secretly pleased with his reputation.

'Two thousand pounds.' Glenfinning answered flatly as though the former banter hadn't occurred.

Charles started. 'That is a great deal of money. He has ruined them for sure this time.'

'That is what I thought.'

Charles turned thoughtful. 'They are likely planning to leave London shortly.'

'Rusticating.'

'That will put paid to any chances Amy Stockton has of finding a husband with enough blunt to pay her brother's debts.'

'That is what Juliet and I thought.'

Charles's eyes narrowed. 'You and Juliet have already discussed this?'

Glenfinning's nodded. 'She feels it is too bad this happened. If George had married Miss Stockton none of this would matter.' His smile turned sly. 'She felt sure you would agree. Perhaps even have a possible solution or be willing to help her in hers.'

Interest flared in Charles. 'Juliet has a plan to help the Misses Stockton? I didn't know she knew them that well.'

Glenfinning shrugged. 'She has observed them while you cavorted with Miss Amy. She is convinced you have hindered the chit's chances in the Marriage Mart and that we must make restitution by arranging for them to be invited to your godmother's house. Lady Johnstone has agreed to host a fortnight-long house party.'

Charles plopped back into his chair, his head whirling with

all the information. 'Juliet certainly worked quickly.' He didn't hide his sardonic amusement.

'Juliet is Juliet.' Glenfinning smiled and love lit his face.

Charles blinked at the change in his brother-in-law's countenance. The man really did love Juliet. Perhaps a rake could change his behaviour.

'So what do you want from me?' Charles finally asked.

'To stay away from the house party.'

'If that is so, then why tell me?'

'Because Juliet thought that when you found out the Stockton ladies were gone, you would find out where and pursue them.' Glenfinning's smile turned apologetic. 'She thinks it better if you stay away.'

'Ahhh.' Charles leaned back in his chair and propped his feet back on the desk. 'I see. Juliet always did think she knew what was best.'

'She still does.' Glenfinning laughed.

'When does this house party start?' Charles asked nonchalantly.

Glenfinning's eyes narrowed. 'This weekend.'

'Well, I don't believe my doctor will allow me to travel by then anyway, so the Misses Stockton are safe from my depredations.'

'Sarcasm accomplishes nothing,' Glenfinning murmured. 'Besides, we both know you will do as you damn well please and the devil take the hindmost.'

Charles grinned. 'True.'

Glenfinning left shortly after. Charles remained sprawled in his chair. His immediate response to Juliet's desire to keep him from the house party was to be the first to arrive. Further consideration made him wonder why Juliet was going to all this elaborate planning. He'd swear she barely knew Emma Stockton and thought Amy Stockton a flighty young woman with no conversation.

But Juliet had a soft heart, and there was no denying that George's not marrying Emma caused great hardship for the

Stockton family. Then again, Juliet also knew that if she told him not to do something, he would likely do it before anything else. He was a lot like Amy Stockton that way.

'Stoner,' he yelled, making Adam the mutt jump up from his bed by the fire.

'Yes, Guv',' Stoner said minutes later, poking his head in the door.

'We are going to the country.'

Stoner rolled his eyes. 'I thought the sawbones told you no travelling.'

'That was four days ago.' Charles softly whistled a jaunty tune, the anticipation of fun lightening his previous foul mood.

Stoner shook his head. 'Shooting or mixed company?'

'Both.' Charles smiled.

He didn't want to imagine what Juliet would do or say. Neither would be fun, but meeting with Emma Stockton, and the look on her face when she realised he would be staying in the same house with her for a fortnight, would more than make up for the scolding his sister would level on him.

Emma looked at the embossed invitation to Lady Johnstone's country house. They barely knew the woman so why would she invite them, and with the Season in full swing?

Still, it was a golden opportunity. There would be other members of the *ton* there so Amy might still meet a suitable gentleman. If they went home to Hopewell, their family estate, Amy would meet no one. There wasn't much choice.

Emma sat down at the desk in her bedchamber and replied in the affirmative. None too soon, either, as Betty was packing up Emma's clothes preparatory to them returning home. Amy's things had been done earlier.

Rising, Emma motioned to Betty. 'Please give this to David and tell him to deliver it immediately.'

Betty took the note and quirked one greying brow.

'It is not for Charles Hawthorne. We are going to a house party,' Emma said. 'Lady Johnstone has been kind enough to invite us.' She smiled. 'You will come as our lady's maid to lend us countenance.'

Betty sniffed. 'As though you need countenance, miss. It is other members of this family as needs that.'

Emma's smile slipped. 'We are not going to discuss that, Betty. Just see that this is delivered.'

Betty's eyes slid away from Emma's glare, but the house-keeper and lady's maid said nothing more. Emma watched her leave the room and wondered what they would do until it was time to leave. They were not due to arrive until two days from now. More than that, how would they get there? There was no money to hire a travelling carriage and going by mail carriage would leave them at the nearest town, not their hostess's estate.

A commotion downstairs caught her attention. What was going on? If it was Bertram... She had not seen him since she confronted him with his latest and most serious losses.

Hair caught in a twist with strands straggling down her neck and back and a grey work dress streaked with dust, Emma stalked from her room. Her patience with Bertram was exhausted. She would make short shrift of her brother.

She reached the foyer, hands clenched in the folds of her skirt, mouth a thin line. Lady Juliet Glenfinning stood in the entry, giving her card to Gordon. Emma stopped abruptly, nearly slipping off the last stair step.

'Lady Glenfinning!'

Juliet looked up at Emma. 'Are we on such formal terms now, Emma? I had hoped that what happened between you and George wouldn't impact on the rest of us.'

Emma was hard-pressed to keep the acerbity she felt from her voice. 'Perhaps if I saw you more than across a room at some function it might have. But I have not seen you often.'

Juliet flushed. 'You are right. I can only plead that my life has been very busy this past year, and I have spent little time in Town.'

Emma knew George Hawthorne's sister spoke the truth.

Juliet Glenfinning was also Charles's sister. What a tangled mess. 'What brings you here?'

Emma took the last step and moved until she was close enough to see the starburst of navy in the other woman's eyes—eyes very like Charles's. Juliet looked unsure, a plight Emma doubted the other woman found herself in much.

'This is very forward of me, to be sure.' Juliet stopped and seemed to carefully consider her words. 'I heard,' she waved one elegantly gloved hand, 'that you and your sister are invited to Lady Johnstone's country estate for a house party.'

Emma stepped back as though she had been slapped. 'Who told you that? I only just now received the invitation.'

Juliet's flush deepened. 'Ah…well, Lady Johnstone.' She sighed. 'Can we go somewhere more private?'

With a start, Emma realised Gordon stood by the still open door. She could refuse to spend time with Juliet, but she had always liked the other woman. Rumour said Juliet's first husband had been too old to care what his young bride did. Rumour also said her current husband was totally reformed and as devoted a spouse as any woman could wish for.

'Yes. Come into the parlour.'

'Thank you,' Juliet said, following Emma.

'Please be seated.' Emma indicated a threadbare chair.

Juliet sat down gingerly. 'Lady Johnstone is godmother to George, Charles and myself.' She seemed more embarrassed than before they entered the room. 'She told me she intended to invite you because she could sympathise with your situation. Her first husband was a heavy gambler, and she only achieved her current stability when she married her second husband. She always says she was blessed her first husband expired before he gambled away the roof over their heads.'

Mortification made Emma blanch. 'Does everyone know?'

Juliet didn't pretend to misunderstand. 'Perhaps not everyone, but many do. Your brother has made no secret of the duel and wounding Charles. He used his success to open previously closed doors. Not since Charles James Fox gambled away a fortune and Brummell fled to the Continent because of his debts has anyone played so deeply that their entire life was ruined.'

'Thank you for putting my brother's actions into perspective,' Emma said dryly. 'I suppose I should be flattered that Bertram is in such exalted company, but I am not.'

'I didn't think you would be.' Juliet laid her palms up as though laying her cards on the table in full view. 'I am making a mess of this. I have come to offer you and Amy a ride in my carriage to the house party.' She smiled. 'I am invited, too.'

Emma tapped one finger on the arm of her chair. This wasn't making sense. These people had no reason to concern themselves with her and her sister unless it was a sense of debt owed over that dratted broken engagement.

'It is best if I speak openly, I think.' Emma waited for Gordon to deposit the tea tray and leave. 'My broken engagement to your brother was over two years ago. Since then, we have seen nothing of your family except your younger brother. Why this sudden interest on your part?'

She poured tea, adding sugar and cream as indicated by her guest, and waited. Juliet took her drink and sipped it. Emma decided she had got to the heart of the matter and Juliet was uncomfortable.

Finally, still holding her cup and saucer, Juliet said, 'It is numerous incidents. Everyone in the family was uncomfortable over what happened between you and George. But we all knew it was best for him. More importantly to me, is the way Charles has been behaving.' Her eyes flashed. 'He is a scapegrace where women are concerned. I believe that had he not encouraged Amy, she would have found another party to interest her. As it is, he behaved shamefully—as I have told him many times—and now with your brother's gambling debts, I worry that anyone else she might become interested in will be scared away.'

Emma choked on a sip of hot tea. 'You are definitely being honest.' She carefully set her saucer down. 'I believe Mr Hawthorne thinks his attentions to Amy will draw the interest of other men to her. I definitely know Amy believes that.'

Juliet snorted. 'That is well and good as far as it goes. Other gentlemen may have noticed her, but if she didn't notice them or—worse—fobbed them off because she was focused on Charles, then his attentions did more harm than good.' She speared Emma with a look. 'Am I correct?'

Emma set her tea cup down. 'Yes, you are.'

'I knew so.' Juliet's tone was one of vindication. 'I told him repeatedly to leave off, and he continued to ignore me.' She leaned forward and put her hand gently on Emma's arm. 'I am so sorry he made things more difficult for you.'

Emma looked at where the other woman touched her. There was a loose thread on the hem of her sleeve. Gently, she pulled her arm free. 'So you decided to arrange this house party at Lady Johnstone's to help remedy the situation your brothers created.'

Juliet's pale skin deepened to a damask rose, but she lifted her chin. 'Yes, I did. Will you help me?'

Emma sighed and wondered when her life had become so destitute that she needed this much and this kind of help. Surely not until after Mama's passing.

She plucked at the loose thread on her sleeve. Someone finally shared her concern over the matter. If only this had happened earlier. Except, a traitorous desire curled through her, she would not have got to know Charles Hawthorne as well as she now did.

Oh, she had met him when engaged to his older brother. Had even attended events where he was, but he had ignored her or watched her with eyes that spoke volumes of disapproval at her engagement to his sibling. She had been haughty to him, knowing he didn't think much of her. Why he started pursuing Amy, she didn't know. Nor did it really matter.

She met Juliet Glenfinning's watchful gaze. 'Yes, we will come.' She shrugged and spread her hands. 'We have very few choices left if Amy is to have a chance at finding a suitable husband.'

Juliet nodded in satisfaction. 'We will accomplish it. Lady Johnstone is inviting several eligible gentlemen.' She smiled roguishly, the curve of her lip reminding Emma of Charles Hawthorne. 'But not the Dowager and Mr Kennilworth. I have seen him with Amy and know she does not consider him.'

Emma laughed, a weak chuckle that barely lifted above the noise of a carriage going by outside the window. Her pride was beaten down by this exchange, but better that than give up on Amy's future. At this moment, she didn't care if the gentleman who took Amy's fancy was wealthy or not. If Amy cared for him and he cared for her, she would support them against Papa. If need be, she would help them elope to Gretna Green.

'Thank you, Juliet.'

Chapter Fourteen

⚜

Emma looked around the bedchamber given to her by Lady Johnstone. It was larger than her room at Hopewell, the Stockton country estate. Finely tooled cream leather covered the walls and deep forest green paint trimmed the corners and ceiling. Elegant furniture in the latest style filled the room in scattered groupings. The bed had satin hangings that matched the ceiling colour. A beautiful room.

She moved to the large bank of windows and looked down on a rose garden in full bloom. In the distance a lake and pagoda took pride of place. Sheep grazed in the bucolic setting.

Tension that had held her shoulders stiff for so long she had forgotten she carried it slid away. Her muscles relaxed and she breathed a silent thank you to Juliet Glenfinning for arranging their invitations.

She moved to the desk where writing paper embossed with Lady Johnstone's crest, several quills and ink sat ready. She should tell Papa where they were, not that it would matter much. But he was their parent. She dipped a quill and began.

'Em.' Amy burst through the door without knocking. 'You will never guess who is about to arrive!'

Thankful she had finished her brief note. Emma carefully folded it and dripped a blob of wax which she pressed down to seal the letter. She turned to face Amy. The girl sparkled. Her eyes glittered like sapphires, and her lips glistened like ripe cherries. Amy was too excited.

A sense of dread and anticipation filled Emma.

She had an awful presentiment of who Amy meant. There was only one person who excited Amy like this. Nor would it be unusual for him to be here since his sister was.

'Do tell me,' Emma said, keeping her tone dry.

'Charles Hawthorne!' Amy did a pirouette, her afternoon dress of fine white muslin belling around her.

'Mr Hawthorne,' she corrected Amy's informal naming.

Emma ignored the thump of her heart as it jumped and seemed to restart itself, pumping faster than it should. She had been afraid of this. Now, if there was an eligible gentleman here, Amy would have no time for him. She would be thoroughly engrossed in pursuing the very unacceptable Mr Hawthorne.

And instead of relaxing in the country, Emma would find herself in the same position she had occupied in London: The spinster older sister whose responsibility was to put a damper on anything that might be even remotely construed as improper. There would be no peace and quiet for her. No respite from constant surveillance. Or chance to have fun. She would be consumed with watching Amy.

Emma sighed and rubbed her temples.

'Em,' Amy stopped twirling and rushed to kneel in front of her sister. 'Are you unwell? I had thought you would like being here. You love the country.'

Emma dropped her hands. 'No, I am fine, Amy. Just tired from the travelling.' She made herself smile when all she wanted to do was grimace. No matter how her body had responded to the news of *his* presence, her mind knew only trouble would come of it.

'Tea is being served soon. We should go down and have some. We can also meet everyone.' Amy stood back up, her slim figure vibrating with anticipation.

Emma remembered this was also Amy's first house party,

other than the type they had exchanged with their parents' friends many years ago. But Amy had not been introduced to Society and had spent most of the time in the nursery. This was all new and wonderful to Amy. Charles Hawthorne's presence added more spice.

Too much spice.

Emma rose. 'You are right, Amy. We should attend. It is expected that house guests participate.' She smoothed down her skirt. 'There might even be an eligible gentleman or two.'

'Like Mr Hawthorne?' Amy arched one eyebrow, evidence that she knew her words needled Emma.

'More eligible than Mr Hawthorne.'

Emma's words were tart even as a sharp stab of anticipation made her stomach tightened. She wasn't interested in the man. Far from it.

'Perhaps,' Amy said archly, 'but not as attractive or as well received. Everyone knows Charles Hawthorne and many of the most important men in England follow his lead.'

'More the fool them.' Emma moved to the fireplace and pulled the cord that would tell Betty she was needed. 'I need to get this letter out before we go down.'

Amy frowned. 'Is that to Papa?'

'Yes.'

'He won't like that we've come here.'

'And why won't he? He should be thankful we have not had to run home with our tails tucked between our legs.' Emma's voice was as hard as the look on her face. 'He and Bertram have certainly done everything in their power to make this a difficult if not impossible Season.'

Amy's eyes rounded. 'Why, Em, I don't think I've ever heard you speak this way. You are always so...so accepting of whatever they do.'

Emma sighed as the exhaustion from the carriage ride settled on her shoulders like heavy bricks. 'Perhaps I am just tired, Amy.'

'Or perhaps you are fed up with what they do. I certainly

am!' She planted her feet and anchored her fists on her hips. 'It is because of them that we find ourselves in this position. Why, if not for Lady Juliet Glenfinning we couldn't have even accepted this invitation. We had no means to get here.'

'So true. Now, please, Amy. I need to lie down for a while before joining the rest of the guests.'

Amy's lips pouted, only to instantly soften into compassion. 'This has been hard on you, Em. I'm sorry. I always seem to think of my own pleasure first—much like Bertram, I suppose. And I definitely don't want to be as selfish as he is.'

Emma paused in midstride to turn back and look at her sister. 'Amy, I think you are growing up.' Pride swelled her heart. 'Mama would be so proud to hear you say that.'

'But Mama isn't here, Em. It is you and me. I am telling you these things because neither Papa nor Bertram cares. But you do.'

She moved to Emma and wrapped her arms around her older sister. Emma, nearly in tears, held onto Amy and wondered when her devil-take-the-hindmost young sister had started to change. Emma had been so caught up in her own worries she hadn't noticed.

Amy squeezed tight and released Emma. 'I am often a chore to you, I know, because I want what I want when I want it. I am sorry for the trouble I cause. I will try to be better.' Contrition knitted her brows. 'But I don't think I will be able to always remember my good intentions.'

Emma laughed, a loud, free explosion of amusement. The release was so liberating she kept laughing until the tears she had managed not to shed when Amy hugged her broke free and streamed down her cheeks.

'Oh, Amy, just to know you realise this much is more than I could have hoped for. If only Mama— But she is not.'

Emma clamped down on lips that wanted to talk about Mama and what Mama would want and expect from her daughters. Instead, she waited until Amy left and then sank into one of the silk-covered chairs pulled in front of a roaring fire—for the country was still cool.

Looking at nothing, Emma thought about her epiphany of minutes before. For the first time since Mama's passing, Emma felt as though she was a person in her own right. No longer was she Mama's daughter, promised to do the best for the family. On her deathbed, Mama had asked her to care for everyone and she had done her best.

She finally had to accept she could not make Bertram stop gambling or force Papa to set a proper example for his son. Nor could she make Amy accept a man she didn't want. Truth be told, and she was finally facing many truths, she couldn't even ensure Amy behaved within the parameters polite society dictated.

Perhaps it was her failure to keep Amy from behaving recklessly or her inability to prevent the duel between Bertram and Charles Hawthorne, made worse by Bertram's celebratory gaming. Maybe it was all of that and the loss of Mama's pearls, the reminder she had worn constantly of who Mama had been and what Mama had wanted for her family. Or it was all of that, but as of this moment, she was done trying to control her family.

All she could do was love them.

With luck, Amy would find a nice gentleman here. After Amy was settled, Emma would look for a position as a governess. Before then, she wanted to enjoy some small part of her life. After she got a position minding other people's children, she knew her dreams and goals would become intertwined with the people she worked for. No longer would she have an opportunity to live her own life.

Bittersweet thoughts. Freedom mixed with future servitude. Emma felt exhausted and exhilarated, opposing emotions.

This urge for freedom and the unfettered desire to enjoy life felt strange and exciting. She wondered if this was how Charles Hawthorne felt, if this was the emotion that kept him doing as he pleased regardless of the consequences. If so, she could finally understand.

She stood and started undoing the ties and laces that held her muslin gown on. Down to her chemise, she climbed into the beckoning bed with its coverlet of spring flowers. A nap was what she needed.

Charles Hawthorne reined in his bay, ignoring the twinge of pain in his shoulder. The doctor had said he was healing well, but hadn't wanted him to travel this far. Charles had ignored the advice and done as he wished, as usual.

He looked over the rolling hills that marked the outermost boundary of Lady Johnstone's land. A day's ride from here was his small estate, Cloudchaser, spread over land as verdant as this. He had plowed a large part of his earnings into his property so that today it turned a tidy profit. Not enough to support a lavish life in London, but enough to provide a comfortable style in the country.

If the success of his import business weren't so satisfying, he would sell it. Several businessmen had offered. The establishment had paid off the last of his gambling debts from several years ago and the remainder was going into the funds. But he wasn't ready to live the life of a country squire. He might never be ready.

Clouds filled up the sky and he smelled moisture. Soon it would rain.

He turned his horse around and made for Lady Johnstone's. Unless he missed his guess, and he was very good at determining the time of day by the sun, he would have an hour or so to change before everyone gathered for tea.

He wanted to see Emma Stockton's face when he walked in for tea. This should be a very amusing house party.

Emma tweaked an errant strand of hair into place and looked critically at herself in the mirror. Her neck still felt bare without Mama's pearls. But she felt free emotionally. She wasn't sure if one was better than the other. She had no other jewellery. She settled a paisley silk shawl around her shoulders and left.

Amy should be ready by now, so she knocked at her sister's door. When no one answered, she peeked in. The room was empty. Amy had gone without her. She swallowed a sigh of irritation. She could no more control Amy than she could control the weather. She needed to remember her thoughts before napping.

She could love her sister and try to guide her. But she could not make Amy do what she did not want to do. She had to stop trying.

Putting that thought firmly in place, she plastered a smile on her face and descended to the drawing room. A footman in scarlet livery stood by the door. She nodded to him as he opened the door for her to enter.

A quick glance showed a dozen or so guests scattered around the room. Her hostess sat pouring tea for Lady Juliet Glenfinning. A young man with blond hair and moderately high collar points above a simply tied cravat sat with them.

Amy stood by the French doors talking with Charles Hawthorne. Emma stopped and took several deep breaths in an effort to slow her racing pulse. It was because Amy laughed up at the man as though he were the wittiest and only male in existence. All her good intentions to let Amy go her own way fled. There was no other reason for her pounding heart.

Instinctively she started towards them.

As though he sensed her intention, Charles looked at her. Their eyes met and Emma wondered why he always made her feel flustered, no matter what the situation. He didn't even need to speak to her to upset her. Or to remind her of his order to kiss him and the knowledge that she had.

She twisted around and headed for the empty spot on the settee next to Lady Juliet Glenfinning. If Amy chose to throw herself at the man, then so be it. She only hoped her headstrong sister would stop short of anything scandalous.

'Please sit here.' Lady Juliet Glenfinning patted the place beside her. 'The scones are excellent.'

Emma made a curtsey to her hostess before sitting.

Lady Juliet Glenfinning said, 'Miss Stockton, this is Lady Johnstone, godmother to the three of us, George, Charles and myself.'

'Thank you for inviting us, my lady.' Emma smiled.

Lady Johnstone lifted a lorgnette to her pale blue eye and studied Emma through it. Emma felt like a bug under a magnifying glass but managed to keep the smile on her face. She owed this woman a great deal.

'So, you are the Miss Stockton. I have wanted to meet you for some time.' Lady Johnstone picked up the teapot. 'One sugar or two? Cream?'

'One. Cream, please.'

Emma began to feel as though she had stepped into a surreal situation. One minute the woman was studying her as though she were some strange specimen and saying she was glad to meet her—as though she were truly curious—and the next she was mundanely pouring tea.

'Yes, I do ramble on, Miss Stockton. But first things first, as I always say, and tea before curiosity.'

Emma accepted the teacup and saucer.

'I was impressed when you graciously called off your engagement to my godson, George Hawthorne. Much as I love the boy, his behaviour was outrageous. He was fortunate you were the one he was betrothed to. Many other women in your circumstances would not have been so generous.'

Emma choked on the sip of tea she had just taken. She started coughing. Juliet Glenfinning took the saucer from her hands before she spilt tea down her dress.

Setting the cup and saucer on the table, Juliet said, 'Are you all right, Emma?' She emphasised her concern by patting Emma on the back.

Emma finally gasped for breath, her spasm over. 'Thank you,' she said. 'I am sorry. I was…' How to say she was shocked without sounding rude?

'You were shocked by my rudeness,' Lady Johnstone said. 'I am not one to mince words. Just as I will say that it amuses me to see your young sister flirting with Charles as though her entire future depends on entertaining him. I can assure you that it does not. The boy is a rapscallion, but a charming one. However, she would do better to exert her wiles on young Chevalier over there. He is closer to her in age and has the money your family needs.'

Emma's eyes widened at the older woman's plain speaking and she was glad she hadn't picked up her tea. Likely she would have spewed it everywhere this time.

'Yes,' Lady Johnstone said, again seeming to read her mind, 'I am blunt. My husband says to a fault. Phah! He pussyfoots around everything.'

Juliet turned to Emma. 'You always know where you stand with our godmother.'

Emma nodded, wondering if it was safe to pick up her tea. She felt in need of sustenance.

'In my day, we called a rake a rake and a loose screw a loose screw. Charles is a rake and he used to be a loose screw, but he seems to have mended his ways in that one area.'

Arrested by the turn in topic, Emma was glad she hadn't picked up her tea. She wanted badly to ask the older woman what she meant, but didn't feel it was her place.

Lady Johnstone's shrewd brown eyes watched Emma like a hawk eyes a mouse. 'Want to know what I'm talking about, eh?'

'I believe I understand about the rake part, my lady.'

'And think you know about the loose screw, no doubt.' Lady Johnstone glanced around the large room. None, of the nearly dozen people, was close. 'But I would wager you don't.'

Emma flushed at the term for gambling.

'Don't like 'wager', eh? Don't blame you.' She took a long drink of her tea and Emma eyed hers wistfully. It was likely cold. 'Well, a couple of years ago, Charles gambled like your brother. Probably deeper.'

Emma's lip curled sardonically. 'I can't imagine anyone being worse than Bertram.'

Even as the disloyal words left her mouth she found she

lidn't regret saying them. She was tired beyond belief of
Bertram's behaviour and no longer willing to either condone
t or try to make light of it.

'Got some spunk after all. I had my doubts. Good.' Lady
ohnstone nodded approval. 'Well, Charles gambled and
vagered again and again. Fortunately he comes from a
vealthy family and George bailed him out so many times I
ost track.'

'Ten,' Juliet put in. 'Each one progressively worse than the
one before.'

Emma looked from woman to woman. 'Why are you tell-
ng me this? It is none of my business. Even when I was engaged to Lord Hawthorne no one mentioned this.'

Lady Johnstone sat back in her chair and studied Emma.
Maybe you aren't as intelligent as I thought.'

'What?' Emma wasn't sure if she should take offence or
vrite it up to an eccentric old woman who was used to doing
and saying what she thought without regard to others. Or…
Is he about to offer for Amy, for I must tell you, his suit will
not be welcome.'

Lady Johnstone shook her silver-curled head. 'It has
nothing to do with your sister. Anyway, George finally let
Charles go to debtors' prison.'

The air left Emma's lungs in a whoosh of shock. 'Let his
own brother be imprisoned? I have heard men die in that place.'

Juliet nodded. 'George didn't make the decision lightly.'

Emma looked from one to the other. 'But—'

'What are you ladies discussing?' Charles Hawthorne's
voice came from behind her.

Heat drenched her face. She had not heard him approach. Nor
had his sister, if the look of chagrin on her countenance was any
ndication. Lady Johnstone looked unchanged. Obviously the
older woman didn't care if he knew what she was talking about.

She looked Charles squarely in the face. 'You.'

'Ah.' He sat beside her without asking permission. 'Flat-
ering me, I hope.'

Lady Johnstone poured him tea with no sugar and no cream. 'No. Telling the truth.'

He looked at Emma, who couldn't meet his gaze. She felt as though they had been gossiping about him—which they had—and the topic had been too personal. Yet she had listened avidly.

'And what did you think about it, Miss Stockton?' His voice was smooth as honey, but underneath was a hint of iron.

Emma folded her hands in her lap to give herself a moment to think. 'It was educational.'

'And about time she knew.'

Emma looked at Lady Johnstone and wondered again why the woman felt she should be privy to Charles Hawthorne's private life. 'I don't think so,' she finally contradicted the woman and made herself meet his eyes. 'What you have done in the past, or plan to do in the future,' she tacked on hastily, 'is none of my concern.'

'Twiddling prat!' Lady Johnstone stood abruptly. 'This generation is made up of namby-pambies. I am going to take a walk in the grounds.' She shot one hard look at Charles. 'I had thought you more honest than this.'

She stalked off, her short, rotund figure held with energetic dignity. She beckoned to the young man she had pointed out earlier as being eligible for Amy. He looked surprised and apprehensive, but came to heel beside her.

'She is a character,' Lady Juliet Glenfinning said.

'Blunt nearly to a fault,' Charles seconded.

Emma released a sigh of relief. Even with Charles across from her and all the emotions his proximity always made riot through her, she felt more comfortable than when Lady Johnstone had sat here telling tales.

'I don't suppose she kept her talk only to my public escapades,' Charles said.

Juliet shook her head. 'Afraid not. She seemed most determined that Miss Stockton learn about the worst period in your life.'

His eyes narrowed and his hand holding the delicate porcelain cup cracked the handle. The cup fell to the floor, spilling tea and cutting his finger.

'Oh, my goodness.' Emma rummaged in her reticule and pulled out a white handkerchief. She handed it to him. 'Use this to stop the blood.'

He paused, studying her before taking the pristine linen square. 'Thank you.'

Emma sensed Juliet looking from one of them to the other. She wondered what the other woman saw. Probably concern on her part and disinterest on his part. More intriguing was what Lady Johnstone had seen that had prompted her to air Charles's dirty linen. Likely she had wanted Emma to know because of Charles's attentions to Amy. She could think of no other reason, regardless of that lady denying that was the cause.

Charles wrapped the material around his finger, but couldn't secure it. Emma watched, itching to reach over and tie a knot, but waited for Juliet to do so. He was her brother.

Exasperation knit his black brows together. 'Will one of you tie this? It should be obvious that I cannot.'

Emma looked at Juliet, who just smiled and shook her head. 'I quit bandaging him years ago. He is too irascible. And he is never grateful for help of this sort, even though as a child he was forever hurting himself.' She frowned. 'The final straw was last week when he took a bullet to his shoulder and yelled at me when I tried to change the bandage.' She shook her head again and rose. 'Oh, no. He will get no help from me.'

Immediate contrition flooded Emma. 'I forgot to ask how you are doing.' Her hands fluttered in her lap. 'My only excuse is that you aren't wearing a visible bandage and are here. I thought Bertram had exaggerated his prowess.'

'Which I'm sure isn't unheard of for him.' Charles's voice was dry.

Emma looked down at her hands and willed them to be still. 'No, it isn't.'

'I am well enough to be here. An occasional twinge, but I hurt more when I broke a leg. At least with this I can ride a horse.'

Emma chuckled. 'I suppose one needs to look on the bright side.'

'I do.' He smiled at her, the devastating curl of lip that promised things she had never experienced. 'Are you going to help me with this or shall I ask your sister.' He held out his hand.

Her previous sense of connection with him evaporated. 'You have a habit of giving me choices with no good ones available.'

He shrugged and the errant lock of black hair fell to his forehead. 'That is your opinion.'

She resisted the urge to push the hair back and instead focused on his hand which he held out to her. Her handkerchief was wrapped around his thumb and kept in place by him holding his index finger against the linen.

'You could hold it like that until you go up stairs and then have your valet bandage it properly.' She met his gaze defiantly.

'I could, but I won't. What will it be?'

His voice was low and provocative, making her think he had used that tone with many a woman before. But she knew he had been offering them something different from what he offered her now. The room seemed overly hot.

She sighed as though heavily put upon. The truth was she was afraid of how touching him would make her feel. She remembered him lying in bed in her attic, demanding that she kiss him. She still regretted the kiss, but even more she regretted not kissing him again.

'You leave me no other choice.'

'I do,' he murmured, 'but you don't like it.'

'True.'

She reached for his hand and pulled it closer. He winced.

'Oh, was that the shoulder Bertram hit?'

'Yes.' He was white around the mouth, but said nothing else.

'I'm sorry.'

'Don't be. You got what you wanted.' He grimaced. 'I didn't hit your brother and it was just bad luck that he hit me.'

Discontent over the past situation dampened any reaction

she might have felt to the feel of his flesh against her. 'Yes, I did, but I never intended for anyone to get hurt.'

'It happens in duels.'

'I know.'

His hand moved in hers, reminding her of what she was to do. His skin felt warm and his fingers were long and strong. They were pale, as though he spent little time outdoors, which wasn't surprising as he was a very fashionable man. His nails were short, clean and well cared for.

Her fingers shook just a little as she unwound the handkerchief. 'You cut yourself pretty deep.'

'Yes.' He shrugged and winced again. 'Habit. I need to stop moving my shoulders until the wound heals. I didn't know until Bertram winged me how much I shrug my shoulders.'

'You seem very philosophical about all this.'

'There are benefits.'

His eyes held hers so she couldn't look away. His hand lay in both of hers. His skin was rough as though he used them for more than cards. She looked down and saw a cut across two of his knuckles.

He saw her look. Pride replaced his former fascination with her. 'I did that landing Gentleman Jackson a facer.'

'You are a Corinthian.'

'I like to think so.'

'What are you two doing?' Amy's voice intruded.

Emma jumped and dropped Charles's hand. 'Nothing.'

He leaned casually back in his chair and allowed his hand to fall onto his thigh. 'Your sister was bandaging my hand.'

Amy arched one blond brow. 'With her handkerchief?'

'Yes.' He looked at the younger girl as though daring her to say more.

'Well, I have a handkerchief, too, and I'm more than willing to use mine.' She looked at Emma. 'It seems you were taking overly long.'

Emma felt flustered and hoped her face wasn't as red as it

felt. 'I was only studying it. It is a deep cut. I was worried it might need to be stitched.'

'Hah!' Amy looked skeptical. 'Let me see.'

Charles rose in one loose, powerful motion. 'I think I will have Stoner attend to me. He is very good with this sort of thing.'

Indignation followed hard on the heels of Emma's previous discomfort. If he had done that in the first place, they wouldn't be in this predicament. As it was, she knew that as soon as he left Amy would start berating her.

Deciding not to get caught by Amy, Emma rose. 'I believe I shall mingle with the other guests.'

She started off only to have Amy grip her arm. 'Em, I want to talk to you.'

Emma put on her haughtiest face. 'It can wait.'

'No, it can't.' Amy looked stubborn.

Emma knew that expression. As a child when Amy had that look on her face and no one immediately did as she wanted, she had thrown a temper tantrum. Even today, if thwarted on something she wanted badly, she was prone to behave on the borderline of acceptability.

'If you insist.' Emma did nothing to disguise her unwillingness.

The two moved to an alcove where Amy squared off. Emma glanced quickly around the room to see if anyone looked their way. The young man Lady Johnstone had pointed out as a possible interest for Amy watched. If only Amy felt the same toward him. Everyone else was busy. Charles Hawthorne had left.

'What is it, Amy?' Emma's voice sounded tired and resigned, much as she felt where Amy was concerned—where her entire family was concerned. A pang of guilt made her force a weak smile.

Amy's rosebud mouth was a thin line. 'Emma, if you are interested in Charles Hawthorne at least be honest enough to admit it.'

Emma rubbed her temple with one hand. 'Of course I'm

not interested in him. He is a thorn in my side. You have chased him brazenly and he has encouraged you. I was only going to bandage his hand because it was bleeding.'

Hands on slim hips, Amy said, 'Something he said his valet could do.'

'That—' Emma stopped. The last thing she needed to do was tell Amy about Charles's manipulation. 'If you would stop chasing after the man, none of this would happen.'

Disbelief sent Amy's eyebrows up. 'Me? If you would leave well enough alone, he and I might be engaged by now.'

Emma blinked in shock. 'He will not propose to you and you know it, Amy Ann. Just as you know Papa would never accept, and you are underage.'

'You don't know that.'

Emma's stomach began to knot even as she realised their voices had risen. She glanced around again. The only person watching them was still the young man.

Exasperation sharpened her tone. 'If you would take an interest in that nice-looking young man, none of this would have happened.'

Amy turned. 'You mean Chevalier? His father's in trade.'

'And our father's in debt! So what if his father isn't from the aristocracy. We cannot afford to be beggars.'

'So we are right back to bartering me to the highest bidder.'

Emma bit back a furious retort. 'This is not the place for this, Amy. If you want to continue this after dinner tonight in the privacy of our rooms, then fine. But right now, we are starting to attract attention and not the kind that will benefit us.'

Amy gave Emma one last fulminating look before stomping off. Relief eased some of the edge from Emma's muscles when she saw Amy stop by Mr Chevalier. At least her young sister didn't find the young man repulsive.

Any silver lining was welcome at this point.

Chapter Fifteen

Emma checked her appearance in the mirror. Her hair was tidy and pulled back with a few tendrils dangling down her nape. She pinched her cheeks for colour, telling herself she didn't want to look like a ghost. Lastly she smoothed down the folds of her lavender evening gown, her gaze skittering to her neck and away.

The pearls were gone. She had to accept that and stop looking for them.

Her paisley shawl was just the thing to cover the bare expanse of her throat and upper chest. She picked it up and draped it so her shoulders were covered.

Determined to think no more about her appearance, she left. She had never been one to primp, and she told herself she wasn't doing so now. She merely wanted to look presentable.

But over the past few days—in fact ever since Lady Johnstone had told her about Charles Hawthorne's past—she had found herself more and more interested in the man. It was not a good thing. She had already been too responsive to him. But to know he had fallen to the greatest depths possible for a gambler and pulled himself out and changed his ways made her respect him. He was far from the self-indulgent dilettante she had believed.

Consequently, he was more dangerous to her emotional well-being.

She shuddered in apprehension, knowing he would be among the other guests. They would be gathering in the parlour for drinks and before-dinner conversation.

Without conscious thought, she glanced back at the mirror. She had done all she could to make herself presentable.

The men had spent the day hunting. Emma had spent the day in Lady Johnstone's extensive library. She refused to worry about what Amy had spent the day doing.

Her new motto was to allow her sister to do as she wished. It helped knowing that the only man Amy seemed interested in flouting convention with was doing everything he could to show he wasn't interested. Charles Hawthorne had spent the last couple of days rebuffing Amy, politely, but definitively. Emma was uncertain what to think.

Leaving her room, she stopped and knocked on Amy's door. When there was no answer, she looked inside. Not surprisingly, Amy was already gone. She was determined to enjoy every minute of this house party and Emma didn't blame her.

This excursion was the last one Amy would get. The girl either found a husband or would be mired in the country for the rest of her life. Emma was thankful she personally had the temperament to be a governess. She was used to putting others before herself. Amy was the opposite.

But knowing her future, Emma was determined to enjoy this house party as much as Amy was. Between the two of them, they would have a lot of memories to store before the cold hard reality of life took over.

Emma stood in the double doorway to the parlour and wished—only for a moment—that she had the wherewithal to look as elegant and refined as the other women in the party. It was a momentary thought only. She was not one to bemoan her fate or envy others. She entered and made her way to her hostess.

They were a party of fifteen women and fifteen men. Lady Juliet Glenfinning was here without her husband. All the other ladies, with the exception of herself and Amy, were here with their spouses. That left three eligible gentlemen. Charles Hawthorne being one of the three, and if the group of women surrounding him was an indicator, the most interesting. Even their hostess swatted him with her fan.

Emma's mouth curled. Older women seemed to be unable to resist hitting him with their fans.

Juliet Glenfinning separated herself from a small group of young matrons and came to Emma. 'I was wondering when you would be down.'

Emma smiled politely at her. 'I napped later than I had planned. It is so nice to be in the country again.'

Juliet nodded. 'Charles mentioned that you prefer country life to the city.'

'He did? I'm amazed he remembered.' Or had paid attention. 'I mentioned that weeks ago when he took Amy and me for a ride in Hyde Park.'

Juliet chuckled. 'Charles can remember the most provoking things. Usually exactly what you wish he would forget.'

'I can imagine.'

'Please come and join us.' With a wave of her hand, Juliet indicated the gathering she had just left. 'Amy is in the midst of the throng around Charles. The rest of us are shaking our heads in amazement at the attraction he holds for so many women. It's not as though he is on the lookout for a wife.'

'That is probably the exact thing which makes him so irresistible,' Emma said dryly. 'The unattainable is always the most challenging and attractive.'

'Well, they certainly don't know what they are after!'

'A rake and a gambler.' The words were out before Emma considered them. Belatedly she realised they weren't the most polite things to say about a man to his sister. 'I am sorry. That was uncalled for. From what Lady Johnstone said, he has done much to change his ways.'

Juliet gave her a sharp look. 'True. He is still a rake, but he's more than that.'

Emma smiled politely and hoped her interest didn't show. It was bad enough that she wanted to know everything about the man. It would be worse if his sister knew it also. 'Such as?'

Juliet considered her. 'I am not his godmother, and I think Charles needs to tell you the rest—if he chooses.'

Instant disappointment, followed by a pang of loss made Emma turn away. The last thing she wanted was for Charles Hawthorne's sister to see she was interested and hurt by the knowledge that there was more to the man and that he might not consider her important enough to tell her. He was nothing to her, and she certainly was nothing to him.

'I think I'll go see what Amy is doing.' Emma moved away, not caring if she seemed rude. Her chest felt tight and the urge to cry was nearly overwhelming. She didn't know what was happening to her.

Amy was still amongst the group surrounding the man who caused all of Emma's problems. She gritted her teeth and managed to slip between two women to reach her sister.

'Amy, come away for a while.'

Amy eyed her before turning back to Charles. She gave him a radiant smile. 'You tell such an amusing story, Mr Hawthorne. Surely there is more.'

His gaze went to Emma. 'Your sister has something to tell you, Miss Amy.'

Amy flicked her hand dismissively. 'It can wait.'

'No, it cannot.' His voice was implacable.

Emma felt the heat mount from her chest to her neck to her cheeks. She wanted to sink into the Aubusson rug under her feet. She wished she had just gone into a corner by herself. Why had she come over here to get Amy?

Through stiff lips, she managed, 'Thank you, Mr Hawthorne.' She turned to face Amy again, her motion jerky. 'Please.'

Amy's rosebud red mouth turned down. She looked at Charles Hawthorne from the corner of her eye, and seemed to realise he was adamant. 'Oh, if you insist.'

'I think she does.' Charles's voice was soft, but no one listening to the tête-à-tête, and there were plenty, would mistake the hard edge.

Pouting, Amy followed Emma to the secluded settee they had used several days before, which now seemed an age ago. Ever since Charles Hawthorne had entered their lives, it seemed she and Amy were at constant loggerheads.

'What now?' Amy demanded before they were barely out of hearing distance.

Emma turned to her. 'Nothing. Oh, I don't know. It seemed the thing to do, come and get you.'

Amazement moved slowly over Amy's countenance. 'You don't know why you dragged me away?'

Emma fingered the silken fringe of her shawl and wondered what had become of her common sense. She sighed. 'No, Amy, I don't. I never intended to get into a public confrontation with you.'

'But you couldn't tolerate watching me flirt with Mr Hawthorne.' Amy's sarcasm cut like a knife.

Emma knotted several strands of fringe. What was wrong with her? She sank onto the settee so she had to look up at her sister. 'Please forgive me, Amy. I don't seem myself lately. I told myself I was not going to interfere with you anymore.'

Instead of sitting beside Emma, Amy looked down. 'Habit. Likely too many nights lying awake plotting how to keep Bertram in line and get me married. As I said, you aren't Mama, and you can't do what she did. None of us will listen to you like we did her. But you've tried so hard and so long that you can't stop easily.'

Surprised at Amy's insight, Emma answered, 'You have grown so much. And, yes, you are right. It is very hard for me not to try and stop you from doing things I don't think are becoming or acceptable. I told myself I would not do so, but…' She sighed. 'Go and entertain yourself, Amy. I will try harder to stay away.'

'Hah!' Amy lifted her brows. 'You will try.'

'Excuse me.' Charles Hawthorne words cut between them.

Amy twisted around and Emma jerked, her fingers already buried in the shawl's fringe got caught so she pulled a strand of fibres loose.

'Mr Hawthorne, I didn't hear you.' Amy's voice was sweet.

His tone sardonic, he said, 'I know. But I heard you.'

She flushed but met his eyes boldly. 'How discourteous of you.'

He stared her down. 'The same can be said of you. Your sister is doing her best for both you and your brother. Both of you behave like spoilt children denied a sweet. No wonder she is exhausted. Then you berate her in a public place.' A muscle in his jaw twitched. 'You are fortunate no one came this way. I managed to head off young Chevalier. He thinks you are perfection, a diamond of the first water is how he described you.' Charles shook his head. 'If he only knew.'

Amy's look of defiance crumbled. Her eyes glistened. 'How dare you.'

Emma shot to her feet, glaring at him. He ignored her.

'How dare you treat your sister the way I just heard when all she is trying to do is help you.'

'Well...' Amy moved away, her back straight as a church pew. Within seconds Chevalier was beside her.

From the look on the young man's face, he was concerned and besotted. Amy would be taken care of. Good. Emma was free to tell Mr Charles Hawthorne just what she thought of him.

'You were out of line.' Her voice was cold as frost. 'That discussion was private. If you were a gentleman, you would have moved away.'

The muscle in his jaw twitched again. 'But you have told me many times that I am not a gentleman.' His voice was a low drawl, at odds with the dangerous glint in his eyes. 'So I did as you would expect me to.'

The urge to berate him was strong. He was so contradictory. 'I would never expect you to interfere between us—particularly not to defend me. Amy is the one you have been chasing.'

Why had she added that last? It didn't matter to this conversation. The only thing that mattered was that he should have stayed away. Now he had hurt Amy's feelings. But…

'Of course,' she continued, more considering now, 'you realise she will not be so attracted to you.'

'I don't believe I shall lose sleep over the loss.' Sarcasm dripped from every word.

She looked up at him, aware of his closeness and the scent of musk and bergamot that was uniquely his. Her throat suddenly dry, she swallowed and nearly choked. 'Really?'

'Really.' His eyes held hers. 'I have learned a lot these last couple of weeks.'

'You have?' Her voice died into a husky whisper.

He loomed over her, his face harsh yet gentle. His shoulders were broad enough to block any curious viewers in the rest of the room. It seemed as though the two of them were caught in a pocket of privacy.

'Yes, Emma.'

She shivered as heat flooded her body to be instantly replaced with nervousness. Her stomach knotted, but in a pleasurable way that seemed to promise even more delight. She felt as though she stood on the brink of a precipice. One step and she would be over the edge. Would he catch her?

The dinner gong sounded, and he edged away from her. Emma blinked as reality set back in. She was in Lady Johnstone's parlour, waiting to eat and nearly swooning into Charles Hawthorne's arms.

She scanned the room looking for Amy. 'Excuse me,' she muttered, edging around the man who made her feel reckless just by his proximity.

She halted beside Amy, who stood talking to Mr Chevalier and another gentleman, Mr George Helmsley. Mr Helmsley was older, a touch of grey in his brown hair and deep lines around his green eyes and mouth.

He smiled at Emma. 'Good evening, Miss Stockton.'

She smiled back, including the others. 'I am ready for dinner, anyone else?'

They all agreed. Mr Chevalier offered Amy his arm and Mr Helmsley did the same for Emma. She hesitated only a moment before lightly laying her fingers on his dinner jacket. Nothing happened. She felt absolutely nothing from the contact.

A quick glance told her Charles escorted his sister. An unwanted sense of relief lodged in her chest.

'Are you enjoying yourself?' Mr Helmsley asked, forcing her to pay attention to him.

They exchanged small talk into the dining room where Emma found herself seated between Mr Helmsley and Charles. A distinct feeling of unease crept over her. Her left side, where Charles sat, tingled and felt flushed then chilled. Her right side felt nothing.

Amy's sat between Mr Helmsley and Mr Chevalier. That was the only comforting thing about the dinner arrangements.

Emma glanced at her hostess and saw a satisfied smile on the older woman's face. Matchmaking. Well, at least Lady Johnstone had kept Charles away from Amy.

Mr Helmsley kept up a steady stream of conversation. He was a landowner in Wiltshire who had been tired of the Season when Lady Johnstone had invited him to visit. He was single and his family thought it time he settled down and produced an heir. He enjoyed hunting and riding and walking. Truth be told, his heart was in the country.

Emma nodded and smiled, all the while conscious of Charles on her other side. He made no attempt to disrupt the flow of information between her and Mr Helmsley. Nor did Charles try to catch Amy's attention.

Contradictory as she was becoming, Emma found herself irritated at Charles for not doing something. Anything. Mr Helmsley was a nice man, an impeccable gentleman, but she had to stifle a yawn even though she enjoyed many of the country pastimes he did.

Dinner ended long past the point where Emma had decided she could stand no more of Mr Helmsley's patter. Fortunately, she had not had to say anything to encourage him. She rose with their hostess and followed the other ladies from the room.

Amy trailed behind, laughing at something Mr Chevalier said. Emma looked over her shoulder and cocked her head to tell Amy to come along. Amy looked through her. Emma swallowed a sigh of exasperation and told herself she was not going to keep pestering Amy to behave. She had made that decision. She was going to stick to it.

Turning away from Amy, she noticed Charles Hawthorne watched her, a sardonic smile on his mouth that told her he expected her to march back and drag Amy off. She notched her chin up and looked away.

There, she had done it. She had refused to nag Amy and had met Charles Hawthorne's unspoken challenge and won. Her steps were lighter as she walked into the parlour.

She considered retiring to her room, but in spite of her good intentions and success in not meddling with Amy earlier, she couldn't bring herself to leave Amy when the gentlemen would be joining them shortly. Accepting that her resolution was going to take time and be difficult to succeed at, she took a chair away from the main group.

Amy chattered away with Juliet Glenfinning and another married lady. Emma breathed a sense of relief. No sooner did she relax than the gentlemen joined them.

Tiredness ate at her. She had not slept well and her afternoon nap had not been as restful as she had thought. She began to think she was more than physically tired.

She put her hands on the arms of the chair and pushed herself up. She should have gone to bed and let Amy do whatever she wished.

She pasted a smile on her face and started toward her sister when she felt someone graze her shoulder. Sparks tumbled down her arm, making her clench her hand into a fist—as though she longed to keep the sensation trapped within herself. She didn't need to look to know it was Charles. No other man made her feel this way.

'Miss Stockton,' he said, moving to block her progress. 'Will you walk with me?'

She stopped so as not to run into his chest and kept her face devoid of emotion. 'Thank you, Mr Hawthorne, but it is dark outside and I am thinking of retiring.'

He bowed slightly, his eyes challenging her. 'Then I will be forced to ask Miss Amy.'

Emma sputtered in frustration and her look of unconcern evaporated. 'Must you always use that threat?'

He shrugged with only a slight wince to show his wounded shoulder still pained him. 'It seems to be the only thing that works.'

From the corner of her eye, she saw Mr Helmsley heading toward them. She could wait for him to interrupt this conversation.

As though he read her thoughts, Charles murmured, 'If he comes and tries to dominate you, I will go do the same with your sister.' His devil-may-care smile lit his eyes. 'I am sure she will co-operate.'

'Most definitely,' Emma said sourly. 'You win, Mr Hawthorne—again. But only because you fight unfairly.'

He extended his arm. 'I fight to win. Anyone who does less is merely wasting time.'

'I didn't realise you were so competitive.'

'There is a lot about me you don't know, Miss Stockton. Just as there is much about you that I intend to find out.'

She cast him a look up through her lashes, wondering what he was at to flirt with her this way, and immediately wished she hadn't. There was a tautness in his jaw and a glitter in his eyes that scared her even as they made her pulse jump before speeding up. She was in a situation she had no experience of. But she could not extricate herself, for she had no doubt he would go to Amy. Nor was she sure she wanted to.

She allowed him to lead her to one of the French doors that opened onto a verandah. Flambeaux cast dancing flames that reached for the stars and sent golden light into the garden.

Twenty steps down and they were surrounded by the heady, musky scent of blooming roses and twining honeysuckle.

He angled her down a gravel path that was bordered on both sides by roses. She dragged her feet, not wanting to go too far. When he put his free hand over hers where her fingers rested on his arm, she skidded to a halt and yanked her hand away—or tried.

He turned to face her. 'I am only holding your hand.'

She stared up at him, noting the harsh angle of his jaw where the flickering and weakening light from the flambeaux emphasised the hollows of his cheeks. 'I did not give you permission to do so.'

He held onto her hand with both of his now. 'Will you?'

She felt as though the precipice from earlier was rushing up to meet her. She couldn't speak. She could barely shake her head no.

His eyes danced with amusement and tenderness. 'I had wanted to pursue you slowly. I see it is not to be.'

Flummoxed by his words, she stood mute, taking shallow little breaths that did nothing to ease the sense that she was racing toward something that would change her life forever.

A warm breeze wafted through her hair and cooled her skin even as his regard heated her body. The scents of growing flowers mingled with the intoxicating smell of the man standing too close to her. But she didn't move away. Her legs were incapable of saving her.

His head bent down so his warm, brandy scented breath fanned her face, caressed her lips just seconds before his mouth touched hers. She stood transfixed.

Sensations cascaded through her. Scents, tastes, hot and cold tingles. Desire.

Her body arced without her conscious volition until her breasts grazed his chest. There might as well be no clothing between them. Her nipples swelled and ached in a way she had never experienced before, never realised was possible.

His arms surrounded her and pulled her closer. One of his

hands dropped to the small of her back and nestled her into the heat that was his hips. Shock sizzled through her at the intimate touch.

She tried to pull away, but he held her firmly.

The world fell away and had it not been for his arm holding her securely to him, she would have sunk to the ground. Never had she thought to experience anything this powerful. This kiss was so much more than their first.

She parted her lips as his tongue flicked along her skin, probing and teasing. He was inside her before she realised what happened. His mouth moved over hers as he probed her sensitive flesh. Her head fell back and he released her lips.

A whimper of loss escaped her only to be replaced with a sigh of pleasure when his teeth nipped the corner where her jaw and earlobe met. He nibbled the nerve-rich area until Emma thought she would swoon.

Her breath turned ragged when he bent her back over his arm and his mouth moved to the hollow that separated her neck from her bosom. He sucked gently on her skin.

When one of his hands moved to cup her breast through the material of her dress, she gasped only to have him gentle her by returning his mouth to hers. His fingers massaged her swollen, aching mound until she whimpered.

'Easy,' he murmured, lifting his lips from hers. 'I won't leave you like this.'

Through the haze of desire she wondered what he meant but forgot when his hand moved to her other breast. Her stomach clenched, starting a pattern of response that mimicked his tongue. She shivered with fire then ice then a hot need that spiralled up with each movement of his body against hers.

'Emma,' he murmured before slipping his hand under the material of her bodice so that the rough skin of his fingers touched the silk of her bosom. 'I want all of you.'

He found her nipple and began rubbing it gently, enough to send sparks shooting to her loins. She felt hot and damp and aching for something she knew he could provide. If only…if only…

The sound of Amy's voice came sharply to Emma's ears. Emma jolted and without thought pushed against Charles's chest. He let her go.

She fell back, gasping for breath, staying on her feet only through luck. She stared at him, eyes wide, mouth swollen.

'What…what have we done?' she asked softly.

He looked as stunned as she. But he was more experienced. 'We have nearly made love.'

'Oh, dear…' she moaned.

'Emma, are you out here?' Amy's voice intruded once more.

A new heat engulfed Emma—mortification. Her bodice and chemise were tucked under her bosom and the cool night air was making her nipples harden just as Charles's attention had so recently. She fumbled with her clothing only to realise her hair was coming down. A red strand caught in her chemise and she pulled it savagely out, wincing when the pain hit her head.

'Emma?'

'Oh, goodness,' Emma whispered. She looked up to see Charles watching her, his face devoid of emotion. 'Go away,' she insisted. 'If she sees you here and sees me, she will know. Just please go away.' Tears of embarrassment threatened to spill as she waited anxiously for him to leave.

Without a word, he pivoted and strode into the night. She was thankful he was going away from the house. He wouldn't meet up with Amy who, from the sound of her voice, was nearly here. Another corner—

'Here you are.' Amy came into view. 'I saw you leave with Charles Hawthorne, but you never came back.' She halted several feet from Emma and looked her up and down. 'What have you been doing?'

Emma swallowed her groan of discomfort. What had she been doing? Allowing Charles Hawthorne to take advantage of her. No, he had not taken advantage of her. She had participated, gone so far as to encourage him. She shivered.

Now she had to lie once more to her sister. 'Nothing, Amy. I just needed some fresh air.'

Amy's eyes narrowed to slits. 'I think you got more than fresh air.' She looked around. 'Where is Mr Hawthorne?'

'I don't know.' Relief that she could answer truthfully eased a small part of Emma's discomfort.

Disbelief filled Amy's face. Emma expected her sister to start berating her again, their previous conversation being only the prelude to Amy's discontent.

Amy brushed past Emma and sat on the nearby bench. 'Em, sit here and let us talk.'

Emma gaped, taken by surprise. 'It is late, Amy. We would do better going inside to talk.'

Sympathy filled Amy's face. 'No, I want to talk here. Now.'

Emma sighed, knowing no good could come of this conversation. Not now. But she sat beside her sister and forced her confusion over what had just happened and her response to the back of her mind. 'What, dear?'

Amy held Emma's gaze. 'I think you need to be honest with yourself, Em.'

Emma raised a brow. 'I am.'

Even as she said the words, she knew she wasn't. There was more to her feeling for Charles Hawthorne than she had allowed herself to acknowledge. But how much more?

Amy shook her head and her curls danced. 'In most things, but not where Mr Hawthorne is concerned.'

The breath caught in Emma's throat as a sense of unrealness moved over her. 'Are you talking about my condemnation of him?'

Amy's eyes became soft and concerned. 'No, Em. Or rather, yes, but not in the way you think. I believe you berate and denigrate him so much because you are beginning to care for him.'

Emma sat straighter. 'I am not.'

'Aren't you? He was with you until I arrived, wasn't he?'

Amy's soft voice felt like a whip to Emma. Surely her young sister was wrong about her feelings for the man. And yet...

And what to say to Amy's last question? The truth? Was she to put still more lies between herself and her sister? No.

Feeling defiant, a totally new emotion for her, Emma said, 'Yes, he was.'

'I thought so. You look…' Amy cocked her head and studied Emma. 'Different. Alive somehow.'

The flush that had engulfed Emma during Charles's lovemaking returned with a vengeance. 'Your imagination is running away with you Amy. All we did was talk.'

'About me? Or Bertram?' A sly look entered her eyes. 'Or did you do something else?'

Emma moved until she sat on the very edge of the bench. 'We talked about both of you.'

'Ahh…'

It was a very knowing 'ah' and Emma knew she had to escape this interrogation before she said something she ought not. She bolted up. 'I am going to bed. Do you want to walk back with me?'

Amy cast one curious look down the path Charles had taken minutes before, but rose. 'If I don't, you will send someone out after me. Not Mr Hawthorne, but someone, so I might as well go with you.'

There was so much smug knowing in Amy's voice that it was all Emma could do not to blush anew. But she was not about to tell her young sister that she had succumbed to Charles Hawthorne's lovemaking. It would do no one any good.

As they moved through the empty garden and cool night, Emma shivered and knew she was lost.

Chapter Sixteen

Emma awoke with the dawn as was her custom.

She felt different somehow. Then memory rushed back and she felt hot and disturbingly excited. She buried her face in the pillow, wishing she could bury her desire the same way.

What had happened between her and Charles had awoken parts of her body she hadn't known existed before. The unspoken acts between a man and woman who were lovers were suddenly part of her memory, part of her body. And, heaven help her, she wanted more.

In an effort to banish the new and unsettling need from her body, she rose and quickly donned a simple gown that needed no maid to fasten the hooks and eyes or tie the ribbons. With a deft twist of her wrist, she fastened her hair in a topknot.

She wanted to walk in the rose garden while the dew was still on the petals and everyone else was asleep. It was the most wonderful time of day for her. At home she did it every summer morning, picking the flowers that were in full bloom. During the fall and winter months she walked amongst the trees. Today it might also calm her mind and cool her body.

She wanted to get away from her bed. Beds were suddenly places where more than sleeping occurred. Yet at the same time, she wanted to experience everything that Charles had only given her a glimpse of last night.

She had never considered herself to be susceptible to the pleasures of the flesh, but last night and now this morning she began to wonder. She might even be wanton. Fresh mortification stained her cheeks.

As she moved through the house, there was a lift in her step that hadn't been there for more years than she could remember. Emma made her way downstairs and outdoors. Fresh, crisp air blew her skirts so her legs and hips were delineated. Her hair lifted in small wisps that escaped her clip. She strode forward feeling strangely happy under the dominating emotion of desire.

Happiness was an emotion she hadn't felt in many years. She was not sure she had ever experienced desire. Yet, the two had many similarities. Both made her feel good, buoyant and full of hope.

An hour later, she returned to her starting point. The sun was fully risen in the east. Several gardeners were about their work. She nodded at them as they pruned bushes and harvested armfuls of blooming roses.

With a soft trill of laughter at the sheer joy of being alive and being desired by a man who made her blood heat, Emma tripped up the stairs to the parlour. Inside it was cool and dim. Breakfast would be on a buffet in the dining room. She was suddenly very hungry.

Her lips parted in a smile of delight, she moved through the house. She had hoped to be the only one up this early and was not disappointed. She took a pot of hot chocolate and several slices of toast and sat down facing the windows.

Buttering and slathering a healthy portion of marmalade on her toast, she pondered why Charles Hawthorne's lovemaking had made such a difference in her. She definitely couldn't marry the man, even if he did ask. Which he wouldn't. He was a rake. She was a spinster with a family heavily in debt. No, it was simply dalliance they were about. But it still felt new and wonderful and full of mystery.

Just a week ago she would have run from his advances. But she was changing. She was going to experience life before she ensconced herself in another woman's nursery. Perhaps she would even go so far as to ask him to make love to her.

Just the idea made her dizzy. It was a thought she would never have entertained even a day ago. Women in her position did not take lovers—ever. Yet…

She finished breakfast in charity with her world. Just as she was rising from the table, Mr Helmsley entered.

'Miss Stockton.' He smiled. 'How nice to see you up this early.' He glanced at her empty plate. 'You have eaten. Will you stay and keep me company?'

Should she? She studied him. His clothing was good and fashionable without being the height of absurdity. His brown eyes were clear and intelligent. He seemed to have a sense of humour. She could do much worse for a morning companion.

No matter that the image of another man rose in her mind. He was only dallying with her to ease his boredom. This man seemed genuinely interested in her.

She sat back down. 'I would be delighted to have a cup of tea.'

He came over and pushed her chair in. His shoulder brushed hers and his scent of pine filled her nostrils. She felt nothing. Mr Helmsley was a nice man. She could and would enjoy his company.

Charles rolled over in bed, taking the mass of covers with him, and reached for a woman who wasn't there. He relaxed onto his back and stared up at the brown canopy. What was happening to him?

In his dream he had made love to Emma Stockton, kissing and caressing her until the pale peach tint of her skin had blazed like the setting sun. Her nipples had been hard nubs, the colour deepening to a dusky richness.

His loins throbbed, and his entire body ached with the need for release.

'Mornin' Guv'.' Stoner's gravelly voice intruded on Charles's misery. 'It's about time you was up. This is the country.'

Charles groaned and sat up, careful to keep the bedcovers over his hips. No one else needed to know the state he was in. 'This is a house party, Stoner. People sleep as late as they wish.'

'Well, your lady is up and about.' Stoner gave him a sly glance while setting hot water on a nearby table.

'I don't have a lady.' If he did, he wouldn't be in this condition. Or more accurately, he'd be in this condition but have a way to remedy it. He was still aroused.

'Good you feel that way, Guv', cause she's with that Mr 'elmsley.'

'What?' Charles jerked to attention, and his embarrassment shrank. After last night's kiss and her response to his caresses, she was with another man? He hadn't thought her the type to encourage two men at once. 'Hmmm… Maybe I should be up and about.'

Stoner grinned without looking at Charles. 'Thought you might change your mind.' He sharpened a razor. 'Got ever'thing to clean you up.'

Charles threw off the covers as his former state subsided, and slipped naked from the bed except for the bandage on his shoulder. He slept naked no matter what the weather. It was a sensual experience he heightened with silk sheets he had specially made to his specification. He was a hedonist and intended to take pleasure wherever he could, and particularly in bed.

He gave himself over to Stoner's ministrations. Nearly an hour later, he went straight to the room where a breakfast buffet was laid and noted both Emma Stockton and Helmsley were missing.

He sauntered to where his sister sat and took a seat. 'Good morning.'

Juliet looked at him. 'You're up early.'

He yawned. 'Went to bed early. Been here long?'

Her smile could have been a smirk. 'I arrived just as Emma Stockton and Mr Helmsley left. They were going for a walk in the gardens.'

Charles's gut churned, but he kept his face inscrutable. 'Really?'

'Yes. Popular place, the gardens.' She spread marmalade on a piece of toast. Munching delicately, she watched him. 'Don't like that, do you?'

He took the mug of ale the footman brought and drank down half. 'Don't know what you're talking about.'

She laughed. 'Of course you don't.'

Lady Johnstone entered and made a beeline to them. She sat down with a thump. 'Good thing we're the only ones in here.' She pinned Charles with her stare. 'Helmsley's got your filly.'

Charles blinked in surprise and nearly sputtered his last swallow of ale. 'My filly?'

'Don't think I invited the Stocktons for my own entertainment.' Lady Johnstone continued. 'Both nice girls, but one's too emotional and the other's too namby-pamby.'

Juliet said, 'You told Emma the other night that she wasn't.'

Lady Johnstone snorted. 'Changed my mind. Although—' she gave Charles an appraising once-over '—I noticed her leaving with you last night and returning without you much later. She looked better than I've ever seen her. And you, my fine buck, look as wound up as a child's top.'

Charles looked from one woman to the other and decided he wished they weren't the only people in the room at this moment. They might have minded their tongues otherwise. He drank the last of his ale and stood.

'Excuse me, ladies, but I have business elsewhere.'

'In the garden if you want the chit!' Lady Johnstone's brook-no-nonsense voice said.

Charles felt heat rise to his face. He made a curt bow to his godmother. 'Thank you for the prodding, ma'am.'

Juliet smothered a laugh behind her napkin. 'She is right, you know.'

Charles scowled at them. 'The lady in question is free to do as she pleases. Just as I am.'

'Ah, a man who doesn't insist on sole proprietorship.' Lady Johnstone's voice cut. 'I imagine that if you had marriage on your plate your tune would be different.'

'Good morning.' Charles twisted on the heel of his Hessian and beat a retreat. He knew when he was outgunned and outmanoeuvred.

Twenty minutes later, he found the couple under discussion sitting on a bench very close to where he had kissed Emma Stockton the night before. He told himself the urge to plant Helmsley a facer was merely the normal reaction of a man who had sampled the delights of a woman. It was not the reaction of a man who wanted that woman exclusively. He could not recall ever wanting a woman to the exclusion of everything else. And he didn't want Emma Stockton that way now.

'Am I interrupting?' He stepped in front of them and just kept himself from stepping between them.

Flushed from something Helmsley had said, she turned to Charles and her face paled. 'Mr Hawthorne.'

Helmsley also looked at Charles. 'Morning, Mr Hawthorne.'

Charles forced a thin smile to his lips. They had not invited him but he wasn't going away. 'May I join or is this an exclusive discussion?'

'Nothing of the sort,' Emma said quickly. 'We were trading stories about life in the country.'

Charles kept the smile on his face. 'Such as?'

Helmsley's eyes crinkled in amusement. 'Fishing for trout and falling in. Mishaps like that.'

An immediate picture of Emma Stockton rising from a stream, her gown clinging to her body and her nipples hard from the chill brought a rush of blood to Charles's loins. He swallowed. It took an effort to drawl, 'How interesting.'

As though sensing he wasn't enamoured of the conversation, Emma said, 'It is time I returned to the house. Amy should be up by now.' She stepped away from the men.

Helmsley immediately offered his arm and Charles checked himself with his hand in the air as though he brushed a speck from the opposite sleeve of his coat.

'Allow me,' Helmsley said, his brown eyes filled with warmth.

Emma blushed at Mr Helmsley's blatant admiration, made worse by having Charles Hawthorne see it. The man had kissed her very thoroughly last night and now he watched Helmsley pay marked attention to her without a glimmer of concern or interest. Obviously, she had been right in deciding Charles Hawthorne didn't care about her, he just wanted the seemingly unattainable. If he ever learned what she truly felt for him, he would run in the opposite direction. Thankfully she hadn't embarrassed herself by pursuing him as she had considered earlier.

She matched her steps to Mr Helmsley and put her fingers on his arm. 'Thank you, but you don't have to escort me if you prefer to stay here.'

He laid his free hand briefly over hers before dropping it to his side. 'With you gone this is just another garden.'

'What an interesting concept.' Charles drawled as he took up position on the side of Emma that Mr Helmsley didn't occupy.

She glanced surreptitiously at him. He looked cool, casual and bored. His fine white shirt was open at the neck and he wore a bandana knotted around his throat in the fashion sported by gentlemen of the ring. His blue jacket fit loosely.

Mr Helmsley's smile faded. 'Ah, Mr Hawthorne. I thought you planned to hunt about this time.'

The look on Charles's face would have made many men pause. 'I changed my mind.'

Emma looked from one to the other, wondering what

was going on. Charles Hawthorne normally had more charm than this.

In an effort to ease the tension that suddenly seemed to fill the warm summer air, she said, 'I am looking forward to...' Her voice trailed off. Bertram strode toward them, still dressed for riding. 'Oh, dear,' she finished faintly.

He stopped in front of them, forcing them to halt. 'I see you are still keeping questionable company.' If looks could slay, his would have eviscerated Charles Hawthorne.

She bristled at his implied criticism of Charles. 'The same could be said of you.'

Bertram's pale face mottled. 'I am a man. I can do as I please.'

She sighed. 'So you are. What brings you here? I thought you were enjoying London.'

Bertram yawned. 'The city is so fatiguing after a while.'

'Rusticating.' Charles's insult cut across Bertram's excuse.

Mr Helmsley cleared his throat. Emma, who had momentarily forgotten him, even with her hand on his arm, wanted to sink into the ground after what had just been revealed. Instead, she held her head up. None of this was her fault. She would not take responsibility anymore.

'Does Lady Johnstone know you're here?' she asked, foreseeing still another embarrassment.

For the first time in many months Bertram looked sheepish. 'I sent a note.'

'When?' Emma told herself again that Bertram and his behaviour were not her responsibility.

'Yesterday.' He looked away. 'I thought that since you and Amy had been invited, I was sure to be welcome also. I am here in my capacity as your brother and chaperone. I am sure Lady Johnstone will understand.'

Emma wanted to scold him so badly her hands shook. Instead she said, 'I see. Well, you had best speak with Lady Johnstone. She might not have room.'

'In which case you and Amy must leave with me.'

Emma stared at him and knew this was one time he was

not going to tell her what to do. She had no intention of leaving this house party now. No matter what Bertram said or did.

'We most certainly will not.' She stepped forward, determined to go around him.

He stood his ground. 'Then you had best speak to Lady Johnstone about a room for me.'

'You are a man, Bertram, and intent on doing as you please. It is your responsibility to speak to the lady.'

Bertram looked as though she had slapped him. 'Well, Em, I had thought you would do that.'

She shook her head, thinking it felt good not to burden herself with Bertram's troublemaking and wondering why she had never exerted herself before. 'I am sure she would prefer to hear from you. She is likely—'

'She is in the breakfast room,' Charles said, a hint of relish in his voice.

Bertram's mouth opened, making him look like a fish out of water. 'But…'

'But nothing,' Charles said. 'I'm sure Lady Johnstone will be surprised to see you.'

Helmsley, who had listened and watched, said quietly, 'I am sure she will find room for you, Mr Stockton. This is a large estate.'

Bertram gave him a grateful look before turning a less than friendly one on his sister. 'I see I will have to fend for myself. Mama would have made all the arrangements.'

Emma blanched. Bertram was absolutely correct. Mama would have made sure there was a room for Bertram and that his bags were taken care of. Mama would never have made Bertram fend for himself. She opened her mouth to say she would take care of everything, but Charles Hawthorne took her arm in a firm grip and pulled her around her brother. Her fingers fell from Mr Helmsley's arm.

'Tell Lady Johnstone it would oblige me to have you stay. Now, good day, Bertram.' Charles didn't look at her brother, just tugged her away.

Mr Helmsley stood for several seconds as though he didn't know what to do. Then he followed them.

Charles gave Helmsley a glower that said clearer than words the man was *de trop*. Helmsley looked at Emma. She gave him a weak smile and shook her head. He fell back.

Emma allowed Charles to pull her away from the other men. When they were out of hearing, she turned on him. 'What do you think you are doing? This is twice you have meddled in my family's affairs—and that is being conservative. I'm not counting your outrageous behaviour with Amy in London or your duel with Bertram.'

The entire time she berated him, he pulled her toward a secluded arbor. The heavy scent of damask roses surrounded them.

'I am standing up for you since you won't do it for yourself.' He scowled. 'I am also making sure Bertram is allowed to stay rather than have him run back to London and continue his disreputable ways.'

She pulled her arm from his grasp. 'I don't need your interference.'

'It isn't interference.' He looked irritated enough to spit nails. 'You allow Bertram to treat you like a servant and Amy to behave as though her actions are of no consequence. Then you shoulder the burden of cleaning up after them.'

She glared at him. 'And you are better than they are?'

'I don't make you bear the brunt of my actions.'

'You don't?' Anger simmered in her stomach. 'What do you call my having to follow behind you and Amy every second to make sure you don't cross the line of respectability with her?'

'I call it poor judgement on your part.'

'What!' Indignation made her sputter.

'Yes. You should have known I would never go to the point where I would have to propose marriage.'

She thought steam must be coming out of the top of her head, she was so mad. 'I should have known that? You are a debauched rake who has led your life the way you wanted with no regard for the consequences you've caused others. And now you are criticising my family.' She paused to take a breath. 'How dare you.'

'I dare because I know how hard Bertram's gambling is on you and on Amy. I care because Amy is rebelling at her fate and who knows where that will lead her.'

'What do you care? We are none of your concern.'

A look of unease flitted across his face. He looked away from her for a moment before saying, 'Because I have made my family miserable in the past.'

'I can certainly believe that.'. She knew the words were cruel, but at this moment she didn't care. He had provoked her beyond belief.

He ran his fingers through his hair and looked as though he was swallowing a bitter potion. 'Please sit down, Emma.'

She glanced at the stone bench near them. 'I am Miss Stockton to you, Mr Hawthorne, no matter what happened last night. And, no, I won't sit.'

'You are one of the most stubborn women I know.' He put a finger under her chin and tilted her head up. 'You were Emma last night. Have things changed that greatly?'

She turned her head away so he no longer touched her. 'Last night was an aberration. It won't happen again.'

'Are you sure?' His voice was low and sexy and deeply disturbing.

She wanted to tell him she was positive, but she couldn't. The heat from his body scorched her, and the intensity of his study made her feel weak in the knees. And she had thought earlier how exciting it would be to have him make love to her—completely. Just once.

She pushed the disturbing thought away and stiffened her back. She had to stay furious with him or she might beg him to kiss her again. 'You are meddling where you don't belong.'

He made a visible effort to appear reasonable. 'Can we try this again, *Miss Stockton?* I am trying to help you even though it is obvious you don't want my help. But someone needs to stop you from allowing your siblings to run over you.'

'That someone doesn't need to be you.'

'Then who?' He spread his hands as though to encompass the world.

She knew the answer. No one. 'Not you. I must do this on my own.'

'Then do so.' He dropped his hands to his sides. 'It bothers me to see what is happening to you because of the way George treated you. And because I know how hard my misbehaviour was on George.'

Puzzled, she waited silently.

Frustration drew his brows together. 'You do remember your short engagement to my brother that you graciously broke so he could marry Rose?'

'Yes. It was the beginning of my latest round of problems.'

'Yes. No one to pay the gambling debts incurred by the men in your family. And now Amy is the sacrificial lamb and she's rebelling.'

Emma nodded. There was nothing to say. He was saying it all.

'The best thing you can do for them and yourself is to step away from their lives.'

He was telling her exactly what she had already decided for herself. How did he know all this? But she said nothing.

'I know.' He paused and there was audible strain in his voice. 'I… This is hard to talk about, although it is no secret.'

Tension formed lines around his mouth, yet took nothing away from the sensual curves of his lips. She wondered that even under these circumstances she still found herself attracted to him in ways that scared her sensible self.

He continued. 'I was in debtors' prison for several weeks.'

She kept herself from saying she already knew. He needed to tell her himself. 'You?'

He nodded. 'I was like Bertram. An insatiable gambler. Among other vices.'

Rumour said he was insatiable in everything. She didn't comment on that even though heat exploded in her stomach at the thought. 'Why didn't your brother bail you out? He is wealthy beyond most of his peers. It wouldn't have been a hardship for him.'

'No, but he had already done so—five, ten times.' Red stained his angled cheeks. 'I was beyond caring so long as I could gamble, thinking each time would be the one where I won a fortune.' He grimaced. 'I understand Bertram very well. I also understand Amy because I have rebelled against every restriction put on me. That was another reason I followed ruin with more ruin.'

'And now you are reformed?' Her tone implied she didn't believe it.

He smiled ruefully. 'Not totally. But the time in jail turned my life around. If George had bailed be out again, I doubt I would be here now. He had to let me experience the miserable results of my behaviour.' He looked her in the eye and took hold of both her arms so she stood in front of him. It seemed as though he meant to use the physical contact to strengthen the impact of his words. 'I would have never had the desperate incentive to change my ways otherwise.'

'You are the strangest man. Why do you think this confession makes any difference to me?' Even as she said the words, she knew she lied. He trusted her with this information which showed a very private and personal part of him. A very vulnerable part.

'Because you allow your brother and sister to continue in their behaviour. You spend all your energy to save them. Let them fall once. The chance is that they won't do it again.'

She sighed. If only he was right, but she didn't think he was. And the fact that she had already decided to do as he suggested for purely selfish reasons was something she didn't want to admit to him. No matter how she told herself he was despicable or disreputable, she was still attracted to him and found she didn't want to look bad in his eyes.

'I must go,' she muttered, twisting her arms to free them. To her surprise he released her.

She whipped around him and sped to the house. With luck she would also miss Bertram and Mr Helmsley. Right now, she didn't feel like socialising. She felt emotionally depleted and confused and totally unlike herself.

Charles Hawthorne did that to her.

Emma entered the house in time to see Bertram paying his respects to Lady Johnstone. He bowed elegantly over the older woman's hand and murmured something that brought a smile to her lips.

It seemed Bertram could charm when he needed to, Emma thought sourly before reprimanding herself. He was her brother and no matter what he did or how he treated her, she still loved him. She needed to remember that because the next couple of days promised to be difficult.

She took a deep breath and let it out slowly, then angled away from the tableau. Her bedchamber seemed the best refuge at the moment.

Chapter Seventeen

Emma smiled as she listened to Mr Helmsley blend his baritone with Amy's light soprano. Half of the house party was in here after dinner, listening to several members play the piano and harp while others accompanied them. The other half was playing cards. Bertram and Charles Hawthorne were not here.

Much as she enjoyed the music, she worried about what was happening in the other room. Bertram was supposed to be recouping after losing too much at the gambling tables. But she knew her brother.

With a smile to the others participating in the music, and noticing Amy looking happy when William Chevalier added his tenor, Emma stood. Much as she had told herself in the last couple of days that Bertram was not her responsibility, habit died hard. Not even Charles Hawthorne's pointed interference was doing much good.

She sighed as she went to the door. The card games were across the hall.

Wall sconces, each filled with half a dozen candles, lit the entire ground floor. It was past midnight and even the summer sun was long since down. She paused in the entrance to see where Bertram was.

Surprise jolted her when she found him. Charles Hawthorne's hand held Bertram's shoulder, and from the look on both their faces neither was happy. Bertram looked harassed. Charles looked furious.

Something had happened.

She had to reach them before they challenged each other again. She sped across the room, dodging furniture and a few invitations to join a group.

She was too slow.

Bertram rose, looking as though he wanted to lash out at Charles. Charles's mouth was a thin line, his jaw motionless as though he held back scathing words. The two moved to a set of open French doors.

Emma passed the table her brother had just left. Faro. She swallowed a groan even as she noticed several men giving her sympathetic looks. Pride lifted her chin even as she gave them a cool smile. Bertram must be losing.

She reached the doors and heard the two men's voices raised in anger. She stopped. She should go outside immediately and stop them before they did anything more than shout at each other. Heaven only knew she didn't want another duel. Charles still wasn't completely healed.

She glanced around. Several people watched her, but looked away when she saw them. No one was close enough to hear what was being said outside—except her. She stepped forward, only to stop when she heard Bertram.

'I should call you out for what you just did,' Bertram sputtered in fury.

'Then do so. You just lost a sum you can't pay back.' Charles's voice was low and cold.

Emma's shoulders slumped. When would it end? The energy that had propelled her to the door evaporated. She stood as though rooted.

'It is none of your business.' Bertram's voice held an ugly note.

'I intend to make it my business. This time I will do a better job of ensuring that you cannot continue to gamble recklessly with no regard for anyone else.'

'Such as Amy?' Bertram's tone was a sneer. 'Or is it Emma now? But it doesn't matter which one, it is all the same. Attention from you does neither of them any good.'

'Changing the subject, Stockton?' Charles's tone was ominous.

'Warning you away from my sisters.'

'Just as you did with your previous challenge?' Silky smooth, Charles's tone dripped derision.

Emma wondered if he was trying to provoke Bertram into another challenge. If so, he was going about it the right way. At the moment, she thought she could easily allow Charles to meet Bertram.

'Don't think I won't.' Bertram's boastful voice carried.

Charles's laugh was cruel and hard. 'I doubt you will be any more successful a second time than you were the first.'

'I hit you!' Bertram boasted. 'It is more than you can claim.'

'True, but then I didn't have a grudge with you. You were and still are merely an irritant.'

Emma gasped. Charles was being deliberately provocative.

'My problem with you,' Bertram sputtered in his fury, 'is that you won't leave my sisters alone.'

'You are a weak man and a fool.' Cream and chocolate couldn't have been smoother than Charles's voice as he delivered that volley.

'I gamble to win enough to pay off my debts.'

'Don't be stupider than you already are, Stockton.' Contempt dripped from the words. 'You gamble because you are addicted to it. Nothing else.'

'You know nothing about it!'

'More than you think.' Charles's voice was bitter. 'And every time you sit down to a game of chance, you make it more difficult for your sisters to find husbands. Soon no man will be able to afford to show interest in them.'

'You have gone too far now.' Emma heard the sound of skin

on skin and realised Bertram had slapped Charles. 'What weapon will you choose this time?'

A heavy thud was the answer, followed by a yelp from Bertram. Belatedly, Emma rushed onto the parapet to see Bertram sprawled on his back, one hand at his mouth. The full moon showed blood on his lip.

'That is what I choose, Stockton.' Charles towered over her brother. 'I have had enough of your whining and disregard for others. I got you invited to this party. I can have you thrown out just as easily if you don't stop gambling.' Charles's voice was flat and carried conviction.

Emma had no doubt Lady Johnstone would do exactly as Charles wanted. He was her godson and Bertram was an uninvited guest who had been allowed to stay. She wondered how much more shame and debt Bertram would heap on their family.

She stepped up. 'Charles. Bertram. How dare you fight out here like two schoolboys?'

They both turned to her. Bertram looked sullen as he scrambled to his feet. Charles looked annoyed.

'Impeccable timing,' Charles drawled.

She glared at him before turning to scowl at her brother. 'Bertram, you are like a little boy. Constantly doing as you ought not. I am tired of it. If Charles, uh, Mr Hawthorne, doesn't prevail upon Lady Johnstone to ask you to leave I will do so myself. First thing tomorrow I am writing to Papa and telling him that you continue to gamble and will ruin our last chance to find a husband for Amy.'

Bertram pulled a handkerchief from his pocket and dabbed at his lower lip, not meeting her look. 'So you are siding with this scoundrel against your own flesh.'

She wanted to hit her brother in frustration. 'No, I am doing what I should have done before. I know Papa doesn't care if you gamble everything away—or everything he hasn't already lost—but I doubt he will be pleased to hear that you are ruining our last chance by doing so here.'

Saying the words out loud made the situation even more

real than just thinking about it. Until now, she hadn't fully realised how much hope she had pinned to this house party. Her palms dampened and she wanted to run from the situation, but knew it would do no good. Something had to be done. She could not allow Bertram to stay if he was going to continue his old ways while here.

For the first time, the defiance left Bertram. 'I will leave if you don't write to Papa.'

She shook her head, amazed he thought he could bargain with her about this. 'No. You will leave, and I will tell Papa. You need to go home and think about what you have been doing, not skulk off to London and continue this ruinous behaviour. It is not just yourself you destroy.'

'Hear, hear,' Charles's admiring voice said. 'That is the first time I have heard you stand up to anyone but Amy and me.'

She rounded on him. 'As for you…' Words failed her. What could she say to him? He was right and they both knew it.

'Yes…?' He drew the word out, one brow lifted, daring her to say her worst.

She turned back to Bertram, a problem she could solve now. 'I want you gone to Hopewell tomorrow.'

'You can't order me around.' He fastidiously folded his handkerchief and held it between his thumb and forefinger. 'I will leave here, but I will go where I please.'

'Then I will write to Papa and tell him Amy and I are coming home early because of your unacceptable behaviour, and just when it appears that a young man is interested in Amy and that she returns his regard. Papa will not like that at all.'

A hunted look entered Bertram's eyes, but he said nothing. Still holding his bloodied handkerchief between finger and thumb, he stalked down the steps leading to the dark garden. In seconds he disappeared.

'Bravo, Emma. You were magnificent.' Charles's voice held admiration.

Emma focused on him. 'False flattery won't achieve anything.'

He stiffened. 'It wasn't false.'

'Huh! I find that hard to believe. But either way, it is immaterial.' Only a small traitorous part of her wanted to believe his flattery was real. She squashed the need.

'I don't think it is. You stood up to him for the first time. Now maybe he will start to mend his ways. And if he doesn't, it is still not your problem.' He took a step toward her, stopped when she stared him down. 'Perhaps things will be easier for you. Young Chevalier might even offer for Amy.'

Exasperation ran along her emotions like a razor. 'If you haven't ruined her with your blatant attentions!'

He stepped back, his eyes hooded. 'Oh, I doubt very much that my attentions have hurt Amy where that young buck is concerned.'

'Only with all the others.' The words were out before she thought. They hung in the air, their falseness obvious. It was Bertram who had hurt Amy's chances, not Charles Hawthorne.

'I very much doubt that. It is your father and brother's reckless disregard for anything but their own addiction that is hurting Amy. And you.'

Shame and fury made an explosive combination. His honesty after her false accusation of him was too much. Emma slapped him.

'Oh, my gosh!' She stumbled back until the stone balustrade stopped her. One hand went to her mouth. 'I am so sorry. I never…'

Words were beyond her. She turned and fled back through the lit rooms, up the stairs and into her bedchamber.

What had she done? She had lost her temper and hit someone who had only been telling her the truth. She flung herself onto the bed, one arm across her eyes and refused to cry. No matter how awful she felt at this moment. No matter how bad the future looked. She was not going to cry. It would do no good.

She also had to find Charles Hawthorne and apologise to him properly. She should have never slapped him. Never. No matter what he said or that it scared her that he had the power to make her blood run hot and her common sense go on holiday.

Lately, it seemed no matter where she went or what she did or what she told herself, he was always involved. He was a bittersweet complication that one moment she wanted to do away with and the next she wanted never to go away.

What a mess.

Charles stayed on the veranda until he was certain the mark he knew Emma's hand had made on his cheek was gone. There was enough gossip about the Stocktons. His dragging Bertram outside had been ill-advised, but he had seen no other way to make the man stop losing large sums of money as though they were nothing.

He finally sauntered into the brightly lit room where games of chance were still being played. He smiled at several of the men, but thought about Emma. She was fighting a losing battle with Bertram's addiction. He knew.

The next afternoon Emma dressed carefully in the lavender half-mourning gown that complemented her complexion. She pulled a few strands of hair free from her topknot and let them drift around her face. She was pale as a ghost. She pinched colour into her cheeks.

She began to shake, starting at her toes. Her lips trembled as though she would cry—or scream.

Her palms moistened and she rubbed them together, not wanting to take the chance of staining her skirts. Her eyes were suspiciously bright. Not because of excitement, she told herself, but because of fear.

What if he turned her down?

'Are you feeling poorly?' Betty's voice came from a corner of the room. Emma had forgotten the old retainer was still here.

'I am fine, Betty. Perhaps too much sun this morning.'

'That would explain the flush,' the older woman said dryly.

Emma suspected Betty knew something was about to happen. But she was not going to tell anyone her plan. If he refused, she would be mortified. If he accepted, she would be ruined—damaged goods.

But she was not on the Marriage Mart, so it wouldn't matter to anyone but her. And she wanted this. One memory outside of time to remember for the rest of her life.

One last look and she swept from the room without looking at Betty. She didn't want to see the expression on the maid's face. She sped past Amy's room, refusing to consider what Amy would say or do if she found out. With luck and discretion, no one but she and Charles Hawthorne would ever know about this.

Reaching the ground floor, she started methodically going from one room to the other. If he was out hunting or riding the area, she would have to wait until after dinner. Nervous anticipation sped her footsteps.

An hour later, she accepted defeat. Disappointment made her move sluggishly. She had been emotionally prepared to approach him. Waiting until this evening, until after dinner in all likeliness, increased her anxiety a thousandfold.

And what if she couldn't speak to him in private? She did not intend to proposition him in a room where there were other people, no matter how far away those people might be. She wanted utter, complete, absolute privacy.

Admitting defeat for the moment, she dragged her feet to the small arbor where just yesterday morning she had stood with Charles Hawthorne while he lectured her on Bertram and Amy. If only she had known then.

She sat on the edge of the loveseat, her nerves too tight for her to relax fully. Her fingers clenched and unclenched in her lap as she rehearsed what she would say. *I want to be your mistress.* She shook her head. She sighed and rubbed her temples.

Her head ached with a vengeance.

Should she ask please? Should she act as though there was no doubt he would agree? What if he said no? Or should she run and burrow into the bedcovers and forget this wild plan?

If he said no, she would be mortified. She had never thought herself a beautiful or alluring woman, but she had to admit Charles Hawthorne's blatant pursuit of her these last days made her feel attractive. It would hurt more than she cared to admit to anyone, even herself, if he refused her offer.

What if he accepted her offer? Her toes curled at the possibilities. Her fingers twiddled in her lap and she stared at nothing, wondering what it would be like to do *that*. She had never much considered it when engaged to Charles's brother, but now she found herself intrigued to the point of wishing she had a fan to cool herself. It must be powerful for men to pay women like Harriette Wilson large sums of money to procure her favours.

'Miss Stockton?' Mr Helmsley's deep voice intruded.

She jumped to her feet, and her heart skipped a beat. Not only was she nearly hysterical with nerves, she was now keyed up and excited about what happened between a man and a woman.

'Mr Helmsley.' Her voice was breathless and a little husky. 'I didn't hear you.'

He smiled kindly at her. 'You were deep in thought and from the look on your face, it was pleasurable.'

Emma didn't think she could be more uncomfortable than she had been, but his words rushed the blood to her face. She waved her hand in an effort to seem nonchalant. 'Oh, it was nothing.'

'Then may I hope you have a moment to speak with me?' Admiration lit his brown eyes.

Apprehension twisted her stomach. Her unease increased, but she couldn't tell him no. He might be here to speak about anything. She remained standing, not liking the sense of vulnerability his towering over her caused.

'Of course I have time, Mr Helmsley.'

He stepped closer. 'Will you be seated?' He took out his handkerchief and cleaned the stone bench she had sprung from.

She watched him and wished she had made up an excuse. After his taking the trouble to wipe the seat, she felt compelled to sit. He sat beside her with just enough space between them so their thighs didn't touch, although his right shoulder brushed her left shoulder.

She felt the discomfort of having someone too close. There were no sparks, no heat, no uncanny awareness. Even his scent of pine seemed to fade into nothing. She sighed in regret.

He cleared his throat, and it was obvious what he wanted to say was important to him. 'Miss Stockton, I know we have not known each other long.'

She gave him a wan smile. 'Several days.'

'Yes.' He took her hand that she had braced on the bench. She gently pulled it away and he allowed her. 'But I have something I would like to say to you—'

Dismay held her tongue. She had thought he might find her interesting but she had not expected a potential offer. Not this soon.

He took her silence as a void to be filled. 'I am not a wealthy man.' His jaw twitched and his cheeks reddened. 'I know the situation your brother is in, and I cannot help with that. But I am comfortably off, and I could provide you with a good life.' He took a deep breath, looking like a man who struggled for every word. 'And I would cherish you.'

She felt miserable. Guilt at allowing him to expose himself like this mingled with disappointment that she felt nothing. She could not give Mr Helmsley the answer he wanted.

'I am very flattered, Mr Helmsley, that you see me in that light.' She angled to look at him and to put distance between their bodies. 'But I am not able to accept. You deserve a woman who will love you or at the very least care deeply. I do not feel I am she.' She trailed off, not sure what to say next. She felt awful.

For a moment he looked stricken before he cleared his countenance. 'I thank you for your honesty, Miss Stockton. I have been importunate and would be ashamed if I weren't so sincere in my admiration.' She said nothing. He spoke into the void, 'I will leave you.' He made her an elegant leg and left.

She watched him go, his footsteps fading as distance parted them. The realisation of just seconds before buffeted her.

She would prefer to be a governess than married to a man she didn't love because she could not have the man she loved. Heaven help her, she loved Charles Hawthorne and he cared nothing for her.

What a fool she was. What a helpless fool.

Hysterical laughter bubbled up from her throat followed by tears of doubt and fear. He did not love her. He would never love her.

She buried her face in her hands.

It seemed only seconds later that footsteps crunching on gravel intruded on her shocked dismay. Emma dropped her hands and sat straighter, hoping whoever was coming her way would pass by on the other side of the hedge and not see her.

She sensed him before she saw him.

Charles Hawthorne turned the corner that led him right to her. She forced herself to smile past the anxiety that had increased to a nearly unbearable degree. Now was her chance to apologise to him, but she was still dazed by the realisation that she loved him.

'Miss Stockton.' He stopped a distance away and studied her. 'Are you unwell?'

Hysterical laughter bubbled up her throat. Her lips trembled in spite of her effort to control herself. 'Of course.'

'Have you been in the sun too long?' He persisted, moving closer.

She shook her head, hoping her voice wouldn't show she had been crying. 'I have just arrived here. I have been looking for you.'

He raised one brow. 'You have?'

She nodded. 'I…I want to apologise for my behaviour last night. It was uncalled for. You did me a service. I should not have repaid it by slapping you.'

He was too close. His musky scent moved over her like a caress. She stood and edged around the stone bench, even as she told herself to stay put.

'You are telling me you're sorry?'

Exasperation began to ease some of her sensual awareness of him. 'I believe that is what I just said—Charles.'

He smiled and the breath left her. She wanted him so much. No, she told herself. He was everything she didn't want in a man. Arrogant. Selfish. Egotistical.

Yet her heart beat wildly because he was near her.

A look of utter disbelief contorted his features. 'You apologised and you used my first name.'

She licked dry lips and made her fingers stop smoothing her skirt. 'Yes. Neither was easy.'

'I can believe that.' He moved closer until only the bench separated them. His eyes were dark, and there was a hint of shadow on his lean jaw.

She shivered. 'I was, um, looking for you.'

He raised one brow. 'In the garden?'

His attempt at humour eased some of her nerves. 'Well, not here. I looked in the house earlier. I ended up here after being unable to find you.'

He gave her his devilish grin. 'Shall we consider this arbour our trysting spot?'

She blinked. He had hit exactly on what she had tried to do. Did he know what she wanted? Keeping her voice light, when her emotions felt riotous, she said, 'Perhaps we should. We seem to end up here enough.'

The smile dropped from his face, replaced by intent hunger as he took her hands and led her around the bench until she was standing next to him. 'Yes, we do.'

She stared spellbound at him. The love she'd just realised mingled in her heart with the knowledge that when they left this house party they would likely never see each other again. Suddenly, Emma wanted more than the kisses they'd shared and the bickering to remember him by.

She wanted so much more. A thrill of danger, excitement, desire, raced through her.

'Will you…' Heat engulfed her, but she said the words, forcing them from a chest grown suddenly tight. 'Will you make love to me? Please?'

His hands released her so he could wrap his arms around her and pull her flush to his body. But even as he held her, his face showed his astonishment. 'Am I hearing right?'

She looked up at him. 'I know I am not skilled, as Miss Wilson, but I will do my best.' The temerity in her tone mortified her, but she refused to look away from the dark emotions reflected in his eyes. She wanted this one last memory of him to keep her the rest of her life.

'I will teach you to please me.'

She gulped. 'Then you will make love to me?'

'Now.' His voice was gruff and commanding.

She closed her eyes, wondering what he would do and being unable to watch him when he did it. His mouth took hers and she gasped, her lips opening. His tongue darted in and flicked at hers.

She tensed.

His hands moved to knead her shoulders, moving down her spine. He worked her tight muscles even as his mouth devoured her. She relaxed into him.

The buttons on his coat pressed into her breasts. The hard length of his loins pressed into the soft swell of her stomach. Moist warmth filled her as she realised he was aroused just by kissing her. A sense of power filled her and for the first time in her life, she felt giddy.

She pressed against him and moved her hips, enjoying the sensation of his maleness. He broke the kiss and pushed her away. She jumped, mortification staining her cheeks.

'What did I do?'

He stared at her. 'Where did you learn that?'

Confused, she frowned. 'Learn what?'

'To move like that?'

'I...I just...It seemed right. Felt good,' she whispered, wishing the ground would open and swallow her. 'I shouldn't have done anything.'

'You did nothing wrong. You surprised me. I hadn't expected you to be so passionate.' He touched her mouth gently with one finger. 'Your lips are swollen from my kiss.'

Triumph lit his face. She wondered how serious a mistake she was making. A warm breeze wafted through the wall of roses surrounding them. She shivered.

'Tonight,' he murmured. 'I will come to you tonight.'

She nodded, unable to speak. Afraid of what might come out. She was scared and excited and eager to experience more of the sensual possibilities his kiss and caress had only hinted at.

'Let me escort you back to the house.'

He held out his arm. Gingerly, wondering if she should change her mind and run before it was too late, she rested the tips of her fingers on him.

Never would she have imagined this.

Chapter Eighteen

Emma pressed her lips tightly together to stop them from trembling. The last thing she wanted was for Betty to question her. As it was, it took all her determination not to tell the old retainer to hurry undoing the hooks and tabs that held Emma's evening dress on. An eternity passed before Betty eased the gown's sleeves over Emma's shoulders. The pale lavender silk fell to the floor and puddled like a rare orchid. Next was her light corset, followed by her chemise.

Emma wondered if she should leave her stockings on. Charles had seemed fascinated by them the one day she'd held him captive.

Betty bent to roll down the pink silk garters. Emma let her. If she kept the stockings on Betty would wonder, and the last thing Emma needed was for anyone—Betty included—to know Charles was coming tonight.

Heat pooled in Emma's stomach at the thought, followed immediately by cold hands and fear that she would be inadequate. He was experienced in all things pertaining to a man and a woman. She was ignorant.

Moving like a wooden puppet, Emma lifted one foot and then the other as Betty took the stockings off. Unable to take more, Emma said, 'Thank you, Betty. That will be all.'

Betty stood up, leaning backwards to knead the crick in the lower part of her spine. 'But you aren't dressed for bed.'

Emma suppressed a shiver of fear—anticipation? 'I am perfectly capable of pulling my nightgown over my head. I am going to read.'

Betty cocked her head to one side, and Emma knew the servant sensed something was not right. All the maid said was, 'Yes, miss.'

Emma stood as though rooted to the spot while Betty left. The faithful retainer closed the door softly. Emma closed her eyes and willed her body to stop shaking.

What was going to happen tonight would forever change who she was. No one but she and Charles would know about it—with luck—but that would not alter what their lovemaking would do to her.

She sat on the nearby chair, thankful it was close. Her legs felt like jelly, and she did not think she could walk if she had to. Naked, since she did not wear the pantaloons favoured by the faster set, she leaned back into the soft embrace of the chintz-covered cushions.

What would it feel like to have a man kiss her and…do other things? Her skin flushed. A light sheen of moisture covered her body.

It was an effort of will to stand up and retrieve her stockings and garters. Careful not to puncture the finely woven stockings, she pulled each one up her calves and over her knees then secured them with the pink satin garters with their lavender rosettes. The garters had come from Mama.

Mama.

Emma pushed that thought from her mind. Mama would not approve of what she intended to do. But Mama was gone, and she wanted more from her life than the loneliness that lay ahead. She intended to store Charles's lovemaking in her heart and take the memory out when the future nights were cold and bereft. It wasn't much, but it would be hers.

Emma went to the bed where her lawn and lace nightgown

lay. She took a deep breath and pulled the delicate garment over her head. She felt as though by donning the nearly transparent gown, she had committed herself to this choice.

She looked at herself in the mirror. Her hair hung to the small of her back, the red highlights nearly golden in the candle light. With her breasts pushing against the light fabric and the *V* of her thighs visible, she looked wanton.

Her expression, however, was that of a schoolgirl caught doing something wrong. She felt like one, too.

Suddenly overwhelmed with heat, she moved to the window and threw open the glass barriers to let in the cool evening air. The soft caress of breeze eased some of her warmth but created a sense of being intimately touched as the wind penetrated the thin material of her gown.

Her breasts ached and her nipples tightened. Her stomach clenched in pleasure as the secret, moist area of her womanhood readied itself for Charles's touch.

Confused and aroused simultaneously, Emma turned back to her room and flung herself across her bed. She didn't know who she was anymore or what she wanted.

Perhaps it was the extra wine she had drank at dinner, the wine Charles had encouraged her to consume. Perhaps it was her sensuality finally asserting itself. Or both.

A soft knock on the door made her bolt upright like a rabbit caught in the sights of a poacher. Her breathing turned shallow. Her heart pounded.

On legs that threatened to buckle beneath her, she moved as though in a dream to the door. She twisted the handle and inched the heavy wooden barrier open.

He stood in the light of the hall candles, fully clothed and looking as he had when she'd left the party nearly an hour ago. Slowly, wondering if she would have the strength to go through with what they intended, she pulled the heavy wooden barrier open.

He slipped inside. She closed the door.

His smile was lopsided, almost shy. But his gaze was bold

and hot as he looked her over. He reached out and ran one palm down the length of her hair, pulling her closer so he could skim the silken strands to their end where they curled over her bottom. He kept his hand on her, cupping her and pulling her toward him.

'Emma,' he murmured seconds before his lips touched hers.

She leaned into him, all else forgotten but the feel of his flesh on hers. She might be naked for what little barrier her gown provided. Her nipples rubbed against the stiffness of his evening jacket, and her stomach pressed into one of the buttons that kept him clothed. His palm was hot on her flesh as he cupped her against his loins.

And his mouth.

His lips moved over hers like a virtuoso on a rare instrument. His tongue tempted and retreated, inviting her to greater pleasure—but at her pace, not his.

Her entire body felt alive like never before.

She opened her lips to him. He entered. She melted against him, no longer thinking of anything but the sensations he created in her.

He pulled away, and she swallowed the whimper in her throat caused by the separation. 'Emma,' he said, his voice low and hoarse. 'Emma.'

She stared up at him through eyes that seemed to see nothing but him. It was as though he had drugged her with his touch and with his kiss.

Slowly, his gaze never leaving her face, he bent down and caught her gown. He gave her a chance to tell him no. When she said nothing he gently lifted the filmy garment from her and let it fall.

She stood before him, naked except for her stockings.

He gulped, his attention moving over her, stroking every portion of her into a blaze. He stopped at her thighs where the garters held her stockings.

In a voice so husky it was barely understandable, he said, 'I have dreamt of this.'

Power such as she had never felt flowed over her. To be able to arouse a man such as him with nothing but the sight of her body. Some of her fear dissipated as she basked in his admiration.

'Emma.' He whispered her name once more, making it sound like a promise as he bent down and swept her into his arms. In three swift strides he was at the bed and laying her gently onto the coverlet.

Eyes wide, body aching, she watched him study her as she lay nearly naked, more vulnerable than she had ever been in her life. His eyes were dark and hungry, yet there was a gentle tenderness on his face that she had never seen before. That expression eased the tension that had held her in a vise since asking to make love with him. She finally relaxed and held her arms up to him.

Charles looked down at Emma Stockton as she lay on her bed, her lovely body no longer hidden by clothing. Just the sight of her stocking legs made him so hard he knew that if he didn't have her tonight he would hurt later. The soft swell of her breast and the hard peach peaks of her nipples increased his ache. He wanted her like he had never wanted another woman. Ever.

'Charles?' Emma watched him study her body and knew her skin was as red as her hair. She had not thought he would examine her. Apprehension and a dash of irritation mixed with the desire raging through her. 'Are you looking at me for a reason?'

He smiled, his rakish, devil-may-care smile that turned her knees to molasses. 'I'm memorising you. You're beautiful.'

She blushed in earnest. Her fingers plucked at the coverlet beneath her. The coverlet didn't budge. In spite of his compliment or because of it, she found herself wanting to cover up. She closed her eyes for a second, telling herself to be bold.

'Are you joining me?' she finally said, looking at him. She

ran her gaze down his body as she had so often wanted to but not done because a lady didn't look at a gentleman in that way.

His smile intensified. 'Yes.'

Slowly, carefully, as though he thought she might take a fright, he shrugged out of his jacket and carelessly tossed it in the direction of the chair. Next he untied his cravat. His attention never left her.

Emma shivered in anticipation as his fingers started undoing the buttons of his shirt. When he pulled his arms out of the shirt and threw it on the coat, she took a deep breath. His chest was broad and muscular. Black hairs spread from one nipple to the next before arrowing to the band of his pantaloons. A bulge showed beneath the fine ebony material and she was woman enough to know he wanted her.

He fumbled undoing his pantaloons and his mouth twisted into a wry grin. 'I'm thinking of other things to do with my fingers besides undress.'

His bold words excited her even as they heightened her embarrassment. When he finally stood naked before her, she licked suddenly dry lips. He was magnificent.

The firelight limned the strong lines of his hips and thighs and threw his shoulders into stark relief.

'Emma,' he breathed her name before lying beside her.

He was fire and ice to her where they touched. Instinctively she moved closer so that her breasts pressed his chest and her stomach pressed the length of his arousal. She closed her eyes and allowed the sensations to engulf her.

He chuckled at her wanton pleasure. 'I knew you would be like this.'

His fingers stroked her neck, down her shoulder and along her ribs. Her breathing matched his caresses. When his rough palm cupped her breast, she felt as though her insides melted.

Then he kissed her and stole her breath away. His tongue slid between her teeth and her mind swirled away into a haze of passion.

Her fingers found his shoulders and kneaded the muscles, her nails digging into his skin. Her hips moved against the hard length of his arousal and she heard him gasp. A smile of satisfaction parted her lips, allowing him better access to her.

When his hand slipped away from her breast, she whimpered in protest only to change to a moan of surprise and delight as his fingers slid along the skin of her inner thigh. He nudged a knee between her legs, parting her to slip a finger along her soft folds.

Shock and pleasure held her motionless as he teased her. Emma had never felt anything like this; had never imagined feelings like this existed. Never in her life had she thought a man would touch a woman the way he touched her now.

Fierce gladness pierced her. 'Thank you,' she whispered when his lips lifted from hers. 'Thank you, Charles Hawthorne, for giving me this.'

He lifted onto one elbow and looked down at her in the dim, golden light provided by the fire. 'Thank you, Emma, for giving yourself to me.'

Shyness moved over her at the intimacy in his gaze. For some reason, having him look into her eyes as though he could see to her very soul was more revealing than anything he could see of her body. Not even his fingers moving rhythmically inside her dispelled her sense that his gaze was more penetrating than any body part could ever be.

He shifted her to her back and moved over her. 'Open for me,' he murmured against the warm skin of her neck.

Gazing into his eyes, she parted her legs and felt him settle so that his loins met hers. His manhood pressed the moist folds of her skin and slowly entered. A brief pain shocked her and she gasped, but it was quickly gone in his suddenly fierce thrust.

She felt full to bursting.

Instinctively her hips moved to match his rhythm. It was as though they were meant to be lovers so easily did they meld.

Whimpers of delight fell from her lips until he bent his

head to catch her pleasure with his mouth. He plundered her in all the ways possible as he took her to climax.

Emma's world shattered as her body pulsated in a pattern as old as the world. She thought she would splinter apart.

His moans of release told her she wasn't alone.

Long minutes later, he gathered her into his arms and kissed her on the chin, the nose, the mouth, as he slid from the slick tightness of her body. Emma let her head fall to rest on his shoulder as she enjoyed the gentle smoothing of his palm along the ridge of her back and flank.

'Thank you, Emma.' He stroked her thick red hair back from the heat of her forehead. 'I have never had such pleasure.'

She smiled sleepily, taking immense satisfaction in the feel of him against her and the meaning of his words. 'I am glad you gave me this gift,' she murmured.

He laughed gently. 'Silly, Emma. It is the man who is always glad the woman allows him to make love to her.'

She kissed the damp skin of his chest, delighting in the taste of salt and the smell of musk. 'I will treasure this memory for the rest of my life.'

He stiffened as though her words had upset him. She lifted her head and gazed at him. His eyes were slumbering and heavy-lidded. His mouth was full and wickedly curved, but he didn't smile.

'Have I said something wrong?' she finally asked when he didn't speak.

'No.' He disengaged himself from her arms and set her aside. 'No, you said nothing wrong, Emma. But the night grows shorter and it is best that no one know what we have done.'

She nodded, knowing he was right. But when he shifted from the bed, she felt cold and bereft. She clamped her lips shut to keep from begging him to return to her side. He would not appreciate her clinging to him, particularly now.

He stayed beside her long enough to pull the covers over her. 'Sleep, Emma. You will find it deep after what we just enjoyed.'

But she could not close her eyes while he was with her. She

atched him dress, intrigued by the intricacies of male clothing.
oo soon he was clothed. She sighed in disappointment.

'You are beautiful,' she told him softly without thinking
hat she said.

He came back to her side and touched her cheek briefly
ith one forefinger. 'Thank you, Emma. But you are the true
eauty here.'

He was gone from the room before she could think of
omething to say. A sigh escaped her. She felt as though some
ecision had been reached, but she didn't know what. Then
leep claimed her love-tired limbs.

Charles slipped quietly from the room. The last thing he
anted was to make a sound and let someone know where he
ad spent the last hour. He did not want to ruin her reputation.

Minutes later, he slipped into his bedchamber.

'Late, Guv',' Stoner said from the chair by the fire where
e'd been waiting.

Charles scowled. 'I thought I told you not to wait up for
ae. Don't you ever do as you're told?'

Stoner shook his head, his massive shoulders swinging
rom side to side. 'You're more addled than normal. If I'd
one below stairs before enough time 'ad elapsed after you
:ft the party, there'd be talk about why you 'adn't needed
our valet.'

Charles snorted. 'Gossip.'

'Well, that's what this all seems about. That and match-
aaking and affairs and such.' Disgust curled Stoner's lip.
More things goin' on 'ere in a week than I seen in London
a a month.' He stepped forward to help ease off Charles's coat
efore the buttons popped off. 'Thought you was addin' to the
un. But yer don look like yer did.'

Charles yanked his arms from the sleeves and then started
pping at his cravat. He was in a strange mood. He should
:el mellow and satisfied instead of tighter than a top and won-
ering why he had allowed his body to rule his judgement.

He slumped into a nearby chair.

This was Emma whom he'd wanted the second he saw her standing by his brother, smiling coolly at the world. He finally understood that from that instant, his only goal had been to get beneath the outer façade of ice she wore like armour.

He had succeeded. But now what?

He stood and yanked his coat off and threw it on the nearest chair. He ripped his shirt, the buttons popping.

'Don't take yer anger out on yer clothes, Guv'.' Stoner tsked, the sound out of place coming from a man of his bulk. 'Ain't like you brought a lot. We was only stayin' a couple o days.'

'And we've been here a week.' Charles yanked his shirt off and moved closer to the fire. 'I know. I know.' He stared into the flames, seeing Emma's fiery hair spread out on the pillow beckoning him to caress her. He kicked the grate.

He didn't want to marry, yet he'd made love to her. He didn't want to be in love, either. But he didn't want to see her become a governess and raise other women's children for the rest of her life. He wanted her to have more experiences like tonight to cherish—not just this one time.

He cursed. 'We're leaving for Cloudchaser tomorrow.'

Stoner hung up Charles's jacket, and his voice came muffled from the wardrobe. 'Better to stay and see it through, if you ask me.'

'I'm not asking you.'

'Right.'

'You can go now, Stoner.' Charles flung himself into the nearest chair. 'I can get myself undressed from here. I have no wish to listen to you further. I will be up early and expect you to follow me after you pack up.'

'Always was too stubborn fer yer own good, Guv'.' Stoner eyed his employer. 'And yer never did know what was good fer ya until it was rammed down yer throat.'

Charles gave him a look that would have shrivelled anyone else. The large man met him head on. 'Good night.'

Charles fell back into the chair's cushions. He still didn't understand what had happened between him and Emma. Surely he didn't love her and he knew she couldn't love him. She had been clear on that point from the beginning.

He let his head drop back and his eyes close. What had started out as a way to ease his boredom was now more complicated than he wanted.

He was not in the market for a wife, even if he had realised a thousand times over that he had wanted her the moment he saw her on George's arm. He did not want a wife.

Emma woke with the sun on her face. Sometime in the middle of the night, she must have put on her nightgown. She shifted and stifled a moan as her thighs twinged. She made a face.

'Are you ailing?' Betty's concerned voice asked.

Emma propped herself on her elbows and looked around. Everything looked the same as it had yesterday morning. It was she who was different. She was experienced. A fallen woman.

The thought should have bothered her, and perhaps it would later, but for the moment she relished the memory of the pleasure Charles had given her. She even anticipated repeating the experience before the house party ended.

She closed her eyes and laughed. She was a glutton.

'Are you sure you aren't ailing?' Betty's worried voice intruded on Emma's pleasant thoughts.

'I am fine, Betty.' She opened her eyes to see the older woman looking askance at her.

'You look different.'

Betty's barely audible words sent a frisson of unease down Emma's spine. Surely she didn't look that different. The last thing she needed was for someone to find out. That would ruin her reputation—

She stopped in the act of swinging her legs out of bed. Oh, no, what if someone did find out? It would not only ruin her, it would ruin Amy's chances.

She sank back onto the pillows. Why hadn't she thought

of that? And what would happen when she saw Charles Hawthorne today? Would her face give her away?

The chamber door banged open. 'Em, you won't believe what has happened.' Amy came in like a whirlwind, her blond hair in disarray. 'Charles Hawthorne left.' She spread her arms wide. 'Just like that. He walked out the front door without a goodbye or anything. The next thing, I saw him riding out as fast as his horse could go.'

Emma turned her head away, not wanting Amy to see the effect the news had on her. He had made love to her last night and left today without a word. Her humiliation was complete. Her pain something she would have to bear with a smile.

'Em,' Amy said, concern entering her voice. 'Are you sick, Em?'

Emma took several deep breaths and willed herself not to cry. She was not a watering pot. She was not. 'I just have a slight headache, Amy. Betty, could you go fetch me a hot chocolate? That will help.'

After the maid left, Amy sat on the edge of the bed so Emma had to look at her. 'You look like you just lost… Like you did after Mama died.'

Trust Amy to speak the blunt truth. 'I had a bad night's sleep, Amy. That is all.'

Contrition clouded Amy's blue eyes. 'Oh, I am so sorry, Em.'

Exhaustion mingled with Emma's despair. She took one of Amy's hands and squeezed it. 'I will be fine when I have had my breakfast and rested a little more. I think I had more wine than I should have last night.'

Amy laughed. 'You positively glowed last night, Em. I thought you would burst into flames.'

Emma's smile was rueful. 'I'm sure I did. But that was yesterday and this is today.' She played with the coverlet on her bed. 'Is Charles Hawthorne gone for good?' She didn't look at Amy.

'I don't know. Seems to be. His servant is packing, or so Betty says.' Amy fell silent. 'I knew you were more interested in him than you would admit.'

'Pshaw!' Emma couldn't meet Amy's eyes. 'Of course I wasn't.'

In a thoughtful voice, Amy said, 'I begin to think he was really interested in you, and I was the means he used to further his pursuit. He always seemed to needle you.'

'He certainly did that!' Asperity lent Emma some life.

'Em—' Amy's voice was serious '—are you interested in him?'

'Of course not. How could I be interested in a rake who pursued you with no thought for the consequences? Besides, he might be wealthy from trade but I doubt he has enough money to satisfy Papa.'

'You could like him—the man.' Amy spoke softly. 'He is handsome and fun and smart. Very stylish.'

Emma snorted. 'He is very full of himself, you mean.'

'That, too.' Amy chuckled then sobered. 'Do you care for him?'

Emma sighed. 'Why do you persist in asking?'

'Because I think you might, and I think he is interested in you.' Amy stood and looked down at her older sister. 'It would be a shame for you to miss out on a relationship that might bring you happiness.'

Emma released the coverlet she had pleated and smoothed it on her lap. 'You are very fanciful this morning.'

'I don't think so.' Amy took Emma's hand and pulled it so Emma had to look at her. 'I think you care for him, and you are disappointed he has left just when it seemed he had decided to fix his interest with you.'

'Nothing of the sort.'

'I believe differently.' Amy released Emma's hand. 'Shall I ask Betty to find out where he has gone?'

'No.' Emma took a deep breath, dismayed she had nearly shouted the word. 'There is no need. You and I shall be leaving shortly. In fact, later today I will send an advertisement to *The Times* listing my qualifications to be a governess. Before you know it, I will be in service.'

'Oh, Em.' Sadness turned down Amy's mouth. 'If you will not go after Charles Hawthorne, you would do better to consider Mr Helmsley. You cannot tell me he has not approached you, for he asked me if I thought you were otherwise engaged.'

Emma flushed to the roots of her hair. 'He is far too bold. Nor is it any of his business. I gave him my answer.'

'But is it firm?' Compassion darkened Amy's blue eyes. 'He would suit you.'

Emma was amazed at Amy's growing maturity and compassion. 'He would, Amy, but he hasn't the means to pay off our family's gambling debts.'

'Pshaw!' Amy flipped her hands. 'Let me worry about that. You may marry where you choose.'

'No.' Emma's disappointment filled the one word. 'No, Amy. Mr Helmsley is a nice man, but I do not love him.'

'When did that matter?' Cynicism clouded Amy's normally sparkling eyes.

Emma gazed sadly at nothing. 'It shouldn't, but I feel that if I marry it should be for fortune or love. He brings neither. I shall likely be happier taking care of other people's children.' Melancholy weighed her down making her disgusted with herself. She pushed back the covers. 'It is time I was up and about.'

If Charles was well and truly gone, then so be it. Her heart would heal. Hearts always did.

Slipping from bed, she pulled on her robe. 'Are you waiting for me?' she asked Amy, who still stood near the bed.

Amy's face pinked. The sparkle returned to her eyes. 'I...I have something else to discuss with you.'

Emma raised one brow. 'Is this the real reason you came to my room?'

Amy's colour deepened. 'It was, until I heard that Charles Hawthorne was gone. But, yes, this is the main reason.'

'I take it Mr Hawthorne hasn't broken your heart.' Emma couldn't keep a hint of sarcasm from her tone. If only he hadn't broken hers.

Amy got redder still. 'No. It is…that is, there is another gentleman.'

'Really?' Emma sank into a chair by the fire.

Amy kneeled at Emma's feet. 'You will think me fickle, I know. Nor do I blame you.' She twisted her fingers. 'I made such a cake of myself over Mr Hawthorne.'

'Yes, you did.' Emma knew she should let Amy's last remark go, but she was not in the mood to be conciliatory.

'You didn't have to agree.' Amy's tone held a hint of indignation, but she knew all too well the chase she had led Emma. 'But I have met the most wonderful man.'

Emma resisted rolling her eyes. Now they were off on another month of pandemonium. She would have to mourn her own loss quickly.

'Who is he?'

Amy beamed. 'Mr Chevalier.' Shyly, she added, 'William.'

Nonplussed, Emma stared at her sister. 'Mr Chevalier? The young man here?'

Amy nodded her head.

Emma felt the onset of a headache. He could not have nearly the money they needed for Papa and Bertram's debts, but knowing love herself at long last, she was unwilling to force Amy to discourage the young man. 'Do you truly care for him?'

Amy nodded again. 'I know you likely think I don't know what I feel. I have been very forward with Mr Hawthorne.' She made a moue of perturbation. 'That is how I am.'

'True.' Emma saw tenderness in Amy's eyes and in the softness of her sister's lips. 'But perhaps this young man is the right one for you?'

'Oh, Em,' Amy grabbed Emma's hands and squeezed. 'He makes me happy. Even when I am in an awful mood over something, he makes me happy just by being with me. I…I can't explain it.'

Emma squeezed Amy's hands. She was not going to force her sister into a loveless marriage now that Amy had found someone she cared for. She had noted the two spent a great deal of time together, but had not given it more thought. She had been too immersed in her own feelings for Charles Hawthorne.

'Then you must do as your heart tells you.'

Despair moved over Amy's mobile face. 'But Papa will forbid it. I told William we must elope.'

Emma groaned. 'That would be the crowning achievement of a Season spent on the thin ice of respectability. Let me speak to Papa before you do anything that drastic.'

'Oh, Em, would you please? William doesn't want to elope. He says it is not the start he wants to his married life.' She dimpled. 'I thought it would be exciting.'

Amy might care for this young man, but she was still reckless Amy. Luckily it sounded as though Mr Chevalier might be a steadying influence on her.

Emma smiled. 'I must agree with Mr Chevalier and thank him for being so level-headed. Besides, I hear the drive to Gretna Green is very uncomfortable. You would far prefer to be married in a small church closer to home.'

'William would be, so that is good enough for me.'

Emma marvelled at Amy. 'You must truly care for him.'

'I do.'

'Then you shall have him, even if I have to stand over Papa while Mr Chevalier talks to him.' Although if their father absolutely forbade the marriage there was nothing she could do. Amy was underaged. Then it would have to be Gretna Green.

'Thank you.' Amy jumped up. 'I must go and tell William.'

'Right now?'

'He is waiting in the garden.'

'He knew you were coming to me?'

'Yes. He wants your blessing as my sister and my chaperone.'

Emma liked the young man more and more. 'Tell him you have it. Now we must work on Papa.'

After Amy left, Emma knew she needed to think of a plan to make Papa agree to Amy's marriage, but her heart wouldn't let her. She kept thinking of last night.

Grief washed over her. She had felt nothing when George

had taken up with Rose and later married her. If anything, it had been a relief to be out of an engagement she had only agreed to because of her father and brother's debts.

Now she felt devastated. It was as though the light had gone from her life. To have him leave without a word.

She dropped her head to her hands.

She loved him, she admitted to herself. She loved him with a reckless passion that had sent her into his arms, telling herself she did so from curiosity. Her lips twisted. Curiosity. It had been passionate love wanting to experience the unity of making love with the only man she had ever loved—the only man she ever would love.

Tears seeped through her fingers to dampen her gown. It seemed she was a watering pot after all.

Chapter Nineteen

Charles reached Cloudchaser after a ride of several hours. His housekeeper and butler met him at the door without a blink of surprise at his unannounced visit.

'Good day, Peterson.' Charles handed the butler his hat and riding gloves. 'Please don't make lunch, Mrs Harper. And I will go into the village for dinner.'

The butler bowed and the housekeeper curtseyed. They were used to his unconventional ways.

'Your room will be ready as soon as I can get clean sheets on the bed, Mr Hawthorne.' Mrs Harper looked eager to be about her business.

'Thank you,' Charles said and turned to go to his office.

The spacious octagon room he used for his accounting was also a well-stocked library. He had spent many pleasurable days here when his grandmother had been alive. She had left him this small estate so he would always have a means of providing for himself.

Then he had nearly lost it with his unchecked gambling. The memory brought back the sense of shame he had felt when he had finally come to his senses. His past was not a place he wished to revisit.

He sat behind the keyhole desk where he had often seen

is grandmother sit when writing letters. The swivel leather
hair she had used seemed to enfold him in the memory of
er presence.

Several hours later, he rose and stretched. 'Peterson,' he
alled. 'Have my horse saddled again.'

'Yes, sir,' the butler said from the doorway he had just reached.

Charles found riding in the clean, country air often helped
im think. He would tour his property and visit with the
enants while his mind worked.

An hour later, Charles reached the small village close to
is property. He dismounted at the Swan and Pitcher, tossing
shilling to the stable boy.

'See she gets oats with her hay and a good rubdown and
here will be more.'

The boy grinned, showing a hole where one of his front teeth
ad been. Charles knew Tom had lost it in a fight the year before.

Charles ducked his head to enter the tap room of the pub.
Candles and a fire made the dimly lit room smoky. He made
is way to the bar and ordered a pint of ale.

'Good to see you, sir,' said Johnny Carter, the bartender and
wner, as he pulled the drink. He handed it to Charles, who
miled as he took it. He drank it half down and wiped the foam
rom his mouth. 'It's good to be here, Johnny. I forget how much
etter your special ale is than that in London.'

Johnny grinned. He made the ale. 'Good reason to spend
nore time at your estate, sir.'

Charles laid a coin on the bar without replying. He smiled
nd moved to sit near a window and watch other patrons play
larts. The alcohol settled in his stomach with a mellowness
hat relaxed him. And he thought.

He had run away from her. He had made love to her and
eft her, scared of the emotions she evoked in him. He was a
oward. He had refused to call off his duel with her brother
ecause he didn't want to be known as a coward, and yet he
ad run from the feelings he had for her.

She didn't love him. Or did she? Would a woman like her

give herself to a man otherwise, no matter what reason sh
used? He began to think not.

Did he love her?

Could he live without her?

He had been gone from her for less than a day and alread
he was thinking of her. This wasn't like him at all. But the
the only thing he had done in the past months that was lik
him was to chase Amy for his own pleasure. And he ha
stopped that because it caused Emma too much trouble.

He realised she meant more to him than his own pleasur
Then she meant too much for him to walk away from her.

But would she accept him? He had to try.

Charles stood, leaving his glass still half full. He had to g
to London. He would need a hefty draught on his bank and th
would take time. He would have to liquidate some of his asset

Two days later, Emma and Amy took their leave of Lad
Johnstone. 'Thank you for having us,' Emma said.

'Please come again,' Lady Johnstone said. 'I imagine the ne
time Miss Amy will be Mrs Chevalier. I expect an invitation.

Amy blushed to the roots of her hair. William Chevalie
stood beside Amy and turned equally red. Two fair people
Two beautiful people who were meant for each other. Emm
intended to see that their happiness wasn't thrown away b
the greed of the men in her family.

They were going home to Hopewell to present Mr Cheva
lier to Papa. Emma hoped that by the time they arrived, sh
would have several answers waiting from her advertisemer
in *The Times* for a governess position.

Mr Chevalier handed her and then Amy into his pos
chaise. He was comfortably well off, but not well off enoug
for her family's needs.

Mr Chevalier took the seat with his back to the horses. /
consideration Emma appreciated although she knew the tw
young people would have preferred to sit beside one anothe
She smiled at him.

He smiled back at her but it was obvious all his regard was for Amy, who blossomed under his admiring gaze. Emma squeezed Amy's hand and Amy squeezed back. Both of them were nervous about what Papa would do.

The time passed slowly for Emma. She listened to the couple talking. She might have not existed except that she was their chaperone. She looked out the windows at the passing countryside. It was beautiful and verdant.

They passed a wrought iron gate with images of clouds chasing across the two portions. On either side of the opening and running as far as the eye could see was a brick fence.

'That is Charles Hawthorne's estate,' Chevalier said.

Emma's pulse jolted. 'Hawthorne? I didn't know he had property.'

Chevalier tapped on the roof of the carriage so the driver stopped. 'He has a small holding that I understand is comfortably profitable.'

'Oh.' She could think of nothing else to say.

'Well,' Amy said with interest, 'I cannot picture him as a farmer. He is far too fashionable and far too debauched to stay in the country.'

'True.' Chevalier tapped the roof again and they moved on.

Emma craned her neck to watch Charles's land as though it held the secret to the man. She too could not picture him living a peaceful, domestic life in the country.

She would feel fortunate beyond words to live in a place such as his property. He was much too vibrant to be mired in a backwater.

He was much too vibrant for her, as he had made obvious when he had run from her without a word. She felt as a doxy must when her client snubs her without reason.

And she loved him.

She turned away from the sight of his country home, the beech tree-lined drive blurring. All it did was make her think of what she wanted but would never have.

She found a handkerchief in her reticule and blew her nose,

blinking rapidly. She was beyond this maudlin behaviour She had to be, for nothing was going to change.

They spent that night at a coaching inn and left early the next day. Three days later they arrived at Hopewell, a small estate in Yorkshire.

The carriage came to a halt in front of the old Elizabethan manor house. Both Amy and Chevalier looked beaten down by the worrying they had done nonstop since starting the journey

Chevalier helped them from the carriage and directed his footman to unload their trunks. Emma had invited him to stay with them. If Papa or Bertram objected, she would stand up to them. After what Charles Hawthorne had done to her, not even the thought of Papa's anger fazed her.

She had never stood up to Papa before. But knowing love herself and knowing the devastation caused by not being loved in return, she would do anything to see that Amy got her chance with Chevalier. Even defy Papa.

Gordon opened the front door. He had travelled here while Emma and Amy had gone to Lady Johnstone's. He barely raised a brow at sight of Mr Chevalier.

'Hello, Gordon.' Emma smiled at him as she went inside 'Betty is following behind with our things. Please see that a room is made ready for our guest, Mr Chevalier.'

Amy bounded inside. 'Is Papa about?'

'I believe he is in the library reading the paper, miss.'

Mr Chevalier came slowly behind Amy. He gave Gordon his hat. Emma saw his hand shake. She looked from one young person to the other. Both were afraid of what Papa would do and say, but both were eager to move forward.

Emma sighed. 'Let me speak to Papa first.'

Amy frowned. 'That—'

'It is my duty— ' Mr Chevalier interrupted.

'It will be better if you let me go first,' Emma said firmly

'Oh, all right.' Amy pouted for a second before nodding her understanding. 'You are going to threaten Papa.'

Emma grimaced. 'I hope not.'

'I say—' Mr Chevalier started again. Amy laid her hand on his arm.

Emma smiled even though she felt like collapsing on the nearest bed and sleeping until morning. It was her duty to make sure Papa accepted Mr Chevalier's suit.

Leaving the lovers in the foyer, she moved to the right and down the hall that led to the library. She paused at the closed door and took a deep breath. This was not going to be pleasant.

She rapped and entered without waiting for permission. 'Papa?'

He sat in a large leather chair pulled near a south-facing window for the afternoon sunlight. A brace of candles sat on a nearby table adding illumination.

He looked up at her and frowned. 'Emma.'

He wore half glasses that perched on the end of his bulbous nose. He once had light brown hair. Now it was completely grey. Whiskers made his round cheeks appear rounder. He wore simple country clothing with a sturdy jacket over his shirt and breeches.

She knew he was displeased with her. She had not got Amy successfully married off. It wouldn't matter that she had done her best and that Amy hadn't co-operated or that Bertram had gambled them out of London. He was still bitter over her refusal to hold George Hawthorne to their engagement.

'Papa, I need to speak with you.'

She moved into the room and took a chair close to his. She wanted to stand, but that would be too much like towering over him and what she intended to do would be bad enough without seeming to come from on high.

'About your failure to get Amy married to a rich man?' He still held the paper showing her he wasn't interested in talking.

She ignored the slice of pain caused by his accusation. 'I did my best, Papa. Sometimes that is all one can do.'

'Humph!' He lifted the paper back up to shield his face.

'I am not leaving, Papa, no matter how you try to ignore

me.' She fought the urge to go away and come back later. But no time would be a good one. 'I need to talk to you about the young man who is courting Amy.'

'Ah.' The paper went on the nearby table. 'You didn't tell me this.'

'Because he is not wealthy and cannot pay all of our debts.'

'Then why are you talking to me? She can't marry him. Simple as that.' He picked the paper back up.

Emma resisted the urge to rip the paper from his hands and tear it into shreds. It was a week old anyway. 'She loves him and he loves her.'

'Love isn't everything.' His voice barely rose over the barrier of the newspaper.

Emma stilled her twisting hands and spoke firmly. 'If the men in this family hadn't gambled us into debt and if they did not continue such behaviour, it would not be necessary for her to marry for money. So instead of sacrificing Amy, why not make Bertram find a wife with money?'

Papa laughed, a great belly laugh. 'Because the guardians of young chits with money won't let them marry Bertram. Now go away, I am reading.'

She had known he would not want to talk about this, but even so, she had not expected him to be so dismissive. His words hurt. 'I am not going away, Papa. I want you to give Amy permission to marry Mr Chevalier.'

'Not going to.'

'Papa, you leave me no choice then.' She was proud her voice was calm and showed none of the hurt his callous words had caused. 'If you will not give your blessing to this union then I will see to it that they elope.'

The paper crashed down and George Stockton shot up. 'How dare you threaten me, girl.'

Swallowing hard, but knowing her father was more bark than bite, Emma stood up to match him. 'I will do what I must. I refuse to let you make Amy miserable for her entire life because you and Bertram cannot control your gambling.'

He stared at her, his brown eyes narrowed over the tops of his half glasses. 'You'd do that to the entire family?'

She nodded. 'Amy loves Mr Chevalier. I told you that. They deserve a chance for happiness.' She took a deep breath and let it out. 'Goodness knows someone in this family should be happy.'

He turned his back to her and went to the fireplace where he kicked the grate. 'I've half a mind to call your bluff, girl.'

Emma's feet wanted to admit defeat and carry her from the room. But Amy's entire life was at stake. And she had her own share of anger and bitterness to pull from for strength.

'Do as you think best, Papa, but you will not be able to imprison us here forever. If you refuse your blessing, then sometime Amy and I will get away and Mr Chevalier will be waiting. And if they elope, I am sure you will get no money from Mr Chevalier. You let Bertram continue to wager sums of money we don't have, then you expect Amy or me to sacrifice ourselves to your weakness. I refuse to help you do that. So, you may give your blessing.'

He turned to face her. 'You've come back hard-hearted, girl.'

She shook her head. 'I've come back stronger, and I hope smarter. Even if Amy married for money, and her husband paid all our debts, you and Bertram would soon be in the River Tick again. I want her to be happy.'

'You really would go through with this?' He eyed her with disbelief. She had never rebelled in her life. She was the child he could always depend on to do as told.

'I am tired of paying the piper for what you and Bertram do, Papa. I am tired of watching Amy be miserable. It has been a joy to see her with Mr Chevalier. I intend to see that they stay together.'

He slumped into a nearby chair as though she had pushed him into it. The chair rocked before stabilising. 'Bring them to me.'

She stood her ground. 'Are you going to give them your blessing?'

He scowled at her. 'It seems you won't let me do anything else. But mark my word, if we are totally ruined you will be sorry.'

All she could do was look at him for a long moment. His words were like a knife slicing through her skin. She had always known he was selfish and bent on his own entertainments and that he allowed Bertram to do the same. But she had refused to see just how callous he was as well. Perhaps if Mama hadn't died it would not have come to this, but here it was.

'No, Papa, I won't be sorry. I am going to become a governess and Amy is going to marry Mr Chevalier. It is you and Bertram who will be sorry.'

She left before he could say anything more hurtful.

Amy and her beau were outside the closed door. She could tell from their faces that they had heard everything.

'He will give you his blessing now, or as close as he can make himself.' Emma smiled wanly at them. She was exhausted.

'Thank you, Em,' Amy said softly. 'We heard nearly everything.'

'Yes, thank you, Miss Stockton,' William Chevalier added. 'I can imagine that wasn't easy for you.'

She took Amy's hand. 'Promise me you will marry this man no matter what Papa says or does.'

Amy nodded and looked at Mr Chevalier. 'I will make him run away with me if need be.'

Emma released Amy's hand. 'That is what I told Papa, but I don't think it will come to that. Papa wants a settlement from Mr Chevalier.' Bitterness seeped into her final words.

She watched them enter the library before leaving. She was emotionally and physically drained.

She headed to the gardens in the back of the manor house. There was a maze and at the center of it a sundial and a bench. She often went there for quiet and privacy. She needed both now.

Within minutes, she was in her refuge spot. She sank onto the bench, thankful for the late afternoon sunshine. The warmth sank into her body.

The past months had been hard in so many ways. She had

changed so much. She had even stood up to the men in her family for the first time in her life.

How much of that strength could she credit to Charles Hawthorne? He had been a thorn in her side from the beginning, but he had also challenged her to stand up for herself. She had finally done so.

She owed him a great deal.

She buried her face in her hands, unwilling even in this secluded spot to cry in case someone might see her. So much had happened. But the hardest was to realise she loved Charles and to know she could never have him.

When he had left her, it had devastated her, but it had made her stronger. If she could lose the one thing she wanted more than anything else, then she could face her father and see that Amy got a chance for the happiness she herself would never have.

At best, she would find contentment. She would have to settle for that.

Chapter Twenty

Nearly a month after leaving Lady Johnstone's house party, Charles drove his high-perch phaeton up the poorly maintained gravel road that led to Hopewell. Emma's home. The Elizabethan manor house was in need of repair and the grounds had seen better days.

His hands tightened on the reins, making his matched pair of bays skittish. He eased his fingers. He knew this neglect. Cloudchaser had been like this during his years of gambling away enough money to fund a grand estate.

He pulled to a stop and hopped out, handing the reins to his tiger. The lad walked the horses while Charles mounted the steps and raised the lion's-head knocker. Many minutes passed.

The door opened and Emma's butler from London, Gordon, looked out. His bushy grey eyebrows rose marginally. 'Mr Hawthorne.' His tone would have frozen a lake in June.

'Good day, Gordon.' Charles kept his voice cheerful in spite of the servant's undisguised disapproval. 'I have come to see Miss Stockton.'

Gordon sniffed. 'I do not believe she is at home.'

The butler moved to close the door and Charles did the undignified thing of sticking his Hessian booted foot forward to stop the action. 'I am not leaving until I see her.'

The servant's mouth pinched into a moue of distaste. 'I will tell Mr Stockton you are here to see his daughter.'

Charles narrowed his eyes. Perhaps it would be better to start with her father. He had some choice words he'd like to deliver. 'Do that.'

Gordon looked like he might open the door then thought better of it. 'Perhaps that would be inappropriate. I believe you should just leave.'

The butler pushed harder on the door trying to close it in spite of Charles's foot. Charles held his ground. 'I shall wait inside.'

He made good on his decision by muscling into the foyer though the butler made it difficult. 'You are not wanted here,' the old retainer finally said quietly. 'You have caused more than enough heartache. Be on your way.'

Servants didn't tell visitors of importance to go away unless they felt their employers would agree. If Gordon felt comfortable trying to oust him, then Charles knew his job of persuading Emma Stockton to consider his proposal would be difficult.

But this was his last resort. All his letters had been returned unopened. And the old retainer had said something about heartache. He knew Amy didn't pine for him since news of her wedding had reached London the day before he had left. Perhaps there was hope.

'Tell Mr Stockton I have a matter of great import to discuss with him.'

Gordon looked down his nose even though he was shorter than Charles. 'I—'

'Who is this?' Amy Stockton's light voice intruded. She rounded a corner and stood looking at Charles. 'Well, well, well. If it isn't Mr Hawthorne.'

He smiled at her. 'My felicitations on your marriage, Mrs Chevalier.'

Her eyes narrowed. 'Are you mocking me?'

Genuinely puzzled, he asked, 'Why would I?'

She shrugged. 'I don't know. It just seemed like something

you would do, mock someone else who wedded. Particularly since everyone knows you have no intention of becoming leg-shackled to any woman.' She cocked her head to one side. 'And since I so brazenly ran after you and you encouraged me.'

He should have expected that from her. He had made it plain he had no plans to offer for her. At one time he had had no plans to offer for anyone.

He made her a half bow. 'Is your sister at home?'

She stepped closer, studying him as though he were an exotic bug. 'Emma?'

He curbed his exasperation, but couldn't totally control his tongue. 'Do you have another one I don't know about?'

A slow, sly smile curved her plump lips. 'No. But I don't think Em wants to see you.'

Her words were like a blow to the gut, but he had not expected this to be easy. 'Perhaps you will tell me where she is anyway.'

She tossed her head so her blond curls danced. 'Why should I?'

Now he studied her and decided to take a risk. 'Because you love her and want her to be happy.'

'Hah! And seeing you will make her happy?' She shook her head. 'Really, Mr Hawthorne, you have a highly inflated idea of yourself.'

'One does one's best,' he murmured with his wicked grin. She giggled at him and he knew he was close. 'Please, Mrs Chevalier.'

'You are begging?' Incredulity filled her voice.

He ignored the butler, who still stood frowning at the situation, and focused on the girl. 'If needs be.'

'Hmmm…' Amy tapped one finger on her chin. 'I'm not sure if she will receive you now.'

'Let her be the judge.'

'Are you going to hurt her?' Her eyes blazed.

'That is not my intent, but I can't promise.'

She closed the space between them. 'Then what can you promise? For I won't let you harm her again.'

'Again?' Hope flared.

Chagrin pinked her face. 'I talk too much.' She sighed. 'Are you here to seduce her only to run away again?'

He focused on the first part. 'So she told you.'

'No, but I knew something happened between you. That is the only thing that would hurt her as she has been hurt.'

'Ah, I am sorry for that. More than I can tell you.'

Amy gazed at him. 'I believe you really are.'

'Well?' He sensed she was close to telling him.

She fell back several steps. 'She is in the garden.'

Relief lifted the corners of his mouth. It was too soon to feel like a winner. 'Thank you.'

Not smiling, she added, 'In the maze.'

Already half turned away, he looked at her. 'The maze?'

She nodded. 'The easiest way is to go out the front door and around to the east wing and follow that to the back. Our garden is not so large that you will get lost.'

He unclenched the one hand that had fisted in tension. He was so close. 'Thank you, again.'

Just as he finished turning, he heard footsteps on the tile. Thinking it might be Emma, he twisted around. William Chevalier. The look on the young man's face as he saw his bride spoke clearer than any words of his devotion. He took Amy's left hand in his and kissed the ring she wore. Charles hadn't noticed the ruby and diamond piece before.

She radiated happiness.

Charles continued out the door, an ache in his chest. That was the sort of love and commitment his brother and sister had found with their spouses. He hoped to find that now.

He made short work of the walk to the back. The grounds would be beautiful if they were cared for. As it was, weeds mingled with late summer roses. The gravel was sparse in parts of the path and the lawn could do with a good cutting.

As Amy had said, the maze was easy to find. It stood out, a building of boxwoods, carved like walls. He stopped at the entrance unable to see above the tops. No doubt Emma was in the center. Would she answer if he called her?

'Emma?' He spoke loudly enough for her to hear. 'Emma.'

Emma roused with a start from the daydream she both wanted and feared. In it Charles Hawthorne always came for her and asked her to marry him. It was a fantasy to pass the time while she waited for a future employer to contact her. In her reverie he had just called to her.

She stood and walked around the wooden bench to stretch her legs. From the sundial that would soon be completely shaded and of no use, she saw she had been here an hour. A blissful sixty minutes without Papa's looks of recrimination or Bertram's smoldering resentment.

Then there were Amy and William. They had been wed last week in a small ceremony in the nearby village. She was happy Amy married for love, for she cared deeply for her sister. Yet, sometimes, in moments of weakness, it was hard for her to watch Amy and William's happiness without feeling envy and sadness for her own lack.

'Emma?'

She froze. Surely not. She had been daydreaming. That was all. That was why whoever wanted her sounded like...

'Emma, where are you? I am lost in this damnable maze.'

Charles Hawthorne. He was here. Searching for her.

Her lips curved up at his choice of words and the undisguised irritation in his voice caused by his unaccustomed lack of control. Joy filled her so she felt light enough to float.

Don't be daft, she told herself. He wasn't here to see her. Still, she could not seem to stop her heart from racing. Quickly, wishing she had taken more care in dressing this morning, she smoothed down the skirts of her lavender morning dress and tucked an errant curl behind her ear.

Where was her hat? She looked frantically for the chip bonnet. It wasn't in sight. Hadn't she worn one? Perhaps not. She was more forgetful of things since returning home.

Well, she couldn't let him continue to wander and call her

name. Sooner or later Papa or Bertram would hear him or be told by one of the few remaining workers and that would disastrous.

'I am here,' she said, dragging her feet to the place where the maze entered the quiet solitude of the center. She moved into the path only to see him turn the corner and head toward her.

'Emma.'

She stared at him, trying to breathe normally and finding it impossible. She felt winded and light-headed. 'Mr Hawthorne.'

All she wanted to do was move to him and have him take her into the shelter of his arms. But she could not do that. He had rejected her on countless times. She wasn't even good enough to be his mistress for more than one night. That hurt.

She stayed put and let him come to her.

When he finally stopped, he was too close. She felt hemmed in by him and by her feelings for him. All her desire and love were his for the taking. The knowledge threatened to overwhelm her. She knew tears would not be far behind.

'What do you want?' She made herself sound calm, as though it meant nothing to have him here.

'Will you sit with me?'

He indicated the bench she had just left. It would barely hold two. They would be much too close. A frisson ran her spine. 'I will stand if you care to sit.'

'Then you may sit and I will stand,' he countered.

Her lips pursed in exasperation. 'Why are you always so contrary?' The words showing such familiarity with him slipped before she thought. She had intended to remain impersonal.

His disreputable smile broke through. 'Because you always provoke me to be so.'

Her fingers, nervously twisting in spite of her efforts, stilled. The entire world seemed to still. She forgot to breathe.

He took a step closer to her. 'Emma?' His voice was barely above a whisper and felt like a caress.

She caught herself leaning toward him and stiffened up. But the effort it took for her to maintain a façade of indifference began to take its toll. Her knees felt like sponge cake.

'Charles,' she finally said, deciding she could not keep up the energy to freeze him, 'tell me why you are here and then go away. I have finally found a sense of peace and am waiting to hear on employment. The last thing I want is for you to stay and disrupt everything.'

'You don't want to be a governess.'

He moved still closer until his warm breath fanned her cheek. He smelled of bergamot and mint and himself.

Befuddled, she said, 'I don't?'

He shook his head. 'No.' He bent down. 'You want this.'

He kissed her before she realised his intention, or so she told herself. She stood still and let his lips move over hers as she drank in the emotions he always created in her: love, desire, pleasure, need; the list was endless. In too short a time for her to store away a lifetime's worth of memories, he stepped back.

'I have something for you.'

Her stomach clenched. What could it be? Nothing of value. Nothing that would indicate a seriousness of affection on his part. She forced herself to take a deep breath.

From the inside of his pocket, he pulled a velvet box. She stared at it. Surely he wasn't going to give her jewellery. That was what he would give his mistress.

'Are you here to offer me the position of your mistress after running away from me?' The words spurted from her, a mixture of pain and anger and hope.

He stopped in the midst of opening the hinged lid. Anger darkened his blue eyes to black. 'No.'

'Oh.' Pain and disappointment joined her relief. She didn't know what she felt or wanted—or wouldn't admit to herself.

'You are not suited to that position, Emma Stockton.'

She sighed. He finished opening the box and drew out a strand of pearls which he held out for her inspection.

'Mama's pearls!' Delight filled her, bringing the dreaded tears. Only these were of joy. 'Mama's pearls.' She extended a tentative finger to touch the necklace. 'Where did you get them?'

He gave her the smile that so many women more experienced than she had been unable to resist. 'From the pawn-broker Bertram sold them to.'

'But how did you know?' Her gaze went from the beloved necklace to his face. The tenderness in his eyes made her gasp.

'I made Bertram tell me.' He moved to her side and then behind her. 'These are for you, Emma. I know how it hurt you to lose them.'

'But I can't—'

'You can.'

She stood stiffly, thinking if she didn't move he wouldn't touch her. She didn't want him to touch her. Except that she did. She drew in a deep breath, thinking that once she had been sensible and had known her own mind—and heart. Now she seemed to flow with whatever emotion this man sent her way.

She felt the heat of his body along her back. His fingers brushed lightly on her nape as he fastened the clasp. The pearls slid along her skin, their warmth familiar and welcome, as a drink of water after a drought.

He felt the same to her. Welcome and precious.

She realised with a flush that seemed to rise from her feet to the crown of her head, that she felt safe with him here. Even as she was scared of what happened to her when he was near.

'There,' he breathed softly against her sensitised skin. 'They are back where they belong.'

'Thank you,' she said quietly, hoping he didn't hear the longing in her voice and realise it was because of him. She reached up and fingered the necklace. 'I have missed them.'

Gently, yet firmly, he put his hands on her shoulders and turned her to face him. Her light touch on the pearls became a clutch. What was he going to do?

He looked at the pearls and then at her face. 'If you grip them much tighter, you might break the strand.' There was a half smile on his mouth that invited her to join him in appreciating the situation.

It took an effort of will for her to release the pearls and let her arms drop to her sides while he continued to hold her shoulders so their faces, their lips, were only inches apart.

He slid his hands down her arms, his fingers caressing her as they moved over her until he took her hands in his. 'Will you marry me, Emma?'

Her mouth dropped. 'What?' Surely she had heard wrong.

For the first time since she had met him, many years ago when she had been engaged to his brother, a look of wariness entered his eyes. 'Will you marry me?'

The heat his touch had created fled. She felt as though an arctic wind moved over her. 'Don't insult me. If you want me for your mistress—which I highly doubt after what happened at Lady Johnstone's—then you definitely don't want me for a wife.' She twisted to escape him. His fingers tightened on hers.

'Don't insult me, Emma. I am not a boy who doesn't know his mind. I wouldn't ask you to marry me if I didn't mean it.'

Tears threatened to blur her vision. She blinked rapidly, determined not to be weak. 'You don't want to marry anyone.'

He sighed. 'I didn't.'

'See.' She pulled but he held firm. 'Let me go. This farce has gone far enough.'

His jaw tightened until a muscle twitched. 'This is no farce.'

'You don't love me,' she said, throwing her final, most condemning accusation at him.

He blinked as though she had caught him between the eyes with a stone. Then his wonderful smile lit his countenance. 'Is that the problem?'

She wasn't sure if it was the only problem, but it was the largest. She nodded.

'If I didn't love you I wouldn't be here now. I ran after making love to you because what I felt scared me. I've never felt like this before.' His grip on her hands eased. He slipped one arm around her waist to bring her closer. 'And I will never feel this way about another woman.'

'You left the next day,' she accused him.

'I was a coward. I ran from a feeling I had never had for a

woman before.' He lightly kissed the tip of her nose. 'Please forgive me.'

'You cannot want to marry me. You don't even like me.' She persisted, thinking that if she repudiated him enough he would finally admit his true reason for this proposal.

He chuckled. 'I think I have always liked you too much. Why do you think I did everything in my power to torment you? I wanted your attention, although I didn't realise that until I had nearly ruined your relationship with your sister.'

'You did?' She sounded like a benighted fool, but could not stop herself. Hope began to blossom.

'I did.' He pressed her close. 'Will you accept me, Emma Stockton?'

'I…I don't know what to say.'

'Say yes.'

'But—'

'There are advantages.' He pursued her. 'I have enough money to pay off most of your family's debt.'

'You do?'

'I have a bank draft in my pocket. It is why I could not come sooner. I needed to have the funds to pay your family's debts so you would have no excuse not to marry me.'

Shock stilled her feeble attempts at freedom. 'You sold your business so you could pay my family's debts?'

He gave a wishful, lopsided smile. 'I think that is what I just said.'

'But why?'

'Emma,' he said softly, gently shaking her. 'Haven't you heard anything I've said? I want to marry you.'

'You haven't said you love me.' Wistfulness filled her with longing.

He groaned. 'I have done everything else.' Exasperation deepened his tone. 'I have done everything you have asked of me and more. If that isn't love, then I don't know what love is.'

'You love me.' She could barely believe it. He had sold his most precious possession for her. 'But I can't let you do this.'

His brows snapped together. 'Do what?'

'Pay off my family's debts. It wouldn't be right.'

He clenched his teeth together and said slowly, 'If that is what I must do to win your hand, then that is what I will do.'

Wonder filled her. Love quickly followed. 'Oh, Charles.' She melted against him. 'I don't want you bailing my family out.'

He rubbed the small of her back before releasing her so quickly she nearly stumbled forward into his arms again. He knelt on one knee. He reached into the pocket of his jacket and pulled out a velvet box, the twin to the one that had held her pearls. He opened it to show a large ivory, pearl and diamond ring.

'Please marry me, Emma. I love you and I promise to do everything in my power to make you happy.'

She gazed down at him, thinking there was nothing more he could do. She felt ablaze with joy already.

'Emma?' he prompted.

She fell to her knees in front of him and wrapped her arms around his neck. 'Charles.'

She lifted her face to his. The kiss was long and deep and very unsatisfying.

He broke away chuckling. 'I think we are better matched than anyone would have thought. But first, this.' He took the ring from its box and slipped it onto her ring finger. 'You are mine now.'

She looked at the sparkling ring and back at him. He glowed with happiness as she knew she did. 'We belong together.'

She leaned forward just enough to kiss him again and once more start the sparks that would keep them warm through any winter night.

* * * * *

Happily ever after is just the beginning...

Turn the page for a sneak preview of
A HEARTBEAT AWAY
by
Eleanor Jones

HARLEQUIN EVERLASTING™—
Every great love has a story to tell.
A brand-new series from Harlequin Books

pecial? A prickle ran down my neck and my heart started to beat in my ears. Was today really special?

"Tuck in," he ordered.

I turned my attention to the feast that he had spread out on the ground. Thick, home-cooked-ham sandwiches, sausage rolls fresh from the oven and a huge variety of mouthwatering scones and pastries. Hunger pangs took over, and I closed my eyes and bit into soft homemade bread.

When we were finally finished, I lay back against the bluebells with a groan, clutching my stomach.

Daniel laughed. "Your eyes are bigger than your stomach," he told me.

I leaned across to deliver a punch to his arm, but he rolled away, and when my fist met fresh air I collapsed in a fit of giggles before relaxing on my back and staring up into the flawless blue sky. We lay like that for quite a while, Daniel and

I, side by side in companionable silence, until he stretched out his hand in an arc that encompassed the whole area.

"Don't you think that this is the most beautiful place in the entire world?"

His voice held a passion that echoed my own feelings, and I rose onto my elbow and picked a buttercup to hide the emotion that clogged my throat.

"Roll over onto your back," I urged, prodding him with my forefinger. He obliged with a broad grin, and I reached across to place the yellow flower beneath his chin.

"Now, let us see if you like butter."

When a yellow light shone on the tanned skin below his jaw, I laughed.

"There…you do."

For an instant our eyes met, and I had the strangest sense that I was drowning in those honey-brown depths. The scent of bluebells engulfed me. A roaring filled my ears, and then unexpectedly, in one smooth movement Daniel rolled me onto my back and plucked a buttercup of his own.

"And do you like butter, Lucy McTavish?" he asked. When he placed the flower against my skin, time stood still.

His long lean body was suspended over mine, pinning me against the grass. Daniel…dear, comfortable, familiar Daniel was suddenly bringing out in me the strangest sensations.

"Do you, Lucy McTavish?" he asked again, his voice low and vibrant.

My eyes flickered toward his, the whisper of a sigh escaped my lips and although a strange lethargy had crept into my limbs, I somehow felt as if all my nerve endings were on fire. He felt it, too—I could see it in his warm brown eyes. And when he lowered his face to mine, it seemed to me the most natural thing in the world.

None of the kisses I had ever experienced could have ever

begun to prepare me for the feel of Daniel's lips on mine. My entire body floated on a tide of ecstasy that shut out everything but his soft, warm mouth, and I knew that this was what I had been waiting for the whole of my life.

"Oh, Lucy." He pulled away to look into my eyes. "Why haven't we done this before?"

Holding his gaze, I gently touched his cheek, then I curled my fingers through the short thick hair at the base of his skull, overwhelmed by the longing to drown again in the sensations that flooded our bodies. And when his long tanned fingers crept across my tingling skin, I knew I could deny him nothing.

* * * * *

Be sure to look for A HEARTBEAT AWAY,
available February 27, 2007.
And look, too, for
THE DEPTH OF LOVE
by Margot Early,
the story of a couple who must learn
that love comes in many guises—
and in the end it's the only thing that counts.

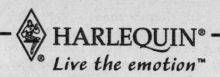

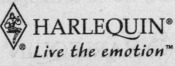

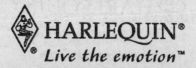

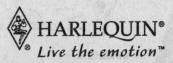

HARLEQUIN®
INTRIGUE®

BREATHTAKING ROMANTIC SUSPENSE

Shared dangers and passions lead to electrifying
romance and heart-stopping suspense!

Every month, you'll meet six new heroes
who are guaranteed to make your spine tingle
and your pulse pound. With them you'll enter
into the exciting world of Harlequin Intrigue—
where your life is on the line
and so is your heart!

THAT'S INTRIGUE—
ROMANTIC SUSPENSE
AT ITS BEST!

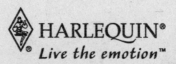

HARLEQUIN®
Live the emotion™